About the

Judy McInerney has lived and work
fessional life. Living in the Middle East, she managed to get lost in the desert, and to live through a military coup. After teaching in Abu Dhabi and starting her own business in Turkey, she returned to London and completed a creative writing course at Goldsmiths. Writing for food and travel guides has enabled her to justify travelling and eating out far too often.

As a frequent traveller to China over the last 30 years she has seen the country undergo seismic changes, from the times of Mao jackets and vast shoals of bicycles meandering along every hutong, to the present day, where there are over 200 million cars in China, and Beijing is far bigger than Belgium. She still travels in China each year to keep in close touch with family there. She also has a longstanding love affair with Italy, particularly the Renaissance cities of the north. Mantua is an undiscovered gem, both magical and macabre.

THE PUMILIO CHILD

THE PUMILIO CHILD

JUDY MCINERNEY

This edition first published in 2018

Unbound

6th Floor Mutual House, 70 Conduit Street, London W1S 2GF

www.unbound.com

ISBN (eBook): 978-1-78965-022-8
ISBN (Paperback): 978-1-911586-03-6

Design by Mecob

Printed in Great Britain by Clays Ltd, Elcograf S.p.A

MIX
Paper from responsible sources
FSC® C018072

To Mike, Lucy, Alice, Greg and Jon for their enthusiasm and support, and for being so quick on the draw with a corkscrew.

Dear Reader,

The book you are holding came about in a rather different way to most others. It was funded directly by readers through a new website: Unbound.

Unbound is the creation of three writers. We started the company because we believed there had to be a better deal for both writers and readers. On the Unbound website, authors share the ideas for the books they want to write directly with readers. If enough of you support the book by pledging for it in advance, we produce a beautifully bound special subscribers' edition and distribute a regular edition and e-book wherever books are sold, in shops and online.

This new way of publishing is actually a very old idea (Samuel Johnson funded his dictionary this way). We're just using the internet to build each writer a network of patrons. Here, at the back of this book, you'll find the names of all the people who made it happen.

Publishing in this way means readers are no longer just passive consumers of the books they buy, and authors are free to write the books they really want. They get a much fairer return too – half the profits their books generate, rather than a tiny percentage of the cover price.

If you're not yet a subscriber, we hope that you'll want to join our publishing revolution and have your name listed in one of our books in the future. To get you started, here is a £5 discount on your first pledge. Just visit unbound.com, make your pledge and type MANTUA18 in the promo code box when you check out.

Thank you for your support,

Dan, Justin and John
Founders, Unbound

Super Patrons

Elza Adamowicz
Jilly & Peter Appleby
Chloe Arensberg
Dianne Arnold
Tay Associates
Charles Bai
Gareth Barnes
Les Beesley
Joseph Beesley
John & Glynis Billett
Sara Birch
Natalie Black
Chris & Helen Brandon-Trye
Clive Branson
Rose Bretécher
Geoff Brown
Annie Burton
Abby Cable
Milla Chaplin
Kerry Cheshire
Pamela Clarke
Carly & Phil Cooper
Ann Marie Cottis
Matet & Niraan De Silva
Madame Defarge
Eleanor Detke
Peter Dunwoodie
Deirdre Ellis
Grace England
Gee Fiege
Jackie Field
Julian Fisher

Kate Freeman
Tricia Gick
Lisa M. Harney
Ray & Jennie Hart
Andrew Hearse
Ben Howard
Michael Jardine
Dave Kermode
Dan Kieran
Tricia Kreitman
Becki Larkin
Kristen Lum
Irene Maisey
Stephen Mayfair
Lucy McInerney
Ian McKendrick
Neil McNaughton
Tina McNaughton
John Mitchinson
Mitzi Nichol
Jonathan Nicolson
Sally O'Malley
Karen O'Sullivan
Hannah Oussedik Sandiford
James Parry
Jon Payne
Nancy Pellegrini
Elizabeth Pickard
Justin Pollard
Medwin Poots
Natasha Quinn
Vicki Rocquelin
Mary San Pablo
Arthur Schiller
Ronald Schouten
Helmut & Barbara Schroeder

Greg Schroeder
Samuel Scotland
Louise Smith
Ruby Soave
Nada Stone
Jane Stone
Hilary Sunman
Natasha Tan
Phyllice Tawiah
Gail Terry
Andrew Terry
Patricia Terry
David Terry
Tiggy Thompson
Bryony Thorpe
Kilian Toal
Guy Ware
Deborah Wheeler
Michael Wilson
Ann Wolfe
Joules Wrigley
Alice Yang
Peter Yiu

'You minimus of hindering knot-grass made.'

Act III, Scene 11, *A Midsummer Night's Dream*,
William Shakespeare (1595–96)

'We want a boy extremely for this function,
kept under for a year with milk and knot-grass.'

Act II, Scene 11, *The Coxcomb*,
Francis Beaumont and John Fletcher (1608–10)

Disclaimer

The wonderful frescos of Andrea Mantegna are to be found online, if you search for 'Images for Frescos Andrea Mantegna Camera degli Sposi'.

All of the main characters in the frescos are portrayed in the novel, but I have changed the identity of one of them. The story is entirely fictitious. The vicious practice of creating pumilios did happen but there is no link whatsoever to Andrea Mantegna. References are made to this process in both *A Midsummer Night's Dream* and *The Coxcomb*. I am neither a historian, nor an art historian nor a linguist, and I have taken liberties for the purposes of storytelling, particularly regarding the pumilio process. The room was only named the Camera degli Sposi in the mid-seventeenth century. Mantegna's paintings are alluded to, but out of historical sequence, as are the hooks, the cage and the use of the word ghetto.

Please find below the modern equivalents for the place names in the novel:

Mantua/Mantova, Venice/Venezia, Padua/Padova, Florence/Firenze, Genoa/Genova, Tuscany/Toscana.

Prologue

Mantova, Italy. 1459.

It looks like a whorehouse. Cheap and run down. Mean little windows in odd places. Dark chunks of timber jutting out. Pieces of masonry, pediments and columns from an earlier age are stuck in the walls like fragments of old teeth.

But it seems deserted. No loud talk, music or raucous laughter when you walk past. No girls about either. There should be a gang of them outside, offering up their tits like apples on a tray. Some shrivelled. Some just ripening.

'Will we be long here, Maestro?'

'Silence. Wait here. Stay outside. Talk to nobody.'

'Of course, Maestro,' Gregorio murmurs, holding the mare still.

'And tell nobody where we have been today. Do as you're told or fear the consequences, boy! Unless you fancy a spell in the cage, eh?'

Gregorio's boyish features drop in fear. He swallows quickly. 'No, Maestro.'

'Clinging on. Swinging about up there. The wind freezing your blood to ice?'

'No, Maestro.' The groom shivers at the thought. He wouldn't be the first to be condemned to a public death in the cage.

'Then keep it shut, like this.' Mantegna bunches his fist together and pushes it against his groom's mouth.

Gregorio flinches. 'Yes, Maestro.' Not daring to look round, he strokes the mare's velvet muzzle. He waits until the door creaks open and Mantegna enters.

'Bastardo!' he hisses. The mare pulls back against the reins, her eyes fearful. She stamps a nervous hoof into the red dust. 'Not you,' Gregorio murmurs, gently pulling on her silky ear. 'No, not

you, little lady.' She blows grassy breath into his palm. He dares a quick glance over his shoulder. 'Him.'

Mantegna pushes on the massive studded doors and slips inside. Five minutes later he is still standing in the arcaded courtyard. Normally he would have stormed off, but he has to stay. Money is tight. He looks down in the direction of an odd shrill noise that seems to be coming from below the filthy floor. He wipes his damp palms down his sides.

'Where's Dati?'

The servant who finally ambles up is a stocky Neapolitan, a shifty-looking peasant who understands none of the Mantovan dialect. The man motions him to wait.

Mantegna's face has set hard by the time Giacobbe Dati makes his way quickly down the stairs.

The man's eyes tighten at the artist's nondescript clothes. No courtly manners. No idea how to dress, no senza vergogna at all. 'No velvets today, Maestro? How wise.' He sounds out of breath. 'Or perhaps necessity.' Mantegna gives him an uneasy glance. It's as if his thoughts are being read. Ludovico Gonzaga has already reprimanded him over his lavish ways and the scarlet velvet jerkin had probably been one ostentation too far. Scarlet. The colour of cardinals and emperors. But he had looked magnificent. He remembers the gasp when he swaggered into court. His glance drops down to his worn tabarro. The jerkin was pawned months ago. He looks round warily.

'Where can we talk?' He wants this over as soon as possible.

'This way.' Dati leads him into a room off the hallway. Mantegna's nose wrinkles. Mildew and something else. It smells more like a stable than a home.

'These are just my business premises, Maestro,' Dati puts in quickly, before he pulls two battered chairs together. 'I entertain here only rarely. So I am unable to offer you vin santo or almond biscuits.' Mantegna looks up at Dati's lean intelligent face. The man is more polished than he thought, but he is known to be *a wily merchant. Shake his hand then count your fingers, that's what he's heard. 'My home is more richly appointed. In fact, I was thinking I might commission you to paint an antique frieze for me.'*

'Ha!' Mantegna tilts back his head with a terse laugh. 'You're all the same, you traders. A classical fresco and a bust of Dante and you think you'll turn into a nobleman.' His glance is withering. 'You couldn't afford me.'

'Really? So you're doing well?' Dati smiles politely. 'The Gonzagas are paying you promptly each month? That's a first.' Dati examines a long thumb nail that is curved like a claw. 'I heard you've been taking on private commissions.' One eyebrow rises. 'Commissions that the Gonzagas know nothing about.'

Mantegna's brow furrows. 'Well, you heard wrong. I might be short of ready money at the moment, but I'll have you know Ludovico Gonzaga is talking of offering me a very large commission. Two major frescos in the Palazzo Ducale, one of the whole family and all their courtiers.' Mantegna flings open both arms. 'And another entire wall to celebrate, God willing, his son being made a cardinal.'

Dati inclines his head, his face ironed of all expression. 'I know. And as you are known to be so very painstaking, Maestro, it will be many years before such enormous frescos will be finished and you get your final payment. And if it's true that you have already mortgaged some of your future earnings against these great works, then your financial position must be a little… difficult.' He gives a sympathetic nod. 'The Gonzagas are known to be as tight as a tick's arse, are they not? Never part with a sessino until they have to. And I've heard of your debts too.' He shrugs. 'You know how these things get bandied about in the piazza.'

Mantegna scowls. He stands and takes two half-hearted paces towards the door. Dati must run an army of spies. 'I didn't come here to listen to this, Dati! I came here with a business proposition, not be spoken to in such a way,' he fumes.

'Sorry. I was only repeating what I had heard. I have no wish to give offence to a man so highly esteemed.' The chair creaks as he leans back. 'So, what can I do for you?'

'I have a friend' – Dati turns away to hide the wry downturn to his lips – 'and this friend of mine has a wife who is pregnant. He already has many daughters to feed and clothe.' He returns to the chair and sits forwards. 'This friend is a cultured man, you understand, who has no wish to give the child away, but if this child were to be a girl-child… then… But only to an excellent home. He might allow the child to be brought up as a servant, but not a slave. In no circumstances can the child be poorly treated.'

'I see. These days are getting difficult. The church imposes more moral strictures every day and the ecclesiastical courts are hounding any poor man whose mistress…'

'I said nothing about a mistress.' Mantegna turns sharply. 'All I said was, he's a respectable man who merely needs to do the right thing and secure the child's future.'

'So sorry, Maestro. My mistake.'

'So could you find her a home? My friend will accept less money if the family will be kind.' He looks across. 'What's so funny?'

'Nothing. Done a lot of business, have you, Maestro?'

'Of course not. I'm an artist not a damned tradesman.' He sits up proudly in the chair. 'Why do you ask?'

'Nothing. No reason at all.' Dati's voice soothes like a stroke. 'Will the child be pretty?'

Mantegna sits very still. 'She will be.'

'Handsome parents?' Mantegna's nod is awkward. 'In fact I might have just the family who would take her, in the event… a patrician family who have recently lost a daughter. The wife is fading fast and the husband wants to help her recover, so he is looking for a child to adopt.'

Mantegna's eyes widen. 'A patrician? And he would adopt a girl?'

'Strange, I know, when there are plenty of beggar families who'll give a sturdy son away for practically nothing, but the wife is pining for her little girl.'

'Speaking of money…'

'Well, they won't pay much. But as you yourself said earlier, your friend will accept less money if the family will treat her well. This family will do a lot more than that. They'll bring her up as their own.'

'I see.' Mantegna looks nonplussed.

'I'll make enquiries for you, shall I?'

'Yes. When will they want her?'

Dati steeples his fingers together. 'Give the child at least two years. Let's see how healthy she is by then. If she is robust, then I can arrange everything.'

'How much can my friend expect, Dati? I must be able to tell him.'

'First of all, I need to negotiate on your behalf. These things take time.'

'Who are they? This family?'

Dati shakes his head with a reluctant smile. 'I'll never be able to disclose that. In my business discretion is everything. That is why you have come to me today, is it not?' He stands and motions Mantegna to follow him out. 'You can trust me. Many men like your friend do.'

Dati waits behind a moth-eaten curtain until Mantegna and the groom leave in a cloud of dust. The big Neapolitan is at his side immediately with a lantern in his hand. When the cellar door opens the stench of raw urine hits the backs of their throats. Dati holds his cloak to his mouth. The murmur of noise stops immediately as they climb down the uneven wooden staircase into the damp straw that lines the floor. A parabola of red light swings out from the lantern, glinting on several pairs of eyes that stare back at them from the shadows, before the whimpering begins. Dati grabs a tiny arm and drags its owner across the rustling straw. 'Come, there's work to be done.'

Chapter 1

Twenty years earlier

The Healers' House, Yiliao Hutong, Beijing

The child's screams sweep across the darkened courtyard, making the finches chitter uneasily beneath the domes of black felt that cover their cages. The nightwatchman hands the bloodied bundle to the healer, then kneels and begins to kow-tow. He hasn't finished the three kneelings, nor even begun the nine knockings of his head on the ground, when he feels a firm hand under his elbow lifting him up and hears the healer's deep voice. 'Come. There's no need for that here.'

'I'm very sorry for the late hour, Dorji sir, but I didn't know where else to bring him.'

'You did well. My door is always open.' The healer nods and gives the man a coin, which makes his eyes widen. 'Where was he found?'

'He'd been thrown on the rubbish cart at the end of the hutong. No one saw anything at all.'

Once the man has left, the healer's wife comes into the treatment room, as he knew she would. She yawns as she tugs a white canvas gown down over her rounded stomach, which curves like a ripe melon under her silk nightdress. 'You should be resting, my love,' he murmurs, moving quickly to stand between her and the crumple of soaking red sheets on the table.

'How can I? Listening to a poor child scream like that?' She leans round her husband and lays a gentle hand on the child's clammy forehead, whispering encouragement down to him. The child's tilted eyes look huge as they swivel round the room. He pants like a thirsty puppy. Her husband grunts in fury when he eases the blood-soaked loincloth down past the boy's narrow hips. Two testicles come away, lost in the sticky folds of the cloth, but the boy's penis lies stuck to the inside of his thigh, like a tiny shrivelled cocoon, still attached by a string of scarlet flesh. Despite blanching at the swampy mess that lies between the child's legs, she manages to keep her voice calm. 'You're being very brave, child. Soon the pain will lessen and you will sleep.'

'If I ever find the butcher of a knifeman who did this…' Dorji threatens, his wide shoulders rising in fury, 'but I don't want you seeing this, Ya Zhi, it can't be good for you so late on in your confinement. The shock might…'

'You won't find him, we both know that.' She glances down at the child. 'How could anyone do this? It makes me ashamed to be Han.'

'Don't be. There are always evil men to be found. We may live in enlightened times with a wise and tolerant emperor, but before the Mings took power, well… life was very different.'

She rests a finger across her lips. 'Shh. Husband, this is no time for a history lesson.' She lays a hand on her husband's arm until the muscles relax, then eases him out of earshot. 'His bladder is nearly bursting, so you will need my delicate little Han fingers to relieve him.' She wiggles them under her husband's eyes and manages a smile, as much for her husband as for the child. Dorji's hands, like his big Mongolian frame, are sometimes too wide and muscular.

'I know, my love, I mean, we must keep in perspective how civilised our society…'

'He might not agree.' Her smile moves from her husband's earnest frown back to the stricken little face. 'Poor little fellow. We don't have much poppy paste left and the Berber won't be here for another week or so.'

'We'll manage.'

He watches her put a dot of paste under the child's tongue before she probes his lower abdomen with an apologetic smile. 'I promise you it will ease soon.' The child's thin ribcage expands and contracts in agony, and the desperation of his trebly screams seems to suck the air out of the treatment room. 'This will be over soon.' She quickly takes out a tiny bamboo quill from a drawer and sharpens one end of it before dipping it momentarily into a bowl of boiling rice wine, then into ice. She waits for the child's eyelids to droop, then quickly explores the pulpy mass with two forefingers. The quill goes in easily and a heavy surge of urine spumes into the glass flask. The child's face collapses with relief before his breathing slows and his eyelids close.

For the next few days, whenever the child comes to consciousness he sees either Dorji's broad face leaning over him or the delicate Han features of Ya Zhi, which always soften encouragingly as she gives him spoonfuls of rice congee and sips of water. The child stares blankly at them as if his heart has been removed too.

'Do you have a name, child?' she asks him on the third night.

'I am called the Fifth,' he whispers.

'I see. Well, you are healing quickly, little Fifth. So we must now try to raise your spirits. Let's start by giving you a proper name. I'm going to call you Chen, after Wang Chen, the most important eunuch at the Imperial Palace. The chief guard of the palace harem, in fact.' She smiles reassuringly down at the boy's empty face on the pillow and drops her voice. 'Listen to me, little one. Wang Chen is so trusted by the emperor that he guards all the empresses to keep the royal bloodline pure. Just imagine that! Being so important! So don't worry, little Chen, there will be many opportunities for you. I can see a great future ahead and Dorji and I will do all we can…' she goes on soothing, but he has already turned his face to the wall.

The following bedtime Ya Zhi's jasmine perfume drifts across his pillow as Dorji looms over him. 'I have good news, child. In two months you will be well enough to leave us and I have already spoken to a friend of mine who works in the pharmacy at the Imperial Palace. He has promised me he will recommend you to one of the most powerful eunuchs at court.'

'No!' The child winces as he tries to prop himself up onto an elbow.

'No?' Ya Zhi's eyes widen. 'But you will have a great future there! The Union of Eunuchs is very powerful, and they will help you find work at the palace. One of them has become an admiral and he sails to Joseon to buy warhorses for the emperor. He has a cellar full of gold! Imagine a life like that!'

'No!' Swimming to the surface through waves of pain, the child locks a pair of stubborn eyes on each of them in turn. 'You can call me Chen if you wish, but I'm staying here. This is my place now.' His eyes drop to the front of Ya Zhi's gown. 'You will need an ayi for the baby.'

Ya Zhi gives a tinkling laugh. 'An ayi? Of course I will. But I have already arranged one, a Bai woman who was my ayi when I was born. Come child, you are a little boy. You can't be an ayi.'

He gasps with the effort of raising a tightened fist. 'Then a guard. A watchman. Look at my muscles. No one will be as fierce as me.'

She shakes her head, smiling. 'Your survival skills must be strong, child. Thinking of your future amid such pain.'

'Yes. I am strong.' He falls back, his face taut against the pillow. 'And I will be fearless. For you and for your family. For your new child.'

Ya Zhi wrings out a cloth and flattens it against his forehead. The grassy scent of artemesia cuts through the smell of sweat. 'We'll see, child. Just rest for now.'

'No. You own me now. I'm yours.' He nods his head determinedly at each of them. 'I belong to you.'

Chapter 2

The Healers' House, 1457

Ya Ling lifts her head from the porcelain headrest. The first rays of the sun stream in through the filigreed carving of her bedroom shutters and form a winking pattern of light on her face. 'It worked, Chen!' she calls. 'I'm awake before you. Come on, lazybones!' Excitement rises in her chest. The thin bedcover pools on the floor as she pulls on her silk dressing gown. Chen lies asleep across the threshold of her room and she points the toe of her embroidered slipper into his armpit and scrabbles it around.

'Too early, Little Sister. Another hour,' he grumbles.

'You expect me to sleep? Today?' She laughs as she hops over him and makes her way to the empty kitchen. She takes down a disc of pu'er tea and crumbles the rim onto a plate. Walking back across the courtyard, she sees that Chen has drifted back to sleep and gives his cheek a good pinch and shakes the point of his chin until he finally pulls himself to his feet. 'The men will be coming soon to put the banners on the ger in the tranquillity courtyard, so you have to be up to chaperone me, in any case.'

'Not at dawn they won't.' He stretches out his plump arms. 'Not even for you, Little Empress.'

She purses her lips. 'I'll take tea now. In the third courtyard. Be quick.' She walks to the outer courtyard where the rock garden with the tiny pavilion, which usually catches every breath of breeze, is now covered over by a big felted tent. Chen carefully puts a tray down on a stone bench and sits down next to her, offering a tiny steaming cup and a plate of bean paste buns. 'It's so stuffy in here now. I don't know why Baba insisted on all of this.' Her eyes look round.

'He wanted your betrothal to be properly Mongolian. So that means a ger.' Chen folds open two of the flaps and ties them back.

She sighs. 'Oh, he's so old-fashioned.' She wrinkles her nose. 'And I don't even like this courtyard.'

'You can't have everything. Even you. Even today. Rumour has it there's going to be a big party in every courtyard tonight.' He turns to her and his features drop as her beauty once again catches him off guard, the way the curve of her lashes casts a shadow on her high cheekbones, the sleek black hair that frames her tiny delicate features. His arm rests protectively behind her. 'What's wrong with this one anyway?'

'Oh, I don't mind the jade rocks so much, or the willow trees, it's just those horrible things.' She points at the miniature *panjin* trees, each species perfect but dwarfed in their tiny shallow containers. 'That banyan tree is the worst. Look at it! With its roots all contorted like that as if grappling for survival in that thin layer of grit. It's just so ugly.' She shudders. 'I once asked Baba how it managed to live like that and he gave me one of his lectures.' Drooping her lips, she drops her voice to a pompous drawl: '"Because it has to, my dear. It reminds us life is not always easy. Life is a struggle and has to be grasped and hung on to." He went on and on.' She rolls her eyes. 'On and on.'

Chen looks away, his tongue clicking against the roof of his mouth. 'You shouldn't talk like this.'

'I tried to change the subject but he was in full flow, you know how he can be. All about the hard times he had when the emperor first summoned him to Beijing. A poor Mongolian nobody among all the hostile Hans.' She wags a finger in Chen's face. '"Soil was often poor for me at court too, let me tell you, my girl. But if you work hard and endure, then like the *panjin* trees you will survive."'

Chen turns towards her on the bench. 'You should respect your father and learn from his words. He is a giant among men, he only—'

'Then the same old tale about having to ask for my mother's hand twenty times. How he had dared challenge the decree against intermarriage between Han and Mongolians, but how he would have asked twenty thousand times if he'd had to.' She raises her eyebrows with a sigh. 'You know what he's like. I feel like I've heard that story twenty thousand times myself.'

Chen's glance at her is sharp. 'Your father is a wonderful man. And your mother is like an empress. You are very blessed to have such loving parents. Many girls—'

'Not another lecture.' She taps her toe. 'That's one thing I definitely won't be sad to leave behind.'

Chen sits in silence. 'But you'll miss all this, won't you? When you leave next week?' His sleeve flaps open as his palm lifts up to the curved roofs where hundreds of green-glazed tiles coil like the skin of a sprawling dragon. His hand sweeps round the marble courtyard surrounded by the latticed arcade, the magnificent red-lacquered columns, the rooms full of dark furniture of carved mahogany, each wall decorated with watercolours of flying cranes and elegant calligraphy. He breathes in the heady perfume of white lilies and pink peonies in their tall cloisonné vases. 'You'll miss us too I hope.' His smile is expectant.

'You? Not likely.' She raises an eyebrow at him. 'No, it's time I left. I'm ready to have my own healing rooms and build my own reputation.'

Chen sighs and shakes his head. 'Don't let your parents hear you say that.'

'But I will miss those.' Smiling, she points at two large yellow porcelain lions that gleam in the early morning sun. 'You got such beatings for letting me slide down those. Remember? How old was I?'

'Two? Nearly three? It was worth it though. To hear you giggle the way you did.'

'Of course it was.' She swings her legs.

Chen looks away from her and clears his throat. 'It seems like yesterday to me. Are you nervous? About tonight?'

Her legs stop and she tucks them underneath. 'Not about tonight. No, not about that.' He senses her sudden stillness. 'Che-e-en?' His name is drawn out like a plea.

He turns, puzzled. 'What then?'

'I don't know what happens, Chen. I don't know what to expect. You know.' She stares ahead and reaches across for his hand. It feels fleshy and soft.

He looks down, horrified, and pulls his hand away. 'Surely your mother...'

'I have done, and she won't tell me.'

Chen fiddles with the pleats on his sash. 'Well, Ayi then?'

'Ayi? She just puts her hands to her face and backs away. She knows even less than me.'

'Well then.' Chen unties his sash and smooths it across his knees several times.

'I asked her about kissing as well, and she said her older sister had practised on an orange before her wedding day. She's useless.' Her voice is so quiet he has to lean forwards. 'Chen, I don't even know what a man looks like down there.'

'But surely the patients you've healed?'

'No! Never that part! You know quite well only married women are allowed to do anything there! So stop pretending you don't.' She leans into his shoulder and feels him shrink aside. 'Look at me, Brother. You have to explain it all to me.'

His hand hovers over her arm for a second, then he folds his belt neatly and pats it into a tight square. 'I'm the last person to ask.'

'Please, Chen.'

He clears his throat. 'No. I cannot deny Altan your innocence. It would be dishonourable.' Her profile stares furiously ahead in silence. 'And I would disappoint your father.' After several moments he sits up briskly. 'So. About tonight. Tell me again who will be coming?'

She scowls across at him. 'I'm not stupid, Chen. You know exactly who's coming. We've talked about nothing else for weeks.'

'Talk to me, Little Sister. Spare me your disappointment in me. Not today.' His voice tries to lighten. 'At least you aren't nervous about tonight. That's good.'

She gives him a long sideways glance. 'You're hopeless.' A deep breath loosens her anger. 'Altan's family and Baba's family are travelling down from Mongolia next week for the wedding, so tonight it's mainly Mama's family and their close friends.' She ticks them off on her fingers. 'The other healers, some of the apothecaries and a few of the spice merchants. They've all known me since I was sliding down the lions, so why would I be nervous?' She gives him a sideways smile. 'Oh, and the scholars Ibrahim and Chaim, they're coming too, and the Berber of course. He's ordered a jade amulet for me to wear tonight. He promised me when I was nine years old and he's reminded me every year since. White jade. He said, for me, it would have to be the very best.' Her voice rises with anticipation. 'A phoenix. He said it's to celebrate my new life.' Her eyes sparkle. 'He was so sweaty with excitement when he told me that the indigo dye from his turban ran blue all down his neck.'

'Did it? Really?' Chen's voice sharpens. 'You only ever call him the Berber. You never call him by his name. Do you even know it?'

Ya Ling gives his shoulder a push. 'Stop being like that! Like a child. In all the years we've done business with him, we've never known his name. No one has. He travels so much to buy his spices and elixirs that he just likes to be known as the Berber.'

'I see. If you say so.' She shakes her head at him. Lacing her fingers together, she pushes them outwards into the warmth of the sun. Chen looks alarmed.

'Cover those up straight away! Tuck them up your sleeves.'

'Oh, stop fussing, Chen.'

'I mean it. It's my duty to protect them. Your six fingers confer so much status and they will be very much on show tonight. They need to be kept pale as bone.'

Ya Ling raises her eyes but slides her hands out of view. 'Happy now?'

'Thank you. Are there any tasks you need me for, Little Sister? If so, I suggest you ask your mother early, because I will be kept busy for much of the day.'

'I need you to accompany me to collect the jade amulet, and then perhaps…'

Chen looks surprised. 'Then perhaps what?'

'I thought we could come back via Altan's workshop.' She doesn't quite catch his eye. 'But as you are so busy then perhaps we needn't tell Baba.'

'No. I can't do that. I can't betray his trust in me. I will ask his permission to take you there and if he agrees we will go. But I will chaperone you the whole time we are there.'

She folds her arms. 'Honestly, I can't wait to leave you behind, Chen. I sometimes think you don't care about me at all. Even after all these years together, even on my special day, you still don't want to please me.'

Chen's face crumbles. It takes him several moments to speak. 'Little Sister, if anything happened to you while you were in my charge, then I would have to take the honourable way.'

She looks at him closely. 'Which way would you choose?'

He answers promptly as if he has given the matter some thought. 'Poison. Or the knife.' He looks down. 'After all, I'm no stranger to that.'

'Would you really?'

'Of course.' He takes both her hands in his. 'I would have to. If anything were to happen to you, even so close to your marriage, I could never look your father in the eye. Not after all he has done for me.'

'Let's not talk of such things today of all days.' Her fingers close around his, her smile guileless. 'So tell me, what is it you think Altan would do?'

'He's a man. I don't know what he might do if you were alone together, even for a few moments. Men are wily creatures.' Anxious eyes scan her face.

She folds her hands back onto her lap. 'How would you know what men are like? Real men, I mean.'

He sits very still for several moments. 'You have been betrothed for two years and never been alone with him. There is a reason for that. His family are wealthy and your family have high status because of your reputation. I cannot sully that.'

'So you don't want me to be happy today?'

He turns to her. 'I have wanted you to be happy since I first saw you. When I was allowed to hold your tiny hand when you were born.'

'Like this?' Ya Ling slips a hand into his. His smile is wary. 'So if we go, and you stay in the room all the time, then we don't need to tell Baba. Because he will only say we are too busy today, but I have to tell Altan something very important.'

'What?'

She presses her lips close to his ear. 'How little I know. How afraid I am. It is only fair he knows. He might not want to marry me.'

'Oh Little Sister. You have no idea how much I am going to miss you. Altan already knows all of that. It makes you even more precious to him.'

'But I still want to tell him. It's only fair.'

'All right then. But I won't let you out of my sight, I warn you.' The creases fan out from his eyes. 'Tell me. Who will I keep secrets with, when you move to Altan's household?'

'Oh, you'll find somebody. Ayi?' Her smile is full of mischief as she nudges his elbow. 'She's as deaf as a doorknob so you'll have to shout up a bit.'

They sit shoulder to shoulder sipping their tea as the dull thud of the kettledrums sounds the last watch from the drum tower. Soon the bells from the bell tower will take over to sound the hours. The banner men arrive with their bales of red silk and the seamstresses come to fit the cushions in the ger. The noise from the kitchen spills into the courtyard. They find Ya Zhi trying to maintain her usual calm in the midst of porters carrying yokes of rice and green bok choi. Pigtailed carters drop cages of indignant ducks, while an army of crayfish try to escape from between the slats of their wooden boxes.

'Mama? What on earth is this doing here?' Ya Ling looks furiously through the window at a large turtle trying to flap its fins in a tight iron bowl. She turns to a row of three caged monkeys with shaved heads and limbs splayed out and wired tightly to the bars, staring out, their faces frozen with desperation. 'I didn't ask for any of these.'

'Shh. Don't annoy the cook. He's from the palace. Baba borrowed him and his assistant specially for tonight.' Ya Zhi puts a finger to her lips.

Ya Ling walks up to the cook and taps him smartly on the shoulder. 'You! Who ordered that turtle outside? And those poor monkeys?'

The cook's eyes narrow in his chubby face. 'People expect them, child. It's a special occasion.' He raises a lofty forefinger.

'Child?' Ya Ling's narrow shoulders surge upwards. 'Well, I'm not having them! I didn't ask for either of them. It's cruel. I'm not having a turtle tortured like that, being cooked alive while I am getting ready for my betrothal.' She pins her arms tightly across her chest.

'You fail to understand the subtlety of my cuisine, child. When the water starts to simmer, the turtle flails his fins around and stirs the scallop broth to perfection.' The cook's hands find his hips.

Ya Ling's slipper comes down heavily on the stone floor. 'Mama! Tell him!'

Ya Zhi pushes back a strand of hair under her black silk cap and spins round to make a grab for a tottering pile of golden bamboo steamers. 'To be honest, I didn't think we had ordered a turtle,' she begins. 'I can't quite remember…'

'And the monkeys too. I'm not having those either. Sawing off the top of their skulls and scooping out their brains, it's barbaric!'

Ya Ling drags on the cook's sleeve until he turns round. He looks thunderous. 'Then let me tell you this, young lady, the emperor himself relishes warm monkey brains.'

Noisy kitchen chatter stops abruptly and the chunk of the cleaver against the wooden board sounds suddenly loud. Her mother's worried glance makes Ya Ling think quickly. 'Then I am sure that it must be a most sophisticated dish, but possibly too refined for my palate. Therefore I am asking for *fang sheng*, for lives to be released, on my betrothal.'

The cook shakes his head. 'No. It's too late. They're part of the yin and yang balance of the feast I have devised.'

'Mama?'

Ya Zhi has already turned to try to pair the hundreds of chopsticks that rise out of a blue and white porcelain vase like giant bristles.

'We have to have them. There's not much else.' The cook looks around unconvincingly.

Ya Ling brings over an abacus and slams it on the table. 'So how many dishes have you planned then?' she demands. 'Come on, let's count them.'

'Lamb. Fish. Duck. Crabs. Swallow's-nest congee, sea cucumber with shrimp ovary…' He tails off, his voice tight in his throat.

'So what's this?' She lifts up a triangular shark's fin out of a mound of ice. 'And I can see abalone, geese, sides of pork, so there's plenty of food. Too much in fact.'

'My menu has never been questioned before.'

'Well, it's about time it was.'

They all turn quickly at a loud yell coming from the far end of the kitchen. The cook's assistant runs across, nursing his arm.

'Here, child.' Ya Zhi holds the arm up to the sunshine to examine a patch of raw skin speckled with wood ash. 'Keep still. I know it hurts. I know,' she soothes.

Ya Ling joins her. 'I'll do it. You're busy and I'm better at burns.' She beckons the boy into the dispensary that leads off from the courtyard. Chen follows them. 'Check the pails of boiled well water and bring over the coldest.' He watches her as she talks with authority to the boy. 'I need to clean the dirt from the wound and to cool the skin to stop it burning you further.' As she talks she lowers his arm quickly into the water. At the sink she ladles a constant stream of clean water down his arm. She takes the stopper from a glass bottle and holds it under his nose. 'Here, smell this. Nice, eh? What do you think it might be?' The boy shakes his head and watches her hands as if mesmerised. 'It's lavender oil and it will stop it hurting. You'll see.' She drips the oil gently on the wound. 'Watch what I do now.' She pours a tiny spoonful of clear honey from a pot. 'Here, taste this. For being brave.' The boy smiles. 'I can't let you have any more, I have to mix it with some cream of goldenseal. What do you think that does?' The boy licks his sticky lips and looks blank. 'It will stop any infection and help it heal.'

His smile shows relief and he nods at her hands. 'I've never seen hands like yours and your mother's.'

'And my father's too.' Ya Ling's shoulders come back. 'I am descended from a long line of healers. Some shamans who have the extra finger claim they have the gift, but most of them don't. They deal in sorcery and the spirit world. But don't worry, you are in safe hands with me.' She nudges him. 'See the joke?'

He returns her smile shyly. 'Wait till I tell my friends.'

She lays a fine muslin cloth lightly over his arm. 'Keep it away from the heat and drink a lot of water. You'll be fine.'

The boy bows his thanks across the courtyard before he returns to the kitchen.

'I forget how grown up you are. Then I see you at work and I remember.' Chen smiles as he puts the bottles and pots in the cupboard. 'It was wonderful to watch you distract him from his pain.'

'If you explain to patients exactly what you are doing then it relaxes them too. Healing the body is just as much about healing the mind. That's what Baba has always taught me.'

Chen sighs. 'So grown up. So sophisticated.'

'You might not think so in a moment.' She tiptoes up to whisper in his ear.

'No, Ya Ling! We can't!'

'Watch me.' The turtle eyes them warily as they look down at it. 'Help me, Chen, you know it's right.' They grunt as they lift the iron bowl and stagger to the third courtyard, where they tip out the green turtle into the fishpond and watch him lift a flipper in a lazy gesture of thanks before he sinks beneath the surface in a wake of silvery bubbles. 'I'm allowed a wish on my betrothal day and so I'm now asking for *fang sheng*. In fact, I'm not asking. I'm demanding it!' she shouts across the courtyard. 'Chen, find me some wire clippers.' The monkeys, released from their cages, waste no time in skittering up across the swallow-tailed eaves and soon disappear over the green rooftops.

Ya Ling and Chen stand shoulder to shoulder under the red-pillared terrace. They begin to laugh like naughty children as the sound of raised voices spills out from the kitchen. 'You go too far.' Chen tries to pull himself together. 'What will I do when you go, Little Sister?' he gasps. 'Who will I make mischief with then?'

Ya Ling straightens herself up. 'Come. Let's go before Mama comes to find me.'

Stepping out of the big outer gates into the busy hutong, their eyes sting from the yellow dust blown down from the Gobi Desert mixed with the brick dust from the new city of Beijing being built all around. Building sites are littered with spades, and barrows full of stones are being pushed by peasants with mud-caked legs, as the new avenues spiral out like tendrils from the 9,999 rooms of the Forbidden City.

'Take care, Little Sister.' Chen quickly raises the red paper parasol and lopes behind her, his arm clamped tightly round her. Walking down the newly paved streets, they sidestep the forest of bamboo scaffolding and wait for an ox cart carrying timber to pass before they cross the road into Tea Delicacies Lane. They pass stalls laden with bolts of silk in rich luminous colours, noodle sellers and strident cries of 'Stinky tofu!', 'Quails' eggs!', 'Teeth pulled quickly!' They walk past the pearl stall where strands of pearls spawn together in tangles, and pause to watch the legendary demon queller, who slaps and shouts at his quivering victim to ripples of applause.

'What did you say?' Ya Ling turns and tries to shout above the clanking of the brass harness of a camel train and the loud cries of the rickshaw pullers. Chen's firm finger on her cheekbone tries to turn her face from the road. 'What?' In the distance they hear the crackling of firecrackers above the strumming of the gongs from the nearby temple. 'What do you mean, don't look? Don't look where?' She turns just in time to catch a glimpse of a courtesan in a sedan chair, her hair pulled back in a large coil studded with ivory combs, on her way to pleasure one of the noblemen in the Forbidden City. Chen leans across Ya Ling and holds the parasol like a shield blocking her view.

Ya Ling holds her hand in front of her mouth and laughs. 'Oh Chen! I know exactly what she is! I have seen them before, you know. My problem is that I don't know what she does.'

'Oh.' Chen's face tightens. 'Don't start that again. Come away.' He pulls them up short in front of the chicken-feet seller. Next to him is a sugared-haws cart. 'Go on. Sweet or savoury? Which one? My last treat.'

'I'm not supposed to. Mama says she has to force you to take any money from her, and you are not to spend any more of it on me.'

'Who else do I have, Little Sister?' A line of sadness tamps down each side of his mouth. 'Who else will I ever have?'

'You have Mama and Baba.'

He nods solemnly. 'That's true. And I look forward to a lifetime of service to them.'

She looks at the skewers of the sticky bitter-sweet red fruit, then back at the chicken-feet stall. One claw raised upwards seems to beckon her. 'And this will be your last chance I suppose. That one then.' Her small white teeth nibble on it like a mouse. Chewy and salty. Delicious.

The jade merchant's shop is cool and quiet. He shows her the amulet, produced from a tiny padded silk box. The jade is pure white and the phoenix is beautifully carved, caught in the moment as it rises from the ashes.

Back outside in the teeming alleyway, Chen raises an eyebrow. 'Let's just go home now, Little Sister, there is still so much to do.' He looks round anxiously.

'Chen.' She slides a hand into his. 'You promised.'

He sighs. 'You must never tell Dorji I have allowed you to visit Altan without his permission.'

She nods and blows him a kiss. 'It won't matter next week.'

Altan's silversmith business is not what she imagined. The jewellery shops his family own are famous in Beijing for their rare stones from Mongolia and for the artistry of the pieces they commission, but the size of the workshop amazes her. Altan comes through immediately with a delighted smile on his face and leads them into a side room. His jet black hair pulled back into his green clan cord emphasises his high cheekbones and the broken ridge to his nose. The way his dark brown eyes hungrily seek hers makes the breath catch in her throat. He takes her hand and, eyeing Chen carefully, brings it briefly to his lips. His teeth look very white against his tanned skin when he smiles. 'What a wonderful surprise!' He turns to Chen. 'Salt tea?' he asks.

Chen pulls a face. 'No time.' He settles into a chair in the corner. 'We must leave in five minutes, Ya Ling.'

'I'll go and get it for you. I finished it two days ago.' The necklace looks very fragile in his big capable hands. 'The silver is very pure, from the mines near Kerulan, and the lapis is from Galshir, the most expensive in the world.'

'Oh! It's wonderful.' She blushes at the mystery surrounding the beautifully worked necklace he drops into her hand. A wedding *zarar*. The silver box under the polished blue stone will remain open until after their nuptial night, when a piece of the bridal sheet that will somehow prove her purity will be sealed inside.

His finger nudges gently into her palm. 'I can't wait,' he murmurs. Both turn in surprise at the grating noise coming from the corner. Chen's eyes are tightly shut but Ya Ling cannot tell if he is faking.

The couple look at each other, delighted. Altan wastes no time. He squares his broad frame, then lifts her chin with a gentle knuckle and dips his mouth down quickly to cover hers. His kiss is slow and skilful, and the feelings it stirs inside make her breasts push tight and tender against the shift under her robe. A warm yearning sensation swells the secret part of her, a flickering feeling she wants to grasp, to hold on to and make its fleeting pleasure last and last. Her hands stroke the silk of his hair and drop to his chest, which stiffens under the soft buckskin of his *dheel*. Something moist nudges against her lips and she realises it is his tongue. What should repel her has the opposite effect. She feels her body opening up to him, wanting more of him, wanting to draw him in. She presses against him, amazed how much her body seems to have a will of its own. How natural it feels, but how terrifying at the same time. Her palms slide against him and press him back and he mutters her name with a rough groan.

A dry cough comes from the chair. They both spin round to Chen, who has opened one eye.

'Have you had the conversation you wished to have with Altan, Little Sister?' he asks dryly.

'No. I'm a bit confused.' Her voice is breathless. 'But I don't think I need to now.'

'Then come. It is definitely time to go.' She feels Altan's jaw grind impatiently against her temple and this gives her an unsettling feeling deep inside.

Altan reluctantly opens the door for them. His deep voice murmurs to her as she passes by him: 'I can't wait for tonight. Or any of the nights to come.'

'Enough of that. Come, we must hurry now.' Chen walks briskly towards home but they both slow down when they turn into Lantern Alley and see the men taking their birdcages into Horse Post Square. 'One last time, Little Sister.' They stand watching the men release swallows with flutes attached to their tails, and watch them go whistling up through the rising heat of the morning air, soaring northwards right over the Imperial Palace, perhaps pleasing the emperor himself with their swirling sounds. Chen leans his shoulder into hers. 'You always loved watching these as a child.'

'I remember.' She pauses. 'Che-e-en? Please, Chen…'

'Oh no. Not again.'

'You know when we saw the courtesan…? And I said I know what she is?' Her voice drops. 'I honestly don't. Although I have heard the word brothel. Is that where they live?'

'Yes. I think they might, but anyway you don't need to worry about anything like that.' He steps aside. 'Tonight is only the betrothal. Your wedding is later. Then after that you can ask Altan any questions of that sort that you like.'

'Just give me a hint. And while you're at it, tell me about the *zarar*. I don't understand that either. About the sheet.' She tugs his sleeve impatiently. 'This is the last time I can ask you. Baba says knowledge is power and you always say I should listen to him.'

'Very clever.' Chen looks round rapidly. 'But we need to get home.'

She stops dead. 'Please, Chen. The sheet?'

'I don't know where it started. It's a custom that came from the Spice Roads, from Moorish people, I think.' Chen takes her hand and turns her round to face him. 'Listen, Altan is a good man and he will treat you gently and if he doesn't then you must come to me. And if he ever refuses to let you use your healer's skills then you must come to me as well.'

'You're doing it again, Chen. Changing the subject.' She frowns as his hand clamps her wrist to his side. She tries to wriggle free. 'Of course he'll let me! He knows how gifted I am. His parents are very proud of me, and my parents made them all swear an oath on that.'

'Your skills are very unusual. Even beyond those of your parents, because you have learned from both of them, from all the Han healers on your mother's side, and from all the scholars from the different countries along the Spice Roads who taught your father.' The swallows swoop daintily above them. 'So you must always use the gifts you have. Promise me.' He points up towards the blue sky. 'Never be like one of these birds. Just piping prettily all day. And you must always use your powers for good.' His voice drops to a murmur. 'Look at me. I'm one whose life has been ruined by a man who used his powers for evil. How different my life could have been if he had taken the right path.'

'Stop it, Chen. I refuse to listen.' Her face creases as she gives a vicious tug away from him but he clings on hard. 'You are spoiling my special day by mentioning such hateful things!'

'Listen to me. Once you are married, it might not always be easy for Altan to accept all the things you have to do to your patients, the men particularly. He might lose face. But you must always do what is right. All life is sacred and you must do everything in your power to uphold that.'

'I've heard enough. Know your place.' Her gaze on him is scathing.

'And sometimes you can be very…'

Their tussling on the pavement starts to attract curious looks. 'Very what?' she demands.

He turns reluctantly. 'This might be my only chance to say this, and I really don't want to…' He pauses, his face anxious, '… not today of all days, Little Sister… but you can be conceited. And wilful. Think of how you behaved today with the cook. How impulsive.'

'But I seem to remember you laughing,' she snaps.

'Yes. And now I'm ashamed of myself.'

She glares up at him. 'Go on! Anything else you have to say?'

His expression is pained. 'Well, you don't always show your parents enough obedience. You must be far more respectful to your husband and his family. There, I've said it.' He lets her hand drop.

She slaps his shoulder hard. 'Stop this! How dare you, Chen! How dare you say such things to me! Just remember your place in the household. And the gutter you came from.' His glance on her is even, but she can see the hurt tightening the lines round his eyes. 'This is my betrothal day and you are doing everything you can to spoil it! I'll be glad when next week comes and I'll see the back of you.'

Ya Ling marches away and Chen follows at a cautious distance. As she swings headlong through the big outer door of the Healers' House, she almost bumps into Mama, who has just started laying out the betrothal gifts on a carved table at the side of the *panjin* courtyard. 'Thank goodness! Why did it take you so long? What's wrong, daughter? You look quite red in the face.'

'It's nothing, Mama.'

'Well, help me lay these out, you have such a good eye. Then you must rest before we prepare you.'

The lid of the big betrothal box creaks open and out of the camphorwood paper Ya Ling unfolds a purple Kashmiri shawl, so fine it can be pulled through a wedding ring. A Qum silk carpet comes out next, so cleverly woven in figure-of-eight knots that it changes colour from different viewpoints. Ya Ling strokes them as she tries to calm down. 'But what on earth is this?' She eyes a large piece of crumpled cotton tie-dyed in a harsh blue and with the pattern picked out in large white stitches.

'Aaah.' Ya Zhi raises her eyebrows with a fond smile. 'Ayi has made you a tablecloth as a surprise. It's an old Bai pattern. It's taken her nearly a year, her eyes aren't so good now.'

Ya Ling holds it out at arm's length. 'Well, it's horrible.'

'Shh!' Ya Zhi tries to still her with a glance.

'I don't care. I'm not putting it out with the other presents. What will our guests think?'

'I'm ashamed of you.' Ya Zhi spins her round just in time to see Ayi's stricken face as she bows her way backwards across the courtyard. 'Go and ask her forgiveness.'

'I can't. Not now. I have to go and rest. You just told me to.' Ya Ling tucks her hands tightly into her sleeves. 'Don't look at me like that! Why is everyone trying to spoil things for me today?'

Ayi has already lined the tiled bath with linen cloths and the steam, perfumed with jasmine oil, rises up invitingly. Ya Ling slips herself gently into the water with a sigh and lies back, soaking until she feels the tension ease away. Later she picks at the tray of steamed dumplings that Ayi has left by her bedside. The silk pillow feels cool on her cheek but she turns restlessly. Poor old Ayi. She imagines her bent close to that terrible tablecloth. Perhaps she could find a dark corner somewhere for it. And Chen. She thumps the pillow, remembering the terrible things she's said to him today. He'd understand. He always does. He knows her better than Mama and Baba, so he must know how anxious she is about leaving home. About leaving him.

There are no patients to see today, so she rests and dozes until late afternoon when her mother wakes her with a smile. 'Come, let's make up. Nothing must spoil your betrothal day.'

Ya Zhi plaits her daughter's hair carefully, weaving the amulet tightly into it. The long-sleeved robe of vermilion drops silkily down from her shoulders, tightly belted and buckled with a heavy gold clasp. Ayi sneezes as she sieves white aloe powder through a scrap of red silk, then she powders Ya Ling's face and paints a vivid red patch on her lower lip. Both stand back and breathe out heavily in delight at their handiwork. They carry the looking glass of polished silver across and Ya Ling nods at it, thrilled with her reflection. They lead her out and show her the entrance where the servants have built tier upon tier of shining red-glass lanterns in the weeping willow trees. Strings of jade beads and scarlet and golden prayer flags loop below the terrace roof. Boxes of fireflies buzz impatiently, ready to be let out once darkness falls.

'It's so beautiful, Mama. I never imagined anything like this.'

Her father comes up behind her and threads both arms round her waist. 'Well, we promised Altan's family a sizeable dowry, the best betrothal and the finest wedding we could afford. In return you can practise your healing skills for as long as you wish.' He looks down at her with a wry glance. 'Though I hear that the feast is missing one or two expensive items.'

She slants her head up to look at his profile. 'You don't mind too much, Baba, do you?'

'No. But you should have asked first. Your mother has had to grovel to the cook all afternoon. You can't behave like this in your new family.' He leans down to kiss her temple. 'I expect Altan will have some fun curbing your headstrong ways. But he'll not change you too much, I hope, my precious girl.'

The ger soon fills with guests who, once plied with glasses of yellow Shaoxing wine, loll back on the cushions and laugh uproariously at the acrobats and the magicians. The drums and cymbals try to keep pace with the rising chatter and the laughter as family members catch up on their news, old friends gather together and acquaintances are remade. Silence falls respectfully for the famed singers from Hangzhou, whose plaintive love songs and lilting melodies make the women dab their eyes as they remember their own betrothals. Ibrahim and Chaim oblige with a rousing Hebrew wedding song that gets everyone clapping. As darkness falls a group of men from Shandong province arrive to guard the gates with their large broadswords strapped to their sides.

'I feel giddy with happiness.' Ya Ling smiles, glad of Altan's strong arm cupping her elbow as he guides her round to greet their guests. The moment he leaves her side to embrace one of his uncles, the Berber approaches Ya Ling to admire the amulet and to wish her well. 'Beautiful as ever.' His eyes skim appreciatively over her as he raises his glass. 'To the start of your new life. I'm enjoying the arak I've brought. Perhaps a little too much.' He winks at her from under his blue turban, which, she notes, is already a little lopsided. As he leans across to peck her cheek she smells the aniseed on his wet breath.

Over a hundred platters of food are laid out on tables in two of the courtyards. The servants carry round bowls and chopsticks and the guests help themselves with sighs of appreciation. A great ewer of rice wine is replaced to polite cheers. The Berber cheers the loudest of all, then flops back onto a pile of cushions.

Cones of incense are lit and a temple gong is rung for silence. Two saffron-robed monks carry through the great double ox yoke to signify that the ceremony is about to begin. As Ya Ling and Altan walk slowly into the great ger, mares' milk is sprinkled on the ground before them. They kneel solemnly down in front of both sets of parents and make their promises of love and faithfulness to each other. At the feel of Altan's smooth cheek pressed against hers, Ya Ling feels again a sense of his frustration, and that strange deep-seated excitement starts to rise again inside. A flush blossoms her cheeks as she wonders how familiar she will be with that other part of his body after her wedding night. She can barely suppress her expectant smile. After the kiss in Altan's workshop, it won't be too frightening after all. The wooden harness is lowered carefully over their shoulders to yoke them together and a great cheer billows out the strings of prayer flags looped across the felted roof. Handfuls of dried cherry blossoms are thrown at them and settle on them like snow.

After several hours of feasting and chatter punctuated by loud laughter, the guests begin to depart. When the ger is emptied, the servants begin to clear away and Dorji and Ya Zhi kiss her goodnight. 'Oh, don't go yet. Stay a while longer.' She pulls Baba's hand, trying to hide her mixed feelings at leaving behind her parents and Chen and Ayi.

'I am afraid we can't, dearest child. See how pale Mama looks. She must be exhausted.' Dorji pats his stomach. 'And too much rich food and wine for me, I'm afraid.'

After they have left, Ya Ling sits outside the ger for a long time, even after the servants have left her unchaperoned. She glances down at her pale unusual hands with pride. Chen is right; she has been blessed with the mark of a healer and is destined for great things. She remembers Altan's mouth on hers, alive with promise. A warm glow of optimism permeates her body as she watches the early morning rays break over the Western Hills before she smooths out the creases on her gown and makes her way wearily up to her room, with hope in her heart.

Chapter 3

The headrest feels cool beneath her cheek and she sleeps heavily until her door is shaken by a loud knocking. Ya Ling is dumbfounded to see the day watchman at her door. 'Are you sick as well?' he demands. 'No one seems to be up and the nightwatchman isn't at his post.'

Ya Ling pulls on her day robe and is surprised not to have to step over Chen, who always lies at the threshold to her room. The house is eerily silent as she runs down the corridor to her parents' room. Her father is coiled tightly in bed and his white face grimaces as Ya Ling leans over him. Her mother's own face looks ashen and she turns to her daughter with a huge effort. 'It must have been the shellfish,' she murmurs. 'How awful if we have given our guests these terrible stomach qualms as well. How will I face them at the wedding next week?' A tear runs down her cheek. 'How are the rest of the household?' she whispers.

Ya Ling quickly runs down the stairs, but everywhere is quiet and still. The kitchen and all three courtyards are empty. A spasm of worry grips her when she sees Chen lying curled in a ball under the shade of the *gingko* tree next to the nightwatchman. He groans and mutters when she slips her fingers across his burning forehead. She takes the stairs back to her parents' room two at a time.

'No one is around at all. Chen and the nightwatchman are both sick with a bad fever. It looks like all of the servants are still in bed.'

'All of them?' Both parents speak in a weak chorus.

Her brows furrow. 'It's very strange, I know. Not all of them could have eaten the crab or the crayfish. In fact not all of them could have eaten the same dishes, there were so many to choose from.'

Her father holds a palm to his chest and shudders. 'Please don't mention food. Go to the dispensary and see how much camomile we have.'

Ya Ling nods. 'And we'll need peppermint and liquorice root too.'

The dispensary is cool and tidy. She picks up a bowl and crosses the tiles to the row of wooden casks. A dry crumble of leaves and a wizened stick of liquorice are all she can find.

'Nearly empty?' Her mother looks astonished. 'But they were half-full two days ago.'

'I know. I thought so too. Never mind. I'll go to the forest. I've been enough times with Baba. I know exactly where to find what we need.'

'But you can't go alone.' Her father tries to lever himself upright off the pillow but slumps forwards. 'You must take the day watchman.'

'Yes, I will.' Ya Ling opens the big gate and the day watchman springs to his feet. She looks back anxiously at Chen's sleeping form. 'You must go to each servant and give them big flagons of water,' she instructs him. 'Keep insisting until they each drink plenty.' The man nods, then his jaw drops as she picks up a big yoke with two wicker panniers at each end and calmly steps out into the street.

'Wait for me. You can't go alone.'

The panniers swing as she turns. 'No! You are needed here. Start giving them water now. That's more important.'

The vast forest that surrounds the new capital city starts at the last alleyway of their hutong. The trees are sparse at first where they have been cut down for firewood or building timber, but soon the pathway leads deep into the forest. Ya Ling glances up at the tall fir tree her father uses as a guide. Soon she finds the big patch of strong wild peppermint and quickly snips off the stalks until the pannier is half-full.

'Ya Ling?' She whips round in astonishment to see the blue turban of the Berber bobbing down the path towards her. 'What are you doing here?' he says. 'All alone, are you? Where's Chen?'

'Yes.' She looks round nervously. 'Chen is ill.' It feels strange to be out alone.

'Well, don't worry. It's only me.' The sweat from his hand penetrates her sleeve.

She steps back. His eyes look very bright. 'Are you all right? Do you have a fever too?' He shakes his head. 'Thank goodness for that! Everyone is ill at home. Everyone! I can't understand it but I need to make a large infusion for stomach qualms for all of them.'

'Everyone? Your parents as well?' He eyes her closely, his voice reassuring. 'How strange that is, child. Look, let me help you. What do you need? I've just seen a liquorice plant nearly as tall as me. Just a bit further in. It must have enormous roots, will that help? Come on.'

She looks doubtfully at the path, which lies ahead like a darkening tunnel. 'Why don't you go and bring them back? I can search for what I need round here.'

'Oh. I thought you were a healer in your own right. I thought you knew what you were doing.'

His voice has a slight edge to it.

'I am. And I do.' Her chin comes up as she hoists up the panniers more comfortably.

'Sorry. But I am worried about your parents. They're such good friends. And Chen too.'

'I know.' She smiles. 'Lead on.'

'Good.' He leads her deeper into the forest until they come to a clearing and she blinks to see the Berber's big mule lift up his head and snort a greeting. The heavy wooden wheels of his cart have made grooves in the pine needles.

'How odd.' Ya Ling smiles at him. 'To bring the cart so far into the forest.'

'Oh, you know how lazy I am.' The Berber reaches to untie the goatskin *tuzluk* from the shaft of the cart. She notices his top lip is misted with sweat. 'All this picking is thirsty work. And I am ashamed to say I have quite a sore head after last night. Was I badly behaved?' He winks as he passes the container to her. The drink tastes sharp like pomegranate. 'Go on, have it all, I've got plenty more, and have one of these too.' He takes a little paper parcel out of his pocket. The hard little sweetmeat has a strong flavour of anise.

'Where is the liquorice bush?' Ya Ling glances around very slowly, and her eyes flare open. All the tree trunks seem to be dissolving into wavery lines around her, and her legs feel suddenly made of cloth and start to fold beneath her. The pine needles scratch through her robe when the Berber lowers her to the forest floor. Her wondering eyes stare at him as he takes out a handful of ropes of different lengths and she watches him tie her up thoroughly and wrap a gag round her mouth, which despite a huge effort she can only open in a frail sigh of protest. He lays her gently inside a pile of rugs in the back of the cart before she hears him clicking the mule on, and the cart creaks as they set off. Her head thuds from side to side with the motion of the cart and feels as if it will explode with pain, but she can't seem to control its movement. She slowly feels pulled down and down into a steep dark well.

When the sun has sunk deeper, the cart stops and a sudden explosion of voices makes her head spin. She gazes slackly into the darkness as several pairs of hands carry her out of the cart and lower her under the woven straw roof of a rice barge. 'Very nice. She looks very expensive,' says a man. She feels a prickle of premonition as she looks up at the approving faces staring down at her from the bank.

'Wait!' She dimly recognises the Berber's voice and feels a painful tugging at her hair and hears him curse as he cuts the amulet free. A hard hand squeezes her breast as she is dragged up into a sitting position and the neck of the *tuzluk* is pushed into her mouth. Her hands flail towards him and she tries to force some strength into them. She spits it out and pomegranate juice spills down the front of her robe. 'I would drink all of this if I were you,' the Berber warns. 'You might be glad of it.' He chuckles in a way that makes her shiver. An image of the courtesan with the ivory combs swims across her mind and her heart races. 'As I promised you at your betrothal, your new life is just about to begin.' Her lips are pulled apart and the juice is poured down her throat. She sinks back onto a pile of hemp sacks, glad to be free of the bumping of the cart and to be floating gently along a calm river. The blood in her temples pounds like a hammer, then gradually the pain in her head slips away and she feels part of the river's gentle flow. Over the next few days it becomes a routine; she wakes in a cold sweat of fear before bread is pushed between her lips, then more juice follows, then she falls again into a long shadowy sleep.

The sound of gulls and the salty tang in the air wake her from the torpor that covers her like a blanket. The guttural tone of a Tianjin accent rouses her and she registers it as important and tries to keep that fact from floating away in her mind.

The cold air as she is lifted into the hold of a big wooden ship stirs her to wakefulness. Glancing up, she sees the white sails snap in the breeze, and she almost sobs with relief as the tight ropes are cut away and she can finally flex her legs. 'Keep still.' The voice is harsh. 'If you behave, then you will be brought up for air tomorrow. You'll find bread and meat below.'

She is lowered to a small shallow room just below deck and before the wooden hatch is slammed down she sees a plate of bread and pork ribs next to two straw pallets. The room smells heavily of peppercorns and cloves. The gloomy light in the room seems to make its small dimensions close inwards and her hot panicky fear of being enclosed makes her heart beat faster and faster.

A sudden scramble lifts the covers of the pallet next to her and a broad face with a ragged haircut leans down. Ya Ling feels an arm under her back trying to lift her up and then a bowl of water is held to her lips. She gulps and gulps and shakes her head, trying to shake off the weariness that weighs her down. Despite the water her voice is hoarse. 'Who are you? Where is this ship taking me?' she demands.

The lopsided fringe shakes from side to side. Underneath it the girl's cheeks are pockmarked and weathered. Her hair looks patchy where it has been cut close to the skull. Ya Ling tries again, this time not using courtly Mandarin. Then she tries two different Mongolian dialects and finally Bai. A wide grin of relief spreads across the girl's face before her words tumble out in a rush. Her accent is coarse. 'I'm Mei Ming. I don't know where we're going but don't worry, it's going to be a wonderful place with a great big house where the captain has found us work. My father told me that. My sisters were sold before me and they sent word to him that they are really happy there.'

'What?'

'I can't wait to see them.'

Ya Ling holds her hand to her face to hide her uneasiness. Her fingers still smell of mint. The Berber. Her eyes look huge as she stares at the girl. That's it. That's why he never told anyone his real name. How easy it had been to target everyone in her family's household. How well he knew all of them. How trusting they had all been. Her fingers tighten into a fist. She must get back to Altan and her family as soon as possible and tell them what the Berber did, so they can have him punished, then no other girl will be taken like this.

'What's the matter, lady? Why are you staring at me like that?'

'Nothing.' When she shakes her head the ship's hold whirls around. 'A big house? And where is it? How far away?' She manages to keep her voice even.

'No idea. But we'll never be hungry again. Look! Meat!'

'No. Take it away.' Ya Ling ignores the plate that is dropped on her lap. Mei Ming chews with gusto. They both look around as the room begins to rock and the sailors begin shouting to each other in brisk purposeful Mandarin and in a strange musical language. Mei Ming huddles her shoulder next to hers. The girl smells of bad teeth. Ya Ling shudders before pushing her away. She tries to stand, staggering with the ship's pitch. The rigging snaps like a firecracker, and after a while the ship rears up like a terrified horse.

Mei Ming starts a spirit chant. 'Join in, it's better if we both do it. Twice as strong.'

'I don't know what you are doing.' Ya Ling braces two hands against the wooden mast in the centre of the room.

'To keep the bad spirits happy. You've got to flatter them a bit.' She continues, her voice nasal and flat.

Ya Ling stares down at her. 'Don't be ridiculous. That won't do anything.'

The girl puts down the plate and lies down queasily. Her voice sounds suddenly like a child's. 'I hope we don't die in here. It's your fault if we do. I hope we don't go straight to the bottom.'

Ya Ling loses her footing and falls on the planking. She cradles her spinning head in her hands.

'Oh! Look at those flowers on your robe!' Mei Ming runs her fingers over the bright red peonies embroidered round the hem. 'Look! They match your shoes. I've never seen anything so pretty.'

'Shh! I need to think.'

'Why did your parents let you keep them?'

'Keep what?'

'Clothes like that! Are they rich?'

'What?' Ya Ling gives a look of distaste as she moves the girl's greasy hand off her hem. 'Yes, of course they are.' Her eyes try to focus as she looks urgently round the room. 'We've got to do something before the ship sails. Find a way out. Or at least leave a message for Chen.'

'Who's he?'

Ya Ling shakes her head as she tries to concentrate. She stands shakily but slumps down again as the ship gives a great lunge forwards.

'Why would you do that? It's too late anyway.'

She sags back into the wooden curve of the ship's side, remembering the way the sailors had looked at her. Expensive, that's what they had said. Her scalp tightens with fear. Around them the timber creaks and groans as the ship rolls on each wave as it picks up speed. Homesickness rises in her chest, stronger even than fear. She looks round in the gloomy light, imagining Altan's tall frame frantically pacing the forest long after the search parties have given up. Of Mama and Baba lying so pale and ill in bed. Who will make the infusions and the tisanes they need? She remembers Chen curled up in pain under the shade of the *gingko* tree. That pain in his stomach will be as nothing compared to the guilt that will rend him in two that he let her go to the forest alone. She remembers her unkind comments to him, the way the lines round his eyes had etched deeper with the hurt she had caused him. Rocking backwards and forwards with the motion of the ship, she can hardly bear to think of her arrogance over Ayi's homemade tablecloth, of her small frame bowing backwards with shame across the courtyard. Tears pour down each cheek as she tries hard to keep each sob stifled inside her chest. Her arrogance has brought bad luck. This terrible misfortune is all her fault. She has to get back and make amends.

'Don't cry. Please don't. You'll set me off.' She feels a heavy arm across her shoulder but the sour waft of sweat makes her shake it off. 'Think how well your family will eat when your father takes the money home. That's what is keeping me strong.'

'No. You don't understand.' Ya Ling lifts up her wet face and shakes her head, making it spin. 'I'm different to you. I was stolen. My parents don't know where I am.'

'Were you? Stolen?' Mei Ming puts down the rib bone she was chewing. 'So they got no money for you? No wonder you feel terrible! Come over here.' Ya Ling feels her pallet being tugged across the planks. Mei Ming's shift, stiff with dirt, crackles as she leans across to pat her arm.

'Don't do that.' Ya Ling tries to move aside. 'I was taken the day after my betrothal party. I am to be married next week.' Mei Ming pats even harder. Ya Ling sits very still, thinking that the kiss that Altan gave her in his workshop, which stirred such longings in her, might be his last for some time. The wedding postponed until she returns. She pushes Mei Ming away and gives herself a good shake. Lying down and crying will achieve nothing. His last kiss for a short time, that's all. 'I need to get back to my family,' she says, straightening her back. She scrubs her face on her sleeve. 'To Altan. I must make apologies to my servants too. I have to find a way out of here and off the ship before it goes any further.'

'Servants? You had servants? Well, you will be able to get back to them. Once you have saved up enough of your wages, you'll be able to go home.' Mei Ming yawns and curls up on her pallet. Ya Ling sits thinking hard. She makes herself stand and begins unsteadily pacing out the wooden walls, feeling her way round the huge circumference of the mainmast in the middle of the room, then she moves along each inward-sloping wall of planks feeling for any hinge or any door handle. There is nothing. The hatch above, buried between the big beams of the ceiling, is the only way out. She bangs hard on it and yells as loudly as she can. Standing precariously on a cask, she presses her ear up to a gap between the planks where the sailors on night watch chat idly to each other. She puts her eye to a knothole and shrieks like a fiend. The sailors glance in her direction briefly, then ignore the noise. Not all the sailors are Han; there are some round-eyes among them too and she must learn some of their words if she is to have any chance of escaping. It's a tuneful language that rises and falls and sounds soft on the ear. After a while she stops shouting and listens hard. Eugenio. Her frame slackens with relief. Now she concentrates furiously, reminding herself of the words she knows and puzzling out those she doesn't. Working out from the tone of the sailors' voices what is the question and what the answer might mean. The men move further down the ship and she moves back to her pallet, trying to ignore the narrow space under the deck that locks her in like a coffin.

She turns to the pallet next to her. 'Listen, I can't do any more for now so we must rest. We'll need our strength for tomorrow when we make our escape.'

But Mei Ming has fallen fast asleep and snores on undisturbed. The wooden sides of the ship seem to be creeping inward. With her hands on her ribcage she calms her fearful breaths until they are slow and deep, turning her thoughts to the Mongolian steppes where she learned to ride as a child when she was taken to visit her father's family to escape from the heat of the Beijing summer. Like a wing-clipped bird imagines soaring in the clouds, she directs her thoughts back to the openness of the Mongolian grasslands, feeling once more the rugged frame of the Ujimchin pony beneath her as she canters across the vast sun-baked steppe, until she can inveigle sleep to overtake her.

'Come on! Up you get! Get some fresh air.' The captain's face at the hatch wakes both of them. A rush of cooler air streams itself into the rising heat as the mid-morning sun warms up their shallow little room below deck. He shouts for a length of rope.

'Can you understand what he says?'

'Yes. He's speaking Mandarin,' Ya Ling whispers.

'A round-eye can speak Mandarin? And you can speak it as well as Bai? How can you do that?'

'And two Mongolian dialects. Some Moorish and Hebrew as well, and I understand some round-eye languages too. In fact I already recognise a lot of the words these men speak. My parents had friends from many countries and they stayed with us when they came to Beijing to trade.'

'Well, you're a lot cleverer than me, so I'm counting on you to keep me safe.'

They both look up at a sudden grating noise. The captain levers himself down between them and hoists them up onto the deck, where two of his men hold them still as they rope the girls' ankles together. Mei Ming looks down in surprise. Ya Ling stiffens her spine and lifts her head high. Pulling on his shirt-sleeve, she holds his glance despite the shock of his blue eyes. 'My parents will pay you a fortune for my release.' Her voice skids on the edge of panic. 'More money than you can imagine.'

His eyes pierce his red salt-chapped cheeks. 'Too late for that,' he grunts in fluent Mandarin as he checks the knots. 'In case you hadn't noticed, we're already at sea.'

The men return to their duties on the ship, leaving the girls space to look around in every direction. Their mouths drop in shock. Already the land has disappeared. All around them great swollen grey waves with lacy white peaks rise and fall on each side of the ship. Clutching each other, they spin round on the slippery deck. There is nothing but the sea as far as the horizon on every side. Ya Ling stares at the waves heaving all around her with a thudding heart. Even Chen will find it difficult to track her down with such a mighty ocean between them.

'Why are we tied together? I'm not running anywhere!'

'Because we're prisoners. We're valuable.'

'But there's nowhere to go.'

'Oh, there is.' Ya Ling swallows hard.

'Where? Where can we hide on here? They'd find us in no time. Then what would we do?'

'Shh. They're watching us. I'll tell you later on.'

They sit down awkwardly on the deck and try to make themselves look inconspicuous. After a while, Mei Ming nudges Ya Ling.

'What are you doing? Staring at the men like that.'

'I told you before, I'm learning the round-eyes' language. I know some of it already, but I need to know a lot more. A merchant called Eugenio used to stay with us when he came to buy silk. There is a big port in a place called Venezia and the round-eyes travel through it to get to the eastern countries like ours.'

Mei Ming looks astonished. 'But I don't understand…'

'You need to listen to the sounds and watch what they do next. I'm going to do this each time we're allowed up here. The captain gives orders in Mandarin first, then he speaks in the other language to the round-eyes. There are over ten of them so he speaks both languages a lot. I already know some of the names of the parts of the ship.'

'No! Do you? Already?'

'And when the sailors' voices sound sad then I know they're talking about family and of home, so I know some of those words too. You should do the same. It's very important.'

'No. I don't need to. Once I'm in the big house I'll only be chopping vegetables and mopping floors, they'll teach me all I need. I bet you'll get all the nice jobs like arranging flowers.'

Ya Ling looks across at Mei Ming in disgust. 'Haven't you learned anything yet, you stupid girl? You're a prisoner. You'll want to escape and go back home to your family.'

'Not me. As long as they keep me fed and give me a full pallet, then I'm happy.' Mei Ming lies on her back and turns her face to the sun.

Something moving idly in the breeze catches Ya Ling's eye. She pokes the girl in the ribs.

'Wake up! You need to help me. Let's move quietly over to the side where that bunch of seaweed is caught in the planking. I need it. It might help us.'

Mei Ming grumbles but shuffles along the deck until Ya Ling can reach out and tuck the strings of leathery seaweed under her robe.

'What's that for?'

'I don't have a knife so I can't make any marks, but I need something to count off the days so I know how long it's going to take me to get home.' Mei Ming shakes her head with a smile.

Each night Ya Ling bites off one of the tiny air pockets that look like brown bobbles along the length of the seaweed, and puts them in a pile. As the pile grows bigger, she becomes more and more anxious. Over the next three weeks the only variation to the long empty days they spend on deck is the weather. Hot days are spent in the shade of the rigging, while on blustery days when the wind blows cool and fresh they avoid the sting of the sea spray by crouching behind the comforting width of the mainmast. They ignore the overtures the sailors begin to make. The whispers, the winks and the gestures. A big-shouldered sailor worries her the most. One of his cheeks has been eaten away by the pox and his pale eyes have a look of desperation as he stands closer to them each day and stares down hard.

'Why is he doing that?' Mei Ming asks. 'Are his trousers too tight?'

'I don't know but don't stare at him.' Ya Ling snatches the hem of her cloak from under his foot. 'Or any of them,' she murmurs, uneasy at the way the men are beginning to get nearer. To get bolder. The only sailor she has spoken to is the oldest, a man with a long grey ponytail and gnarled hands who agreed to ask the captain for a bucket of clean water, for soap and two cloths and for a chamber pot to be lowered into the hold and changed each night. The following day he approaches them, holding two moth-holed fustian cloaks. He points to himself. 'Me Agostino. Got these for you. Put on.' His Mandarin is well pronounced. 'Big wind today.' He mimes as if shaking, then hands them over. As he scurries away she remembers how often he has managed to station himself between them and any of the rougher-looking sailors when they approached. Ya Ling eases out the length of rope that binds them together, apparently chatting to Mei Ming, but all the time listening hard, repeating each sound the round-eyes make over and over to herself. The language slowly cedes its structure to her and she stores every new word she learns, pulling each one close.

The sea turns stormy one day and their legs have trouble keeping them upright on the heaving deck. Mei Ming tumbles heavily and brings Ya Ling down with her. The captain curses the nearest sailor. 'I don't want the taller one bruised,' he orders in Mandarin. 'She's going to be a private sale. The other one doesn't matter. No dockside brothel's going to be that fussy.'

Ya Ling clamps her lips together and drops her eyes in case her face betrays the horror that surges inside.

'Aye. She'll get plenty of bruises there.' The sailors suddenly crowd round the women. 'No perks on this trip, Captain?' one asks. The sailor rubs his pocked cheek. 'Go on. Who's to know?' The other men mumble in agreement, the smell of sweat and longing steaming off them like the miasma off a swamp. Agostino hovers anxiously and tries to squeeze into the crowd but is pushed backwards.

'Get back, you lot.' The captain nods at his two henchmen. Their swords give a grinding whisper as they leave their scabbards and the men step back. 'Don't waste your time even thinking about it. Not even the ugly one. And the taller one is too good for you, you can all see that. They'll fetch a much higher price as virgins. You know that by now.' He repeats his orders in both languages, several times. 'Any man going anywhere near them will pay a very heavy price.'

Ya Ling tries to stand but her legs tremble violently as she processes the stream of Mandarin. Virgins? Her stomach churns as her thoughts spill out. The Berber's timing had been perfect. Trying to kneel, the deck comes to meet her as a vast rolling wave sends a spray of water that gushes over each side of the ship. The captain pulls her to his feet and his arms tighten round her. The greedy look in his eyes confirms her worst fears. She is going to be sold to a man she doesn't know and forced to marry him. Or even worse.

Once back below decks Mei Ming finishes off a plate of dried ham. 'I wonder if they'll feed us like this in the big house?'

'Mei Ming, I need to talk to you.'

The girl looks up at her, her cheeks slick with fat. 'Oh no! Look at your lovely slippers.'

Ya Ling looks down. The embroidery is coming off in whorls and a button has sheared off, making the strap flap about when she walks. Ayi would be horrified. Her eyes well up.

'Never mind that.'

'Why? What's the matter?'

Ya Ling tries to keep her voice steady. 'There is no big house, Mei Ming,' she begins slowly. 'We're going to be sold to men who will pay to do anything they like with us.'

'Don't be silly.' The creases deepen on Mei Ming's low forehead. 'You don't know that...' Her voice rises into a wail.

'I do. That's what I overheard the captain say just now.'

'But my father would never have...'

'He wouldn't have known what was going to happen.'

'But my sisters...' Mei Ming slumps down to the floor. 'What happened to them?' Ya Ling stares at the floor. 'But I'm not even pretty.'

'I don't think that matters to them.'

Mei Ming covers her face with her hands. After a while she looks up, her face slackening with relief. 'You can't be right, because why would the captain have cut my hair off and sold it to the wig man? If he wanted me to look my best?'

A dockside brothel. That's what the captain had said. Ya Ling's voice feels locked in her throat. 'I don't know.' She looks away.

'Are you sure that's what the captain said?'

Ya Ling nods. 'I'm telling you the truth. Why would I lie to you?'

Mei Ming gives a deep, wrenching sigh. 'I believe you. My father isn't a clever man.'

'Come here.' Ya Ling steels herself and bends down to put her arm stiffly round the girl's waist, watching her fingers fuss with a corner of her pallet.

'Well, there's nothing we can do about it.' She rubs her face with the hem of her shift. 'We can't run away. We'll just have to get used to the idea. At least we'll be together.'

'No. There is a way. We're going to be dishonoured, so…'

'So?' says Mei Ming. 'What can we do?'

'When we next go on deck we must both jump over the side.'

'But I can't swim! I've never even been in water before.' Her eyes dart around in panic. 'And don't forget we're tied together.'

'I can swim. I'll help you.' Ya Ling keeps up a look of composure for as long as she can. 'Promise me you'll come with me. Dishonour is worse than death. And I can't do it alone.' Mei Ming looks across, her swarthy face streaked with tears, and nods.

That night neither sleeps or speaks much to each other and the air feels very close. Just after sunrise the captain opens the hatch. From the deck Ya Ling tries for Mei Ming's sake to keep her face calm and stares steadily ahead. The sea looks wild, the waves more quarrelsome as if pitching their mighty power against each other, but she knows they have no choice. As Ya Ling pulls Mei Ming gently towards the side of the ship, the rope opens out between them. 'Come on! Now!' She runs headlong and manages to get one hand on the ship's rail before the rope tightens and pulls her up short. She feels a leaden weight behind as Mei Ming digs her heels into the deck, and hears her squeal as sharp splinters dig in. Ya Ling strains and manages to get her other hand on the rail again before two sailors run across the deck and drag her back. The captain arrives quickly but before he can get to the girls one of the sailors calls him to one side.

'Hold out your hands.' Ya Ling holds them out with a proud smile, which soon drops at the captain's unexpected reaction.

'Gesù Cristo!' He stares hard at her as if blaming her for a shameful deed, before both girls are bundled roughly down into their hold and the hatch is rammed down over their heads.

'I'm sorry,' pants Mei Ming. 'I'm not brave like you. I never will be.'

'Then pay the price for everything that lies ahead, you stupid girl.' From that point on, Ya Ling blocks all attempts Mei Ming makes to speak to her. They are not allowed on deck for two days and the heat in the small space begins to infiltrate every pore. Strips of hot sunlight filter through the gaps in the planking and fibres from the hemp sacks float idly in the stifling air. The fiery smells of the spices in the cargo hold burn the back of their throats. 'Hot enough for you?' She smiles as if delighted at the patches of sweat that deepen all over Mei Ming's shift. 'Thirsty enough?'

Each night Ya Ling spends with her ear to the hatch, listening to the sailors speaking on their watch, whispering the phrases to herself over and over again.

One morning they are woken by the hatch being levered off. 'You two don't deserve this. Any favours from me at all. I'm only doing it so you are in good shape when you arrive!' the captain shouts down after a grille has been hammered into the space. A cooler breeze stirs the sweltering heat in the small room.

The following evening the captain brings Ya Ling up on deck and leads her into his cabin. A half-empty bottle of *baijiu* liquor stands on the table and the captain's speech is slurred. Ya Ling glances nervously round the room. It is surprisingly clean and spacious.

She straightens her back. 'Where is the ship going?'

'Venezia.'

'Venezia?' Her heart surges with relief. 'You mean the place where there is a big port where many merchants trade?'

The captain looks impressed. 'Yes, it's a massive trading port. How did you know that?'

'The one where traders from the Spice Roads travel through?'

The captain's smile is sharp. 'You're a clever girl, I'll give you that. But don't build up your hopes. Your chances of getting back to Beijing are less than nothing. No man will let you out of his sight.' He gives her a brief smile. 'I know I wouldn't.'

'But you're wrong.' Her chin comes up. 'You have no idea. Chen will find me. He'll cross the world if he has to. He'll stop at nothing until I am safely home.'

'Well, good luck to him.' The captain shrugs with a weary smile. 'Whoever he is.'

'But I'll get home on my own, if I have to.'

'Of course you will.'

She thinks for a moment. 'Listen to me, if you honestly think I will never get back to my own country, then you must give us some lessons in the language of this place Venezia. The older man called Agostino, he could do that.' His strange blue eyes widen at her challenging tone. 'It will make us much more valuable when you sell us. Won't it?'

'And make your chances of escape a little better perhaps?' His chair scrapes against the floor as he stands quickly and calls for a decanter. 'I'll think about it,' he mumbles. 'It won't be my problem then, in any case.'

Facing her across the table, he gives her a glass of strong wine. His eyes drop curiously down to her fingers, where they cup round the curve of the glass. The wine tastes vaguely familiar and helps settle her nerves, so she allows him to refill it again. 'How can you do this?' Her Mandarin is tight and clipped. 'How can you sleep at night?'

He glances up towards a darkened porthole, then shrugs and looks away. 'I have a family. Men to feed. It's a cargo like anything else. Just more expensive than most.' He touches his chest as if trying to locate a reservoir of decency that once might have lain inside. Picking up the decanter, he waits, poised, until her head begins to drop forwards. He calls out and she stirs, trying to force up her head, which now feels incredibly heavy, and falls backwards against the wooden headrest of the ship's chair. 'Not such a lady after all, eh?' The captain smirks as she manages to let rip one of Chen's more colourful curses at her own stupidity. Two sailors come quietly into the room and one ties her hands to the arms of the chair, while the other one puts a small sawn-through log of wood on the table in front of her. Her eyes swim as the rings of the wood flow inwards and outwards like the ripples in a pond. A gag is tightened round her mouth. One of her hands is untied and her little finger is pulled apart so widely on top of the log that it hurts and she hears a voice protest that sounds a little like her own. The captain and the sailor bear their weight down on her so she cannot move at all. 'Get rid of them both. The last one from each hand. Do a clean job,' the captain warns. 'I don't want it to show.'

She sees the axe blade come down in a swift arc and when her hand is lifted away, she sees her sixth finger lying on the block. The shock and the outrage pluck a scream from deep within her chest and make her teeth work furiously into the gag. She tries to summon enough strength to pull her other hand away from the block, but her limbs are overcome with a lassitude so overpowering that all she can do is watch the axe's rapid descent and stare at her two precious extra fingers, which now lie parallel on the block in the middle of a pool of blood. Before she faints, her teeth sink into the gag and her curses are muffled within the confines of the captain's room.

The throbbing of her hands wakens her at dawn the next day. Holding them nearer to her face in the half-light, she sees the bloodstained rags wrapped round each one, and she realises it wasn't a nightmare.

Mei Ming squats in front of her, her face frozen with worry. 'Oh, you're alive. I'm so glad!'

Ya Ling glances down at the patches of scarlet that ooze out of the bandages, then she manages to speak through gritted teeth. 'Untie the rope wound round that empty sack.'

Mei Ming turns in surprise. 'This one?' She shakes it open and a few cloves spill onto the floor, releasing their spicy smell.

'Now tie my hands above my head with my fingers pointing upwards, and don't untie me no matter how much I might beg you to.'

Mei Ming's face crumples in sympathy. 'Oh, I couldn't do that! I was always the soft one in the family, the one who could never wring a chicken's neck even though I was desperate to taste it, and I always cried when—'

'I'll bleed to death if you don't. I have to stay like that for at least two days.'

Ya Ling cries out as she shifts her position to look upwards, watching when Mei Ming throws the rope round a rafter and gently pulls each hand up higher and higher. 'I'm sorry. I'm sorry.' Her face is blistered with tears.

Ya Ling spends the next agonising hours trying to rise above the pain by remembering every detail of her betrothal party, the feel of Altan's warm palm at her waist as they walked through the courtyards to talk to their guests, the pride in her parents' eyes and the sight of Chen, the wine jug poised ready, attending to every detail. She remembers the labels on each of the glass phials in the dispensary and recites to herself what the contents were used for. Mei Ming constantly fusses over her, dabbing away her own tears and bathing Ya Ling's face with water.

When dusk filters through the grille on the second day Ya Ling summons her strength. 'Carefully open the bindings and see if they still bleed.'

Mei Ming pulls a terrified face, but does as she is asked. 'No. I think it's stopped.'

'Then untie my wrists carefully please.' Her voice is faint and she winces when she gingerly stretches her aching arms and lowers her hands.

Mei Ming's eyes are lost in her waterlogged cheeks. 'You were right. I should have listened to you,' she sobs. 'We should have jumped.'

Ya Ling cries out in pain as she rests her hands back on her lap. 'Yes. You should, you stupid little fool. We've missed our chance.'

'I wonder what they're going to chop off me?' Mei Ming's voice rises in hysteria.

'Nothing. They won't do anything to you. I had six fingers. The mark of a shaman or a healer. They didn't know which I am, so they had to remove them. That's all. To make me more saleable, I bet.'

'I noticed them before but I didn't dare to say anything.' She bites her bottom lip. 'So which are you?'

'A healer. Like my father and mother. It's in their bloodlines.'

'Are you sure? Because I've been terrified you might be a shaman.'

'You don't need to worry. The gift of healing is a privilege and it comes with strong obligations. My family use our gifts only for good. Sorcerers still worship the sky god Tengri, but my mother's family worship Buddha, and my father's family have been Muslim for many generations. We are good people.'

'I'm glad you've told me this because I've been so scared.' Mei Ming sighs in relief. 'I'm just so sad for you. It must be really painful.'

Ya Ling nods, her face pale. 'It is. But I am more afraid they have taken away my gift. Shout for the captain.' When his face appears over the frame of the hatch, she demands a bucket of fresh seawater, a bowl of clean salt and fresh bindings. 'I'll know over the next few days. If I'm not able to heal the wounds to my hands, then they will have taken my healing powers as well.'

She soaks her fingers in the strong mix of salt water for as long as she can bear. Gasping in agony, she eases a strip of skin and flesh over the bony nub on each side of her hand and binds it close. Two days later she sags in relief against the pallet when the flesh round each small wound begins to heal pink and clean.

To her surprise, when they are next brought up on deck they are given words to learn by Agostino. He looks down at her hands and his face falls in sympathy. He speaks Mandarin with an educated accent and his vocabulary in the round-eye language of the ship is very precise.

'When do we land?' Ya Ling asks straight away. 'And is it Venezia?'

'Hard to say. It all depends on the winds and the tides.' He gives a tight cornered smile. 'How long we wait at victualling stations. How much sickness we have on board. But yes, we're heading for Venezia.'

Her eyes search his face. 'From your experience then, how long?'

He sucks in air between the gaps in his teeth. 'At least six more months. Perhaps seven.'

She looks aghast. 'So when we get there, we're going to be eight months from Beijing?' Chen doesn't like travelling. He likes what he knows. For life to be quiet and calm. But he will. For her. To the end of the earth. She has no qualms about that.

Agostino nods. 'Possibly, could be less, but it depends on storms and currents and docking for ship repairs. Things like that.'

Her eyes narrow. 'But we must be stopping quite soon, Agostino. We've been eating dry biscuits for days now and the water tastes brackish. There will be sickness if this continues.'

'Yes, we'll be stopping off for victualling soon to take on water and meat and vegetables, perhaps a few hens if we're lucky.' His smile is kind. 'Fresh eggs, eh? You'll like that.'

She nods as if thrilled. 'And what else will happen?'

'More cargo. I think a load of indigo at the first one. The crew need to rest up a bit as well. We'll stop at five stations on the way.'

'Really?' Ya Ling's eyes widen, but she keeps her voice casual. 'I wonder what will happen to us when we dock. Do you know?'

His look across is shrewd. 'Nothing. Captain's orders. You'll both stay on board, but he'll let you up on deck for air when it's dark. Heavily guarded. He can't take any risks with you.' There is grudging admiration in his voice, which drops low. 'My advice is to learn as much as you can from me, then try your luck in Venezia. I can't do any better for you. It's the best advice you'll get.' His mouth droops.

Deep in thought, she wraps her arms round her knees. Her eyes search his intently, and find only kindness and regret. She nods dispiritedly and thanks him.

Learning with him each day, his enthusiasm for her progress spurs her on. On the days when she struggles hard with complicated new words and sounds, his shoulders look as though they would be comforting to lean against. She can almost feel the brush of Altan's buckskin *dheel* against her cheek and feels a lump rise in her throat. Mei Ming only tries a few words each day, then gives up, settling her back against the warm planking of the deck and snoozing. Ya Ling always shoots her a look of disgust. Their days settle into a deadening routine with Ya Ling listening hard and learning. Soon the deckhand corrects her only occasionally as they begin to hold long conversations, which are always punctuated by Mei Ming's loud snores. The captain rarely comes out of his room.

By the time the ship has pulled out of the third docking station, the seaweed bobbles have run out and Ya Ling begins to save rice from her rations. After the fifth station, when the combined total of days is nearly two hundred, Ya Ling feels near to despair. She remembers the impatient edge to Altan's voice. 'I can't wait for tonight. Or any of the nights to come.' The sense of energy suppressed in him. How handsome he is. How eligible. Once they set foot on dry land she must escape immediately. Mei Ming turns over on her pallet, muttering in her sleep. Ya Ling turns her head in the darkness. If Chen isn't waiting for them in Venezia, then it will be up to her. Somehow she must find a way to save Mei Ming and get her to safety as well.

A week after the last victualling stop she senses a different energy on board. Pressing her ear tight against a knothole, she hears two sailors talk about landing, and later on deck she sees one of them doing a vulgar mime and guesses they are talking about the women waiting for them. Perhaps in one of the whorehouses the sailors talked about before. Chen has got to be there waiting for her, but realistically it might take him a few days more. She glances across at Mei Ming and feels a wave of pity for her before she pushes a fist against her chest to stem the rise of panic she feels for herself. An image slips into her mind of Ayi bowing backwards across the courtyard, of Chen's face when she insulted him. If Chen arrives later, she can't let Mei Ming go to face whatever lies ahead before they can rescue her, without making amends. When they are next allowed on deck she picks up a strip of knobbly seaweed that has just blown over the side, and offers it to Mei Ming. Before she can take hold of it Ya Ling squeezes one of the leathery air pockets until it gives a loud pop. Mei Ming jumps backwards, then laughs. 'Can I have a go? Are we friends now?'

Ya Ling nods briskly. 'Yes. Yes. Of course we are.' She pats the girl's shoulder briefly. 'You can keep it.'

The next day a much bigger bucket of water is lowered through the hatch. 'What's this for?' Mei Ming looks at it doubtfully.

'Tell her to wash herself and you come with me.' The captain won't catch Ya Ling's eye.

'But I've had a wash every now and then. I'm all right.'

'Better do as he says.' Ya Ling tries to keep her voice light as she follows the captain into his room.

He nods to a wooden barrel half-filled with warm water and hands her a piece of soap and a strip of linen. 'I'll lock the door and wait outside, I can't afford to be tempted,' he says over his shoulder. A clean hemp shift lies on the bed.

Ya Ling purses her lips. 'I don't want that. I want to keep my robe. It's all I have left of my parents.'

'You'd best forget about them.' He sighs. 'It's worth too much. Don't argue with me. Don't make me take it off you. And leave your slippers too.'

'But what will I—' but the door has already slammed.

The barrel is large enough to climb into and she holds the soap, inhaling the sweetness of its faint lavender perfume with delight before she ducks down, letting the water close over her head. She soaps and rinses her hair vigorously several times before reluctantly stepping out of the warm water. The coarse weave and dark brown colour of the shift make her wrinkle her nose and the neckline chafes her neck but at least it covers her well.

The noises on board ship slowly quieten as the din from outside becomes louder and louder. Ya Ling presses her face to a porthole but can see nothing but a series of red-tiled roofs and wooden wharves coming closer. Back on deck Mei Ming is brought up blinking out of the hold, her face still striped with dirt. She looks very young and afraid. 'Come here.' Ya Ling licks her fingers and leans down to wipe her face clean.

'Better now?' The girl's smile is determinedly hopeful. 'A bit prettier?'

'No. A lot prettier.' Ya Ling scans the dockside anxiously as far as she can see. No sign of Chen anywhere. She fumbles for Mei Ming's hand and holds it tightly to her side. 'I'm sorry I couldn't keep you safe, Mei Ming.'

'It's all right. Nobody could.' They turn at the rasping of the thick hemp hawser as it drops the anchor, then stand shoulder to shoulder, staring at the noisy crowds of round-eyes on the wharf in front of them. They all speak in the same rolling language as the sailors on board and, like them, they seem to use their hands as much as their voices. 'But we'll be all right. You and me. As long as we're together. As long as I get to see you every day…'

Ya Ling quickly runs a knuckle under her eyelid.

'You all right?' says Mei Ming.

'Just dust. That's all.'

Ships' captains shout loudly as they supervise the unloading of the vessels moored along the quaysides. 'It's busy here, isn't it?' Mei Ming leans into her for comfort as they watch merchants swarm over piles of sacks, gesticulating and complaining loudly. Boxes are jemmied open and the smell of cloves and peppercorns and dried fish spills out into the crowd.

'Look up there!' Ya Ling nudges Mei Ming and they both look upwards, astonished to see a huge mule lifted through the air with a strap under his belly, braying an indignant complaint. They look at each other and manage faint smiles despite their fears. Ya Ling leans down and plants a kiss on her cheek and the girl burrows herself into her side until she is suddenly wrenched away by one of the deckhands and bundled down the gangplank, screaming and struggling to turn round.

'No! Stop! Leave her alone!' Ya Ling strains forwards to shout goodbye but the other girl's small square frame is already swallowed up by the crowds.

The captain quickly steps in front of her and, glancing down at her hands, nods in satisfaction. 'They've healed well, but I'd still keep them hidden until the scars have gone.' He looks away. 'For your own sake.' He shouts out across the quayside. 'For God's sake come and take her. Be quick.'

Two men with identical blue cloaks come aboard. One stares at Ya

Ling with interest, before he nudges the other man. 'This one's a bit different.'

The man looks up from the thick white docket he is signing. 'She'd better be healthy. That's all I'm interested in.' He looks warningly at the captain. 'The boss has paid enough for her.'

'I've kept her fit.' The captain looks down at Ya Ling, who slips her hands into the pockets of her shift. 'She's bright, this one.' He tips the money purse out into his cupped hand and counts the heavy silver coins, then nods at the men before he holds out his hand for a brisk handshake. 'You need to watch her.'

The men look at each other in amusement before they walk towards her. Without the rope tethering her to Mei Ming, she can run fast and has pounded halfway down the deck before the men corner her.

'Fit enough, is she?' The captain chuckles as they lead her down the swaying gangway, one closely in front, the other tightly behind. They walk over a series of small bridges across canals until the salty smell of the quayside is replaced by a damp smell of wet stone. The cobbles feel cold and slippery beneath her feet. Despite the men's proximity, when they cross a wide square Ya Ling is fondled and squeezed by several hands as they pass through the clamorous crowd. She cries out in fury but the men don't seem to notice and nudge her forwards. The uneven bricks laid in a herringbone pattern across a large open square dig into the soles of her feet. She bites her bottom lip until it hurts.

Chapter 4

A breeze from the lagoon ruffles Gregorio's fringe. There's a market to the side and he glimpses some bales of shiny fabrics and some big pottery jars with blue and white flowers on them. He must try to remember to tell Genevra about those – she'll want to know every detail. The scent of some strange fruit makes his mouth water as he leans his head back and stares round, his jaw dropping in amazement. The back of Mantegna's green velvet cloak swings from side to side as his pace quickens ahead. They turn into a bend of the Grand Canal and the groom can only glance quickly around at the airy merchants' houses that sit right up to the water's edge. They have plaster in bright colours and pointed arches and seem to be held up by impossibly skinny columns. Nothing like the dark fortified houses he's used to in Mantova, with their big forbidding doors set into high walls. These folk must be very confident in their powerful families. Or very well protected.

They cross over a grey stone bridge and he hears men grunting beneath his feet before a galley with twelve boatmen pulling on the oars appears from the side. 'Look, Maestro! See how they avoid the mudflats and skim over the shallows.' One man sings to keep the pace and Gregorio looks on in admiration at how the men's powerful muscled forearms attack the water with such nonchalance. 'Look at their muscles and their manliness!' He doesn't see the rough edge to the cobble that sends him flying.

'Gesù Cristo, boy!' Mantegna rushes back to him and rescues the rolls of canvas before they get muddied. 'Can't you do anything right? Why can't you look where you're going?'

'Sorry, Maestro. I've just never been anywhere like here before.' A group of men with red and white striped turbans and gowns to the floor walk past them, chatting together in a strange tongue. One has a curved silver dagger tucked down the front of his belt. 'Look! Look at his gold earring! A man wearing an earring! Wait till I tell Clemente.'

As his head turns back he feels a ridge of knuckle under his chin. He winces at the menacing tone of his master's voice. 'You don't say anything to anyone about what we are doing here. Anything you want to say to Clemente or Genevra, you tell me first. Or the mistress. Especially her. I've told you that three times already. So let's see if you can remember for once.' He steps even closer. 'So go on then, what are we doing here, Gregorio?'

It's hard to speak with the pressure under his chin. His voice comes out cut off and clenched. 'We are visiting four patrons to sell them two paintings that were agreed two years ago. That is...' he hesitates, 'before you were employed by Ludovico Gonzaga.' The knuckles force his head backwards with a sickening jolt.

'How can I please four patrons with two paintings? If you spent more time listening and less time staring round like a village *buffone*, then you might remember.'

Gregorio screws up his eyes. 'Two patrons with three paintings?'

'God help me.' Mantegna stares heavenwards. 'Why do I keep you on?'

'For your immortal soul, Maestro.' Gregorio hunches up. 'Honestly, I've been trying to keep up with you but I'm having trouble with this lot.' He shifts his grip on the bundle of paintings under one arm and attempts to stop the paper pinned to the easel under the other arm from creasing. 'To be honest I'm terrified of getting lost. It all looks the same round here.' He gazes sullenly around him; churches everywhere, big rich houses set right by the canal's edge and lots of narrow twists and turns over countless little bridges. Most of them slippery with pigeon shit too.

'Well, try harder!' Mantegna snaps. 'Use this!' He taps his temple furiously.

'I've tried. I keep trying, but this city is so huge.' He points to a richly embellished *contrada* flag set in a sconce in the wall. 'I thought these might help, but they're nothing like the ones in Mantova, they're much flashier and brightly coloured. And the symbols don't mean anything to me. I'll never get my bearings here.'

Mantegna points to the bell tower of the Basilica di San Marco with its wooden roof pointing up above the roofline. 'Use that as a landmark. You stupid boy.' He looks across in irritation. 'And don't crush them like that against your side.' He takes three rolls very gently out from under Gregorio's arm.

'Sorry.' Gregorio's stomach gives a loud rumble. When the maestro is in a selling mood, then he thinks of nothing else. He watches the maestro's long curls bob down his back as he approaches yet another grand house, then he looks about, giving a click to any pretty girl passing. They always look askance at the emblem on his livery. It's not from Venezia so they ignore him. But it doesn't stop him trying. There looks to be only one roll when Mantegna comes out with a smile on his face.

'How many to go, Maestro?' Gregorio ventures.

'Nothing to do with you.' Mantegna looks from side to side.

'Of course not.' It's all very strange. It looks like the rumours must be true. Normally the customers come to the house, the ones the Gonzagas let him sell to, and the maestro and Nicolosia put on a bit of a show in the big room upstairs. The last time they'd offered expensive sweet wine from Alba, and biscuits. He'd pinched a sip taking the flagon upstairs and had rolled the honeyed sweetness round and round in his mouth for as long as he'd dared. For a man as fussy about his reputation as Mantegna, this selling from door to door like a tinker is worrying. He'll have to ask Clemente when they get home. But the maestro seems happy enough.

'Set up the easel over there in the shade, under the scaffolding on the side of the Doge's Palace, then find me something to sit on.'

'There?' Gregorio looks across at the noisy tavern on the corner with men spilling out unsteadily over the cobbles. 'Won't it be noisy?'

Mantegna turns sideways to see the hawk-like profile of one of the men. He's in a good mood, five paintings sold, so he feels kinder. 'You're right, Gregorio, you see all kinds here. From all over the world. I'll get some good faces. Different to Mantova.'

The groom's frame slackens in relief. 'Well, they'll be relaxed,' he ventures. 'Coming out of there, that's for sure.'

Mantegna stares at a priest walking by and notices the hem of his soutane is soaking up the wet from the cobbles. 'Some good details too. Something I can show the mistress when I get back.'

'To keep her off my back for a while,' he murmurs to himself.

'She'll like that.' Gregorio's smile puffs out his cheeks. 'She'll be pleased about all the paintings we've sold as well.'

Mantegna folds his arms and drums his fingers. 'Did you not listen to what I said earlier?'

Gregorio flinches at the change in his tone. 'But I didn't think you meant… I didn't…'

'I said don't tell anybody anything until I have agreed to it. Only I will tell Signora Mantegna how many I've sold. Only me. Is that clear?'

'Yes. Only you. Sorry. Look, if I put the easel here then you can sit on that low wall.' He snatches off his cap and lays it on the top of the wall. 'It won't be damp if you sit on this.'

'How long have you worked for me?'

'I don't know, Maestro. Many Pentecosts, I know that.'

'And where did the priest find you?'

'In the church doorway. I remember that. I do remember that.'

'And what did he say to Signora Mantegna?'

'Something about me making a good servant…?' The young man mumbles, his cheeks aflame with pride. 'That my thinking had been touched by God and that He would bless you both if—'

'A loyal servant. Do you know what that means?'

'Working hard.'

'That too. But what it really means is that when I tell you to keep your mouth shut that's exactly what you do. Or face a spell in the cage.'

Gregorio's knees buckle. 'Don't say that, sir! Not the cage!'

Mantegna's finger prods his chest. 'There's something shifty about you sometimes. Something I don't quite trust. You might feel you owe Signora Mantegna a great deal because she brought you home and looks after you far too well, because she fears for her immortal soul, but I don't fear any priest as she does.'

'I'm more stupid than shifty, Maestro. Honestly. My loyalty always lies with you.'

'We'll see, my boy. We'll see.' He spins round at a sudden murmuring from the side of the Piazza San Marco. A flock of pigeons flaps skywards grumbling in viscous bubbles of sound. He notices two men leading an exotic-looking girl across the rough cobbles to where he is standing. 'Stop! Wait! Let me look at her!' He stands up behind the easel. 'Turn her towards me.' The men ignore him. One gives the girl a push in the small of her back. Mantegna leans forwards as she is led past him into a large pillared building, and he stares at her. He tries to cup her chin in his hand but she veers her face away out of his grasp, her dark almond eyes sparking angrily at him.

He hears her give a gasp of relief as she steps onto the cool tiles of the entrance hall.

Chapter 5

A noisy crowd of men waits outside a big panelled door. The two men guarding her step aside to allow all of them to have a good look.

The whitewashed room is quiet after the uproar of the dockside and the bustling crowds in the piazza. A line of three posts waits at the front of the room and Ya Ling is chained by the waist in between two tall muscular men, who seem covered all over with a shiny black paint. Their skins look much darker even than the Moors who used to come to sell her father musk and hashish, and their curls are sheared close to their skulls like the fleece of a black lamb. She stares at them both in amazement, then struggles against the chain, turning to try to heave it from the post behind.

A group of men wearing clothes of expensive velvet and wool are sitting in tiered rows facing the three of them. A few surge down the aisles to get to her and they stand in a semi-circle in front.

'Mother of God! Look at her.'

One man steps forwards to run his hand through her silky hair and whispers an admiring aside to the man next to him. 'She's eastern, isn't she? Are they all as delicate as this? As beautiful? Never seen hair like that before.'

'Blue-black like a raven's wing.'

'Poet, are you?' He grins at his friend. 'My needs are a bit more down to earth. She's got a nice tight little body. That'll do for me.' He nudges the man next to him and they both laugh.

A man in a lush red velvet cloak pulls down her shift and tries to slip his hand down to feel her breast, making the dark-skinned slave to her right hiss in disgust. She manages to land a kick in the man's stomach. The men around him laugh and jeer and, red-faced, he steps forwards and slaps the side of her face hard with the back of his hand. She reels back in shock, putting her hand to her cheekbone, looking round instinctively for Chen.

'Don't mark her,' the auctioneer snaps. 'She's not yours yet.' The two men on either side of her rear up in disgust and one tries to mutter some soothing noises to her.

'Stop! I'll take her!' The short man who had been drawing outside pushes his way to the front of the queue.

'That's not how it works,' the auctioneer explains with exaggerated patience. 'We bid until we finally get to the man who bids the most. She's a virgin, so she won't come cheap.'

Mantegna stares at her as if thunderstruck. In all the paintings he has ever studied, he has never seen beauty like this. And her demeanour. Even here, brought as low as this, there is an elegance to her, a grace in her posture. He knows what they say about him at court, a runty little nobody, son of a carpenter from a muddy little village outside Padova that nobody has ever heard of. No family. No breeding. No taste. Well, they won't be saying that again. Not with a beauty like this waiting for him at home.

The auctioneer takes out a scroll and reads out the slave contract. 'This confers on the buyer all full powers to hold, sell, exchange… and… enjoy' – his voice luxuriates in the last word and he raises one envious eyebrow at the men clustered around him – 'and to do with in perpetuity whatever may please him and his heirs in accordance with his own pleasure.' As the auctioneer drawls out the last word, Mantegna feels a sharp tug of arousal. 'Gentlemen, are we all agreed?'

'Doesn't she have a reserve price on her?' the artist insists, rolling up the sheaf of sketches and tucking them under his arm.

'Of course she does.'

'Then double it.'

A surprised murmur rises around the room. The man who was kicked looks furious. 'Treble it,' he snaps.

The artist sees the fearful glance she gives the men on each side of her. 'And another *mezzo ducato*.' His eyes gleam in triumph when the other bidder shakes his head, his lips tight.

The artist nods. The chain slithers from her waist and the painter reaches up for her hand and makes to lead her out. He hands over a money purse that the auctioneer tips out onto his desk. 'I'll bring the rest by this afternoon.'

The auctioneer looks annoyed at the pile of coins. 'I need a bigger deposit. What's your name anyway?'

'My name is Mantegna. Andrea Mantegna.' He puffs out his chest. 'Painter.'

'Painter?' The auctioneer looks unimpressed.

'I've got some walls at home that need whitewashing,' one man jeers, making the crowd laugh.

Mantegna's face mottles in fury. 'I'm a painter to the court.' He looks round pleased when the laughter quickly subsides.

'Here? In Venezia?'

'No. Mantova.'

'Oh. I see. Mantova.'

'Yes. To the court of Ludovico Gonzaga, and I am soon to be formally commissioned for two major frescos at the—'

'Soon to be. Soon to be. That's what they all say.' The auctioneer turns to the crowd. 'Any firm bids? No timewasters. This time.'

'I've already told you I'll bring the rest this afternoon.' Mantegna squares up to him. 'One word from me to the Gonzaga family and you'll be shut down. They have powerful connections here. Trust me. You don't want to cross them. Or me.'

The room goes silent while the auctioneer looks at the pile of coins, then back at Mantegna. He purses his lips. 'You had better be back by close of business,' he says quietly.

Mantegna leads Ya Ling to where a young man is dismantling his easel and rolling sheets of parchment under his arm. His jaw drops at the sight of Ya Ling. 'Wake up, boy.' He rifles through the canvases and takes two out. 'Take the rest of the paintings and sell them. Try the merchants' houses on the lagoon side. Any left over plus the sketches today, sell in the piazza.'

'The piazza? Sell your work in the piazza? But Maestro…'

'That's what I said. Are you deaf as well as daft? Get as good a price as you can, then take the money to the auctioneer. Ground floor. In that building with the pillars. Mention my name. Got that, Gregorio?' He points in the direction of the piazza. The servant cannot drag his gaze from Ya Ling and Mantegna has to repeat himself, giving him a cuff round the ear. Gregorio finally walks away with the easel under one arm and the roll of sketches under the other, stopping every so often to stare back at her.

Mantegna sees an inn sign and throws his last two coins to the landlord in the entrance before he pulls her upstairs. The room has a rank smell but he pushes her over the threshold 'Come, maid. We don't have much time. My groom will be back soon with the mule cart.' He jerks his head casually towards the straw mattress in the corner.

Ya Ling watches him as he lays the two sketches very carefully one on top of the other on a rickety table, as if they are made of precious ivory. Once he sits on the bed and begins to pull off his *tabarro*, she runs across the room, picks up the sketches, drags open the door and takes the stairs in three reckless jumps. She manages to get to the doorway.

'Not so fast, little whore.' The landlord grabs her hair, pulls her up short with a sickening lurch and hands her back to Mantegna, who has run puffing down the stairs after her. Both of them hustle her back up the stairs. Mantegna locks the door, then steps up to her and unties the lacing at the neck of her shift. Breathing hard, she braces her feet and shakes her head angrily. Her heart thuds against her ribs. His shortened breath and his avid gaze on the front of her shift make her stomach knot with fear. 'No.' The word is spat out. 'No.' She shakes her head again and her eyes rise up to hold his in a furious gaze.

'I have just bought you.' He rubs his fingers with his thumb. 'Do you not understand? You belong to me.' His brown eyes narrow on her and his ragged curls shake as he gives a humourless laugh. 'So why do you think I've paid all that money for you? Eh? I've got servants enough at home.' He pushes her gently back onto the bed and her flood of black hair covers the pillow. 'I'm a good master. I won't hurt you. I don't get any pleasure in that.' He leans towards her and she slaps him so hard across the face it makes his ears ring.

'Hey! Now that's enough of that,' he warns. 'You go too far, striking me like that, little maid. Nobody gets away doing that to a man. Not to me anyway.' Pinning her hands together over her head, he lifts up the front of his *tabarro*. She struggles her hands free and pushes against the big curve of his chest until the veins stand out beneath the skin of her temple. His face is damp with sweat. 'For God's sake, stop this. You're making this situation worse for yourself. I'll be a lot kinder to you than any of the other men at the auction. Don't try to kid me you haven't pleasured more than one sailor on the way here.'

'No. No.' She shakes her head angrily.

Impatience rises in him as he tries to drag the hem of her shift upwards. Her face screws tighter with determination as she digs her nails into his chest. He pins his two elbows down on each side of her and forces his knee between her flailing legs. 'Stop acting so foolish and just let me get some relief. Nothing you haven't done before.' She feels a vicious pinch of panic as something hot and rigid is rammed between her legs. As his weight lands down on her chest she feels the air pushed from her lungs. A sudden pain spears inside like a fork of lightning. She lies rigid with shock. Now she knows all about the man's part. Shaped like a sword and made of wood. The shame of his hot dense flesh inside her is worse than the pain. He makes a deep rumbling sound that rises and rises until he suddenly relaxes and lays his wiry cheek against her breast. After a while he slowly rolls off her and looks down in surprise.

She curls away from him but he pulls her back round to face him. Her eyes flick from side to side, wide with shock. How will she be able to tell Chen when she sees him that she has not died of shame? She must take the honourable path, but if she does, then she will never be able to apologise to him or to Ayi. Or find Mei Ming. Her spirit will be restless with guilt and will plague them all.

Mantegna runs two fingers along the cleft between her legs and holds them up. They are coated in blood. 'Jesus help me! I thought the auctioneer just wanted to up the price. I wouldn't have been so rough if I'd known.' Her face is impassive. Only her eyes give any indication of the jagged feeling that tears her heart. Altan. She thinks of the flat golden planes of his face. Of the wedding necklace, of how the lapis lazuli stone looked such a vivid blue against the palm of his hand. Altan. The pride he took in her purity. How could she face him now? Sullied and used. Her stricken glance takes in Mantegna wiping his fingers on a rag he has pulled from his pocket. The *zarar*. Suddenly she understands.

Later that day Ya Ling lies in the back of the cart watching the cream hessian awning flap against the wooden frame. Her heart feels frozen and her thoughts spill back to the shock of what happened in that dingy room in the tavern. Mantegna sits next to her and she curls away from his hand resting on her hip. Gregorio's tuneless whistle coming faintly from the front of the cart and her muffled sobs compete with the creak of the cart and the clop of the mare's hooves. She feels numbed by the taint of shame.

The jolt of the cart as the wheels hit a deep rut brings her wandering thoughts to order.

'That blasted boy!' Mantegna bumps her as he moves forwards to sit with Gregorio.

Her nimble fingers quickly begin to work loose the threads round one of the awning's eyelets until it gives her a space big enough to look out. When the cart rumbles to a stop, she watches Mantegna go into a large house on the outskirts of town with the two paintings held out carefully. He comes out and the dust flies up as he crumples one of the canvases and stamps it into the red dust. 'Somebody won't pay,' she whispers to herself. 'But you will. One day.'

She stares at the tall hedges and the rolling countryside, which has grapevines strung across the hillsides like washing. The people here never seem to be still. In the fields and in all the small villages they pass through, their gestures look flowery and exaggerated whenever they speak.

That night, the cart is pulled into a copse of trees and she is handed a slab of bread and a piece of dry, sour-tasting cheese. 'Don't worry, little maid, I'll feed you better once we get home,' he says, his voice hopeful. 'You wait till you taste some of Mantova's finest wine. You won't be wrinkling your pretty little nose then.' She turns her back on him.

For the next four days neither Mantegna nor his groom ever leave her unattended and she is loosely tethered to the wooden frame of the cart all the time. Even at night, Gregorio sleeps at the front of the cart while Mantegna sleeps with his arm tightly clamped round her. Ya Ling lies awake, hating his touch. 'Are you still sore, maid? Do you still bleed?' When she nods, he sighs heavily but takes his hand away and tries to make himself comfortable between the wicker travel chests and the easel.

The following afternoon the mule's pace picks up and, above the grinding of the wooden wheels into the dust and the jingling of the bit, she starts to hear the sounds of other carts and the cries of fruit sellers. Ya Ling carefully works the hole in the awning even wider. The town looks a primitive place and the constant ringing of bells makes her senses swim. The cart wheels stir up clouds of red dust and as they venture further the tall towers and the buildings, many with barred windows, look dark and forbidding, as if the whole town is a prison. Finally the mule halts outside two heavily studded doors and the groom gets down to rap for admittance. The cart clatters inside. Her watchful glance takes in the way the curved courtyard is hemmed in on all sides by a high wall. Mantegna unties her from the cart and helps her down. She drops his hand quickly.

Chapter 6

Although the kitchen is warm, the welcome she receives feels like a breath of ice blown across the winter wastes of the Gobi Desert. Mantegna's wife hates her on sight, just as she expected. Not that the wife shows it. Not a jot. From the moment he leads her into the courtyard and loudly calls 'Nicolosia! Nicolosia! Come and see what I've bought! A new servant for you,' the wife's reaction is unexpected.

The slave woman risks an upwards glance at Nicolosia. She isn't wailing. No promising to be a better, more obedient wife if only the master will sell her on. No sobbing or beating her breast like a thwarted child. Unlike the other round-eye women Ya Ling has seen so far, this wife stands very still while her eyes run over Ya Ling. There is something Confucian in the tight rein she keeps on her emotions. Something admirably bold in her calm stance. A foil against all her husband's swaggering. The way her sturdy upright posture gives nothing away. Cunning. Playing him along. Mantegna's wife could almost be a Han.

'I see.' Nicolosia's glance on her is slow. She presses her thumb down Ya Ling's long elegant neck, which rises gracefully out of the brown shift, then digs it in sharply, following the line where the coarse hemp has rubbed a raw red necklace into her pale skin. The slave woman barely winces. 'For me? How kind,' she says, looking her over from the black matted hair down to the bare feet coated in reddish dust. The wife manages to be submissive but to provoke him at the same time, Ya Ling considers. It's good to see.

Ya Ling keeps her eyes low, the better to hide any flicker of interest in what is being said around her. The grit grates between each of her bare toes. What an archaic country this is, barely paved.

She dares a glance round the kitchen. Wooden platters and bowls lie along the dresser shelves. A blackened pot swings over an open fire. No fine blue and white porcelain plates. No tureens of pale green celadon. No attempt at refinement anywhere. The heavy outer door creaks. Footsteps patter on the tiles.

'Not yet, Genevra. Wait outside until you are called. Stay in the courtyard with the men.'

The woman puts down a small knife on the tabletop. Her hands are red and raw-looking. 'Yes, Maestro.' As she hurries outside the servant gives her mistress an apprehensive look before she closes the door behind her, leaving Ya Ling with Mantegna and his wife.

Ya Ling quickly glances down, remembering her father's lesson about how he managed to succeed when summoned to the court of the Zhengtong Emperor. 'You must look and learn, child. Every day. Listen hard and learn. Different customs. Different ways. Miss nothing. Information is more valuable than salt.' If she is ever to escape then she needs to heed his advice. To be vigilant. To miss nothing.

Judging from the trace of flour on the front of her shift, that servant with the red flaky lips must also be the cook. It is hard to tell the cook and the mistress apart, Ya Ling observes. Both have the same shapeless build. Like sacks of rice tied round the middle. The same plump faces pitted with brown eyes like currants set deep in doughy cheeks. But the mistress has a lace cap and a chunky plait that sticks out behind like a fist. And that air of stillness to her, of course. Genevra is older, the unruly brown curls that escape from her kitchen bonnet are shot through with grey, and yet, Ya Ling registers, she is pregnant.

'It doesn't need to be like this, Nicolosia.' Mantegna's voice is oily and suggestive. 'Not all the time anyway. If you were a proper wife to me, I would never have bought her.'

Ya Ling watches the stoic set to Nicolosia's broad back as she sits down heavily on a kitchen stool and opens a green tapestry bag, taking out a series of wooden bobbins and arranging them by colour until the embroidery silks lie along the pine table in a long rainbow stripe. 'I just can't. You know the pain I've suffered, husband. Another stillbirth would kill me.' Her low reasonable voice belies her shaking fingers, which fiddle up and down the line of silks.

'But I need more sons. Sons I can apprentice to keep my legacy alive.'

'I can't.' Nicolosia's plait shakes from side to side. 'I couldn't go through that again. And who'll take care of Cecco when anything happens to me?'

'Cecco? He's far too much of a mother's boy. You spoil him. You always have,' Mantegna says bitterly. 'You've made him that way. Sickly and unmanly. When I was eight I used to do a full day's work, labouring for my father, stacking wood and sawing. I'd barely turned eleven when I was apprenticed as a painter to Squarcione and I've worked like a dog ever since.'

'He has a weak chest. He can't help that.' Nicolosia struggles to keep her voice calm. 'He can get very ill in no time. If you would let me buy more expensive cures from the apothecary…'

'He's weak all right. And he's idle.'

Nicolosia's tone turns icy. 'What kind of example is this for him? A father bringing a whore into the family home?'

Mantegna crosses the kitchen to where Ya Ling waits. 'It's about time he saw how a real man lives. Many famous artists have one. But none as fine as her.' Ya Ling folds her arms tightly.

'Not these days they don't.' Nicolosia sighs. 'And did you tell Gentile you were buying this whore when you were in Venezia?'

'What? That strait-laced brother of yours? And get a lecture! What do you think?'

'Then I will write and tell him of the shame you are bringing upon my household,' she ventures quietly. 'He'll know what to do.' Nicolosia's voice is light and easy. She might have been discussing the price of peaches. Ya Ling's lips twitch, but then the smile quickly freezes. The wife's composure speaks of careful calculation. Of cruelty to come.

'And do you honestly think he'll travel all the way from Venezia again for a fight? I can tell you now that he won't. He's just started a big commission, so he'll not want any damage to his hands. And I haven't touched you for nearly six months now. Have I? Eh?'

'Touch me?' she demands over her shoulder. 'I don't remember much touching, husband. But I do remember that time when you tried forcing. Believe me! I remember that all right.'

'It was a moment of madness. And I'd been drinking. You know that.' He shrugs by way of apology. 'I need sons. I felt I had no choice and I've never tried again.'

'You don't need another son.' She swivels round to look him full in the face. 'I could help in the workshop like I used to help my brothers. When there were a lot of commissions we all pitched in, and I can grind pigment as well as any man.'

'Giovanni might allow you to do that, but Gentile? He'd never let you do anything like that now. He's become very strict in his household. Very proper. The priests in Venezia are tightening their grip and your brother has suddenly discovered how pious he is.'

'Pious? It's not just him. That's how the world is turning these days. And yet you risk it by buying a woman like her and bringing her into our home?' Nicolosia walks across the room and opens a low door. 'How much did the whore cost?'

'A lot.'

'So how much did you make in Venezia?' Her head suddenly turns to him.

Mantegna's voice affects nonchalance. 'Not much.'

'And it all went on her?' Her voice rises as she points inside the cupboard. 'Well, perhaps you would like to come and look at the bare shelves in here.' She points upwards at the row of hooks on the ceiling. 'Look. Empty! We need hams and salami hanging up there, and my flour sack is barely half-full.' Her voice has a thin anxious edge. 'Have you pushed Ludovico about the frescos yet? For a firm commission? Asked him about when you start?' She makes a click of disgust when he shakes his head.

'I can't push him. There are plenty of artists who would do anything for his patronage. Never forget his family keep us safe here, so I have no option but to wait on him. But he has said he might give me some land to build a house.'

'When?'

Mantegna waves a lofty hand. 'At some stage.'

'That's all well and good but how will we pay for the builders?' She looks around. 'This place is too small, I know. We need more artists working for you and there isn't the space, but the crucial thing is the starting date. Once we know that, then if you let me grind the pigments, it will free up Cecco and Settimio to help you make a start. In fact I can go to the apothecary and get the pigments myself. Cecco is far too shy to haggle and you are too proud. I'm not. I can't afford to be.'

'I have asked the marchese and he's got no spare money at the moment.'

Nicolosia wags a plump finger. 'Well, he's got plenty to spend on that palace of his. Takes up most of the Piazza Sordello.'

'And he's got foreign wars to fight. He has to keep Mantova safe…'

'I'm not that gullible, husband. I've heard rumours he's paying you plenty.' Her voice hardens. 'And he pays you every month. I know that! So where does it go? Velvets for you, and costly ornaments for the house that we don't need, that's where!' She turns furiously to face Ya Ling. 'And now her!'

'I have my reputation to keep up, and never forget I've had to create my own.' His thumb jabs into his chest. 'Unlike you, I wasn't born into privilege. I've had to earn everything I've got by hard graft and by my brilliance. An artist is about a lot more than just his paintings, particularly an artist of my stature.' He throws his cloak towards the back of a chair with a grandiose gesture. Nicolosia catches it before it lands on the floor and smooths out the creases before she folds it carefully.

'You need to care less about your reputation. To be less sensitive, husband. Court cases cost money and surely your reputation can stand a few critical remarks? And the expensive clothes, the velvets and the emerald ring you just bought. Leave those to the ignorant nobles at court who dare criticise your talent.' Her voice becomes soft and pleading. 'No one can juggle creditors as well as me. And keep your reputation up. But it's hard to do that when your shoe has a hole and your stomach grumbles. But I try.'

'Stop this. I've heard enough.'

'But you said yourself, the frescos could take ten years, and we can't live like this with you spending the money as fast as it comes in.' Her eyes rake his face. 'Did you get any commissions in Venezia? What did you manage to sell?'

'Enough, wife! Enough!' Mantegna shrugs angrily. 'I'm not answerable to you. And I warn you now, my temper is rising.'

'You need to get a firm commission on the frescos, then you can ask for an advance. But you've to show the Gonzagas that you're keen to start. As you say, there are plenty of other painters who would love their patronage. To step into your shoes.'

Mantegna cocks an ear to the sudden silence from the courtyard. 'I'm not discussing this here. We can talk in the marital room. That will be novel for you, wife, won't it? To go in there?'

He cups her elbow and leads her towards the staircase along the back wall, but she pulls her arm away and goes back to the table and sits down. 'And what about our good name? Eh? You, who's always so worried about his status, about keeping up appearances. The Mantegna reputation! And now you dare to bring one such as her into our family home. Parading her like this in front of me. You should be ashamed.'

Mantegna utters a harsh expletive and rams a fist down on the kitchen table, making the bobbins roll around in disarray. Nicolosia simply stoops and gathers up the bobbins that have rolled across the tiles and drops them back in her bag. The slave lifts her glance when she hears the soft slap of the wife's slippers as she approaches. 'Where's she from anyway? This… this… new servant of mine.' She sounds almost amused, but Ya Ling notices the fine hatchings of defeat that fan out from her eyes.

Mantegna's voice, when he recovers it, is more resigned. 'She's a Mongolian. The dealer told me she's so slender she must have some Cin in her as well.'

'So this is where all the money went? How much? How expensive was she?' The wife could have been enquiring about a brace of partridge. This self-possession makes Ya Ling think hard. To reassess what her approach might have to be. 'She certainly looks expensive.'

'Yes she was. Very. And she's a runner. Any chance she gets.' His voice thickens in admiration. 'But not with me she won't.'

'But yet you still bought her? Even with our fortunes the way they are?' Only the whitened row of knuckles that peak along each clenched fist gives the slave woman any idea of the depth of the wife's feelings.

'Of course. Once I saw that face I had to. Buy her. Have her.' As Mantegna continues to goad his wife, Ya Ling's heart plummets. She can guess what this will mean in the future. How hard it will be to mend. But she will just have to keep on trying until it does. 'No, I just couldn't resist her. Who could? Looks like hers will always command a high price. The auctioneer told me not many men would dare to buy such a beautiful eastern woman for a household slave. For other things perhaps.'

'No doubt.' The slave woman glances up at the wife's coolness. It's as if her emotions are rationed. No drama at all. No pleading. No waving her arms about. Not like the rest of them she has seen so far in this primitive land. 'But as my father always said, you're a fool with money.'

There is a harsh intake of breath. 'I'm sick of hearing about your wonderful Bellini family and all their rich commissions. You show me no respect. You'll pay for that remark.' Mantegna kicks the embroidery bag clean across the kitchen floor, then he follows it and grinds it hard with his heel several times until the bobbins crack in protest as they crumble to dust. Nicolosia sits very still with her hands clasped tightly on her lap. He lets out a furious sigh. 'Then be it on your own head, Nicolosia. Call them in.'

The three servants come in quietly and line up below the window that looks out on the yard. After Mantegna has introduced them, they stare and stare at Ya Ling as if she is a spirit. A djinn from the underworld. As if they have never seen anything like her before.

Ya Ling pushes her hands deeper into her pockets. Genevra keeps tucking her hair in her cap and her bottom lip looks raw as she gnaws at it. The one called Clemente, a big solid man with sloping shoulders, purses his lips in embarrassment, then tactfully examines each black-rimmed fingernail in turn. He keeps glancing between the mistress and Genevra as if his concern is shared equally between both of them. He stills the cook's agitated hands with a squeeze. So he must be the husband. A kindly, thoughtful one at that. Gregorio the young groom she already knows, but his boyish features still drop whenever he stares at her. He turns towards Nicolosia with a look of concern. He brings in the smell of the stable with him. She thinks of the Mongol trickery her father told her about, of warriors dividing loyalties, the better to pick off targets.

'Her name is Ya Ling. She is to be my new servant,' Mantegna announces. 'One with special duties.' He pauses. 'And who will be answerable only to me.' The servants give each other awkward sidelong glances. Nicolosia simply looks on when Mantegna instructs Gregorio to clear out the harness room along the corridor from the kitchen. She stands before the jumble of reins and whips and old horse blankets that spill into a heap on the floor, as if she is looking through odds and ends on a market stall. Her husband watches her.

'Burn these,' Mantegna snaps.

Nicolosia raises her eyes to the ceiling and murmurs to herself.

'Burn them, Maestro?'

'Are you deaf, boy? As well as stupid?' Mantegna grinds out angrily.

'But why?' Out of the tangled pile he pulls a handful of brown strappings. 'There's a newish night-halter here, it must be worth at least…' Gregorio falls silent at his master's livid glance.

'Why? Because I can, boy. That's why. Because I'm master of this house, and my word is law.'

Ya Ling glances at the wife. Perhaps the wife is too proud to get word to her brothers and ask them to send money. Family loyalty seems to count for nothing here. Ya Ling thinks hard, analysing everything she has learned so far about Mantegna's household and working out how she might manipulate these people to effect her escape. Work on the cook first. Then Gregorio the groom. Obviously she will have to keep Mantegna happy, learn what gives him pleasure, keep him thrilled with his new purchase, however repulsive that might be. A shudder ripples her slim frame as she watches him cross the kitchen.

'See how she shrugs at us, Mistress! As if we're not good enough,' the cook whispers out of the side of her mouth. 'The little madam! Who does she think she is? Don't you worry. The maestro won't be at home all the time, now will he? We'll have some fun then.'

Ya Ling keeps very still. No. Mantegna must be her priority. First she has to learn what she must do to keep him satisfied long enough for her to get to work on the others.

'Come, maid,' says Mantegna. She blinks as he leads her inside the harness room. 'I don't want to be disturbed,' he shouts over his shoulder as he closes the door. The room is narrow, and lined with dark-red brick. The dark-beamed ceiling seems to lie low on the room.

Her heart plummets when he undoes the lacing to the neck of her shift but she manages a wan smile. His hands on her are more gentle now but his unshaven face rubs the tender skin of her breasts like glasspaper. She dismisses all thoughts of Altan's smooth high cheekbones. When he eases himself into her, despite her best efforts she moans and inhales on a shaky breath. That seems to please him. He grunts in approval and grinds his hips faster against her until she feels his heavy weight fall on her chest as he lies spent and breathing heavily. 'See, little maid. You are already starting to enjoy my lovemaking.'

'Yes.' She pulls the nearest horse blanket closer and burrows her wet cheek into it. Make a noise. Moan a bit. Breathe loudly. A lesson for next time.

He rolls over and pulls her across his chest. 'I knew you would.'

Her breath ruffles the thick black hair on his chest. 'Yes, Maestro,' she murmurs. 'Of course.'

He's easy to fool and so will be the others. Already she knows a lot about this family. More valuable than a whole barrel of salt. She allows a small smile to play along her lips. Mongol endurance and Han cleverness. None of them will be a match for that.

Chapter 7

The Gonzaga Palace

'Marchese Ludovico, I think it would be prudent to conceal your day-to-day expenditure from the painter.' Marsilio Andreasi lifts an open scroll from the pile scattered across the table. His manner is courteous and soldierly. His eyes scanning the list are sharp but half-closed, giving his face an expression of sleepy cunning.

'Why?' The Marchese Ludovico's voice is deep and good-humoured, imbued with the dignity of a man secure in his dynasty.

'Not until we have secured the terms for his commission for the frescos.' Andreasi runs a finger down a list. 'This one is fine. Wages for lawyers, accountants, muleteers, jailers, blacksmiths, saddlers, falconers, kennelmen. All everyday expenses. Nobody could argue with that.'

'Argue?'

'Marchese Ludovico, forgive me. I just meant that the other invoices, the one for musk to scent your gloves, and for the velvet collars for your hunting dogs and the three jewelled rosaries, these might seem a little…'

Ludovico strokes the silky stripes of a tiger skin that lies across the back of a chair upholstered in figured blue velvet and patterned with gold studs. 'Luxurious… perhaps?'

'Forgive me, Your Grace.'

'But that's where you are wrong, look, this invoice only shows the expenses of the falcons.'

'Indeed, Marchese Ludovico. It shows the cost of raw meat per day for each bird. More meat than even the household staff here can expect in a week and, thanks to your generosity, they are all exceptionally well fed.'

'I think you are being ridiculous.' The marchese drops the scroll on a side table with a dismissive shrug. 'And I'm not entirely happy about your attitude.'

Marsilio Andreasi turns to him with an uneasy smile. 'It's just that now is an excellent time to negotiate with the artist. My spies tell me that his extravagant ways are running through the monthly stipend you pay him so generously like a hot knife through butter.' He gives a courtly bow. 'Marchese, your financial interests are always my first concern.'

Ludovico gives him a shrewd look. 'I always welcome your counsel, as you know. Nobody has ever been as discreet and careful in my more... sensitive dealings than you. Nobody can broker marriages between loyal Mantovans like you, or secure amnesties or diffuse vendettas, and I have a lot to be grateful to you for, I am aware of that, but I do think on this occasion that you are being quite ridiculous. The man is an artisan. A mere painter. What I choose to spend my money on has nothing to do with him.'

Marsilio Andreasi's voice holds the velvety manner of a diplomat. 'Mantegna is becoming one of the most celebrated artists in the land, and his work will prove to be an excellent investment for the future. He has no family money to fall back on, so he will be delighted to be paid a little inducement to embark upon such a large commission for the frescos you so desire. The question is, how much? If he thinks your finances are boundless then he will expect your generosity to be so as well.'

'You encouraged me to employ him as painter to the court.' The Marchese Ludovico walks over to the walls and inspects two paintings. 'So I hope he is the genius you have described.'

'Yes he is, Your Grace.' He quickly moves over to the marchese's side. 'His draughtsmanship, the way he paints vistas receding into the background, is magnificent. Look at the way he can suggest space and depth, no one can better him, and he's currently not too expensive either.'

'But so sombre. Everything so hard and sharp. Never any voluptuous ladies. Nothing sensual for me to enjoy looking at.'

'That's not his style, Marchese. Look at this one, he calls it *The Martyrdom of San Giacomo*, see the winding path leading up to the castle? How does he create such depth on a canvas? No one else can do this so well. It's almost unbelievable.'

The marchese's fleshy lips turn downwards. 'But with the saint being beheaded in the foreground, it's hardly cheerful now, is it? Not going to raise my spirits?'

The private secretary takes down the other painting. 'And this one, *The Agony in the Garden…*' he says in a tone warm with reverence as he holds the picture to the light.

'Yes, yes. I know he likes doing those. But one can have a little too much agony, don't you think?'

'But Your Grace, look at the illusion of the hills and peaks stretching back to the horizon.'

'Too many bodies in tragic poses, if you ask me.' He shudders.

'But Your Grace, they are merely sleeping in Gethsemane, they are not dead.'

'They're foretelling death, Marsilio.' His glance is cutting. 'As a child I had as much scripture battered into me as you had. Probably more.'

The private secretary lowers his head. 'Forgive me, Your Grace. Indeed you are most reverent.'

'Am I?' The marchese's mood turns and he nods in sudden good humour. 'I must be, I suppose. I narrowly avoided a crucifixion from Mantegna' – he turns with an expectant look – 'not literally, you understand.'

Marsilio Andreasi laughs loudly on cue. 'Very witty, sire.'

'But too much death and gloominess in it. He tried to sell me one of his San Sebastian portraits, with the poor old saint pierced by so many arrows he looked like a hedgehog. Forgive my levity. But really…'

Marsilio Andreasi gives an uneasy laugh. This kind of heresy could cost a life, courtesy of the ecclesiastical courts. Could get a common man swinging on a gibbet. He shudders, thinking of Lauro, the loudmouth potman at the tavern, and his drunken remark about the Virgin's birth. Not all who die in the cage are murderers and thieves. He hangs the picture carefully back on the wall and stands back to view it again. 'Still, as investments they will be incomparable.'

'Well, you have done well for my coffers so far. But you need to maintain your reputation, to keep me happy. You know that.' The threat in his voice is lightly layered.

Marsilio's smile is humble. 'With God's grace.'

'I just resent having to play-act my supposed poverty. Look at my appearance, Marsilio. Shall I take off this black velvet hat? Or simply remove the cockade of peacock feathers and the ruby brooch? Shall I take off my fine Spanish leather shoes and meet him barefoot like a peasant? Or we could always strip the room of the Flemish tapestries, the ivory sundial and my gold inkwell. Perhaps we should make the room as bare as a novitiate's cell?'

Marsilio's mouth tightens. 'It will be worth it. I promise you that.'

'All this effort just to secure terms with an artist whose style is rather too austere for my taste. I hope for your sake I haven't made a mistake choosing him for frescos.'

'Of course not, Your Grace. It was merely a suggestion to make him understand that our finances are not infinite.' Marsilio Andreasi watches him, his eyes careful.

'I don't need reminding of that!' Marchese Ludovico snaps. 'Although, some of my mistresses might.' He reaches out and lays a hand on his private secretary's back and feels the big mass of muscle relax. Marchese Ludovico smiles. His lips are full and soft with a hungry sensuality. He loves wine and he likes delicate and submissive women. Barbara, his wife, is neither. When there is a knocking on the door the men nod to each other. They retire quickly to an anteroom and wait until the visitor has entered and the papers they have left so visibly have rustled for long enough.

'Good morning, Mantegna,' says Ludovico, entering the room.

The artist moves away from the scrolls. 'Good morning, Your Grace.'

'And what can we do for you this fine morning?'

Both men note how Mantegna's gaze trawls the room from the walls hung with tapestries and silken arrases to the carved crystal reliefs hung between them, and the great astrological globes that flank the Marchese Ludovico's chair like a pair of ducal guardsmen.

Mantegna bows deeply. 'I have come to ask you when the commission for the frescos in the Camera degli Sposi will be formalised. And if I may ask, on what terms?' Mantegna walks to the wall and stares at his two paintings. 'These two works have been praised for my mastery of illusion but I promise you, Your Grace, that the ideas I have for the frescos will surpass anything ever seen before.'

The Marchese Ludovico purses his lips. 'In that case I would like to see a preliminary outline as soon as possible. Then I will decide.'

Mantegna shrugs. 'I have examined the room several times and firstly I need a window moved to widen the space I require, then I can begin.'

'The marchese has many expenses rebuilding the palace. He really doesn't wish, I'm sure, to undertake more building work.'

Mantegna waves a languid hand as if batting away a tiresome insect. 'Then I must petition for an advance, just for materials.'

'How is your new mistress?' Marsilio Andreasi asks innocently. 'I've heard she looks very expensive. Perhaps she came from Venezia when you were there recently. I've heard your groom was seen selling paintings to the public while you were there, but I doubt that very much. Malicious gossip, surely. After all, with the generous stipend you receive from the marchese, it would demean his status for his court artist to behave in such a way. If this fresco commission were to take place, then of course any private commissions taken during this period would be regarded with the utmost censure.'

Mantegna tries hard to stop his eyes widening in despair. 'Of course. That is understood.'

Ten years. That's how long the frescos could take. Ten years of scrimping. He thinks of the many debts he has already run up. The lavish furnishings he has ordered for the house. Reneging on any of these would ruin his reputation. Private commissions are the only way he can survive and he must have paintings ready for discreet patrons before he agrees to any starting date.

'Or perhaps you were merely overheard boasting about her. Of course one shouldn't listen to gossip.'

The marchese raises his eyebrows. 'But, Marsilio, at court it seems to be the main pastime.' He gives a bark of a laugh. 'One could say the only one.'

'She is well.' Mantegna folds his arms.

'Of course these days we are all having to be more careful to guard our reputations, with the Marchese Ludovico's son Francesco being considered for a cardinalship,' says Andreasi.

'Yes indeed. For a while at least, we have to be. The ecclesiastical commission is watching us all very carefully. My new mistress thinks I have joined holy orders myself.' The marchese smiles, as he waits for his humour to be applauded. 'But it pays to be discreet.'

'I understand, Your Grace.' Mantegna walks over to a side table and picks up a gold crucifix, encrusted with rubies like pustules. 'But about my advance...'

'Maestro, as I'm sure you know, by inviting celebrated artists like yourself, I am trying to make my palace look less like a fortification and more like a place of culture and refinement for my family, and for the glorification of Mantova. This clearly is stretching my funds.' The marchese pauses. 'And let us not forget my promise to give you a plot of land in the future, for you to be able to build a house. A very substantial house at that.'

The private secretary steps forwards. 'In fact, Maestro, we've been wondering if the dimensions of the Camera degli Sposi and the stonework already in there might perhaps be too difficult for you? Too much of a challenge?' His voice is low and silky. 'So the Marchese Ludovico mentioned to me that he was wondering if he should show the room to other painters?'

'Difficult? Too much of a challenge?' Mantegna turns with a swagger. 'My artistry doesn't even recognise these words! On the wall just above the fireplace, a great swathe of curtain will be pulled back to show the court in all its glory.' He unfurls an arm in a grandiose gesture towards the door. 'While on another wall, I will depict your beloved son Francesco, hopefully to celebrate his cardinalship. I will bend all the features of the room, the mantelpiece and the doorframe, even the ceiling itself, to my will.' His voice resonates loudly. 'No one will know where the stonework ends and the frescos begin. There will be lunettes beneath the corbels decorated with ribbons, with glorious intertwining leaves and mythological symbols. Beautiful cherubs holding wreaths, medallions with busts of Roman emperors, Tiberius, Caligula, Julius Caesar, Nero... It will be a work of brilliance. The ceiling itself will be like nothing ever seen before.'

'The ceiling?'

'Yes. No other court in the world will have ever have seen anything like it.'

The Marchese Ludovico slips an arm through his. 'Tell me more.'

'I intend to call it the oculus, for it will train the eye up to the heavens. It will look open to the elements and, standing underneath it, the artistry of my illusion will make you feel the breeze itself wafting in. But it will take a great deal of time to plan.'

'I am intrigued.'

'As I am sure you know, Marchese, being such a cultured patron, frescos are better painted only in spring and autumn. On hot days the plaster dries too fast, on freezing days the ice forms on the wall.'

'But other artists manage.' Mantegna feels the arm tighten against his side.

'It will be like nothing I have ever done before, and I only need—'

'I am glad you say that, Maestro, because sometimes I find your work, though undoubtedly touched by greatness, a little… how shall I put it? Rather severe? A little too stony, too sculptural, perhaps too precise. The palette a little sombre.' His arm falls. 'For the frescos I must request more life, and more colour.'

'Life? Colour?' Mantegna keeps the glint of anger from his eyes as he raises his palms outwards. 'There will be optical illusions, and perspectives that no artist has attempted before. The likenesses will be brilliant with colour! I even intend to paint a touch of humour in the ceiling. My frescos will do your court great justice, and show it in all its opulence and splendour. All I need is—'

'So if formally commissioned, when can you begin?' Marsilio Andreasi persists. 'The marchese needs to know.'

The marchese beckons his private secretary over to him and turns with a bland smile. 'Spare us a few moments, Maestro.' Mantegna strains his ears but their voices only murmur together until they both turn back to him.

'The marchese agrees to move the window in the tower to give you more space for one of the frescos. The builders will be diverted from other works at the palazzo as soon as is practicable.'

'And my advance?' Mantegna glances distractedly at the Marchese

Ludovico, who steadfastly refuses to catch his eye. He realises he will have to play for time and sell as many paintings privately as he dares before he begins such a massive undertaking. His glance takes in the cockade at the side of the marchese's cap. 'I need some peacocks to study first,' Mantegna says quickly.

Marsilio Andreasi shakes his head with a thin-lipped smile. 'Peacocks?'

'Yes.' Mantegna turns to the Marchese Ludovico. 'Your Grace, as I promised you, opulence and splendour.'

'And where will you get peacocks from? And how much will they cost?'

'Oh I'm sure you will manage to get me some, Marsilio,' the Marchese Ludovico says smoothly, 'with your usual efficiency. Anything else, Maestro?'

'An enormous quantity of pigment, brushes of every dimension, verdigris for the gilding and a sack of dragon's blood.'

Marsilio Andreasi shakes his head. 'Dragon's blood? Now this is getting really ridiculous.'

'It's a red resin, Signore. As any artist will tell you. This perhaps shows the difference between an artist and a private secretary.' He taps the painting on the wall with a proud flourish. 'And of course, it will be far cheaper if I purchase all of these items myself, but it will take some time.'

'Agreed.' The Marchese Ludovico looks at the leather purse he has just lifted from the table and picks up a heavier one, which he passes to Mantegna. 'Take this in payment for those two paintings, and as the down payment for the frescos. You must live within your means from now on. As we all have to do in these straitened times.'

'So kind, Your Grace.' Mantegna nods to the private secretary, his brown eyes aglow with triumph. 'Such a wonderful patron.' He gives a courtly bow.

Marsilio Andreasi watches him hurry out. 'As you so wisely said earlier, my lord, Mantegna is not stupid.'

'No but he is clearly no match for me.' The Marchese Ludovico arranges a tray of expensive cameos until they sit in two perfect lines.

'Order two peacocks, just to be on the safe side. We don't want any more hold-ups.' There is a faint accusation in the voice.

'Of course, Marchese.' Marsilio Andreasi maintains his usual careful expression. 'I will make arrangements immediately,' he murmurs.

Mantegna nearly slips on the marble stairs and kicks his horse into a canter, leaving Gregorio trailing in his wake. The money purse inside his jerkin feels chunky against his chest. Plenty in there, and he knows just where he'll spend it.

Chapter 8

For three days, Mantegna keeps Ya Ling in the harness room, bringing in plates of food and a bucket of water for her to wash. She learns fast. Using every skill she has acquired so far, she uses her mouth and her tight cleft to arouse him and keep him teetering on the rim of release until he squirms beneath her as if he will die of pleasure.

Lying over her, he pushes his fingers through her shiny hair and holds her face firmly in his hands. 'You hold sway over my heart, little maid.' His face is tight with longing. 'Inside you, I feel like a god,' he mutters, lying heavily on her, while his cheek, metallic with stubble, needles her breast. Each breath sounds heavy with satisfaction. 'Not so much the short-arsed son of a carpenter from a shitty village near Padova now, eh? Not with a *principessa* like you underneath me.' His hand squeezes her breast. 'Just knowing you are waiting for me, sighing my name in that sweet foreign way of yours, and I know I'm better than any of those plotting bastards at court.'

'Yes, Maestro.'

'I don't care how much you cost. You're worth every *grossone*.'

For almost an hour she teases his body and holds him in thrall. Her soft murmurs of delight convince him of the effect his fingers are having on her too. Finally he lies back, exhausted. Her fingers toy with the dark pelt on his chest until his breathing slows to normality. Pulling her into the crook of his arm, he dozes contentedly for a while before dragging himself up from the pallet. He throws her shift on top of her naked body and tells her to dress quickly. When he returns, her smile quickly fades as a stranger enters behind him, holding a long tape marked with numbers.

'Don't worry, maid. I have no intention of sharing you with another man. Now, stand up for me,' orders Mantegna.

The next day he opens the harness room door with a flourish. 'I'm trusting you, little maid. You may go into the kitchen as often as you wish.' Ya Ling hears the outer door bang and a horse's hooves crossing the cobbles. She walks quietly down the corridor and looks through the gap by the door hinge, waiting until the kitchen is empty. Her face falls when she realises that the outer door leading to the courtyard is locked, but her eyes, quickly scanning the kitchen, notice a large brown dresser. One drawer contains only squares of old cloth, another is empty but gives off the greasy smell of tallow candles. A heavier drawer jingles and she slips a hand inside and pulls out a handful of spoons. Choosing the sturdiest one, she places the rest back carefully in the drawer and rushes back into the harness room, where she begins to sharpen the spoon against the stone window frame, remembering how Chen had sharpened the knives for the cook. Prising the spoon against the bricks in the dark corner of the wall behind the straw mattress, she begins to loosen two of them.

When she enters the kitchen again, Genevra and Clemente are chatting by the sink. Genevra turns her back with a loud hiss. Clemente manages an awkward nod. Ya Ling returns to her room, not ready to face any of them until she has to.

Three days later Mantegna arrives with a long parcel under his arm. The paper smells of cedarwood and the dress he pulls out of it is magnificent. She tries hard to keep the dismay from her face. 'For you, my little empress.' He holds the fabric under her chin and gently scrapes the rich nap of the velvet against her skin. 'Feel the quality of that.'

The more her eyes roam over the expensive details the more uneasy she feels. 'But your wife, Maestro?' she enquires.

'Nicolosia? Quality like this would be wasted on a lump like her.' He drops a kiss on Ya Ling's neck. 'Come, little maid. Put it on. Let me show you off to the others.'

It's difficult to hide the surprise Ya Ling feels at the reaction to her entrance into the kitchen. She had expected anger. Jealousy. From what Mantegna has told her, she knows that Mantovans set great store by possessions. By cloth. Paintings. Statues of worked marble. But she expected nothing on this scale. Nicolosia's pink homely face recoils in shock. Real shock. As if she has just received a blow to it. Gregorio shifts his weight from one leg to the other. His brow is set with creases. 'No! Not that! Not your dowry velvet!' says Genevra, her hand clasped to her mouth.

A beautiful dress of Florentine velvet, the colour of Chianti, and lined with a fine linen shift to protect the tender skin of Mantegna's new possession. Both women exchange a look that Ya Ling finds hard to fathom. Surely they couldn't be more distressed by the dress than the terrible slur to the wife's honour of Mantegna so openly enjoying his mistress in the family home? A Han woman of good birth would have poisoned his rice. A Mongolian woman would have waited until he slept, then cut off his penis.

Both Nicolosia and Genevra look as if they have just been snared by the same memory. A memory of a happier, more hopeful time, perhaps, when Nicolosia had a full dowry chest and a new husband she loved. Ya Ling keeps her eyes on her new chamois slippers.

'So, wife. What do you think?'

'She looks very fine.' Nicolosia's voice is like a breath.

'How you disappoint me, wife,' Mantegna drawls. 'You're always telling me that being brought up in the Bellini household, with your illustrious father and your two famous brothers, none of whom paint as well as me by the way, and helping in their workshop has given you such a keen eye for beauty, so now is your chance to prove it.' Mantegna presses the slave woman under her chin with his finger, raising her face upwards. 'Look at her more closely and tell me properly what you think.'

'Of course, Maestro.' Nicolosia's glance slowly travels up the length of the dress. When their eyes meet, Ya Ling doesn't react at the flare of fury as the wife's eyes bore into hers.

Mantegna leads Ya Ling over to the window where she stands as if framed by it, like a portrait. 'Look at her skin, the colour of the finest olive oil. See how it is lifted and tightened by those high cheekbones. Look how those dark upswept eyes are brought into dramatic relief by that thick fringe of eyelashes. See how the planes of her face hold so many shadows, show so much more character than any of the bland Mantovan faces I see about me. I long to paint her.'

'That's not wise.' Nicolosia's voice is crisp. 'You need to paint good Christian scenes. The Madonna and Child. Lives of the Holy Saints. A painting of a slave woman, especially a heathen like her, won't sell at all.'

'I know that, wife,' he snaps, 'but to please her I'm going to paint an Adoration of the Magi and put Gasparre's gift of gold inside a little Chinese bowl. As a reference to her. She'll like that.'

'She'll have no idea what you're talking about. She's a heathen. You're being ridiculous. And we don't want to risk annoying the marchese.'

Mantegna takes an angry step towards his wife. 'So you're the expert now, are you?'

'Well, my father and brothers taught me well.' Her face upturns to his with a cool stare. 'And they seem to be doing a lot better than you.'

The room goes silent. Clemente clears his throat and Genevra nervously fusses with her apron strings. Mantegna looks at his servants and clenches his jaw. 'Go on, wife. Look at her properly when I tell you. Admire her beauty.'

Nicolosia stares deep into the woman's eyes. Beyond the beauty of her small delicate features, the slave woman's stance looks fearless and her shrewd tilting eyes hold an expression of intelligent curiosity beneath that impassive stare. 'I think you need to be careful, Maestro. Her eyes speak of heathen ways. Mysterious customs and cunning ideas, perhaps even cleverness.'

'Really? You think I have met my match?' Mantegna's ripe laughter fills the kitchen. 'That a slave woman once chained up in a market can outwit me?' He gestures with his hands as if calligraphing his words in the air round him.

'Who knows, Maestro?' Nicolosia says politely. 'Perhaps. And perhaps others, too, need to be watchful. To take care.' Her stubby finger prods painfully along all the expensive details of the dress. The gold braiding at the neckline woven in and out with ruby silk ribbons, the slender gold cord that laces the sleeves to the bodice. 'Great care.'

Mantegna's brow furrows. 'What do you mean?'

'Try this.' She turns to hand her husband a wine glass. He takes a sip, then tips it further back, before looking down as if surprised at the already empty glass. 'Just a taste. A new barrel came today.' She smiles pleasantly. 'I didn't want to mix the old with the new.' When Mantegna walks across to the alcove where the new barrel lies on its side and leans down to hold his glass under the brass tap, Nicolosia leans close.

'I don't know how much of this you understand, but I know you can tell a lot from my tone of voice,' she whispers urgently. 'Whatever goes on in that room, I can see you haven't been cowed. He hasn't broken you yet. And I'm glad.' Ya Ling pushes her hands deep into her pockets and stares down hard at the floor. She measures each breath in and out. 'Because soon it will be my turn. And I won't fail.'

Mantegna walks over to the window and holds the glass up to the light. 'Not bad, wife. You have chosen well.' He lets his glance drift across to Ya Ling. 'As have I.' He takes a loud appreciative gulp. 'Decant me a bottle for later, Clemente.' The servant nods. 'Tomorrow I leave for Firenze with an envoy from the marchese. He wants me to see a couple of bronze pulpits Donatello is starting for the Medicis. Rumour is he's on his last legs so I'm aiming to pick up a commission or two on the sly. I'm taking Cecco with me. Good practice for him, and the astrologer says now is a good time to travel.'

Ya Ling swallows hard. She sees a slow flush begin to stain Nicolosia's neck, though her face remains calm and interested. 'And how long will you be away, husband?' Her deep-set eyes follow him across the kitchen.

Mantegna shrugs. 'A few weeks. It depends on how much work I choose to do there. How quickly I get to see the bronzes. Donatello is not much of a rival, unlike your exalted family of course, but I might want to do a few sketches for reference.' He pauses in front of Ya Ling and gives a slow proud smile of ownership.

His hand encloses her breast, leisurely kneading its soft curve as if testing a peach for ripeness. She hears a collective intake of breath from Nicolosia and the servants, and her cheeks burn. Any sympathy any of them might have felt for her would be wiped out by this action. This public humiliation is more wounding than anything he does to her in private. And will take a great deal more to undo. 'Ya Ling may be given some light duties, but I don't want her fatigued when I return. And I don't want a mark on her, wife.' His index finger moves down inside her bodice to the soft hollow between her breasts. Gregorio exhales a gritted breath. She stands aside quickly as if Mantegna's touch burns. 'Clemente, while I am away I leave you to keep the house secure. You are responsible for that.' He unwinds the leather strap from his neck and gives Clemente one of the keys. 'But take this one too, and lock her in the room we share each night. Never let her out of the house.'

Nicolosia ignores the slight to her authority. 'So you will be away a few weeks, husband?' she enquires. The contempt in her voice is controlled. 'Then I will make the necessary preparations for you immediately. Please take care of Cecco, be mindful of his chest.' Mantegna nods impatiently. She turns to Clemente. 'Decant a dozen bottles of the new wine straight away.' Her smile doesn't falter as she watches the way her husband's hand reluctantly leaves Ya Ling's velvet bodice before he picks up the wooden funnel and follows Clemente over to the barrel. The flush has spread upwards from Nicolosia's neck and now flames across her broad cheeks. Her sideways glance is cold and knowing. In a whispered aside heard only by the slave woman, she hisses 'A few weeks? That's more than enough. I only need a couple of days.'

Chapter 9

In the sudden calm after all the shouting and bustle of Mantegna's departure, Ya Ling sits on a corner of the pallet in the harness room and looks around the small space. All of a sudden she doesn't want to leave it. Her fingers pluck nervously at the sleeve of her brown shift. The door looks comforting in its heaviness but soon she will have to breach it. She expects a few flicks of boiling water from Genevra, perhaps a knife dropped on her foot, but she knows that Nicolosia's violence won't be so crude. More considered. But cruel no doubt. She rubs her clammy hands together and stands suddenly. Beijing is a mighty journey from this land, but she won't bring it any closer by staying inside here. Chen will be out there looking for her. She will find him and together they will find Mei Ming, then they will all get back to Beijing, however hard the journey. She centres her thoughts on Chen, imagining his face lit with indescribable happiness before he prostrates himself at her feet. The look of joy on Altan's face as he races down the hutong alley to her father's house. Crossing her arms, she chants Confucius to herself. *Moving a mountain begins by carrying away small stones.* Mustering her courage, she takes a deep breath and grabs hold of the handle.

The servants turn curiously as the door to the harness room opens. They stare at her.

'She's waiting for something.' Clemente's voice is kind. 'She doesn't know what to do.'

'Is she? Oh poor thing. My heart bleeds.' Genevra walks towards her with a hand on each ample hip. 'She's all we need. A heathen in our midst. Still...' she pauses, looking Ya Ling up and down with a sneer, 'she's not quite so grand today, is she? Eh? In her shift? Not quite so exotic?'

'You hungry?' Gregorio mimes chewing.

'Don't you dare! Stupid boy. Not if you know what your job's worth.' Genevra turns and points. 'You. Yes, you. Just stand here and don't move. Signora Mantegna? You understand? Eh?' She points upwards. 'I'm going for her.'

Ya Ling looks at her without expression, just watching her climb the stairs.

Both men stare at her as if mesmerised. Clemente's voice sounds far off, as if he is daydreaming.

'I've never seen hair as black as that, apart from our Rosina's.' His voice tails off sadly. 'I wonder if it feels as silky as hers did when she was little.'

'Don't think like that, Clemente. She's different. From another land. She's led another life. Not pure like Rosina was. Just think what she must have done. Where she's been.'

'What she's done might not have been her choice.' Clemente's glance on her is thoughtful.

'It would be mine all right.' Gregorio slips a hand under his *tabarro*. 'Did you see the way the maestro kept fiddling with her *tette*? Christ! I couldn't sleep last night. I was hard all afternoon. I could hardly walk. I'm surprised nobody noticed.' He sounds very aggrieved.

'Oh Gregorio. You don't change.' Clemente laughs and leans over to tweak the end of his nose. 'Your purse will always be too light for one like her.'

Ya Ling stands suddenly taller, her lips pulled into a tight straight line. 'She looks fierce. I'll give her that. She's not given in without a struggle, I bet. She doesn't move so easily now.'

Clemente lowers his voice. 'I wonder what he's done to her.'

'I'll give you three guesses.' Gregorio sniggers. 'Everything any man would like to do to her. Me, ten times a day. Oww!' He stumbles forwards, rubbing the back of his head.

'Stop that filthy tongue of yours, boy!' Neither of them had seen Genevra come back into the kitchen. 'It's upsetting enough for the mistress as it is.'

They turn as Nicolosia bustles briskly down the stairs. Her upright demeanour makes her look as if she has grown overnight. Both men move away sharply.

'What would you like her to do, Mistress?' Clemente asks. 'The maestro said she could do some light work.'

'Good,' says Nicolosia, stepping into the room wearing her best yellow brocade dress, 'then she can move the shit pile.'

'But the midden cart is due this week.' Clemente glances out of the window at the pile of dung and straw towering high against the wall outside.

'Didn't you hear me, Clemente?' Nicolosia folds her arms. 'The whore can earn her keep.'

'But with the cart coming…' Nicolosia's extravagantly opened palms stop his tongue. 'Move it? Yes. Yes, of course. But where to, Mistress?'

Nicolosia holds out two pink hands at full stretch. 'About that far. To the left. Give her the old fork, the one with the splintery handle. That should do nicely. You'll have to show her what you want her to do, although I don't think she is anywhere near as stupid as she pretends. Then leave her to it.' She makes for the stairwell, then turns as if in afterthought. 'Oh, and it's a cold wet day. I don't want her catching a chill.' Nicolosia speaks with quiet satisfaction. 'Tell her to wear the velvet dress.'

Clemente's eyes widen. 'The velvet dress?'

'Well?' Nicolosia demands.

'Yes, Mistress. Of course.'

'And the chamois slippers too. Can't have her feet catching cold. Can we?' The way Nicolosia stands with her hands on her hips and her chest puffed out makes her look like a little bantam fighting cock.

'No, Mistress.'

'And one last thing. Go and get the hobble.'

'The mare's fine now.' Gregorio shakes his shaggy hair, puzzled. 'She's not so skittish any more.'

Nicolosia drums her fingers on the handrail. 'It's not for the mare, you stupid boy.' She inclines her head towards the slave woman.

'Hobble her?' Gregorio's mouth falls open.

'Then bring it here and I'll do it. She'll run away if she can and there'll be hell to pay if she's not here when the maestro gets back.'

'I think the maestro might have given the hobble away…' Clemente's voice tails off as he takes in Ya Ling's frightened gaze.

'Don't worry, Mistress, I'll go.' Genevra gives her husband a filthy look, then bustles across the yard before handing the rope to Gregorio with an air of triumph. Shamefacedly he demonstrates to Ya Ling that she should lift the hem of her shift before he kneels and wraps the rope round her ankles in a taut figure of eight.

'And tell me the moment she has finished shovelling. Idle hands make mischief. And she looks like she knows all about that.' Nicolosia gives a wintry smile before she leaves.

A heavy drizzle comes in with the mist that blows cold off the River Mincio. Ya Ling looks up at the shitpile. It looks mountainous and each sodden forkful weighs heavy. Four rats have already skittered out of the pile and squeezed themselves under the door to the stable. The last one ran in panic over her foot and made her stomach clench in fear. The dress is soon dragged down with moisture and feels as tight and icy as armour and the chamois slippers feel slimy inside. In no time the rough wooden handle scores deep grooves into her palms.

After the terce bell rings for mid-morning, Ya Ling comes back into the kitchen and collects the wooden slop bucket and takes it to the well. The chain grinds its way through the pulley and it's hard on her hands to keep winding the bucket down, but she perseveres until she hears the splash as the bucket hits the bottom of the well, then she draws up enough water to wash out the bucket thoroughly. She repeats the process until the water in the bucket is clean enough before she plunges her filthy hands into the icy water and lets them have a moment's respite before the cold bites into the blisters on her palms. Clemente sees her look down in despair at the stinking stains that have soaked up from the hem of her dress. 'Quick! Be quick! Come inside for a bit.' Her wet slippers leave rank footprints on the floor, which Clemente wipes up behind her. 'Wait here by the fire.' He comes back from the stable with a length of hemp sacking and saws off two strips with his knife. They look clean and dry. He mimes wrapping them round her hands. 'It'll keep the worst off.' When he sees the bloodied mess of her palms he doesn't look so sure.

'Thank you,' she says behind a curtain of wet hair that now steams in the warm kitchen.

Genevra comes bustling in and gives a sharp intake of breath. 'What the hell do you think you're doing?'

'I'm giving her a bit of time before I tell the mistress she's finished. Letting her catch her breath,' he says sheepishly.

'Oh really? Are you? Eh? Well, I'm not!'

'Come back here, Genevra. Show her.' Clemente holds out his hands. Ya Ling awkwardly shakes off some of the sacking but is careful to show only her palms. She allows her face to register the pain she feels and unclenches her jaw far enough so that her teeth rattle against each other.

'I don't care! I know where my loyalties lie, and if you want to keep your job here, Clemente, so should you!'

'Be quick. Over here. Drink this down.' He hands her a bowl of warm water, which she swallows hungrily; then she coughs as it begins to thaw her frozen windpipe. 'God help us. You're only a slip of a thing. Wait.' He saws a slice off the big millet loaf and mimes at her to eat quickly.

Nicolosia's heavy tread comes immediately down the stairs. 'She's finished? Then why is she hanging about in here?' she snaps. Walking up to the slave woman, she sees crumbs on her bottom lip and slaps them away before she looks at each of them suspiciously. Pushing Clemente to one side, she snatches what is left of the slice of bread from within the wet folds of the dress, opens the door and throws it out onto the cobbles. A large rat darts up and starts gnawing it straight away. 'Now tell her to move it back.'

'Back, Mistress? What do you mean, back?'

'The shitpile! To exactly where it was before, and then tell me the moment she has done that. And give her nothing more to eat. Or else!' She stomps away.

The creases on Genevra's face deepen. 'What the hell do you think you are playing at, Clemente? You are too damned soft for your own good! Do you want us to join one of the bands of beggars out there?' Her hand cups her stomach. 'We can't risk annoying the mistress. You know how queasy I've been recently. How tired I get.'

'It's more than that, wife. More than tiredness. Over three months gone and still sickly.' He eyes her keenly. 'I couldn't bear it if we—'

'It's all right.' Genevra winds her rosary round her wrist. 'You must stop fussing. I'm going to be fine.'

'Well then, teach her a bit then she can help you. Help her understand.'

Genevra raises her fist. 'I'll help her understand all right.'

'But wife, have pity. Just look at her. Her hands are raw. She's frozen through! Doesn't she remind you of anybody?' His voice lowers. 'The same height? Same build?'

Genevra spins round to him. 'What? You talk of our blessed Rosina, our little rosebud, in the same breath as one like her! Our daughter was pure. A little saint! Suffering as she did with never a complaint. The fevers that burned her little body and the ague that chilled her to her marrow. You dare compare her to a heathen whore like that one.' Her back heaves as she burrows her face into her apron. 'I just hope you remember your foul mouth when you're next at confession.'

Clemente runs his hand across the few wispy strands on his bald head. 'And what will you have to say to Father Anselmo?' he reproves gently. 'She might be a heathen and she might be a whore, but you're going to have to confess that you stood by and watched her suffer.'

'I don't care.'

'And we'll need the priest to intercede for us to keep the new child healthy.' Clemente pats her stomach gently. 'You know we do.'

'I'm not having her helping me. Ever.' Genevra looks at Ya Ling's shivering frame, then sighs as if she has run out of steam. 'You. Just get outside,' she says wearily.

Apart from a shaky intake of breath, Ya Ling walks uncomplainingly to the door. She looks up at the tottering mound in front of her and winds the sacking round her blistered palms as best she can, wincing at the weight of the wooden handle against them. Taking a deep breath, she murmurs one of Baba's favourite sayings from Lao Tzu. *He who conquers others is strong. He who conquers himself is mighty.* She works solidly on, trying to alternate the weight on each raw palm as she distances herself from the pain by thinking hard about how to escape.

The big outer doors are tantalisingly near but she needs no reminding of the hobble, which chafes her ankles with every move. Under the pretext of straightening her back she memorises every crevice of each door for footholds. Then she turns her attention to the house. All the windows have thick iron bars and the grand entrance doorway on the first floor is hidden round the curve of the wall. The lock on the kitchen door looks heavy and solid.

'Give me that! I've not got long. But I'm strong as an ox. Just watch me.' She jumps when Gregorio takes the fork from her and digs like a demon into the pile. Gregorio. He will be next. She lets her eyelashes droop onto her cheekbones and leans briefly against him with an exhausted sigh. A shudder runs the length of him. He keeps stopping to look over his shoulder and when Clemente waves to him from the window he hands the fork back with a muttered 'Best I can do. More time and I could finish the job for you,' and hurries to the stables.

The sky darkens as if bruised and heavy rain begins to fall. She doesn't need the ringing of the sext bell to remind her how hungry she is but, after a further hour's toil, when she goes back indoors she waits silently, dripping, by the door. Pride makes her feign oblivion to the noisy chatter round the table that suddenly tails off. Faint with hunger as she is, only strong willpower helps prevent her glance from straying to the sound of tearing bread and the sharp savoury tang of goat's cheese, which makes her stomach churn loudly. But she won't beg. She will never kow-tow. She will wait to be asked. But Nicolosia has chosen that day to have lunch downstairs with her staff and merely orders her outside to move the shitpile once again.

The courtyard is almost dark when Ya Ling comes back inside. She immediately picks up the bucket, takes it to the well and draws up a clean supply of water. Wincing, she pushes both hands under the freezing rim, but the dung has set hard under her fingernails. Back inside the kitchen, she stands by the sink and asks for the thing she wants even more than food or dry clothes. The smell of lye and tallow had drifted under the door of the harness room, so she knows the servants have recently made some. She points to a bar of soap on the sink.

Clemente hands her a thin yellow slice of household soap before his wife can object. They all watch her carefully pick off every trace of shit and straw that has dug into the raw skin, then carefully scrub each crease. Genevra watches her.

'Well, at least she's clean,' Clemente says encouragingly.

'Not in the harness room.' Gregorio snorts. 'I bet she's as filthy as anything in there.'

'Don't you dare start that again.' Genevra's voice is shrill. 'Or I'll be using the soap on your smutty little tongue. See if I don't.'

They turn at the mistress's tread on the stairs. 'So, she's finished. Why wasn't I told? Now tell her to scour the cauldron. The big one.'

'The big one?' asks Clemente. Nicolosia nods as if it is an everyday request. 'Come on, lad. I can't shift it on my own.' Both men grunt as they drag the huge metal cauldron across the kitchen floor. It's big enough for a man to climb into and thick with rust.

'Another part of my dowry, but at least this hasn't been given away to a whore. The maestro isn't known for laying on a banquet for his friends or feeding the poor on a saint's day, so a good clean is long overdue.' Nicolosia picks up a piece of sharp twisted wire carefully between a finger and thumb and pours a handful of brown salt onto a platter. 'Don't stop until it shines like that.' She points at the tiny copper mirror on the wall. 'Or risk a beating,' she says over her shoulder as she locks the bread and cheese away on the big flint shelf in the pantry. 'No one speaks to her. Or gives her anything to eat or drink. Anything at all.'

Genevra nods in approval.

'It's a damn shame,' Clemente murmurs. They look across at the sodden dress that seems to drag down Ya Ling's tiny frame, the reeking water that drips from the hem. The slave woman grimaces as she picks up the wire and begins slowly scraping away at the surface.

'Well, I'm not having her dribbling all that muck from outside all over my nice clean floor.' Genevra wrings out her floor mop, then gives the slave woman's shoulder an angry shove, which is abruptly shaken off. Genevra spins round to her husband. 'See? She's doing it again! I'm only trying to get her to move over and she spurns me with that cocky little shrug of hers!' Ya Ling turns in despair, stiffly straightens herself up and stumbles forwards.

'Stop it, wife. I don't know what's got into the mistress.' Clemente moves across and peers down. 'Or you either.' Genevra bristles at the disappointment in his voice. 'Tethering her like an animal. Making her suffer like this.'

'It's the velvet. I'd be furious too.' Genevra scratches her scaly lips. 'It cost Gentile the profit from two commissions to buy it for her dowry.' Ya Ling rises and puts her hand in the small of her painful back, then slowly turns round to listen. 'They went to the cloth merchant together to choose the colour. It's from Firenze. It's the most expensive velvet money can buy, and she was saving it for Cecco's wedding. It's priceless. And he's given it to a whore. I'd be livid too.'

'Well, I think it's a damn shame, what's happening to you.' Gregorio traces a toe across the tiles, then looks earnestly across at Ya Ling.

'She can't understand you. Well, I say that...' Genevra frowns as she looks across. 'She's got a really cunning look about her. And she's so watchful all the time, as if she's listening to every damn word we say.'

Clemente shakes his head. 'I just don't want her thinking we're savages.'

Ya Ling turns back to her task as if she has understood little of the explanation, her lips tightening as she manoeuvres the sharp wire back into the salt.

'Savages? What? Like her, you mean?' Nicolosia asks tartly. They turn in shock. 'Didn't I give orders no one should speak to her? Or show her any sympathy?' She stands halfway down the stairs and pulls herself as tall as she can. 'Go on! What were you just saying?' Genevra's mouth gapes like a fish.

'I was only telling her to work hard. To keep at it,' Clemente puts in quickly.

'I see.' Nicolosia's sewing box thumps on the table and she pulls out her embroidery ring. Both servants quickly resume their duties. Ya Ling is conscious of the occasional glance Gregorio sends her way as she works on. 'Lay a place for me down here tonight, Genevra. I'm sure we are all hungry. All four of us.' They can hear the growl of the slave woman's stomach as the delicious smell of the evening's beef stewing with carrots and garlic, and the buttery polenta warming in the pot by the fire, permeates the room like a promise. She stops only once, to plunge her hands into a bucket of water and then rinse out the rags and tie them round both hands before going straight back to work. The servants' supper is punctuated by the grating sound of metal on metal as Ya Ling labours away in the corner. There is none of the usual banter, no expressions of delight at the rare treat of a platter of steaming meat that Genevra places on the table.

'If there's money for an expensive dress for the whore then I don't see any reason why we shouldn't enjoy a little luxury ourselves.' Nicolosia looks at the servants expectantly and they murmur their thanks, but both men keep turning to see that the hessian wrapped round each of the slave woman's hands is becoming more shredded as it darkens with rust stains and blood.

Clemente keeps a small slice of meat tucked under a piece of bread on his plate. Gregorio notices but doesn't ask if it's going spare. Nicolosia finally yawns and takes a pear from the green maiolica bowl. 'Nobody gives the whore any food tonight,' she orders and bids them all goodnight.

'Be quick! I can't stop your pain, but I can stop your stomach complaining at least.' Clemente watches anxiously up the stairs as Gregorio takes a piece of bread from his pocket and wraps it round the slice of beef. Ya Ling wolfs the food down.

'You're both mad, the pair of you! I don't care what you lot say. There's something not right about her. She's bewitched the maestro all right. And you too, Gregorio.' Genevra turns to her husband. 'And you can take that innocent look off your face and all. You're worried sick about her, I can tell. Even mentioning our blessed Rosina in the same breath! And another thing, the way she's withstood pain… and hunger too. No whining. No complaints. Eh? It's just not natural. I'm beginning to think she's a witch.'

'Hold your tongue, wife!' Genevra jumps at Clemente's angry tone. 'Do you know what happened to the last one accused, eh? Fed salt then strung up in the cage in the burning sun. Is that what you want? And that other one was hung up by her wrists on the hooks under the bridge near the Piazza Broletto. Luckily she was so fat the wrist binds broke away after two days but that wouldn't happen to *her*, would it? There's nothing to her. She'd dangle in agony up there for a very long time. Do you want that on your conscience?'

'No, husband.' Genevra swallows hard.

'Then let's have no more dangerous talk of witchcraft. Our blessed Rosina didn't ask for her suffering and perhaps neither did she. Get to bed. I've got to wait up and lock her in once she's finished.'

'Please?' Ya Ling fishes out one of the leaves left on a smear of beef gravy at the bottom of a bowl and holds it out to Genevra.

'What, one of these?' Genevra looks puzzled as she crosses over to the dresser and lifts down a canister of dried bay leaves. The slave woman nods with relief. Genevra watches her curiously as she carefully counts out ten leaves and lays them on the table. 'What's she up to?' Then the slave woman opens the wooden box of honeycomb that lies on the sill and gently rubs a thin smear of the golden liquid on the wounded skin of each palm, then lays five bay leaves on top and awkwardly winds the strips of bloodied rust-stained cloth round each hand. Genevra leans down and stares saucer-eyed at what appears to be a small bump just below the little finger at the side of each hand. 'I knew it!' Her voice stutters a Hail Mary as she backs away, twisting her rosary tightly round her fingers. 'I told you, and there's the proof. Look there! On her hands.'

'Nothing. Is nothing.' Exhaustion and pain have made her forgetful. Have overridden her keen sense of survival. Ya Ling tries to lose both hands in the damp velvet of her skirt but it's too late. Cursing her stupidity, Ya Ling turns back to the cauldron and slowly continues scouring in slow agonising strokes. She needs to think hard how to rectify the blunder she has just made.

'Saints preserve us! I'm going to tell Nicolosia straight away, and she can call out a priest. He'll know what to do.' She gives Ya Ling a fearful glance.

'No. I am no witch.' The unexpected pride in her voice makes them all spin round towards her. 'I am a healer. I know nothing of spells or evil things like that.'

'See, I told you!' Genevra's voice is shrill. 'All this time she's been spying on us. Listening in for some heathen reasons of her own.'

Clemente gets to the stairwell before his wife. 'You know it's practically a death sentence to accuse anybody of witchcraft and I'm not going to confession with that on my conscience. And neither are you.'

'But—'

'No buts, wife.' Clemente puts a finger to his lips. Gregorio kneels down and loosens the hobble and Ya Ling lets her hand linger on his shoulder as she steps out of it. She makes a point of rubbing the red rope marks on her ankles. Clemente watches her, then unwinds a key from his neck and holds it out ready.

She thinks quickly. 'Please, I want to finish. Or Nicolosia will be angry tomorrow.' She walks to a cupboard and motions turning a key in each lock, before giving Clemente a shy smile. 'You can leave everything locked. Then what can I do? Only work.'

'Go on.' Gregorio nudges him.

Clemente looks at his wife, who gives him a stony stare. 'Don't look at me. You never listen to a word I say.' They hear her angry footsteps echoing down the corridor.

Clemente locks the kitchen door and the cupboards and stifles a yawn. 'Well, I don't suppose you can get up to much now.' Ya Ling sighs and sprinkles cold water on her ankles. 'And you've had enough imprisoning for one day. I'm too tired to wait up till you've finished, so I'm not locking you in the harness room tonight, I'm trusting you. Do you understand?'

Ya Ling gives him a timid nod then and looks on admiringly as Gregorio attacks the rust on the cauldron with muscular strokes. 'That all right?' His hopeful smile makes him look even younger than he is.

'Thank you.' She puts a hand round his wrist as he walks by. 'My friend.'

His face reddens. 'Get yourself some rest. Ready for tomorrow.'

As soon as he has left she waits in the harness room for the bell announcing nightfall, then once the house is dark and silent she takes the key and creeps down the corridor, then tries to use it to unpick the lock of the kitchen door. Easing the sharpened spoon from behind the bricks in the harness room, she tries with the handle of that. After an hour of patiently trying, she feels her way to the back wall and up the staircase and in the darkness finds the lock of the grand outer door. Strong and stubborn, that lock also refuses to yield. Her head drops in defeat but she forces it up again. Tiptoeing back down the stairs, she allows herself a wry smile. 'Let's hope Gregorio won't be quite so stubborn,' she murmurs as she gives the metal curves of the cauldron one last polish until they finally begin to lighten and shine.

Chapter 10

'Let her do it.' Clemente's face softens. 'You're too sickly today. She's quick on the uptake too. Go for a lie-down while you've got the chance.'

'Yes, she's that all right. Two months here and she knows as many words as me.' Genevra's pale face looks scathing. 'I don't know how she's done it. It's not natural.'

'She's just willing. Trying to do her best. So off you go and rest.'

'Willing? Well, we all know that, don't we? The little tart.' Genevra steps aside. 'Well, just this once. But don't expect me to thank her, that's all.'

Looking down at the pile of wizened white turnips on the wooden chopping block near the sink, Ya Ling sees how her hands have become red and ingrained with work, her palms dotted with hard calluses. At least the scars where her fingers were taken off are now healed and lost in all the roughness. She looks at her fingers, remembering Chen's devotion to her. How pure his love for her had been. How he would never let her sully her pale beautiful hands even with sunshine. A ragged sigh comes from deep inside her chest. Like him she has become a slave, answerable to others for every action she takes. She wonders how Altan might view her now, so demeaned. A servant whose hands have shovelled filth and emptied chamber pots. A humiliated woman, one who has lost face and fallen far from purity. Wiping her eyes on her sleeve, she chops the turnips' white flesh ferociously, ignoring any thoughts that might divert her determination.

The turnips give off an earthy smell. Ya Ling's stomach growls as she feels a sudden sharp longing for the strong tastes of home. For the flavours from the spice market. For the fine white noodles hot with ginger and Szechuan peppers that her mother so enjoyed. Nothing like the lumpen yellow pasta that people in this godforsaken country have crudely copied, and try to call their own. Her mouth waters remembering the Mongolian food her father loved, the creamy walnuts and salted pistachios, the aubergines and the mutton marinated in spices, then roasted and served on a platter of chickpeas crushed with cumin. The fruit syrups and the sorbets. The picnics in clean mountain air, unlike here, where the humid air from the swamps brings flies and strange rashes that bubble under the skin. A wave of emotion rises in her chest as she remembers the times when the women in her father's family had all gathered to cook together. A joyous time enjoyed by them all, but not so promising for the fat-tailed sheep tethered under the birch trees ready for the sacrifice before the Eid feast. The births. The betrothals. The laughter. The joy of being together. The protection of her father. And the firm smooth feel of Altan's cheekbone held fleetingly against her own. The clean smell of peat smoke that infused the diamond padding of his winter jacket. The way he had drawn her hands inside it to warm them against his hard chest. The first brief taste of his lips on hers. The only time they had been left alone together, his tender palm had explored and lifted up her breast... she shifted against the sink, reliving the feeling inside her when her flesh had blossomed under his touch. His calm unruffled smile when Ayi had bustled back into the room. The pain of memory almost stops her breath. The knife clatters down onto the block.

She glances up out of the window. Gregorio's precious songbird trills from the little reed cage tied to one of the outside bars, the tiny fluting sound drowned out by the raucous cry of the tripe seller from the other side of the thick courtyard wall. The washing flaps and drips onto the cobbles. In the space between something catches her eye. An extravagant scarlet cord holding two goat horns swings boldly in the breeze where it is tied to the latch of the big outer door. There seems to be a little scroll tied under it. Ya Ling stares hard.

Gregorio's tuneless whistle comes across the yard, the kitchen door opens suddenly and he strolls in. Ya Ling goes into the larder and throws a brass jug hard against the flint floor. 'Oh no! Look what I've done.' She holds it out to Gregorio. 'See. I spoiled it. Nicolosia will be very angry with me.'

'Don't worry. I'll go and hammer the dent out of it. It'll take me no time.' She watches him duck his head between a row of washing, then turn right and disappear into the toolshed. Once the banging starts, Ya Ling snatches up the peeling knife and hurries into the courtyard. She saws viciously on the cord, then quickly loosens the string round her neckline and tucks the strange object down the front of her dress. Once in the quiet harness room she pushes the hidden spoon further back into the deep hole she has carefully carved out behind the two bricks she has loosened and slips the horns inside before she rushes back to the kitchen.

'It looks like new! I am very grateful to you. Here. Have some water. It's the only present I can give you.' She fills the water jug and holds it out to Gregorio with a smile.

'Well, there is something you can do for me.' He scuffs his toe along the join of a tile. She looks warily at him. 'Oh no! Nothing like that! The maestro would kill us both.' He gives her a curious sideways smile. 'It's just… I want to know what happened to you. How you ended up here. Clemente and I have talked about how on earth your parents could ever sell a lovely girl like you.'

With Genevra sickly in bed and Clemente tending her, this is it. The perfect moment. The one she has been waiting for. But it will be hard to relive. 'I will be happy to tell you and please tell the others – especially Genevra.' She takes a deep breath. 'My parents didn't sell me. They would never do a thing like that. They love me, they always have. I was stolen from them by a man they trusted, a man they traded with, a Berber. He used to bring us cures we couldn't find anywhere else, bark from a special tree and henna from Basra, foxglove powder for the heart, musk, that kind of thing. I've known him since I was a baby. The Berber had planned it. Given my father a potion, given one to everybody in the household, at my betrothal party. There were a hundred people there.'

'Betrothal party?' Gregorio looks stunned. 'A hundred people?'

'Oh yes. My parents are rich. I had a wonderful life ahead of me,' she says bitterly. 'But how were we to know the Berber was so evil? So…' Her hands clasp nervously together, then she stiffens herself upright. 'So… I went into the woods with my big willow baskets, and I never came back. My family must still wonder why. A wild pig? Or a bear? Who knows what they think? All I do know is that they would have searched for me for a very, very long time. Perhaps they still do. And perhaps they still see the Berber, and other children in the hutong are in danger from him. But I think he is too cunning to return to a nest he has fouled.'

'The bastard! If I ever get anywhere near him I'll finish him off.' Gregorio punches a fist against his palm. 'So what happened to you then?'

'I was put in a ship's hold and I was at sea for many days with another girl. A poor girl who ended up even worse than me.' Her face falls as she remembers Mei Ming struggling against her captors. 'Then we arrived in Venezia and Mantegna bought me.'

Gregorio shakes his head as if dazed. 'You've plenty of courage. I'll give you that.'

'No, I was very frightened. The boat jumped about like an angry stallion.' She walks up to him and rests a hand on his arm as if she needs him to anchor her.

'It's like a tale told by a storyteller,' Gregorio marvels as he looks down on her. 'But listen, you're safe now. I'll look after you.' His face shines with sweat and devotion.

'Please tell the others. Tell Nicolosia too, make her listen. I expect Genevra will tell her, but I want to make sure she knows.' She rests a hand on the side of his cheek. 'Tell them everything.'

Gregorio puts a hand where hers has been. He feels his cheeks burning. The brown leather bridle lands on the kitchen table and Gregorio takes a piece of cloth and a pot of tallow and starts rubbing it in furiously.

The onions prickle her eyes before she throws them in the pot quickly. She giggles. 'We look like an old married couple, Gregorio.'

'I wish we were.' His smile is wistful. She notices how relaxed he is as he sits in the chair, as if he is content just to be with her.

'Tell me…' She keeps her voice low and even, smoothing the shake of excitement. 'I heard the mistress talking to a friend about horns. Something about them hanging outside a house? Tied with a little red rope? Something like that.'

Gregorio stops unbuckling the cheek straps and drops the bridle in his lap, his eyes alight. 'No! Who? Who was it? Which family?'

Ya Ling gives him a vague shake of her head. 'No name, just something she heard in the market, I think.'

'Oh.' His face falls.

'Go on. Tell me. I told you my story. Your turn now.'

'It's a set of cuckold's horns. A terrible slur on the honour of the master of the house. It's telling him that his wife has been unfaithful.'

'Unfaithful?' Ya Ling feels her heart thud in her chest. 'And what does the master of the house do then?'

'Most men would lay a vendetta when they find out who's responsible. Obviously they have to find out if their wife really has been up to anything first.'

'So the maestro would do that? Cause violence. Doubt his wife?'

'He'd be so angry we'd all suffer! But he'd never need to doubt the mistress. But he probably would. I'd bet a week's wages – not that I've had any for a while...' He shakes his head. 'You only need to look at Nicolosia and you can tell she'd never lie with another man. But he would be furious with her in any case.'

'But why?'

'Because he'd feel humiliated. That's how it works. And he's got a temper on him like an angry bull.'

Ya Ling thinks hard and chooses her words with care. 'It must be awful for a woman to be accused of this sin, if she is faithful to her husband. But that would never happen, would it?' Her sideways glance is guileless.

'Oh yes. It does sometimes.' He nods with a grim smile. 'If a man has enemies then the horns are a good way to get at him.'

'Well, we're lucky the maestro has no enemies...' Her voice rises softly but Gregorio just spits on the rein he is polishing and rubs even harder. 'Has he?' The groom unbuckles the shiny bit and soaks it in a bowl of water. She smiles prettily. 'Go on, tell me.'

The groom crosses the kitchen to bring his head low and near to her. 'Shh! Between the two of us, he has a lot of enemies. Merchants. Other artists. And he's not exactly popular with a lot of the Gonzaga courtiers either. He thinks people look down on him and he takes offence at everything. And he takes people to court if they criticise his work. I've taken a beating many times defending his honour. Not many servants do that these days but he knows I'd defend his name even if it killed me.'

'You are very brave.' She smiles at him from under her lashes.

Gregorio's voice drops low. 'I have to, I have no choice. There are plenty of servants starving out there.' He jerks his head towards the door. 'But I'm lucky. Nicolosia will never let the maestro get rid of me. Her priest promised to intervene with God to make sure Cecco doesn't die from his illness if she looks after me here. So I'm safe as long as she believes that.' He looks closely at her. 'I'm daft, but I'm not as daft as they think, you know.'

'I never thought you were.' She smiles up at him. 'And the other two servants?'

'They're safe too. Genevra's family have always worked for the Bellinis. Her mother looked after Nicolosia from when she was a baby, then the Bellinis let Genevra and Clemente move here with her when the maestro started work for the Gonzagas, so if the maestro ever tries to get rid of the pair of them, then the Bellinis will want to know why.'

Ya Ling looks up at him with an admiring smile. 'Well, they are very lucky to have you. So brave and so strong.'

'Aye, I am that. Look!' He pulls a clenched fist up to his shoulder and points to the mound of muscle. 'No one can beat me for heavy lifting.' He drops his face down into her silky hair. 'And I'll look out for you too, whenever I can.'

'Dusters? Yes, Mistress. I'll get them.' They move apart when the banister creaks as Genevra makes her way downstairs, grumbling to herself. 'There's only a smear of beeswax left and it's not my fault. I couldn't be more sparing.'

Gregorio grabs the bridle and slips through the outer door. Ya Ling rushes into the harness room and wedges the door shut before she allows herself a long sigh of relief. She pushes her palm against the bricks, as if keeping what lies behind them even safer. *Guanxi*. Obligation. Power. That's what the strange contraption of horns contains. More power in the household than she has ever dreamed of. The possibility of freedom unfurls inside her chest, as exhilarating as if she has just taken a large glass of the sweet muscatel wine that Mantegna knows she loves and brings her back from the market. Power. All she has to do is bide her time and think carefully when best to use it.

The next day Mantegna's loud voice is heard shouting at the top of the stairs. 'What kind of welcome home is this?' Ya Ling looks upwards with a sinking heart, watching as Clemente and Gregorio rush up the stairs. 'Thank God for Ya Ling, at least she'll be ready to welcome me! Get the staff together down in the kitchen now.' When they are all gathered nervously in the kitchen Mantegna comes down the stairs and walks straight up to Ya Ling. 'There you are, my beauty. Go and get ready for me. Put the dress on. I've been imagining you wearing it all the time I've been away.'

The push catches her in the middle of her back and propels her forwards. She steadies herself and nods obediently.

She dresses in the harness room. The garment still feels damp to touch; she has washed and soaked it many times and has left it dripping for several days over the stool in her room, but the fabric still weighs heavily with moisture. Ya Ling shivers as she feels its clammy touch brush over her hips. The bodice has shrunk slightly and her rounded breasts rise over it. The panniers at each side now dig into her slender hips as the wet skirt hangs heavily down. She delays long enough to allow a slow build-up of fear in Nicolosia and the servants.

Mantegna notices straight away. His eyes darken. 'What in God's name has happened to the dress?' he demands. 'What have you done to it?' He moves quickly across to her and snatches a handful of the sleeve. 'It's damp! The colour's gone patchy. All the sheen, the richness has gone out of the fabric! Have you any idea how much that velvet was worth?'

Ya Ling tries out a pretty smile, but her lips shrivel back from her teeth. 'It's my fault. I'm so sorry, Maestro – you told your wife to give me some light work, so on the day you left…' She pauses long enough to send a quick glance to encompass them all. A log shifts in the fire, sending out a spray of sparks up the chimney, but no one turns to look. '… you see, I was missing you very much, so when the mistress asked me to carry the laundry basket I was so sad thinking of you being so far away from me that I fell over in the courtyard, not far from the midden. I was very heartbroken…'

Mantegna glances at his wife. 'I don't believe you.' He studies the others in turn, noting the way Genevra's palms keep rubbing together until Clemente squeezes them to stillness. The way Gregorio gnaws at a fingernail. The way his wife's features have gone taut with dread. 'There's something going on here. I can tell. Everyone seems to be holding their breath. What's worrying you all? Why aren't you all eager to blame my mistress and see her getting a beating?' Each servant drops their glance in turn and looks away.

'But Maestro, you listen to me! Let me explain and say how sorry I am… I promise I will make it up to you later.'

Mantegna holds up a hand. His eyes darken as they move from Ya Ling's winning smile to the slow flush rising like a tide up Nicolosia's neck. 'You haven't survived so far without having your wits sharpened on a whetstone. That dress was worth more than you will earn in a lifetime. You'd never have worn it to do household tasks. What do you say to this nonsense, wife?'

Nicolosia takes out her rosary and begins to turn the pale pink stones over and over between her hands. Her voice spins out like a thread. 'I wouldn't have minded anything else but the velvet. And you knew that. It was the last valuable possession left from my dowry and the most precious to me. Gentile saved up a long time to give me that. He took me to the cloth merchant and we chose it together.'

'So you decided to deliberately ruin it? Knowing how much it was worth?'

Nicolosia nods. 'You disgraced me,' she says quietly. 'You knew I was saving it for Cecco's wedding.' Her chin comes up and her plain features seem to brace themselves. 'And it wasn't yours to give.'

Mantegna's derisive laugh makes them all jump. 'Oh, you own property now, do you? You're married, you fool! Everything belongs to me. Only a Bellini born and bred would dare to think otherwise.'

'If you behaved more like my family then we would be a lot better off…' Her voice tapers to nothing.

Mantegna glances round the kitchen at the servants all staring at the floor, scarcely daring to breathe. 'Really? In what way?' His voice has a bitter edge.

'In every way.' Nicolosia raises her head and looks into the middle distance, refusing to acknowledge his sharp exhalation, then she draws back her sturdy shoulders. Ya Ling dares an admiring glance. It seems women here lose more than their freedom when they marry. Husbands seem to take everything. Mongolians would fight a clan war over a bride's dispossession and a Han family would never condone the public loss of face of a brother's personal dowry gift being given to a concubine. Judging by her dignified stance and unbowed head, neither apparently does Nicolosia.

'We need to discuss this in private.' He points a shaking finger at the staircase. 'Upstairs in the marital room. Come with me now. *Wife*.'

The staff follow the progress of Mantegna and his wife up the stairs, then all make the sign of the cross. Loud voices are heard, and they glance upwards in unison at the sound of something heavy landing on the tiled floor above.

The rest of the afternoon is spent in limbo, as if waiting for the Last Judgement to fall on them. Most of all, to fall on Nicolosia. Genevra sits at the kitchen table, too weak and nauseous to do anything but glance up at the ceiling and wait in trepidation for her mistress to come down.

Ya Ling takes the opportunity to go through the store cupboard and gather together a pile of dried herbs, which she dampens with honey and sour wine. They watch her strip the leaves from the vase of yellow arnica on the windowsill and simmer them slowly, then wring them out and simmer them again and again until she nods when she smells them. She wraps the herbs in the damp leaves and keeps softening them in her hands until she reduces them to a malleable green parcel.

When she finally appears, Nicolosia looks worse than they expected. Refusing all help, she holds the banister rail tightly as she makes her way down to the kitchen with a slow painful dignity. Her lip is split and one eye is half-closed in the middle of a mound of reddened skin. Purple bruises are beginning to bloom along her jawline. Ya Ling pulls apart the green poultice and rolls each half round in her hands and then slaps them into two flattened circular shapes. She indicates to Nicolosia to hold one to her swollen eye and the other against the broken flesh of her mouth. 'What's this?' Nicolosia says through her inflamed lips. 'The whore is trying to poison me now? Is that it?

Not that I'd mind,' she grinds out. 'You can take my place completely and you're welcome to it.'

Ya Ling tears off a few shreds from the poultice and, holding Nicolosia's lopsided stare, deliberately chews them. Nicolosia shakes her head and, snatching up both poultices, throws them in disgust onto the wooden draining board by the sink. With difficulty she pulls a sealed roll of parchment from her pocket and gives it to Clemente. 'Take this to Signora Trionfetti. The maestro has gone to the palace until late. Tell her to get it to Gentile as soon as she can.' She turns to Ya Ling. 'Tell him! Go on! Tell my husband I am sending for my brother! Do what you want. I no longer care. Giving you my velvet and parading you in front of me has hurt me far more even than a beating like this.'

'I know, Mistress.' The slave woman looks at Nicolosia with her impassive stare.

'Get out of my sight! Don't imagine that I will ever feel grateful because you tried to take the blame over the dress. If you weren't here, my velvet would still lie safe in my dowry chest. Don't imagine that I will ever forgive you.'

Ya Ling looks at her with a quiet optimism. The Mantovan way can't be all that different from the emperor's court. Reputations saved. Favours given. Nicolosia will hate to be beholden to her, but she definitely will be. 'I have something to show you. Something important.'

'Some trick of a foreign whore? You expect me to fall for that?' Nicolosia's stare is withering.

'I need to speak with you alone,' she mouths, giving a slight sideways nod of her head in the direction of the servants now murmuring together in a tight trio on the far side of the kitchen.

'My word, your knowledge of our language has really improved since you've been here. Hasn't it?' Nicolosia's voice stiffens in fury. 'Genevra has warned me how clever you are. How you must have enjoyed spying on us all this time and reporting any household gossip back to my husband.'

'No, Mistress. I have told the maestro nothing I have seen and I can prove it to you. Send the servants away and I will show you.'

'You think I'm stupid enough to fall for some heathen mischief?'

The words sound blurred, as if it is painful to get them past her lips. She walks decisively over to the sink, picks up the two poultices Ya Ling has made and throws them contemptuously into the slop bucket. 'Be warned, whore. I will never ever give you a moment's peace in this house. Now get out of my sight.'

Despair embeds itself in Ya Ling's chest. Keeping her expression polite, she manages a confident nod before she opens the door of the harness room. Lying on the pallet, she clings to the words of Confucius to help shore herself up against a wave of disappointment. *Our greatest glory lies not in never falling, but in getting up every time we do.* She has acted too quickly, that is all. Too impulsively. *When it is obvious that goals cannot be reached, don't adjust the goals, adjust the action steps.* Her moment will come if she is patient.

She lies back and swallows down the slight rise of nausea that she has felt many times recently. Her heart constricts. There is no escaping what has worried her for several days. She has never been late before. Time isn't on her side. She feels her throat tighten, her blood pumping as she spans both hands across her stomach.

When Mantegna comes to her that night his lovemaking is urgent, as if making up for his absence. Her smile drains away as soon as he leaves. Her heart feels swollen and tender in her chest. She brings her knees up and wraps two arms round them and lies curled into the straw mattress. Her emotions swing in a violent arc. In her mind, she hates the child growing within her. It is part of Mantegna, of his forcing himself upon her. In her heart she pities the child. Like her it is blameless. Loneliness wells up from deep inside her and she curves her arms round her stomach like a chrysalis protecting the tiny scrap of life inside. She imagines how it will feel to have a new life stirring inside. Her mother's benign face and her soothing touch seem a lifetime away. The pillow dampens under her cheek. Suddenly fearful for the child's safety here, she feels her pulse racing and drags a deep breath into her lungs, then releases it with a powerful sigh. The baby is safe for the moment at least. Abortion is a mortal sin here, she knows that from the chatter in the kitchen. As long as no one finds out too soon, then somehow she will manage. But escape is now vital. She has to think her way out of this, and quickly. Every day counts.

Chapter 11

'How do you feel?' Concern etches Clemente's face as Genevra walks quickly to the sink. 'You're not still being sick, are you?'

'No. Not really.' Genevra shakes her head. 'Only a bit.'

Ya Ling notices her shoulders making small heaving motions. She hands Clemente a bowl of water and a damp cloth. 'Let her sip water and cool her face.' Glancing out of the window, she notices the yard is empty and hears the clank of the milking bucket from the stable. Gregorio must be helping with Genevra's duties. 'Where is the mistress today?' she asks innocently.

'With Signora Trionfetti.'

'And what time will she return?'

Genevra sits down heavily on a stool. 'Later. I don't know.'

'Then why don't you go back to bed? I'll take over here. Again.' Ya Ling picks up a large field mushroom from the basket and begins to wipe the earth from its cap. 'You won't want to cook feeling sick like this. I can do these. What are they called? Mushrooms?'

'Yes. That's it. You learn so fast.' Ya Ling nods prettily at Clemente, who beams across before helping his wife down the corridor.

She opens the kitchen door and holds her breath when it creaks. The milk cow gives a soft lowing sound as she creeps quietly past the stable door before she picks up her skirts and runs headlong towards the heavy gates. Her fingernails crack and splinter as she frantically grabs for any handhold she can, pulling against the beams hammered into the wood, prising and hauling herself higher and higher until she manages to straddle a leg over the top.

The bucket clanks on the cobbles. 'Martyr's blood! Clemente! She's running away! Come and help me get her back!' Gregorio jumps up and catches her by the heel, but she kicks hard and hears his hand bang heavily into the wood before she slithers down on the other side. A family leap back in astonishment when she lands on the floor in front of them. Picking herself up, she rushes past them, their two children laughing and pointing at her. Her feet drum against the dusty road and she hears two sets of feet chasing her. 'Stop her! Grab her, somebody!' Gregorio's voice roars behind her as she turns down a side street and nearly collides with a flock of sheep that spread out like a woolly grey cloud across the road. The flock divides into two and the sheep bleat in panic as she flounders among them. The angry shepherd raises his staff to her and lands a blow on her hip that makes her falter sideways. Neighbours scream from the balconies above, shouting out directions to Gregorio and encouraging jeers to Clemente, who is red-faced and doubled over, gasping for breath.

The terrified sheep skitter in all directions and as Ya Ling runs parallel to a row of fruit barrows she slows down just enough to tip over a sack of red apples that roll around the sheep and make them stop to forage among them. The stallholder shouts in fury, picks up an armful of oranges and tries to pelt her with them, but she has already turned off into a small alleyway that leads out into a piazza with a big mulberry tree in the centre. There she sees a sight that brings her to a standstill.

Coming down the staircase of a merchant's mansion is a group of tiny humans, who laugh and joke with each other. They posture and preen, showing off their expensive clothes. One of the females is even wearing a velvet cloak, which she throws over one shoulder with a piercing laugh. They strut across the cobbles as if there is nothing remarkable about them being there at all. They turn to stare at her with bold curious glances. One pulls both of his eyelids sideways and says, 'You should try looking in a mirror before staring at me like that.' They chuckle and move towards her with little menacing steps until they stand in an arc around her.

'Wh-who are you? What are you?' Her voice wavers as she steps backwards. Two arms like iron bands grab her tightly from behind and she recognises Gregorio's loud panting in her ear. 'You little bitch,' he gasps. 'I trusted you. And so did Clemente. We felt sorry for you and we did our best for you. But you'd have us all in the cage, would you?'

'But what are these? I've heard of them but never seen one before. Or are they demons? Or djinns? Gregorio, tell me!'

'Don't you worry about them. The maestro will be demon enough when we tell him you've tried to run away.'

When she sees Clemente and the man from the fruit stall striding furiously towards her she realises that struggling is futile. The stall owner grudgingly accepts a coin from Clemente. Gregorio keeps a tight hold of Ya Ling until he and Clemente can link arms through hers and march her quickly back to the house.

The following day no one in the household dares question why a brawny blacksmith suddenly arrives, bringing with him his brazier and his skinny bellows boy, and why both disappear into the harness room. The blacksmith comes out and pulls Gregorio round to face him. 'More kindling, boy! Tell me – are the logs in the stack outside well seasoned? I need them to burn as hot as hell.'

Gregorio looks at Nicolosia for instructions. She shakes her head. 'You can't have all of that, it's all we have for winter.'

'Maestro's orders. And nobody argues with him. Tell your boy to bring it in.' He nods at the bellows boy waiting by the door. 'I'll have this too.'

'No! Not the charcoal. It's my last sack.'

'I need it to build up the heat. Going to take a while. Your husband told me to take whatever I needed.'

Nicolosia looks as if her face has marbled over when the sack is dragged across the terracotta tiles, snaking a trail of black dust that stops abruptly at the harness room door. The heat inside the room belches out each time the scarlet-faced bellows boy comes out for jugs of cold water. No one says a thing.

'What's he going to do to her?' Genevra finally whispers.

Nicolosia stares at the harness room door. 'I'll stay down here and organise my linens today,' she says, pulling a stool over to the tall linen press in the corner. She works steadily, folding and refolding the heavy white sheets and embroidered cloths on each shelf over and over again, as if oblivious to the fearful curiosity that seems to thicken and clot around them all in the quiet kitchen. They see her occasionally turning her coral rosary beads and murmuring patiently to herself.

When Mantegna brings the slave woman into the kitchen she stares in shock at the clanging and the smoke. 'No! No!' Wild-eyed, she lunges away from Mantegna, nearly toppling him over as she manages to drag him halfway to the door, his feet paddling on the tiles. She erupts with all her strength, her flailing fists bringing a whole row of pewter platters crashing down from the dresser. They all look on in terror at the stream of alien words she spits into the face of the blacksmith as he struggles to overpower her. Her straight black hair swings violently like a whip.

'Go on, you two! Don't just stand there. Grab hold of her! Mantegna steps aside. 'I can't risk my hands.' Gregorio, Clemente and the muscular blacksmith manhandle her through the doorway into the furnace of the harness room. The blacksmith binds her thrashing wrists and winds a rag round her open mouth to stop her savage bites and stem the frenzied curses that stream out. She makes a keening noise liked a trapped animal before Mantegna pushes both terrified servants outside. The last thing Ya Ling sees before the door slams shut is Clemente patting Genevra's back while she makes the sign of the White Christ over and over against her chest. The kitchen holds its breath, but nothing is heard from the slave woman above the whooshing of the bellows and the metallic clanging of the hammer. As the afternoon darkens into evening the blacksmith comes out of the room and hammers a much bigger iron lock into the harness room door. 'Here, Maestro.' He hands over two substantial keys to Mantegna, who ostentatiously threads them both onto a leather cord and ties it round his neck.

Over the next three days Mantegna spends long hours during the day and each night in the room. Relieved he hasn't carried out the worst of his threats, Ya Ling uses every trick she has learned since her capture to keep him contented. Wincing, she tries to ease herself away but he burrows deeply into her with an irritated growl. She tries to wriggle out from beneath him.

'Do you want me to call the blacksmith back? I don't want it to be like this, but he can do far worse than he's done already.' He lifts his head and glares down at her. 'I own all of you. Don't you understand that? And yet you dare to make me a laughing stock in my own *contrada*. Losing face before all of my neighbours. You are going nowhere now. Understand?'

'Yes Maestro.'

Her eyes hold his with a narrow elliptical stare until he looks away; then he digs his hands furiously into her hips and drags her slight frame on top of his. 'Then do what I've paid for.'

She presses her tongue to the roof of her mouth and holds it there until she dares trust her voice. 'Of course, Maestro.' *You'll pay all right*, she promises herself. She takes a steadying breath and carefully bears her weight down on him. *Knowing how to yield is strength.* With a leaden smile, she looks down at him until his features slacken back into the pillow, then she curls away from him on the pallet, tears bubbling behind her lids as she scans the tight space of the room. Years and years of this stretch ahead. The rough handling. The threats. Then, even worse, perhaps more of the awful penitent tenderness when he is replete, when he tries to kiss her and she has to fight her revulsion. Intimacy like that will never be for one such as him.

He only leaves the room with demands for food and wine, which he brings back inside at regular intervals. 'Give me two big bowls of ragu,' he demands. 'Fetch a large jug of *vino nobile*, and some of those pastries with caraway seeds,' he shouts, strolling across the kitchen and scratching his bare chest.

Ya Ling has to move carefully, not just because of the chinking noise that now follows her every move, but because of the pain her ankles already give her.

Mantegna padlocks her chain to the wall and prepares to leave her for the first time in three days. Ya Ling doesn't care where the hell he is, as long as he isn't on top of her. 'You need to eat something,' he says, raising his eyebrows with that rueful look he shows when his conscience bites. 'You'll need all your strength when I get back.'

A plate of bread and apples, a bowl of yoghurt and a pitcher of water lie ignored on the floor. Her throat gives an involuntary swallow but she pulls her gaze away from the jug. 'It's probably well water, and the fool won't have the wit to boil it in any case,' she tells herself to stiffen her resolve.

The room locks her in like a tomb. She flicks a fearful glance around it. Not room. Cell. That's what it is. A cell. The red-horned Satan who terrifies them all in this godless place must know what crime she has committed to be punished like this, because she certainly doesn't. The chain slithers out as she walks gingerly as far as she can. The manacles dig into her flesh where it thins above the ankle bone. Every muscle aches where she has controlled her flesh so as not to retract from his exploring fingers and his probing tongue. The air feels cloying inside her bruised chest and the walls seem to close in. Pacing from wall to wall might help stem her rising panic, but now she can't even do that. Breathing quickly, she strides to the bolt in the wall and, shortening the chain, she puts her feet on the bricks on each side and heaves and heaves until the veins stand out on her forehead. A sifting of brown dust comes down but the bolt doesn't move at all. '*Bastardo!*' she shouts at it, then comes out with every curse she has ever heard on the streets in Beijing, from the sailors on board the ship and all those she has heard since she first arrived in this uncivilised land. After the bolt is cursed, next comes Mantegna, the blacksmith and most of all the Berber.

She falls back on the bed, closing her eyes tight shut to keep the walls from moving inwards and smothering her. This is worse than anything she could have imagined. Worse than any horror that has happened so far. This is hopeless. Chen will never find her here. Mei Ming will never be rescued. Terrified of small spaces as she is, she imagines years and years of being buried alive in here with Mantegna taking her whenever he chooses. Between these dank walls. In the half-light. A sob rises up from her aching chest and in the warm foetid atmosphere the tears remain pooled on her cheeks. She feels emptied inside. Dried-up and fragile, like a snakeskin sloughed off.

There is only one way to escape. To get inside her mind and go back. To pull herself through a slit in the fabric of time, and discover the still and central place where mind and body can meld together in harmony. To ride again across the Mongolian grasslands on her stocky Ujimchin stallion, feeling the rhythmic tattoo of his galloping hooves on the sun-baked earth, hearing the swish of the parting plumes of grass that billow all around like the waves of a mighty ocean.

A soothing lethargy begins to creep up each limb as she lies back, impassive with exhaustion. Now she disciplines her mind, leading it back to Beijing, to the family house, sitting with her mother embroidering the brightly coloured bedspread for her dowry chest that flows around their knees. Her mother keeps patting her hand and smiling as they admire the curves of the purple peonies and the ruby pomegranates that grow beneath each other's tiny stitches.

Ya Ling slowly breathes in *qi* and drifts down from reality into the release of dreams. Now she is with her father, listening to his solemn instructions as she crushes fennel seeds with the white marble pestle in his consulting room. Next she polishes the brass scales and the row of weights that stand in ascending order on the shelf, from light as a maiden's whisper to heavy as a *jin* of lead. She drifts, all the time pulling herself inwards, making memories reality. Hiding inside them for longer and longer periods. Dying is going to be easier than whatever lies ahead. Oblivion. Release. She longs for both. She feels weak and boneless. Dizzy with hunger and fighting the urge to snatch up the jug, she lets a weariness seep into her soul. She shuts her eyes tighter, welcoming it, drawing it in.

No longer dirty and debased in her dreams, she can allow the soft swell of memory to take her back to an intimate memory of Altan. To his keen eyes and his smooth golden cheeks. The muscular spread of him under the soft buckskin. The straw whispers as she leans back into it as if welcoming his tall frame in beside her. They have never lain together, only been alone together that one wonderful time when Ayi had briefly left the room and he had kissed her for the first time. His lips on hers had been warm enough to thaw an ice-ghost. Does he still think of her? How long did he patrol the forest looking for clues? How long after the search parties had given up hope and gone back gratefully to their own families?

She turns restlessly. Altan. Beloved Altan. Afraid of nothing. Hotheaded to the point of madness as a youth, he'd once come across a group of much older boys trapping sparrows for fun. He'd taken them all on. All seven of them. 'Not sparrows! You can't do that! Let them go! Sparrows won't be caged. They won't eat or drink. If they lose their freedom they choose death every time.'

An hour later he had arrived at their compound with two black eyes and a badly broken nose. And a handful of empty cages. She remembers her father showing her how to bathe the grazes on Altan's face, and the sweet medicinal smell of artemisia coming off the damp cloth. The first flickering between them had begun that afternoon. So innocent. So tender. It seems a lifetime ago. Pushing her face into the pallet, she sobs until her ribs ache. Artemesia. A lot sweeter than the smell that comes off her at the moment, she thinks, looking down at her stained shift with disgust. But what was the point of trying to be clean? Mantegna would be back soon, his filthy hands dragging off her shift, then pawing and roaming all over her again. She rubs at the dull pewter of the jug and stares hard to see her likeness in it. The outline is blurred, as if the contours of her face have suddenly dissolved with age. The thought no longer worries her. At this rate she'll be dead of starvation and thirst long before Mantegna loses interest.

Staring at the wall, she tries to get back to Altan but he won't cooperate. Tough and stubborn. Like all Mongolian men. He just refuses to appear. Just his hazy shadow drifts past, then it moves behind another man and pushes him forwards violently.

The Berber. Ya Ling sits up so suddenly she winces and clutches her sore ribs. The Berber. With his lopsided blue turban and his greasy smile.

Her hands ball into fists. Her glance takes in the suffocating dimensions of the room.

She might be caged but she will never be like those spineless little sparrows. Instead of pining and starving she will eat and drink and store up as much strength as she can. Her stomach gives an approving gurgle. She looks at the plate of food. She must store away knowledge too. Find out more about how this rough-and-ready Mantovan society works, so that when the slightest opportunity comes she will be ready to grasp it. A clever, well-thought-out escape plan, not just a stupid mad dash for freedom. And she'll make it work. She begins to break down her plan into stages. One stone at a time. Getting out of this filthy room is the first stage. Repairing the damage to the way the servants feel about her is the next. Leading her mind into Confucian thinking, she can almost hear her father's deep voice murmuring in her ear. *It does not matter how slowly you go, as long as you never stop.* The chain is dragged out to its fullest length and she begins to pace out the room, restoring the strength to her limbs. The steps are already painful, but she will no longer lie back stewing in misery. Strength and good health. That's what she needs to build up. Her mind must be as strong as her body. The shift comes over her head and she knots together a handful of straw. After soaking it in water from the jug she wipes herself down until she has scoured away all traces of Mantegna from her body.

Memories of her parents' blue-tiled bath filled with warm water and scented with rose oil are firmly banished. Life in all its complexity begins to pulse in her veins. *Qi* surges inside her, like a stream in spate, flowing almost uncontrollably. People in this household need her skills, so she will see where that takes her. She feels her calling, calling her. The gift lies within waiting to be used.

Chapter 12

'I don't like it, husband. I don't like it at all. How can we trust her? Eh? Not after last time. Running away like she did. She'll land us all in the cage.' Genevra drops the knife and leans both hands on the kitchen table until the nausea subsides. She pulls a face as she pushes away the string of garlic.

'I'm worried about you. It's over eighteen weeks now, isn't it? The sickness shouldn't be lasting as long as this. Listen to me for once. You have to let her help you so you can rest before the baby arrives. To give it the best chance. Our last chance.' He runs a hand through his sparse hair. 'The maestro has lengthened the chain and he lets her stay in the kitchen more. Some days he can't stand the sight of her, others, when he wants her, he's like a lovesick calf. So we must take advantage.' Clemente's voice is firm. 'What else can we do?'

The clinking noise that always accompanies the slave woman is heard as she enters the kitchen from the harness room. Ya Ling takes up the wooden crusher and peels the papery skin off several fat garlic cloves. Genevra leaves the kitchen quickly, her hand to her lips. The noise of coughing is heard from the floor above.

Clemente watches Ya Ling as if deep in thought as she squeezes a lemon into a bowl of hot water and adds honey and a pinch of ginger. 'Give her this and make sure she rests. Stay with her.' Ya Ling shrugs, lifting the hem of her shift. 'I can't run. Not with these. And all the doors are locked anyway.' Clemente gives her a sympathetic nod before he leaves.

Cecco comes slowly into the kitchen, his hand pressed hard against his chest. His pale face reddens as his breath becomes more laboured. Nicolosia follows him in and begins to slice bread and cheese and lay them out on a clean muslin cloth. 'Four slices. I need to build you up.' She smiles but her face looks drawn.

Ya Ling continues brushing the breakfast crumbs from the tabletop into the slop bowl, then lifts up a sack of polenta. Cecco's burlap tool bag lands with a rattle on the floor. He clings onto the back of a chair to keep his balance while he coughs and coughs. Great bubbling noises surge from deep inside his squat torso. Ya Ling listens quietly to the way the effluvium on his chest sounds as solid as stone. It's exhausting listening to the boy trying to force his breath past it.

Standing noiselessly at the sink, she begins slicing a pumpkin into golden crescents on the draining board and separating the seeds out onto a wooden tray ready for drying and salting. Ya Ling works quietly through the cook's list of tasks as well as her own. *Guanxi.* Favours given. Obligation. Reciprocation. Genevra might not like it, but she is already indebted.

'You mustn't go to the workshop today.' Nicolosia looks through the window at the thick fog that has blanked out each window. 'The damp air coming in off the lake seems to make your chest worse. Your father is away for a couple of nights so it makes sense for you to go back to bed and rest. I'll send Clemente to Settimio to tell him to take over for a couple of days.'

'No, I can't.' Cecco gasps. 'Father's left a big sack of pigments to grind and Settimio can't do it all on his own, so I have to go. You know what he's like.'

'But you'll make yourself ill again, standing all day in the cold with that terrible plaster dust settling on your chest.'

'No. I've got to go. I've had enough sneering from him recently.' Cecco pretends to count on his fingers. 'We're behind with the work because Settimio's lazy. Because I'm sickly, and spoiled.' He pauses for breath. 'And neither of us have any artistic talent at all. Oh, and compared to the hardships he went through, we both have it too easy. Have I missed anything, Mother?'

'It's true that I spoil you.' Nicolosia smiles. 'But that's the only bit of his nonsense that is.'

'What? Like you're doing now?' He shakes his head good-humouredly as his mother kisses his forehead and leans down to tuck a thick piece of felt down the front of his *tabarro*.

'Plenty of goose grease on this.' She winks at him.

The fat from a goose? Ya Ling turns to stare, then turns back, rolling her eyes.

'I'll send Gregorio with some hot pumpkin soup at noon. Your favourite. Oh, and take some kindling so Settimio can make a fire.'

'No, we can't, you know how smoke discolours the plaster – but bless you, Mother.'

'He won't know! Who's going to tell him?' Nicolosia's face furrows.

'He'll just know, and he'll take it out on Settimio.'

Cecco pauses at the door as a fresh wave of coughing overtakes him. The blood rushes to his face as he tries to drag in great gulps of air. Ya Ling freezes in horror. The sound of the terrible wheezing reminds her of the blacksmith's bellows and gives a sickly rise to her stomach. After an initial period of staring at her, Cecco has chosen out of decorum and deference to his mother to ignore her entirely, so offering her help is difficult. Nicolosia strokes a circle on his back and makes soothing noises. The coughing goes on for longer than Ya Ling can ignore. She scoops out a bowl of water from the drinking bucket and makes a move towards him, but he leaves the room. A look of fury from Nicolosia sends her clinking awkwardly back to the sink.

For the next couple of hours, Nicolosia paces the kitchen, looking out across the yard whenever the scaly branches of the plane tree knuckle the window. Suddenly the door bursts open, bringing in an icy blast and a swirl of crisp leaves. Settimio struggles in, his legs buckling under the dead weight of Cecco slung across his back. 'He's been taken bad, Signora. I got him home as soon as I could.' He drops a shoulder as both Nicolosia and Ya Ling rush across to take the weight off him.

'Here. Put him on the rug by the fire.' Cecco curls up his stocky frame, trying to defend his chest as his breaths come out in panicky bursts.

'He's suffering, Mistress. What do you want me to do?'

'I don't know. I've never seen his colour as bad as this. Look at the veins standing out on his forehead. Get him nearer the fire. God help him.' They tug his frame until the heat rises over his face. His breathing suddenly becomes slower. His chest must ache with exhaustion. 'Light a candle. Quick, Settimio.' She sinks to her knees by her son's side. 'Pray with me. Send a prayer up to San Rocco, then you need to run to the astrologer as fast as you can.'

Her son raises a pair of dark fearful eyes. 'Mother. Help me. I can't... I can't...'

Nicolosia snatches up one of his hands and holds the icy fingers to her cheek. 'Stoke up the fire!' she shouts at Settimio. 'Get any wood you can find, the last bit of charcoal – anything.'

Ya Ling feels her lips tighten as she looks on and listens. Prayers? Candles? Astrologers? These fools are hopeless. They know nothing. She moves over to stand above them. 'No! Stop this straight away!' Nicolosia looks up outraged at the way the slave woman stands over them with such an air of confidence. 'Put water on to boil, Signora, then the apprentice must help me lay your son across the table.'

Nicolosia bridles at the woman's tone of authority. 'How dare you give me orders? A filthy *puttana* like you!'

'The air can't get past the congestion that fills the breathing sacs inside his chest. We need to get rid of it from his body. And he needs wet heat, not dry, and the smoke is making it worse,' she says flatly, pointing down at the short tight gasps coming from Cecco as he beats his fists ineffectually against his big bowed chest. 'We have little time.'

Nicolosia glances down at her son, then, after a few moments of watching him struggle for breath, raising his eyes to her imploringly, as helpless as a huge landed carp, she slumps over him for a moment, her hand on his brow. Her voice is low and defeated. 'Do as the whore says.'

Settimio fills a small cauldron and lifts it onto the fire. Nicolosia watches anxiously as he and Ya Ling raise Cecco's almost inert frame and lay him face down on the table until his fringe of black hair flops down about a foot above the tiled floor.

'Get this off him.' They wrestle him out of his heavy woollen *tabarro*, then Nicolosia and Settimio gape as the woman tears at the tight back of his chemise with her teeth and rips it from hem to neckline. She quickly examines the patches of rough skin on his back, criss-crossed with livid scratch marks, before she presses hard on his spine. At the sight of Ya Ling's hands massaging her son's pale back, Nicolosia tries to drag the slave woman's slight frame away. Ya Ling prays to any god who might be listening for the strength to keep going. Keeping her balance, she continues pummelling softly along the long dimple of Cecco's spine. The hard cupping movements of her hands as they drag downwards over the table begin to make weals in his roughened skin. 'Get me oil quickly!' she orders. Cecco struggles to get his breath uphill and it seems for a moment as if he has given up. Nicolosia stares hard for several moments at her son's straining back, then she nods abruptly and hands across a jar of olive oil. The woman wrings her hands in the oil, then continues her strong downward strokes. 'What else do you need?' Nicolosia asks brusquely.

'Crush a handful of fennel seeds into the boiling water and put the bowl right under his face. Settimio, remember the third tree along outside? The tall wide one? The one with a broken branch that leans down? Run and pull down a branch for me. Quickly.' Settimio leaves the kitchen at a clumsy run.

Nicolosia lifts down several canisters and sniffs each one. 'I'll have to go for Genevra, she'll have to get off her sickbed for this. Cecco's needs are much greater than hers—'

'No, we haven't time.' There is no panic in the slave woman's voice, just a deep urgent demand that makes Nicolosia feel as if her own spine is being stroked by an icicle. She holds out the first canister. 'No, no, that's cinnamon bark. Try another. Look for small curved seeds, smell like liquorice. Yes, perfect. That's what I need. Now crush them. Be quick! I can't stop what I'm doing.'

'Why? What are you doing to my boy?'

'Loosening his chest. So air can pass. His breathing tubes are inflamed, so we need to calm them. Hurry!' Nicolosia flattens a pile of seeds with a big copper ladle and as Ya Ling flings a handful into the boiling water the kitchen is filled with a sweet spicy perfume. 'Hold his head over the steam – not too close or it will burn him.' The slave woman steps back and shouts down to Cecco, 'Try to take small breaths in when I take my hands off you, then breathe out when I push down along your back! That will help move the pestilence along.' Cecco gives a deep groan of acquiescence. 'When Settimio gets here with the cedar branch then it will get easier. Until then keep trying. You must keep trying.'

Nicolosia grasps his hand. 'Try, son. Breathe, breathe.'

Settimio staggers into the kitchen carrying a large branch, dense with dark green needles. He looks at the slave woman enquiringly. 'Strip two handfuls off, careful, they are sharp.' She hands him the big ladle. 'Then bruise them with this and throw them into the water.' A deep, aromatic herbal smell fights with the perfume of the crushed fennel seeds. 'Come on, Cecco, you have to work hard now.'

'What else can I do for him?' Nicolosia's voice trembles.

'Get a bowl to catch the slime. Make sure it doesn't slide into the boiling water. It will spoil it, and make it bad, and we will have to begin again.' The span of Cecco's breaths seems to be becoming slightly deeper and more regular.

'This bowl?' Nicolosia's eyes darken with panic. 'How will I know what to do?'

'You'll know,' Ya Ling says grimly. 'When it begins to happen, you'll know.'

Nicolosia notices the muscles beneath her son's plump back begin to tense and ripple as the deep coughing begins. He shudders. 'Now! Use the bowl now!' Ya Ling feels a wave of nausea as Cecco's foul-smelling green mucus slides down into the bowl as he retches convulsively for several minutes, but she ignores the sudden queasy feeling and focuses her mind on drawing long strokes down his back until he finally finishes shuddering. 'Take the bowl away.' She stands back to instruct Cecco to keep breathing in the steam. 'It will prevent the corruption from coming back for a while,' she says quietly, draping a cloth over his head so that no precious steam can escape. 'You need to keep him away from smoke and dust. Some flowers will inflame his tubes also. You need to watch him and see his reaction, then keep him away from them. The rash on his back is part of the same disease.' She senses Nicolosia staring at her in amazement before she bends her plump frame to pick up her son's hand and hold it to her cheek.

For what seems like a long time they stand there, listening to Cecco's increasingly deeper breaths until he finally waves a weary arm to tell them he wants to be lifted up. He sinks onto the stool, his face scarlet and running with sweat. His mother dabs at it until the usual pallor returns to his plump cheeks, then leans down to kiss each one. Cecco looks up at the woman and smiles, giddy with relief, then reaches out a hand towards her. 'You saved me. Like an angel from—'

'Enough of that.' Nicolosia moves quickly between them.

'But Mother, if it wasn't for her—'

Nicolosia's face tightens as she looks at Ya Ling. 'How do you know such things? I've never seen anything like it. A woman curing like this.'

Ya Ling thinks quickly. 'I haven't cured him, Mistress. This lung ague has no cure. All I can do is keep him alive when it happens. And make him potions to soothe his chest.' Her voice is quiet and authoritative, and her gaze remains calm as it locks onto Nicolosia's flushed face. 'He will need my help again.'

'Oh, very clever. Keeping me indebted to you. Part of a whore's stock-in-trade to be cunning, isn't it?'

Ya Ling turns towards Cecco. 'There are nail marks on your back. Does that rash pain you? Does it itch?'

Cecco nods. 'All the time. On warm nights I can't sleep for the burning.'

'But you never said!' His mother snatches his hand.

'Because you worry about me so much.' His voice saddens. 'And it makes Father so angry when I complain.'

'I can make a salve to soothe it. Perhaps even take it away.' A swell of optimism surges inside Ya Ling's ribs.

'Then tell me what you need and Settimio can go to the apothecary.'

'You can help his skin by giving him bone broth and the liver from white fish. You can dab it with salt water too, but to help soothe his chest ague, I need special things. I can also help Genevra as well. When her time comes.'

'I've already said! Just give me a list and Settimio can go today.'

Ya Ling shakes her head. 'That won't help, Mistress. I don't know the Mantovan words for the herbs I need. I need one herb with tiny white flowers, another that has yellow, another that has blue berries. When they are dried, they all look alike. For many others I need to see the different leaves growing. To gather them myself. It's better when they are fresh.'

Nicolosia gives a bark of a laugh. 'Oh. I see your game. You expect me to sink to my knees, my brain addled with gratitude because you have cured my son? To let you go wandering round the forest? If I let you out of this house you'd be off like a hare before hounds.' Her angry tone causes Settimio to turn in surprise. 'How could I trust a *puttana* like you to come back?'

Cecco tries to get up off his stool but falls back. 'For shame, Mother,' he remonstrates, raising a weak hand. 'After what she's just done for me.'

'Shame?' Ya Ling murmurs, casting a saddened glance over towards the three of them. 'What do any of you know about that?'

Chapter 13

The bread lands on the floor between them with a thump. 'What are we, wife?' demands Mantegna. 'Peasants? Gnawing on wood?' He walks over to the fire and sniffs the cauldron. 'Boiling up old bones?'

'It's a broth for Cecco. He needs to rest. He was taken bad two days ago.'

'Again?' Mantegna rolls his eyes.

Nicolosia beckons the servants. 'Go and clean the maestro's room upstairs. Strip the bedlinen. I've let the maid off the chain so she can help more. Earn her keep. Here.' She passes Genevra a transparent sliver of wax and a cloth. 'But be sparing.' Ya Ling takes two sheets from the press and carries them upstairs. When they have left, Nicolosia picks up the bread, which lies on the kitchen tiles in a flurry of dry crumbs, and puts it back on the table before she turns to face her husband. 'It's bread made from bran, husband. It is the best we can afford. The miller refuses me any more credit, and I had to practically beg him for this.' She opens the larder door and her open hand trails down the shelves. 'There's nothing at all for supper. You will have to go today. Get a date to start the frescos.'

'That's the last thing I want. To be locked in for years on a stipend. Taking private work at great risk.'

'Then ask for an advance.'

'I've already had one.'

Nicolosia bristles. 'When? How much?'

Mantegna waves her away. 'The problem is, this household is too costly to run. I'm going to have to get rid of Gregorio.'

'But you can't. I promised the priest after he interceded for Cecco's health.'

'Well, it doesn't seem to be working, wife, now does it? The boy seems as sickly as ever.'

'Don't say that!' Nicolosia snatches her rosary from her pocket and murmurs for several moments. 'It's tempting the devil.'

'Then it will have to be Clemente and Genevra, who never seem to do much work recently.'

'What? I could never lose Genevra. She's part of my family. And my brothers' too. It was a real wrench for the family to let me bring her to Mantova.' She arches an eyebrow. 'And what would my family think? That we cannot afford a proper household? They have plenty of help in theirs. All worthy artists have.'

'Do they now?' Mantegna fumes.

'And think of the gossip at court.'

'And what of my mistress? I'm curious you haven't mentioned her.' Mantegna puts his head to one side. 'She's another mouth to feed, isn't she?'

'I haven't made my mind up about her yet. She's useful. For the moment, that is.' Nicolosia hastily smooths down her skirt. 'Until Genevra has her child. But you will have to go to the palace today, I can't conjure meals out of thin air.'

Mantegna rubs his hands through his wiry curls and sighs heavily. 'For all the good it will do me,' he grumbles. He goes to the big buckled chest in the marital room and takes out a sheaf of paintings. When he reaches the courtyard, Gregorio leads the mare to the mounting block and Mantegna notices how worn and stained his livery looks. 'You're not coming,' he snaps. 'There's no point.'

The air is biting and the empty branches of the birch trees are silhouetted against the sky like candelabras as Mantegna trots along the wide banks of the Mincio. Mist rises over the milky waters. He keeps the paintings carefully tucked under his arm.

Marsilio Andreasi looks up in surprise as Mantegna taps on his door. 'The Marchese Ludovico is out hunting. I don't know when he will be back.'

'Where shall I wait?' Mantegna demands.

'Sit, Rubino!' A huge russet guard dog with a thick collar embossed with silver bounds over and sniffs Mantegna's feet, then goes back to curve its big frame under the Marchese Ludovico's chair.

'His library is always quiet.' Marsilio Andreasi's glance down his prominent nose is knowing. 'And discreet enough for you.'

Mantegna looks round the opulent library. He sniffs the heavy perfume of beeswax, then sighs heavily, thinking of the yellow tallow candles they use at home, the spluttering, the smell of rancid fat. A set of Valencian leather hangings, stamped and gilded, hang from the walls, and on the table sits a manuscript of the scriptures covered in black leather with a clasp of gold, and a page marker strewn with rubies. Next to it lies a silver leaf mirror, enamelled with green leaves and scattered with pearls to look like dew in a sylvan glade. At least it is quiet in here, Mantegna thinks. Private. Away from the silliness of court, the love-intrigues, the fooleries of clowns and the romantic ballads that always make him feel unversed in chivalry and ill-prepared.

'Darling?' Mantegna spins round to see a beautiful woman wearing a dress of shiny yellow taffeta, with her hair braided and held up in a net of amethysts. Earrings shaped like cornucopia flicker below her pale plump jawline and hint at her fruitfulness; they almost rest on the creamy upswell of her breasts, which curve high over her bodice. Her face drops into a sulk. 'Where is he?' she asks.

The private secretary follows her in, then takes her hand, trying to lead her back to the door. 'Tiziana, you've been told I don't know how many times.' His face is firm. 'And been paid a small pension too.'

Her voluptuous mouth drops like a child and she taps him with her fan. 'But it's not enough, I've heard he's keeping Floriana on, and he's bought Orabella a sapphire pendant, so why—'

'No, that's not true. You are all going to have to go. There will be no more jewellery for anyone, not even for the Marchesa Barbara herself. You know this quite well. He even sent away the Slav dancers last week. Come, leave the maestro in peace.'

The whining tone tails off as he leads her down the corridor. 'Did it work, my sweet?' she enquires. Her lips are soft and full.

He nods before handing her a gold coin, which she bites with a mischievous smile that cracks the white lead paste on her cheeks like an eggshell. 'Well done.' He pats her on the bottom.

Mantegna waits for two peals to pass and just as he is about to leave, a flourish of trumpets and a drumming of hooves announce the return of the hunting party, cantering up the shallow steps outside the palace. The Marchese Ludovico's face is red and windblown and the slender pageboy who accompanies him carries two handfuls of dark-brown birds, and wears three ropes of tiny thrushes wound round his neck like feathered necklaces. The marchese hands one ring of birds to Mantegna with a magnanimous bow. Rubino comes in and sniffs at the birds delicately, and tries to slip one into his mouth as if trying it for size. 'You wicked hound!' the marchese says with a laugh before rapping the dog's snout with his knuckle.

'Good morning's fowling, Your Grace?' Mantegna manages a hearty smile.

'Excellent! A good day for plovers. Partridges too.' He swings off his coat of thick velvet lined with ermine. A waiting-boy comes in with a tray of wine and candied quinces. 'I'm glad to see you, Mantegna, because those damned peacocks have just arrived and my dear wife tells me she wants them painted quickly, then they can be the centrepiece of our next banquet.'

Marsilio Andreasi coughs discreetly at the door. 'Not that the Marchese Ludovico is planning many banquets at present. We are all tightening our belts quite stringently.'

'Exactly. But you must paint them soon. There must be no more delays – they keep Barbara awake at night with their shrieks. She tells me they sound like wounded souls in torment.'

Mantegna smiles politely and opens his big canvas bag. 'In fact, in the meantime I have brought these for you to admire. A few paintings to adorn the palace, which I have only just completed. Some subjects come into an artist's mind and simply demand to be set down.' He notices the knowing set of the private secretary's lips. 'They won't be expensive but I thought you should have something of mine to enjoy before I devote myself to planning the frescos.'

The marchese fans out the top two paintings. 'Look at this one, Christ descending into Hell.' He sighs as he holds the picture close to his face. 'Very dark, isn't it?'

'It's a dark subject, Your Grace.' Mantegna keeps his voice reined in.

'And this one too. The sacrifice of Abraham. Look at that poor terrified lamb. The father poised with the knife at his son's throat.' The marchese looks up. 'The style, though, I concede is magnificently executed, but it is very… explicit again, isn't it?'

'I see.' Mantegna struggles to keep his temper tight in his chest as he collects the two paintings and lays them back in his portfolio case.

'Not so fast. Now, this last one is a bit more like it. A bit more colour to it. An Adoration of the Magi. A far more cheerful subject to look at.' The marchese walks over to the window and holds the painting outwards. His smile lowers. 'At least it should be.'

'Marchese?' Mantegna turns towards the light, trying to keep his expression polite.

'But dear Maestro, look at it! This one is obviously a more modern style – with a few nice rich touches here and there, like the turbans – but look how sad all their faces are! Is the bald one supposed to be Gasparre?' Mantegna gives a terse nod. 'Well, if I was giving the Holy Child a pot full of gold, then I would look a lot more cheerful about it.' Mantegna's lips narrow as he rolls the paintings up.

The private secretary clears his throat. 'Your paintings are very worthy though, Mantegna. I am sure all three are of estimable quality as usual.'

'Yes my dear Maestro, not so fast. Don't be too disturbed by my judgement. I'll still take them.' Mantegna bows low. 'But as we have discussed, I want something in a different style for the frescos. Something more true to life. No more whey-faced Madonnas. I want my private secretary painted in an attitude of diplomacy.' Marsilio Andreasi bows his head in thanks.

'Of course,' Mantegna says through a tightened jaw.

'And my family painted true to life.'

'Perhaps not entirely true to life,' Mantegna blurts out without thinking. Tension blows into the room like a cold draught and fills the waiting silence. Mantegna shoots an apprehensive look at the marchese.

'I said true to life,' he says loftily. 'And I meant it. Their minor imperfections are testament to their breeding. They are the mark of the few who can claim a truly aristocratic lineage.'

'Something commoners like us do not always appreciate,' Marsilio Andreasi says quietly.

'Of course, Your Grace. Of course. I didn't mean to imply anything other than—'

'Enough.' The marchese holds up a hand, then passes the paintings to his secretary.

'I will take these. Marsilio will work out the details, but I warn you I won't be paying a great deal for them. Times are increasingly hard here, and I must now insist that you begin the frescos. Planning them at least. You have already had an advance from me on top of your generous monthly stipend. The window will be moved as you requested – at great expense I might add. My patience is wearing thin, even for a genius like you. I hear rumours of your extravagant ways, the costly furniture you buy, the velvet dress you had made. Was this for the exotic mistress you have taken, I wonder? Perhaps these are all funded by the private commissions you are reputed to be still offering. As your patron, I insist that these must now stop. I will pay you a little something for the paintings you have brought today, but this will be the very last disbursement you receive from me until the frescos are well under way.'

Mantegna murmurs his thanks and takes an even deeper bow. 'But Your Grace, I don't think you understand the years of work that lie ahead for me, the planning, the finding of the perfect faces among the servants. Sourcing rare pigments. There is damp in one corner of the room that will have to be traced back to its source. Then the replastering and drying out…' He notices Marsilio's slight head-shake, but decides to plough on. 'And most appreciative though I am of your stipend, and your offer of a piece of land, for the building work alone, I will have to find—'

'Tiziana came to see you earlier,' the private secretary suddenly interrupts.

'Did she?' The marchese looks across at him. 'I wasn't seeing her until Thursday.'

'No, don't you remember? You're having to let her go. With the others.' The marchese turns to face his private secretary. 'And the Slav dancers too.'

Mantegna glances from one to the other. The Marchese Ludovico walks to the window and stares gloomily through it at the empty garden. 'Of course. Don't remind me. Those lovely harem girls, dressed in their golden veils. Bodies so young. So firm. So supple. What a pity. And my other ladies having to go as well. My special favourites.'

'How does your mistress fare? Only, seeing that little blue and white bowl in the painting reminded me of eastern lands.' Marsilio Andreasi's face is open and enquiring. 'Does she prosper?' Mantegna gives a brief nod. 'A beauty like that must be costing you a fortune, so you will understand the expenses we are referring to.'

'Yes indeed. It seems ironic that I am having to let my mistresses go, yet my court painter can afford to keep his.' Mantegna puts his hands behind his back and keeps his eyes on the floor.

'But it's not just the expense either, Mantegna, as I told you last time. Now that my son Francesco is being considered for promotion to cardinal, the Gonzaga court must be seen to be pure. That is another reason why I am regretfully saying farewell to some of my ladies.'

'All of your ladies,' the private secretary insists. 'The Office of Morality is prosecuting prostitutes and sodomites again, and increasingly they have in their sights any woman who is reputed to be of loose virtue. We cannot take any risks.'

'Priestly sermons thundering every Sunday about the sanctity of marriage, the inviolability of vows made before God.' Ludovico's mouth tightens in distaste. 'Hypocrites, all of them.'

'Indeed, Your Grace, but the ecclesiastical courts are really tightening up on morality and many a man has fallen foul of a vendetta and been denounced as a satyr,' Marsilio Andreasi puts in. 'The punishments are cruel. Razor-sharp implements. Long and slow, I've heard, and centred on the fleshy area that drags poor sinners down to temptation.' Mantegna shivers.

'Indeed so. We all have to be more pious now. Or the consequences will be too dreadful to contemplate.' The marchese's plump hand feels for the jewelled cross on his chest. 'I find this helps remind me of my duty. There is a piece of the true cross in here given to me by the pope himself.' His hand flicks open a prayer book full of bright miniatures. 'I refer to this, too, in moments of temptation.'

'See here, Your Grace. I've found what you were looking for yesterday.' Marsilio Andreasi hands him a scroll. 'The ascetic life of Santa

Caterina of Siena.' Mantegna feels a cynical smile tugging down his lips and walks quickly to the window.

'Yes, we could all learn a great deal from her life of poverty and renunciation. That's why I give so much of my income to the poor for masses, and to pay for corn rations for poor clerics.'

'And the widows…' Marsilio Andreasi prompts.

'Yes, and firewood and candles for widows.'

'And the major expenses of Christmas…'

'Ah yes. Christmas.'

Mantegna turns to them both and gives a tense nod. 'Thinking of that, I am hoping to give my groom new livery, and my cook is with child, so that is why I have to ask for Your Grace's generosity regarding the paintings I have brought today. And perhaps in a week or so another advance to set against payment for the frescos.'

'But we all must cut our cloak according to our cloth,' says Marsilio Andreasi smoothly. 'Hard on the heels of Christmas, the feast of Epiphany will soon be upon us, won't it, Your Grace? All those white robes for the flagellants…'

'Exactly. And the gifts, the banquets I lay on in every piazza.' The marchese runs a weary hand across his forehead. 'It doesn't bear thinking about.'

Mantegna settles his sceptical features into an aspect of humility, then bows his head. 'I understand, Your Grace.'

'Marsilio will pay you as generously as I can afford for the paintings. You can be sure of that. And I may even bestow an honour upon you. Elevate you to the nobility. A Knight Cavaglieri, perhaps.' Mantegna blinks. 'But no more advances.'

The money purse feels disappointingly light as Mantegna pushes it into his pocket. A beggar runs alongside him on the Piazza Sordello and taps on his knee and receives a kick on the shoulder for his pains.

Nicolosia comes to the threshold when she hears the outer door creak and waits there hopefully. Her husband's sullen expression and bitter tone silence her. 'His Grace talks of possibly giving me an honour in the future. Of elevating me to the nobility perhaps.' He sighs. 'Once I would have been overjoyed but now all I can think of is the expense.'

'Well, still, I am pleased for you. For the honour bestowed,' Nicolosia says cautiously. 'But I agree, it's little consolation when the shelves in our larder are empty.'

Mantegna drops the ring of thrushes on the table. 'Not much meat on these,' he snaps, 'and not much weight in this.' She nods with a wan smile when the purse is dropped on the table. 'So make it last,' he grinds out. 'I've managed to stall him on the frescos, but I'm going to have to be very careful taking on commissions. There might not be much coming in for a long time.'

Chapter 14

Genevra's bulk overhangs the kitchen stool when she sits down on it heavily. 'All the Christmas preparations to do, then Gentile's visit not long after.' She arches her aching back. 'I don't know how I'll cope.'

Ya Ling turns in surprise. 'Nicolosia's brother? He is coming to stay? The one from Venezia?'

'For a week or so. Nothing's been fixed yet.' She sighs. 'As if I didn't have enough to do.'

'Then I will help you all I can.' Ya Ling works as if pursued by a djinn. Taking on most of Genevra's duties as well as her own, no matter how tired she feels, from the moment Mantegna leaves the house to go to his workshop until his loud imperious voice is heard in the evening demanding food and wine and her presence, she never stops. Beginning at the top of the house, she works her way down, until each room on the upper floors has a faint smell of lavender soap and the kitchen is scrubbed until the pewter platters shine along each shelf and the floor tiles sparkle. No matter how much the rancid smell of Parmesan cheese makes her stomach heave, she takes great care to replicate the bland Mantovan cuisine that is Genevra's stock-in-trade. One evening Mantegna compliments Genevra on her hard work in front of them all and the cook manages a weary nod, having steered her unwieldy frame into the kitchen only moments before his arrival. Clemente smiles and gives Ya Ling a playful push on her shoulder, ignoring Nicolosia's angry intake of breath.

'It's going to be a lean one this year,' Clemente observes one afternoon, watching his wife take out the figures neatly packed inside the crib and start polishing them and tweaking their costumes.

'I know. But the maestro has sold those two big vases from upstairs. You know the ones? Patterned in blue and gold, inlaid with brass. I heard the mistress persuading him and now they've gone. So we'll still have eels for the Eve and a suckling pig for the Day. Only a small one, but still.' She carefully arranges the figures on a bed of golden wool on the hall table. 'Do you think they'll manage any gifts for us this year?'

Clemente shrugs. 'I doubt it. Still, we've got the procession to look forward to, and' – he steps alongside his wife and cups her swollen belly in his hand – 'we've got our own special present to look forward to in the new year.' He brushes a kiss on her temple. 'One that money can't buy.'

A gasp of shock is heard behind them. Both turn to see Ya Ling staring at the figures. 'Are these creatures from the spirit world?' she asks.

'Don't be so stupid! Just fancy, calling our blessed Holy Family spirits! What a dreadful thing to say. I'm going for the mistress. She needs to hear this!'

Clemente pulls her arm. 'No. Don't do that. She can't help being a heathen. Don't get her into trouble at this time of year. And she's been such a help to you.' He nods at the crib. 'No, not spirits. This is called a crib and it was carved in Modena. Explain the holy figures to her, wife. How else will she know, if you don't tell her?'

'Honestly! I don't know what good it'll do.' Genevra tuts and raises her eyebrows. 'All right. I suppose we should.' She picks up a tiny doll, unwraps the golden tissue that curves round his pink body, takes off the tiny crown and blows the dust off it before she kisses its forehead. 'This is the *bambino*.'

Ya Ling gently lifts it from Genevra's reluctant hand. 'The White Christ? As a baby?' she asks. Genevra nods abruptly. 'And are these his emperors?' She picks up an oriental-looking figure dressed in velvet and brocade with a wrought golden crown.

'No, you silly girl, that's Gasparre, and you see the casket in his hands? That's gold for His crowning.' She picks up another figure wearing a shiny purple robe. 'Now Baldassarre here, he's bringing incense for His worship, and this last one—'

Ya Ling snatches the figure up and stares at his blue headdress. 'I know what he is, he's a Berber. He's a *bastardo*!' She curses, almost under her breath but loud enough for Genevra to hear. The other woman's face pulls tight.

Clemente takes it quickly from her. 'No. He's not called that. He's called Melchiorre and he brings myrrh for the Christ child's mortality.'

'Oh I know him. I know just what he brings,' she mutters. 'He brings evil.'

'Well, this is going down well, husband, isn't it?' Genevra smiles acidly across at him. 'This preaching to the heathen?'

'And this one?' Ya Ling picks up a figure in blue satin that bends slightly in a drooping posture.

'This is the Holy Mother Maria, and I don't think we need to make any remarks about her,' Clemente says hurriedly, then presses a finger to his lips. 'In fact I think you two need to get back to your kitchen preparations.'

Downstairs Genevra plunges her hands into the bucket of eels and slops them into a bowl, watching them writhe and struggle for air. They slip through her fingers and wriggle off the chopping board no matter how often she wipes the slime off her fingers with a kitchen cloth. 'You're going to have to help me with these.'

'Of course. Sit over there. You've gone very pale. Are you still sick?'

'Don't tell Clemente.' She runs a weary hand over her face.

Ya Ling picks up a kitchen mallet and dispatches each eel with a firm thwack to the head. 'What now?' she asks.

'Gut them.' Genevra's hand shakes when she pours herself a bowl of water.

'The baby needs to come soon. I can help you. You know what I did for Cecco.'

'How?'

'I need some things. They won't cost anything.' Ya Ling gives a propitiating smile. 'Just plants I can find.'

'What?' Genevra's expression is guarded. 'I could never get you out of the house. I wouldn't dare.'

'No, I know. But I am worried about you. I know exactly what I need. The longer the baby stays inside you the worse it is for both of you.' Ya Ling quickly prepares the vegetables and the pasta. 'You could ask Nicolosia,' she murmurs as she begins rubbing down the little pink carcass of the piglet with a handful of salt.

Nicolosia comes down the stairs, followed by Clemente. 'Why isn't Genevra seeing to that?' she snaps. Genevra lifts her head up from her folded arms and gives a wan smile.

'She was. I've only just taken over.'

'I see.' The deep-toned bells ring across the town. 'The procession will pass by very soon. I need to lock the woman in the harness room, but I can't find the key. Clemente?'

'Can't she see the procession?' Clemente's voice is mild. 'She'll never have seen anything like it before. And she's worked hard.'

The door bangs as Gregorio comes in. 'Aye. We'll stand on each side of her, Mistress. She won't run anywhere with me holding her down. I'd like to see her try. And it's Christmas after all…' He tails off sheepishly.

The mistress looks from one to the other, her face set hard. 'I see.' She holds up both palms in front of her. 'Then God help the pair of you if she runs. Christmas or no Christmas.'

They pinion her tightly between them as they wait on the street. Ya Ling feels the warmth from both of them seeping through the sleeves of her thin shift as she glances around. Both men nudge her nearer to the brazier of the roasted-chestnut seller, though the smell makes their stomachs ripple with hunger. Sweetmeat stalls decorated with orange lanterns line the street; those selling marchpane tarts have great golden stars tied above their awnings. The noise of lauds being sung wafts across the frosty evening air, underpinned with the noise of drums and the brassy burst of trumpets. The thunder of horses on the cobbles makes the crowds surge forwards expectantly. Ya Ling tries to slip her arm imperceptibly out of Gregorio's grip and distract him with her sweetest smile, but he looks down at her in the dusky light with a knowing look and tightens his grip even more.

A golden star held high and carried by two priests leads the procession, and this is followed by all the figures Ya Ling has seen on the hall table. When Mary carries the baby past them, he gives a plaintive piping cry like a newborn lamb and the crowd all say 'Aahh!' in unison. A Berber passes by with a turban like the one the little statue was wearing, but in the tumult no one hears the loud hiss and the curses that come from Ya Ling. A large ape on a chain is walked past, then a horse that has been painted in black and white stripes, which stuns the jostling crowd to silence.

'Look, the Gonzagas!' The men bow and all the ladies curtsey as a series of men dressed in rich velvets and ermine capes walk past and wave airily to each side of the street. Ya Ling notices the powerful ducal bodyguards who walk alongside them, hemming them in. 'Look, there's the maestro!' They all wave and call his name and Nicolosia smiles very proudly as he drops her a bow as he passes. When the women of the Gonzaga court walk past, their ropes of jewels catch the light from the flaming torches leaning from the city walls. *Look and learn. Listen and learn. Information is more valuable than salt.* 'Who's that big plain woman? With the split in her chin?' she asks.

Gregorio looks down at her in horror. 'For the love of God, Ya Ling! Keep your voice down! That's the Marchesa Barbara of Brandenburg! The wife of the Marchese Ludovico Gonzaga. She'll have your head off for a comment like that!'

'And what's wrong with some of the children? They have big bumps on their heads.'

'Be quiet! If anybody overhears you saying things like that, we'll burn. Now I mean it!' He clamps her painfully to his side.

She turns to Clemente. 'Who is that?' A tall dark-haired man walks under a canopy of silver cloth held aloft by two straining priests.

'That's the Marchese Ludovico's second son, Francesco. With any luck, he'll be made a cardinal one day. It will be a great honour for us all to have a Mantovan in the Vatican.'

As he passes, the heavy taffeta cloak swings to one side and Ya Ling notices the outline of a hunchback under his soutane. 'But doesn't he have a—?'

'Enough! You need to stop asking questions.' The two men squeeze her tightly between them.

'Sorry.'

Next come the trumpeters, the capering jesters and a giggling group of the little people who had so terrified her on the day she tried to escape that she had stopped running. She shrinks back from the road. 'Clemente? Just one last question, please. What are these little beings? Where do they come from?'

'Don't ask.' His expression is set firm. 'It's better not to.'

'But...'

He bends down, his breath hot on her ear, his tone sharper than usual. 'They are pumilios from the court. Now don't ask any more questions.'

She looks up at him with a frown. 'What's a pumilio?'

'Ssh.' He draws his finger across his throat.

Right at the end of the parade, after the troops of soldiers and the lines of priests carrying their *contrada* banners, come several terrified oxen, slipping and sliding over the cobbles, followed by a timid little ass.

Clemente and Gregorio lead her back through the large outside doors. 'Now what did you think of that?' Clemente asks her with a proud smile.

Ya Ling pushes away all thoughts of the processions she has seen in China, with thousands of soldiers in silver armour marching with slick precision, their silken banners filling the sky. The golden sedan chairs, inlaid with ivory and jewels, which held aloft the Imperial Family. 'It was wonderful.' Her smile is artless. 'Thank you for letting me see it.'

Back in the kitchen they rush to complete the preparations before Mantegna returns from the palace. Genevra pauses and beckons over the two men. 'Shall we do an augury? Oh go on! While the mistress is upstairs.'

Ya Ling looks puzzled. 'Pumilios? Augury? So many new words, and I don't know what they mean. Genevra?'

Genevra looks hurriedly from Clemente to Gregorio. 'Well, you don't ask anybody about the first one – I mean it, it's asking for trouble – but if you watch and keep quiet, then you'll soon find out about the second.' Her pale cheeks dimple as she gets a knife and peels an apple carefully. The peel is thrown onto the tiles.

'What does it say?' Clemente nods at his wife expectantly.

'C. Of course.' Genevra shakes her head with a smile. 'I don't know why I'm doing this, I've no need to. I know who my true love is. I've always known.' She pinches Clemente's cheek.

Clemente throws next. 'It's a G. Who else could it be for me? And no. That doesn't mean you, Gregorio.'

Gregorio grins and goes next. 'It might be a P,' Clemente offers. 'What's that girl in the tavern called? Perlita?'

'Give over.' He glances at Ya Ling and stomps across to the fire, then walks back to them, his sulk quickly over. 'Go on, Ya Ling. You have a go.'

Ya Ling picks up the knife and an apple. In her excitement her fingers feel stiff and wayward and the knife keeps biting into the flesh instead of slipping easily beneath the red peel. The peel comes away in a series of small tiny slivers. She gamely throws them onto the tiles, but they scatter into pieces.

'Is it an A?' she asks eagerly. 'In your language. Does that say A? It must be that.'

All three turn their heads from side to side as they look down.

'Perhaps it's eastern writing,' Clemente offers, his tone kindly.

'No. It's not.' Her voice is shaky. 'Not Mandarin. Or even Bai.'

She feels Genevra's hand tentatively pressing into her back. 'Whose name is it that begins with A? Is it somebody important to you?'

Ya Ling drops her head, then picks up the pieces of apple peel from the floor. She dabs her face with the back of her hand. 'Nobody,' she says fiercely. 'It's nothing.'

'Is that him? The one you were supposed to marry?' Gregorio pats her arm awkwardly.

They watch in silence as she wipes the stickiness off the floor with a cloth before she straightens up and splashes her red-rimmed eyes with cold water. They exchange glances as she stirs the simmering pot of eels and begins to collect the plates together into a pile ready to carry upstairs.

They hear the maestro's voice rumbling down the stairs. Genevra smiles excitedly. 'Come on, it's time.'

They line up in the grand reception room upstairs. The maestro hands Genevra a small box of candied plums and she curtseys her thanks. He walks past Ya Ling with a brief awkward pause, then gives Clemente and Gregorio their gifts of new pairs of hose, which they both hold delightedly in front of them. The servants all turn to Ya Ling and then look expectantly at their employers, and there is an uneasy break in the merriment before Clemente and Gregorio quickly roll up their gifts. Ya Ling feels her cheeks burning and swallows hard. Mantegna walks quickly out of the door.

Cecco's voice cuts through the uncomfortable silence. 'Isn't there anything for…?'

Nicolosia shakes her head. 'No. She is enough of a drain on our coffers as it is.'

'But after what she did for me?'

Nicolosia turns to the others with a gracious wave of her hand. 'You may leave now to enjoy your gifts.'

She grabs her son in the empty room. 'Cecco, listen to me. You must keep silent about her helping you. No heathen woman should have such knowledge. If she was respectable, a good Catholic woman with powerful friends, then it would be different. I've told you before, if we need her to heal you again, then you must tell no one. Not even your father. Now go and get him.' She nods at the beautifully laid table with its damask runner embroidered in scarlet and green, and walks over to light the tapers. 'Then we can eat.'

In the kitchen Ya Ling feels the box being pressed into her side. 'Go on. I'll let you have one.' Genevra's smile is almost warm. There are only six plums in the box. The candied fruit is succulent and sweet. It reminds her of the sticky red haws on the skewers that Chen used to buy her when she lived with her family on the other side of the world. She remembers her rudeness to him, her lack of gratitude when he spent his paltry earnings on her. She wonders how her Mama and Baba are. If they ever recovered from the Berber's poison. What they are doing tonight. How different it might have been to be sitting together for a family meal round the big camphorwood table with Chen and Ayi bringing delicious plates of spicy food, with Altan giving her his proud possessive smile and with Mama and Baba beside themselves with excitement at celebrating the arrival of their first grandchild. 'Lovely, aren't they?'

'Thank you.' As she nods, her tears splash down onto the backs of Genevra's hands and she turns suddenly, leaning down to burrow her face into the other woman's plump shoulder. Two warm hands span her back and pull her in closer.

'Well, I think it's mean not to have given her anything.' Gregorio folds his arms. 'She works as hard as any of us.'

Clemente says quietly, 'I don't think it's just that. Is it, child?'

'Me neither. Are you thinking of your family tonight? Your parents? It can't be easy for her, now can it? On Christmas Eve.' Genevra's face creases in sympathy as she speaks to the others over Ya Ling's head.

Ya Ling lifts her damp face. 'And Altan. And Chen,' she mumbles.

'Aye, she's a long way from home.' Clemente briefly rests against the two of them.

'No wonder she tried to run. I'd have done the same.' Gregorio clasps his forearms tighter. 'But I'd have run faster.'

'Altan? Is he the young man from the augury, beginning with A?' Clemente's voice drops in sympathy. Ya Ling's nod pushes her forehead deeper into Genevra's shoulder.

'Will you talk to Nicolosia, husband? I think she might be dithering. Cecco's coughing is getting worse, and the mistress will think more kindly of her if she helps him get well again. And you never know' – Ya Ling feels herself pulled tighter into Genevra's ample frame – 'she might find something in the forest to help the birth if the mistress allows her to go.'

'Good idea. But she'll have to go with somebody.'

'I'll take her. She won't get any tricks past me, will she?' Gregorio's dark eyes watch her carefully. 'We can all trust you, now, can't we?'

Ya Ling's eagerness cuts through the catch in her voice. 'Of course. I won't let you down. Where could I run to? A woman without protection here?'

'She's right.' Genevra holds her at arm's-length and lifts a strand of Ya Ling's damp hair where it has stuck to her cheek. 'Now hush, child. We must cheer you up. You can't cry tonight. Be thankful instead. You're in a Christian family at Christmas time, not among heathens. And we've got bread and a pot of eels to look forward to. Now what could be better than that?'

Chapter 15

It is nearly mid-morning and Genevra hasn't appeared. Ya Ling slips down the corridor with the usual bowl of lemon juice sweetened with honey. 'This will help your sickness a little but peppermint and sage would make better tisanes for you. What I really need is tansy and rue or other herbs that help a baby to come.' She puts her hand on Genevra's forehead as she sips cautiously. 'Do you feel dizzy? When you use the chamber pot, is it dark?'

'Yes. Yes to both of those.' She shakes her head, her eyes rounded with despair.

'When are you due?' The urgency of Ya Ling's voice sends a flicker of fear into Genevra's eyes.

'Only a few weeks now. It's hard to say. Our little Rosina came very late.' A tear rolls down her cheek. 'Clemente doesn't know how bad I've been. I daren't tell him. He longs so badly for a child. After we lost our little Rosina he was so…' She gnaws away at her bottom lip.

'Then you must tell him and he must ask Nicolosia straight away.'

'He has done it three times and each time he got a telling-off for his pains. He daren't ask again.'

'Then I will have to try.' Ya Ling stands decisively. 'She's upstairs, isn't she?'

'God help you.' Genevra kisses her fingers and holds them to Ya Ling's mouth. 'But thank you for trying.'

Upstairs in her room, Nicolosia sees Ya Ling take a deep breath at the threshold. She puts down her sewing with a cynical smile. 'I know why you are here. Clemente gives me no peace. But the answer is definitely no.'

'It will only take me a few hours. Cecco is coughing again. I need herbs as well, to keep me strong so I can be a better worker. But Genevra urgently needs special herbs to help bring the baby along, and they need a week to work. The doses have to be very gentle to be safe. The longer the baby stays inside, the more danger both are in.' She folds her arms tightly.

'Cecco's cough has been far worse than this. And as for the baby, how do I know that you are telling me the truth?'

'Just look at her. You can see how ill she is.'

Nicolosia picks up her sewing quickly and the needle slips out. She pats the tabletop to find it. 'Come here.' Nicolosia looks up and her glance is severe. 'Even if I trusted you enough, which I don't, how would you get to the forest without anyone seeing you go out of the house?'

'I can wear Genevra's old cloak and borrow a veil from you. I can ride as well as a man, so all will be calm.' Nicolosia's eyes narrow. 'And Gregorio can keep me on a leading rein all the time,' she adds quickly.

'So you have this all planned out, eh? So scheming, so wily. I know nothing about you, apart from some tall tale you told Gregorio about your parents being tricked and you being taken from them. You won't find me so gullible.'

'What I told Gregorio is true. My parents are well known for their healing skills and my family were educated and of good standing. Mistress, think what I did for Cecco.'

Threading the needle takes a long time. 'I find it impossible to trust you, with all the strange knowledge you have. It's not normal. And now you tell me you are an expert horsewoman too. One who could gallop away, no doubt. That's not natural either.'

'Yes. I ride well. I could pretend to you that I have never ridden a horse before, but I won't lie.'

Ya Ling feels pride swell in her chest, but convincing rather than boasting is what is needed.

'I learned to ride on the plains of Xilinhot, north of the Great Wall. It is a very mighty wall with many turrets, and it curves like the peak of a wave over mountains and valleys as far as the horizon, and then the horizon beyond that.'

It doesn't seem to be working. 'Well, I've never heard of it!' Nicolosia snaps.

Ya Ling drives her nails into her palms. She pauses, trying to think of a way to keep Nicolosia's interest. Then she stretches her arms as wide as she can and lifts her voice. 'The Great Wall. It's hard to describe. So big, you can't imagine—'

'What? Even bigger than the city walls of Mantova?' Nicolosia demands with a wry glance.

'Oh, a thousand times. A thousand thousand times.'

'Really? As big as that?' Ya Ling is not surprised at Nicolosia's ignorance. At the disbelief in her voice. It's impossible to even try to explain the scale of her homeland. And not enough time to do it justice – but the truth doesn't seem to be what is needed. 'And who taught you to ride like a man?'

'My father.'

'Really? The one who was careless enough to let the Berber take you?'

'Not careless. I told Gregorio the truth. He was tricked by a man he thought was an old friend. A man he had traded with for many years.' Her chin drops. 'My life has been terrible since. Can you imagine the shame I feel?'

Nicolosia stares hard at the slave woman for several moments. 'Go on. I thought you lived in a city. Now you tell me you rode horses in some wild place with mountains and this vast wall. How can I believe anything you tell me?'

'Mistress, I lived in both places. Most of the time we lived in Beijing, where my parents were healers, but some years we travelled north to see my father's Mongolian family. We took a huge felt tent with a skylight that opened to the blue sky, and it was full of embroidered rugs and quilts. The beds were covered in bearskins with claws that clicked on the floor when they were pulled back.'

'What? Your family sleeps under animal skins?' Nicolosia pulls a face. 'Like savages.'

Ya Ling remembers the pungent smell of the animal hides but decides to keep that to herself. 'We had to cross the Great Wall. It runs for thousands of miles and reaches up higher than this house, but there are still a few gaps where the Ming workers hadn't finished repairing the battlements, so we always—'

'Enough of this nonsense! These ridiculous tales of a primitive land!' Nicolosia snaps. 'These lies have not helped your case at all. Get back to work.'

Ya Ling stares at the sky above the courtyard wall, willing thoughts of the grasslands back into her mind to strengthen her resolve. To see the white gers again, clustered together and dotted on the vast plain like tiny islands, surrounded by their flocks of sheep and goats. Where endless plumes of grass wave and bow like a mighty ocean all around them. And where eagles soar in the blue infinity above. She thinks hard until she grasps the exact Confucian thought. *They must often change, who would be constant in wisdom.* Her voice is firm. 'Yes Mistress. It is a primitive land. That is why I want to remain here in Mantova. Where it is civilised and where great artists live nearby. Like your family, the Bellinis. That is why you can trust me to come back.' She holds her hand to her heart and locks eyes with Nicolosia, just as she has seen Genevra do. Nicolosia's returning glance is cool and surprised. Ya Ling feels a sheen of sweat on her forehead. 'Mistress, I have to go to the forest. You know exactly why. This is Genevra's last chance to have a child and I know how fond you are of her. I have to bring the birth forwards or she will be in danger. And so will the baby. You have to trust me.'

'Are you mad? With your reputation for running away?' Ya Ling is watchful. Nicolosia's sewing is picked up and dropped on the table again and her sudden bustling around the room would fool nobody. Thinking time, that's what lies behind the opening and closing of drawers, the repeated straightening of the headcloths at the backs of the two armchairs.

Ya Ling stands very still. Options are being weighed up. Cecco's future health. Genevra's life and that of her unborn baby. The pewter lid from the salt cellar is carried from the table over to the window, where Nicolosia holds its rim up to the light and polishes it with her skirt. 'And you said you need medicine for yourself. Why? Are you sick? You seem pretty indestructible to me.'

'Only for these.' Ya Ling raises the hem of her shift. The manacles have dug two purple circles into the thin skin round each ankle.

Nicolosia's eyes widen. 'I'm sorry. But I can't.' Her words quicken. 'The more I think about it, the more I'm convinced that the apothecary in the Piazza delle Erbe will have everything you need, and no one will be suspicious if Gregorio goes in there for a long list. Every family suffers sickness at this time of year and—'

'I cannot be sure the herbs are fresh. Or even if they are the right ones. When they are dried they all look the same.' Ya Ling keeps her voice steady and insistent. She can see Nicolosia hesitate. 'But the apothecary hasn't been able to help Cecco, has he? Only I can do that.' The keys in Nicolosia's pocket jingle as they are turned over and over. Ya Ling's breath stills in her throat as she waits.

Suddenly Nicolosia's hand comes to rest on Ya Ling's shoulder. Her fingers feel icy through her shift. 'You will come back, won't you? Promise me that.'

'Of course. Where else can I go?' She pauses at the door, as if a thought has just occurred to her. 'And when does your brother arrive?'

'Gentile? In two days. Why do you need to know that?'

She flicks up the hem of her dress. 'Because we might need his help. Do you have the key for these?' She lifts her skirt. 'Because I cannot ride with my legs chained together like this.'

'No, the maestro took it back. He wears it round his neck.'

Ya Ling thinks hard. 'How many candles can you spare?'

'Not many, I need to be frugal.'

'Well, give me as many as you can and all the candle stubs as well.'

'What? Immediately? One might think you were the mistress of the house all of a sudden.' Nicolosia bridles.

'Mistress, time presses on us.'

Nicolosia listens to the patter of the slave woman's feet going down the stairs. Following her down, she takes out a hessian bag of yellow tallow stubs from the dresser drawer and puts in a fresh candle. The bag bounces gently in her hand. She glances in, then puts in two new candles, descends the stairs and opens the harness room door.

That night Ya Ling listens until the peal of the next bell before Mantegna's snores settle into a pattern, then she rolls over and carefully pulls out the ball of wax that she has tucked between the pallet and the bedframe. Holding her breath, she begins to knead it until it feels soft and supple. She then splits the wax into two.

'Lie still, maid!' Mantegna snaps. She waits, frozen, trying to still her racing pulse. The straw rasps as she leans over the warm curve of Mantegna's chest and feels for the keys round his neck.

'You're restless tonight. I need my sleep,' he grumbles, then rolls over, away from her. In the darkness she counts to 200, then she moves noiselessly round the end of the pallet and crouches down on the floor. The keys have fallen away from Mantegna's neck and lie tumbled on the cotton pillow. She leans carefully down until she feels the rhythmic blast of his wine-soaked breath, then she gingerly lifts the first key away from his sleeping form until the leather thong pulls slightly behind the back of his thick neck. Pacing her breath into tiny even strokes, she presses both sides of the key into one of the balls of wax. Then, cupping the rest of the wax in her hand, she repeats it with the other key.

In the darkness she feels along the wall, surreptitiously counting the bricks, then she removes the two she has loosened, pushes the horns right to the back and slips the two wax impressions inside before replacing the bricks and climbing back under the woollen blanket, where Mantegna's hands are already feeling for her. She turns her back on him and slips down a hand, resting it gently over the curve of her stomach.

His hand slides over hers. 'You are becoming plump.' His voice is puzzled. 'Yet you are never still.' His hand on her breast is heavy. The first time she moves it away, he grumbles; the second time, his voice tightens with annoyance. 'You're getting above yourself, maid,' he warns. His thumb bears down on her chin until her mouth opens for him and he slants his face down to hers. There is a slight bitter taste beneath the mint she chews to scent her breath. He lifts his head. 'Are you sick, maid?'

'No, Maestro.' He feels the thud of her heart against his arm.

'Light a candle.'

The taper feels slippery in her hand and almost falls into the fire. It takes her two attempts to slot the candle into the wooden candlestick before she shields the flame and carries it through. He holds up the flickering glow to her until she can feel its warmth. His downward glance takes in the rounded curves of her breasts. 'When was your last bleed?'

Ya Ling feels a spasm of fear. 'I have only missed one, Maestro.' She manages a pretty sideways smile through lowered lashes. 'It's nothing.'

Worry chases across the angular planes of her face. Noticing the droplets of sweat on her top lip, he sits up heavily on the pallet and rests his head in his hands. 'Maria, Mother of Christ! Is pregnancy contagious in this household? Like the plague? You've definitely missed only one? You're sure?' She nods. He stares at her for a long time, then his eyes narrow as if his thoughts have taken him elsewhere. He turns away, but she pulls the back of his nightgown until he turns back, bringing his face close to hers, his expression unreadable.

'It's nothing. But if it is, then I will be giving you another son for your workshop. A free apprentice for you, Maestro.' Her voice is soft with entreaty. 'I thought you wanted that.'

'If it's a boy. But there's no guarantee of that. And what happens if it looks like a heathen?' Mantegna grumbles, running a hand through his thick curls. 'Mother of God, another thing to worry about. These blasted frescos are going to take me years, and now another mouth to feed.' He cups her chin roughly and pulls her face across the pillow. 'You are going to have to be very careful. Tell no one. Not a soul.' Ya Ling nods. 'The church courts are very active at the moment. Even Ludovico Gonzaga himself is being a lot more discreet.' He sighs. 'Or so he says.'

'I will tell no one, Maestro. No one.' Her smile drains away as soon as he leaves. Her heart beats fast as she lowers her palms to rest on her stomach. Now Mantegna knows, she has to get to the forest fast. Fearful of the censure of the Gonzaga family, he can't be trusted. As long as Gentile is prepared to help then there is a slight hope. Her thoughts veer wildly until they come to rest on a terrible decision. She clamps her arms tightly across her ribcage. She feels pity for the innocent scrap of life growing within her, but she knows she can never return to Beijing as she is. Altan would never forgive her for giving herself to another man. Chen would never forgive himself, and would be duty-bound to take the honourable path. Her teeth clench together tightly at the thought of what she must do. One dosage for Genevra and a far stronger one for herself.

Chapter 16

Gentile Bellini arrives the following day. Mantegna has been increasingly tetchy in the run-up to his arrival and has been particularly kind to Nicolosia, but he is still full of his usual bluster. 'Your brother won't dare issue a challenge on this visit. I know that. He's just got a big commission for some church in Venezia, so he's going to be too worried about his hands to start throwing punches.'

'A big commission?' Nicolosia folds her arms. 'Then it might be a good time to ask him for a loan.'

'Stop interfering, wife! What, and get a patronising lecture about being frugal? From a tight-arse like him? Never! You keep your advice to yourself.'

Down in the kitchen she finds Ya Ling layering slices of mutton with rice and spices into a big earthenware dish. 'What's this?'

'It's called a pilaf.' Ya Ling pauses, the big brass ladle overflowing with fresh mutton stock that she dribbles over carefully to moisten the rice. She scatters a handful of dried grapes over the top. 'In my country we make it for a celebration. I used to watch our cook make it.'

'Cook? You had a cook?'

Ya Ling nods sadly. 'Yes. We had many servants.'

Cecco comes in, sniffing the air appreciatively. 'Something smells different.' His breath whistles in his chest.

'Well, I hope it tempts your appetite. You're picking like a bird at the moment.' His mother ruffles his dark curls. 'Don't be late tonight. Your uncle is looking forwards to it.'

'Tonight?' His brows draw together. 'But I've arranged to see some friends, after I finish at the workshop.'

Nicolosia moves across to stand in front of him. 'Where? In some tavern, I don't doubt! Your chest still isn't properly healed yet. And at this time of year!'

'I know. Sorry, Mother, it's just, you know…' He grins, then opens the flap of his tool bag and tucks his lunch into it before he leaves.

'The air is too cold on his chest at night.' She runs her hands down each side of her skirt. The scent of powdered cinnamon bark and hot peppercorns makes her nostrils twitch in the warm kitchen. 'And another thing, my brother is old-fashioned in his taste. He's very particular about his food…'

The mistress looks very on edge. 'Don't worry. Everything will be all right. I will make medicine for Cecco and keep him safe, and your brother, he will enjoy the meal. It's good to try something new.' Ya Ling keeps her voice soothing, and her thoughts to herself about the monotonous repertoire of tasteless oily dishes that these people seem to love.

Gentile doesn't look as if he's a particularly fussy eater when he arrives that afternoon. Quite the contrary. His broad heavy frame takes up most of the stairwell, and the way the front of his *tabarro* bulges outwards is testament to how much he enjoys the fruits of his many commissions. Ya Ling's quick glance at him takes in the family resemblance to his sister and her son; the same wide faces, studded with small brown eyes.

'Haven't you seen an eastern woman before?' Mantegna says as if amused. Ya Ling notices the way Gentile's features quickly rearrange themselves to the usual level gaze he reserves for his brother-in-law. 'You're practically salivating.'

'Yes. Of course I've seen one or two before.'

'But none as beautiful as this one?'

Ya Ling takes a black suede bag off him and braces herself to carry it up to his room. She is conscious of his eyes following her and the faint chinking noise she makes. 'She's strong.' Gentile's voice is neutral. 'That's all you need.'

Genevra's glance takes in the steaming pans on the stove, the strong smell of cardamom that Ya Ling sprinkles onto the tiny spatchcocked quails before threading them on skewers and roasting them over the flames. 'When do you go?' she asks anxiously.

'The day after tomorrow. So not long now. Here, drink all of this honeywater, and that jug of it too.' The stool creaks as Genevra sits down heavily. 'Keep drinking a lot of well water but boil it first. Then your headache will go.'

'How did you…?' Ya Ling raises an eyebrow, then smiles as Genevra sips at the bowl.

'I'll serve them at table tonight. I insist.'

Genevra rubs her palm up and down the slave woman's wrist. 'Feel these. My hands have never felt so soft for years,' she confides. 'Usually they feel as rough as pigskin, but with you doing all my work they feel like I'm wearing silk gloves. I think you are filling out a bit too, but I don't know how.' Ya Ling tries hard to keep her smile from fading. 'Not with all the rushing about you have to do.'

Ya Ling looks away quickly. 'I'm fine,' she murmurs. 'Greedy? Is that the word?'

After the meal Gentile sits back in his chair with a satisfied groan. He finishes off the last mouthful of pears poached in sweet muscatel wine and licks each sticky finger. Ya Ling places a bowl of warm water at his elbow with a square of cotton folded underneath, and what looks to be yellow flower petals floating on the top. He looks at it, confused. A tiny bowl stacked with thin pieces of wood puzzles him as well. He watches Mantegna grin at him before he dips his fingers in the bowl and wipes them on the square of cloth. Then Mantegna leans back and loosens a morsel of meat from between his front teeth with one of the fine slivers of wood. 'She is teaching us some of her refined Beijing ways,' Mantegna drawls. 'She never ceases to surprise.' Gentile looks protectively across at his sister, but she nods back with what appears to be agreement.

'And what of the food, brother? What do you think of that?' Gentile is astounded that Nicolosia would ask such a question so warmly, and with no apparent sign of resentment.

'Not bad.' Gentile leans across to pick out a sliver of wood and cautiously inserts it between two bottom teeth.

'No. Come on. It was delicious. Admit it,' Mantegna says. 'Like her.'

Gentile stares, astounded, at his sister, who has merely drawn her lips together as if at some private joke. 'This is not appropriate,' he growls. 'Not in front of your wife.'

'Well, if your sister was a better wife to me, then I wouldn't have to look elsewhere. To venture to the exotic places I do.' Gentile watches the woman quickly place the heavy pewter salt cellar on the carved buffet, then gather together a pile of platters and carry them out of the room. He picks up a bowl and makes to follow her.

He stiffens as his brother-in-law's sardonic voice trails after him. 'Don't be long, Gentile. I know exactly what's running through your mind.'

When the bowl lands on the tabletop in the kitchen, the slave woman jumps. Her almond eyes slide away from his. 'Thank you. The food was wonderful,' Gentile says quietly. Her eyes blink in surprise. 'What's the matter? That can't be the first compliment you have been given? I have never eaten a meal like that anywhere before.'

'I don't often hear thank you. That's all.'

The felt soles of his indoor shoes make little noise on the tiles but she can sense him crossing over to her. She turns and is startled to find herself looking straight into the flickering glare of the candlestick he has picked up from the table. As his fingers cup her tiny chin and lift her face towards him, she flinches in anticipation. 'It's all right.' His eyes absorb her face as if storing in his memory the way the shadows accentuate its unusual planes. 'Be still. I'm not a violent man. Not like him.'

Gentile steps back as Mantegna's footsteps are heard on the stairs. 'So there you are. Seen enough of her yet?'

Gentile's smile fades. 'No I haven't, but not in the way you think. I would like to paint her, that's all. Just as an exercise. The structure of her face, it's just so… extraordinary.'

'No. Don't even think of it. Not for a moment.' Mantegna's voice deepens in irritation. 'You're not going anywhere near her. She's mine. Come back upstairs.'

Nicolosia comes down later as Ya Ling is sliding the big meat platter into the groove on the shelf. 'The men need more wine.'

Ya Ling puts the flagon below the tap on the barrel. 'Will he do it?'

'Of course he will. He's my brother.'

Ya Ling's slender features relax into a smile. The manacles jingle and dig in as she moves swiftly to the harness room and retrieves the two wax shapes. 'Tell him to take them to a blacksmith in a different *contrada*. Not the one your husband usually uses.'

'I had already thought of that.' She wipes the lip of the flagon with a cloth. 'I'm learning a great deal. In a week or two I'll be as cunning as you.'

'And Signor Gentile won't say a word to anyone?'

'No. He's a good man. When I told him how you were kept chained like an animal, he was very upset. He knows nothing of the rest of our plan. And I'm using him. Using his kindness.' Nicolosia's voice is pointed. 'I just hope I don't live to regret it.'

Ya Ling concentrates on polishing the table, eking out the last yellow sliver of beeswax, until she hears Nicolosia's footsteps withdraw. *Learning to be cunning? Like me?* Cloth in hand, she smiles at her reflection in the table. It won't be long now. She can almost feel the surge of the ocean beneath her feet. Smell the sharp salt-licked air. Her father and mother ordering more Shaoxing wine for the wedding. Chen helping her keep the cook in his place, and the turtle safe in the fish pool. The feel of Altan's cheek, unspoiled by the straggling facial hair that plagues all the men in this godforsaken country. His impatience, his longing for her. It will happen. As long as Nicolosia doesn't change her mind. She's an amateur in the art of deception. They all are.

Chapter 17

'How long will you be at the palace, husband?' Nicolosia keeps her voice casual. 'And will you be requiring dinner this evening?'

'I'm there until very late. Gentile wants to see the dimensions of the Camera degli Sposi and my initial sketches for the frescos, and Barbara of Brandenburg wants to meet your famous brother, so we'll be dining there.'

Gregorio comes into the kitchen. 'Full livery today, Maestro?' he asks.

'No. You won't be needed. The marchese is kindly sending two grooms across with two of his finest horses.' He looks at Gentile as if expecting applause. 'Ludovico often bestows such favours on me,' he boasts. 'In any case, your tunic needs a clean.' Mantegna looks momentarily shamefaced. 'Arrange it, Nicolosia.'

Both women exhale in relief, giving each other a furtive glance. They only rush to the window when they hear the loud rumble of the outer door.

Ya Ling scarcely dares breathe. 'The timing is very good, Mistress.' She surreptitiously runs her hand over the slight bulge in the pocket of her shift where one of Nicolosia's veils lies folded.

Nicolosia turns her head reluctantly. For several long moments she stares at Ya Ling's profile.

'I pray to the Blessed Virgin that I'm doing the right thing.'

Ya Ling holds her penetrating look without blinking. 'You can trust me.'

'I have no choice. For Cecco and for Genevra.' Her sigh is deep and heartfelt. 'I'll go and tell Gregorio to saddle up. You go to my room.'

She has hidden the keys under the needlepoint mat in front of her shrine to the Virgin. They shine against her pink palm like newly minted coins. The first one doesn't work. Nicolosia's fingers shake like a maple leaf. Ya Ling remains outwardly calm. 'This must be the one for the door. Try the other.'

The manacles spring open like a pair of tiny jaws. Ya Ling sighs with relief as she eases her feet out of them. She gives them a resentful kick and they slide across the wooden floor. 'Careful!' Nicolosia warns. 'Give me the key. We must be ready to put them back on the moment you get back here, in case the maestro returns early.' Her eyes narrow. 'Assuming you do come back, that is.'

'Of course. I'm sorry.' Ya Ling's expression doesn't falter.

Reaching for her sewing bag, Nicolosia produces two strips of cloth. 'Here! Put these round your ankles, so the stirrups won't rub you. They look raw enough as it is.'

'You are very kind.' Ya Ling pretends to wind them round and round, but when Nicolosia's back is turned she tucks the strips into the pocket of her shift. New cloth is too valuable to pass up. 'We won't be long.' She picks up the thick, nondescript brown cloak and pulls the veil over her face. 'See? It's quite safe. No one will know.'

When she reaches the courtyard, the mare flicks an ear forwards as Ya Ling cups the silky cheek in her hand. 'What do you call this breed?' she asks conversationally.

'She's a Barbary.'

A Berberi? Ya Ling looks across at Gregorio in surprise. 'From the lands where men wear blue turbans?'

'Wear what?' He shrugs. 'How would I know?' *A Berberi.* Ya Ling leans her face into the mare's mane to hide her smile of delight. How wonderful. To ride a Berber horse on the first part of her journey to track the bastard down. 'I only know the name. That's all.' He clips on a leading rein and leans towards her, bending his elbow. 'Put your foot in here.'

Shaking her head, Ya Ling mounts easily and unaided, glad that this morning she has loosened the bindings she ties each day to disguise her ripening stomach. The feeling of firm horseflesh beneath the saddle sends a shiver of anticipation through her.

Once out of the thick walls of the Mantegna house, they trot along the street. The sense of space after all the time spent in the confines of the harness room makes her drag in deep thankful breaths. Apart from the half hour to watch the Christmas procession, Ya Ling has been indoors for months. Suddenly her ears are assaulted by the cacophony as merchants haggle dramatically, insults are hurled and challenges laid down, while women shout coarse encouragement from the balconies. Pigs root and squeal among the vegetable peelings and the rotting stable sweepings, as tiny songbirds trill piteously from their straw cages. The church bells boom across the town, announcing masses, or deaths, or the birth of a boy-child, and the opening and closing of the many different markets. The stench from the public cesspit scores the back of her throat. Looking around, she sees Gregorio watching her every move and keeping a check on the leading rein he has clipped to her bridle. Each time she leans down to stroke the mare's neck, she glances around, taking in every detail, as they ride straight across the cobbles of the Piazza delle Erbe.

'Wait, I want to show you something,' says Gregorio suddenly. Ya Ling nods, being careful to keep her distinctive blue-black hair tucked well back inside the big hood. She knows exactly where he will take her. Better to humour him, she thinks, better to let him trust her, then his reactions will be slower later on.

'See that big tower over there?' he says. 'Well, that's where it is. It won't take a minute and you'll never have seen anything like it before.'

'If you wish.'

Riding into the Piazza Sordello, they rein in on the left below the Torre della Gabbia. 'Look up there. See the poor soul inside?' Ya Ling holds on to the sides of the hood and as she tips her head back her senses swim. She can't afford to feel sick now. She clutches at the mare's mane until the nausea passes and she dares to look up again. A ragged body has been stiffened by the freezing wind into the same pose that she has seen nailed onto the crosses of wood. An image of the holy man, the one her people call the White Christ. The man's arms are held straight out sideways as if frozen onto the metal of the cage. His face is set into a snarl of agony. His body looks rigid, as if carved out of pale stone. A shudder of sympathy ripples through her own cold body. 'I'm not a coward, but I've never liked looking at the cage, and the maestro always makes us come this way.' He bows his head and reaches into his pocket for his rosary. 'Imagine how he feels, his flesh slowly turning solid up there.' His voice shakes with an urgent undertone. 'And it's no better in the hot weather. One thief last summer was so crazed with thirst he kept flinging himself at the sides of the cage until he was black and blue. The crowd loved it, but I still hear his screams some nights when I can't sleep.'

She senses his anxious eyes on her. 'How awful, Gregorio. That would give anybody night terrors.'

'I'll tell you the worst thing that ever happened up there.' His thumb jerks upwards. 'A woman once gave birth in the cage.' He shudders. 'All on her own. Her screams attracted the biggest crowd ever. Hundreds, there were.' Gregorio looks up fearfully. 'I heard that the baby was too slippery for her to keep hold of, and she was too weak, so it slipped through the bars. The rooks were on it as soon as—'

'Stop, Gregorio!' Her hand comes up to her mouth. She takes in several deep breaths. 'So if you don't like looking at the cage, then why did you bring me here?' Gregorio looks down at the rosary wound round his fingers. 'It was the mistress's idea, wasn't it?'

He nods. His freckles splash dark across his nose and his eyes look huge in his wind-scoured face. 'Yes. You see… If you run away…' He shrugs helplessly. 'The maestro would be beside himself. He'd be vicious. He'd show no mercy. He's done it before. This is where I'd end up. We all would. Clemente and Genevra too.'

'What? Mantegna has had people put in the cage?' The hood slips as she swivels round in amazement.

'Two that I know of. And neither was in good shape when they were let out. He's a very powerful man. He has the full protection of the Gonzagas.' Gregorio's voice is earnest with truth.

'I see.' They both glance fearfully upwards as they ride beneath the cage. The view is even more horrifying up close.

Trotting quickly through the streets, Ya Ling's keen eyes miss nothing. She doesn't know how much time she has. They urge the horses across a drawbridge near to two tall towers. 'See that tower on the right? That's where the maestro's frescos are. Soon those windows will be out of line because the marchese is going to have the middle one moved to give him more room to paint. That's how powerful the maestro is. He can make people do anything. Even alter palaces.'

'Yes. We do well to please such an important man.'

The road leads on to clay ramparts that take them high up across a strip of water where the two lakes meet. The cobbles end abruptly and a series of cinder tracks lead into a lane of packed earth full of hard ruts that big wooden cartwheels have carved into the mud, but the mares are surefooted and they canter towards the big dark mass of the forest that lies ahead.

'Look over there.' Gregorio points to an icy ribbon of water. 'You'd never think to look at it now, but in summer that will be full of fat brown trout. When the maestro is away, Nicolosia lets us come here sometimes. Gives us bread and fruit. Clemente is handy with a rod and Genevra cooks them over a fire. You'll never taste anything so fresh. My mouth's watering just thinking of that crispy skin.'

'That sounds wonderful.' Ya Ling manages an enthusiastic smile. Gregorio is so obvious. She can't bear to hold the hopeful expression in his eager brown eyes and leans down to stroke the mare's neck. 'I hope I'll be joining you this summer, if the mistress lets me,' she murmurs.

Relief floods his voice. It's hard to look at him. 'Oh, I'm sure she will. I'll ask her as soon as we get back.'

The air smells damp and fecund. She nods to him and dismounts, pretending to examine a clump of mallow. She picks at random handfuls of feverfew and goldenseal that have been sheltered by the spread of a holly bush, and the bags are soon half-filled. 'Over here.' He holds out the last empty sack ready as she forages among the leaves and under the fallen logs to show willing. Pale bracket fungi cling to the sides of the older trees deeper into the forest, where green shoots lean towards gaps in the tree cover. 'Unclip the leading rein. I need to go further in and there's no room for both horses to turn round.'

He shakes his head. 'I promised Nicolosia.'

'But what can I do?' She holds out both hands to him. 'I'm on foot!' She leans across and unclips it herself.

The forest trees spread their huge pine-scented arms around her as she leads the horse deeper inside, and, for a moment, as Gregorio concentrates on tying the sacks to each side of his pommel, she is completely obscured from his view.

Now! The orange moss on the trees tell her which direction lies northwards, where the big river waits, and she has only to keep riding slightly to the east of the spatterings of moss to reach it. She will have to sell the mare for less than her worth, she knows that, but it will be enough for a few loaves of bread and to pay a series of boatmen to get her along the quiet byways and then on to the port of Venezia. Going by the smaller rivers will be much safer than going by road. Mantegna won't expect her to travel so slowly. Clemente had naively answered her questions, telling her about all the rivers that feed into the big basin at Venezia, and she reasoned that Mantegna can't afford to have them all watched. Transformed by her cloak and veil, like a respectable Mantovan woman looking for her missing sea-captain husband, she will make sure she is received sympathetically. There will be plenty of sea captains there she can ask about how to get to Beijing. As a realist, she thinks that once on board, if she doesn't have enough money for the voyage, she will do whatever it takes to keep the captain happy. Just as long as he gets her back to a port in her homeland.

Using the stirrup like a springboard, she mounts quickly. The warm flesh of the mare tenses beneath her, sensing the rider's legs tighten with a sudden urgency. The mare surges forwards in little bouncing moves, held back only by Ya Ling's strong hands on the reins. 'Now! Go!' The mare takes off, dodging through the treeline, delighted at the unusual instructions, the possibilities and freedom this skilful new rider is giving her. She guides the horse in an arc, predicting that Gregorio will panic and blunder on straight ahead. Images flash by as quickly as the trees in the forest. The golden dust that blows in from the Gobi Desert. The rosy dawn flooding the hutong roofs, the rhythmic drumming from the drum tower and the deep sense of safety knowing Chen lies asleep outside her room. Ayi's cheek, as wrinkled and soft as new leaves when she plants a firm kiss on it. The turtle raising his green scaly flipper in welcome. Altan's deep growl of a laugh will make everyone within earshot join in too. Once they are married, his arms tight around her, he will never let her go.

It is only faint on the wind, but the sound of raw despair resonates through the enclosed woodland. 'Ya Ling! Ya Ling! For the love of the Virgin, don't do this to me! To all of us!'

The mare digs in and after three shortened strides easily leaps the stream. There will be no picnic this summer. Despite herself, she reins in and turns. The mare tries to push forwards but Gregorio's echoing voice, reverberating through the maze of trees behind, makes Ya Ling lean back to haul her in. The mare seethes beneath her, slippery with excitement.

'For the love of all that is holy!' She can almost taste the salt breath of the sea on her lips, feel the planks on deck rise and fall beneath her feet. 'For all the saints in Heaven!' The voice sounds fainter now.

The mare champs furiously at the bit as she tries to canter forwards. The sound reminds Ya Ling of the noise the manacles make and, feeling the throb of her raw ankles, she instinctively turns away from Gregorio's shouts, wheeling round to give the mare her head. She kicks her hard. A dark cloud of rooks rises up in front of them, swirling like black smoke against the frosted trees. Ya Ling has a sickening image of them greedily swooping down onto the slippery mass of Genevra's baby on the cobbles below the cage. Of Clemente forced to watch his wife's suffering until it is his turn. Of the blood in Gregorio's veins slowly turning to ice. The beating Mantegna gave Nicolosia would be nothing compared to the savagery that awaits Gregorio when he returns home without her.

A gust of air slaps her cheeks back into the present and she hauls on the reins; summoning all her strength, she saws on the bit until the mare finally slows to a trot. The worst realisation she has kept until last. Altan. A sudden knowledge sears into her heart. The journey home will take a long time, and he might not have waited for her. Not a strong virile man like him. Rich. Eligible. Handsome. Admired by so many women in Beijing. And even if by some miracle he has waited, it will be difficult to face him honourably. Used as she is. Even after the herbs have done their work. The idea of using them lies heavy on her conscience. All her years of training have taught her the sanctity of life. Chen's words come back to her. She lays her forehead against the mare's warm damp mane and cries anguished tears. Mantegna must suffer for all that she has lost. Her ragged sobs drag in gulps of air until her chest feels tight and constricted.

She finds Gregorio in a clearing, his back pushed against a tree, his head on his chest. He springs up in relief when the horses whinny a greeting to each other. 'Oh! Ya Ling! Thank you! For the love of Sant'Anselmo, thank you! I was going out of my mind! I couldn't have faced the others if I'd let you escape. The maestro would have ruined us all.'

'Tie that on properly.' She points with a shaking finger at the empty sack flapping on the pommel of Gregorio's saddle. 'I've got work to do.' Handfuls of wild anise seeds go in the bag to soothe Cecco's chest, along with the first pale comfrey shoots and dried yarrow for his skin. Peppermint and sage grow sheltered by a big holm oak and will do to make tisanes to help Genevra's sickness. With a sinking heart Ya Ling forces herself to pick some crisp leaves of rue and pennyroyal that lie near a pile of brushwood, and several stems of tansy and angelica, which she slips into her pocket. In mild doses these will encourage Genevra's baby to start the journey to life. She cups both hands across the slight swell at the front of her tunic. In stronger doses they will do exactly the opposite for her own child. Only then can she return to Beijing. The bags are soon half-filled and they remount.

'Let's go back,' she says, wiping her eyes on Genevra's cloak, 'before I change my mind.'

Gregorio is stunned with gratitude. 'I won't tell any of them. What you did. I won't say.'

'No!' She clicks the mare ahead of him along the brown pine needles that coat the path as they make their way back to Mantova. 'Tell them all. That I had my chance but I still came back.'

Chapter 18

The potion is working well for Genevra. Her cheeks look pink and her eyes are alive with anticipation now that the sickness has abated. The occasional downward twinge below her stomach makes her grasp Clemente's arm with delight.

In the harness room Ya Ling looks at the bowl of darker green liquid that she has made for herself. Her nose wrinkles at the acrid smell that comes off it. She brings it up to her lips and closes her eyes. She imagines the tiny life budded deep inside her and the terrible shock that awaits it. An echo returns of Chen's advice on her betrothal day when she was young and impetuous. When she treated him with disdain and insulted him with abandon. It seems years ago. A different life that happened to someone else. She remembers his anxious face and every word he said. 'You must always use your powers for good. Look at me. I'm one whose life has been ruined by a man who used his powers for evil. How different my life could have been if he had taken the right path. If he had made an honourable choice. All life is sacred and you must do everything in your power to uphold that.'

She doesn't even know the right dosage. Her child could live but be deformed. She remembers the occasional broken little body brought to her parents and their distress that nature had been so cruel and that they could do nothing to help. She quickly stands. The contents of the bowl leave a dark stain on the midden as she flings them outside quickly before she can change her mind.

Options have to be weighed, and fast. Mantegna does not want the child and she fears what he might do when her pregnancy becomes obvious. Gentile lives in Venezia. She remembers all that open sea racing into the lagoon. The tall ships tugging patiently at their moorings in the vast area of the port, some with their prows facing eastward. And Gentile is a man who fears God. A man who might not turn out a pregnant servant. And once the baby is safely born she will have to lie to Altan and her family, to tell them that her child is one she has befriended.

'Mistress, I need to talk to you alone. I have something very important to ask you.' Nicolosia turns from arranging flowers in the dining room, surprised by the undercurrent of tension in the slave woman's voice. 'And I must do so while your brother is still here.'

'My brother? Then tonight. Before the men return from the palace.'

Clemente and Genevra are delighted by the chance of an early night. Both women sit in the firelight waiting for Gregorio to finish outside. The kitchen is quiet apart from the occasional rattle of the windowpane when the night breeze gusts through the courtyard. Nicolosia sits with a half-finished table runner spread across her knee, the spools of her embroidery silks lined up neatly in the basket at her feet. Ya Ling counts each breath in and out as she waits. She picks up a tiny bonnet she's making out of a scrap of kitchen cambric for Genevra's baby, and indicates the basket of silks. 'May I?'

Nicolosia nods and watches the slave woman as she unravels a line of yellow thread and snips it with her sharp white teeth, and begins to embroider a delicate pattern round the bonnet brim with deft cross-stitches. Out in the courtyard the pulley clatters down into the well with a dull grinding, then Gregorio's footsteps cross the cobbles and the stable door opens. Water sluices into the horse troughs. She drums her fingers on her knee before she turns.

'So, what do you want to ask me?'

'I would like you to ask the maestro to let me go to Venezia with your brother. To let me work for him.'

Nicolosia turns in astonishment. 'The maestro would never agree!'

'I think he will. He is losing interest in me and I am another mouth to feed. Signor Gentile is rich and could afford to pay a great deal. And I don't think he is happy for his sister's reputation that she has one like me in her household.'

'You don't miss anything, do you? Your cleverness unnerves me.'

'Also I think Signor Gentile would be a kinder master to me,' she adds quickly.

'What about Cecco?'

'I will show you how to make the potions he needs. I promise you, Mistress, that I will teach you everything I know that can help him before I leave.'

'Anyone can make a potion. But there is more to it than that. Some special powers. It keeps me awake at night wondering where your powers come from, and if one day you will use them on us.'

'Never! I am a healer who only—'

'Listen to me. I scarcely know where to begin.' She begins to pace the kitchen, turning the runner over and over in her hands. 'Cecco's chest is clear again. Genevra looks transformed. Even my prudish brother's glances linger after you. You make food that tastes like nothing from our soil, you sew like a seamstress, you ride like a soldier and you are tiny yet as strong as an ox...' She turns abruptly. 'How is all this possible in an ordinary woman?'

Gregorio comes in and, looking surprised at Nicolosia's accusing voice, he stands in the middle of the kitchen, turning his cap in his hands. 'Mistress, can I just say something about the slave woman? She could have run off when she had the chance and then we would all have been—'

'Enough, Gregorio.'

'And some terrible things have happened to her. Stolen from her family, she was. Right before she was getting married.'

'I know. Genevra told me. Get to bed. Now!' His lips droop as he leaves. 'Before you came, my servants were all completely loyal to me, but now...' She shakes her head. 'You must have put a spell on them.'

'No, Mistress. Nothing like that!'

Nicolosia points a stubby finger. 'All the things you are capable of really worry me. I can't sleep at night thinking of them.'

'Well, that can be remedied.' Ya Ling keeps her voice low and reassuring. 'Because if I leave with Signor Gentile, then—'

'But then am I putting my own brother at risk from witchcraft?' Nicolosia's fingers begin fiddling with the folds of fabric at her waist beneath her *cintura*.

'Witchcraft? No, Mistress. No one is at risk from me. Let me explain—'

'Wait!' Nicolosia holds up a commanding hand and hangs the table runner over the back of her chair, then, striding to the firewood basket, she throws a large log on the fire, pressing it harshly down into the flames until a sweet pine scent overrides the greasy kitchen smell of meat and oil. Ya Ling looks at the hungry flames flickering their way along the pale wood, watching how they flare and spurt when they burn the sticky resin. Witches burn. That's what they do here. Or put them to the hooks, or the *strappado* to get them to confess. Ya Ling looks helplessly into the crimson craters of the fire, trying to banish all thoughts of the conversations she has listened to many times in the kitchen. Of crowds gathering round the neat bonfire stacked up in the Piazza delle Erbe. Of the hooks waiting high up the vaulted arch next to the Piazza Broletto. Of the cage being lowered from the Torre delle Gabbia and its door swinging open. Perhaps, one day, for her.

Panic pinches inside her chest as she imagines the flames licking their way along her body, spitting when they reach her blood before gnawing into flesh and bone.

'Tell me, why shouldn't I take the safest path and ask the ecclesiastical court to try you as a witch?' Nicolosia holds out the reddened poker in front of her, the heat coming off it in waves.

The bonnet drops onto Ya Ling's lap as she chains her arms round her body, and holds them so tightly her breath grazes the inside of her chest. Her voice drops low and urgent. 'I am a healer, Mistress. That is all I am.'

Dark shadows play across Nicolosia's stern profile as she bends into the fire. 'Though I fear for Cecco's health, I am also afraid for the safety of all of us. If you can't answer my questions tonight, then I will report you to my priest. He'll know what to do with you.' She leans forwards and rams the poker back onto the log. Subtlety has never been her strong point, but Ya Ling's heart still pounds with fear. 'So where did you learn all of your heathen tricks and potions?' she demands.

The bonnet feels damp as Ya Ling picks it up and turns it over and secures the needle to it. Her words come out in an anxious rush. 'My father is Mongolian, and for many generations his family learned healing skills from the scholars and merchants who travel along the Spice Roads. When his reputation reached the ears of the emperor in Beijing, he was summoned to attend the royal court for several years. He met my mother there. Her family have been famous Han healers since the time of the Yuan dynasty. So ever since I was a child my parents have taught me all they knew. About herbs, balancing *qi* and using fine needles to cure.'

Nicolosia snatches up her needle. 'What? Using these? To cure sickness? And perhaps embroider a pattern on the patient at the same time? What nonsense you speak! More tall tales of yours. This is not helping.' The guttering of the tallow candle on the mantel over the fireplace casts Nicolosia's face in deep shadow. Her voice is the only indication of her feelings and it does not sound promising. 'Beijing. Beijing.' The way she repeats the foreign-sounding word makes it sound like an incantation. 'It sounds an unholy place to me.'

Gregorio's songbird tied to the bar outside gives out a pitiful cry. Both women jump. It's unusual for the little bird to cry out like that into the darkness.

'It's just the name of a city, Mistress. The biggest in my homeland.' Ya Ling tries to keep her voice measured and reassuring.

'What? Bigger even than Mantova?' Nicolosia asks, her lip already curled in disbelief.

'Oh yes. Much bigger than Mantova.'

'I thought it might be.' Nicolosia's tongue clicks against the roof of her mouth.

'No, it is. Believe me, Mistress! It has a beautiful palace with curved roofs and gardens, where there are fountains full of golden fish that come to be fed when they are called.' She thinks of the contrast between the openness of the Ming emperor's palace nestled in its landscape, like a pearl on green silk, and the dark forbidding outlines of the Gonzaga Palace with its thick, threatening walls.

'Stop all this wild boasting.' Nicolosia's sideways glance is hard.

'In my country, the gift of healing is only given to those who are honourable. We use our gifts only for good, otherwise they are taken away. Shamans worship many gods, but we don't do that. My mother's family worship Buddha, and my father's family are Muslim. They each have their own book to worship, just like the Jews and the Christians like you. My country is tolerant of all beliefs and my family have friends of many different faiths.'

'Different faiths? Surely not! How can they keep their own faith pure?'

'We believe we can learn from everyone.'

'So in that case, you believe in the Holy Virgin? I don't remember seeing you at mass!' Nicolosia snaps.

Ya Ling thinks for several moments. 'I might not believe in her exactly as you do, but my family believe in all the things she represents. We're the keepers of the old ways and traditions. Real healers. We don't believe in the power of charms or love philtres, or telling fortunes by throwing knucklebones or cowrie shells. We never chant spells or pretend we can raise djinns from the underworld.'

'I'm glad to hear it.' Nicolosia's voice sounds hollow. 'My priest will be very relieved.'

Ya Ling decides on something less threatening. 'You mentioned the food I have prepared for you – well, as I told you earlier, my family had a cook and I used to watch him, and sometimes my mother taught me her favourite family dishes too, so that's where I—' she begins.

'Your skill at that unsettles me too. Those strange dishes that make all who eat them demand more.'

'But that's only because I use different spices. That's all. It isn't magic.'

Nicolosia holds the cambric cap out so that the firelight shines through and shows the delicacy of the embroidery. 'And was it your mother who taught you such fine stitching?'

'Yes. My mother. We were working together on a bedspread…' Ya Ling decides to keep quiet about the luxurious betrothal gifts she had been given, the Kashmiri shawl as fine as a cobweb and the silk carpet that changed colour as you walked around it. 'Before I was taken, my mother and I were embroidering a bedspread—' Ya Ling stops suddenly as the back of her throat tightens as if being welded shut.

Nicolosia shoots her a curious glance. 'Go on.'

'It is a custom that comes from the far west of my country. The mother and daughter make a bedspread together…' Her voice ripples upwards. It is several moments before she can continue '… for her daughter's dowry but they leave a little part of it unfinished, so that when her daughter has her own daughter then they will complete it together. And so on, down the family line…' She clears her throat as her mother's kindly smile swims before her. The cosy companionship of sitting together, admiring each other's artistry, chatting about her future with Altan. Warmed by the embers and by their close companionship. 'We sat together by the fireside. Like this. But not like this at all…' Her voice tails off to a thread.

Nicolosia stares at her bowed head, then pulls the table runner back onto her lap and folds it into a neat rectangle. 'I find it very hard to believe you were dowried. And allowed to roam about where you could be taken.'

'His name is Altan. I was betrothed to him.' Ya Ling crosses her arms and holds each forearm tightly, and begins rocking backwards and forwards on the stool. 'He is very tall, and when he laughs he throws his head back…' Her black hair falls down her shoulders as her own head makes an involuntary tip backwards. 'It's such a joyful laugh, it makes everyone nearby want to join in. My father raised a big tent in our courtyard in Beijing, so our betrothal ceremony was properly Mongolian.' Looking into the middle distance, she can see it clearly again. 'It was so beautiful, made of cream felt with scarlet silken banners flying from the top. Altan and I kneeled down together and our families threw so many white rose petals at us that they swirled around like a snowstorm. I wore a specially embroidered gown and when Altan looked at me he said he had never—'

'A charming story. It all sounds very quaint.' The wind murmurs outside, and a draught lifts the rug from the tiles. 'I've never seen you weep before.' Nicolosia waits, staring uncertainly, until the girl's breath stops catching and the only sound in the kitchen is the ashy subsiding of a log in the grate. 'Perhaps acting is another of your skills. But my priest will no doubt see through you.' She pulls Ya Ling to her feet.

'Please, Mistress.' Ya Ling tries to still her racing thoughts, and slow the fear that churns inside her head and prevents her from thinking clearly. A deep breath draws in *qi* and calm flows outwards around her chest. Lowering her eyes, she focuses on letting the life force enter and feeling its gentle peace flow along her bloodstream.

'Off you go.' She hears Nicolosia's slipper tap impatiently on the tiles.

There is no rush. All will be accomplished if she uses logic instead of allowing fear to overwhelm her. The answer is within her grasp if she can allow it in. Gazing into the crimson craters of the fire, her memory is jolted and begins to make a connection. *Keep breathing and thinking*, she commands herself.

She puts her hands to her hips, her stance suddenly convincing. 'Sit down, Signora Mantegna. And wait.' The steel in her voice makes Nicolosia take a step back. 'I said wait.' She moves noisily up the stairs and across the landing, then opens two drawers of the big dresser and slams them shut again loudly for Nicolosia's benefit before she creeps silently into the harness room and untangles the scarlet cord from beneath the horns. The bricks go back in seamlessly.

She drops the cord casually onto Nicolosia's lap. 'Saintly Mother Maria! Where did you get this?'

'It was tied to the door outside.'

The creases around Nicolosia's eyes deepen. She runs two hands down the brown folds of her fustian dress. 'When? When did you find it?'

'The day the maestro returned from Firenze.'

'Yes. Of course. That makes sense,' she says bitterly.

'Exactly. No point accusing you of lying with another man if the husband is at home. It's better to accuse you when he has been away. Adultery – is that the word?' Ya Ling keeps her voice calm and businesslike.

'Yes it is. I should think you know all the words for such goings-on. A woman like you.' Nicolosia's eyes narrow in accusation.

'Mistress, it is true I've had to live on my wits since I arrived here. To keep my eyes and ears open. I miss nothing, but I also know when to keep silent,' she says with quiet emphasis. 'As I have done over this.'

'But where is the rest of it? The scroll? And the horns?'

'Hidden.'

'But for how long, I wonder.' Nicolosia looks askance at her.

'I told you that I had something important to show you before but you didn't believe me. So now I will make a bargain with you. Persuade Signor Gentile to take me to Venezia and I will give you the horns.'

'I told you, the maestro would never agree to it.'

'Then you will have to make sure he does.' She leaves Nicolosia staring at the fire.

While Ya Ling is lying on her pallet with her eyes fixed on the brickwork, she hears Nicolosia's heavy tread on the floor above and the noise of her frantically opening and closing all the drawers. What had Nicolosia once said to her? 'In a week or two I'll be as cunning as you.' She gives a tight shake of her head and settles down to sleep.

Chapter 19

Two days later she waits for the summons, her hands clasped as tight as clams. Already she's had to loosen the gathers round the waist of her shift twice, despite the tight bindings she wears each day, so there is no time to waste. She puts her ear to the door of the upstairs sitting room. The voices are so muffled through the thick polished wood that she can't tell which way the conversation is going. Occasionally she hears a higher, pleading, feminine voice, then the grumble of men's voices as the bargaining goes on. Footsteps come striding purposefully across the wooden floor towards her and she springs back.

'Come in.' Mantegna's voice oozes confidence, as oily as olives in a press. Gentile sits upright on a highly carved oak chair that would not look out of place in the marchese's palazzo. Nicolosia sits on its twin on the other side of the hearth. Ya Ling looks anxiously at Nicolosia, who casts her glance quickly down to her lap. 'My brother-in-law has made me a very substantial offer for you, maid. He wants you to join his household as a… as a… How shall I describe her position, Gentile? Believe me, she knows every position there is. And plenty you'll never have imagined.'

'As a servant.' Gentile looks at Ya Ling. 'I merely think it would be more appropriate for her to join my household retinue. More respectable. I think it would make life easier for my sister.'

Gentile looks at the reddened cheeks of his sister and the way the slave woman's slender fingers are hooked nervously together.

Mantegna looks carefully round the room. The Persian tiles with the hunted fawns beautifully painted on them and the ruby red epergnes of Limoges enamel have already gone. His eyes gloss over the space where the two big blue and gold cloisonné vases used to sit, his mouth downturning at remembering how magnificent they had looked set against the Arras love tapestry. There are only two items left from Nicolosia's dowry, and he daren't sell either of those. The wedding chest with its irritating perspectives was painted and signed by each of the Bellinis and the della Robbia plaque with its sickly blue and white Madonna was made for them by the vast Robbia clan. Too many tongues would wag. His gaze turns to the two magnificently carved chairs that have cost him three commissions to buy and his spirits lower. They're next on the list to go to the moneylender.

Then his eyes skim across Ya Ling's narrow shoulders, the soft golden skin of her downturned face framed by a sleek curve of black hair, and his hungry glance slides up and down. His most prized possession of all. One that belongs only to him. One he can take whenever he likes. Having forgiven her for her escape attempt, he now adores her once more. Worth more than any mere object, however luxurious, however fine the beaten brasswork or how delicate the enamel inlay. Gentile's money purse would come in very handy, but he could never part with her. Despite her unwelcome pregnancy and the scandal that might bring to his door. His eyes travel to his plump wife, who slumps untidily in the grand chair. She looks diminished, as if overawed by its dimensions. 'So what say you, wife?'

Nicolosia picks up the *cintura* that attempts to define her waist, and holds the tiny latticed box of potpourri at the end of it up to her nose before she clears her throat. 'I agree with Gentile. It is better for our reputation if she leaves. With the way things are, I feel it is time.'

Mantegna turns to his brother-in-law with a courtly nod of his head. 'I do understand why Gentile suddenly feels a sudden urge for the services of this maid. She gives me sudden urges all the time.' Mantegna's voice coarsens with amusement at the scowl of disgust his brother-in-law gives. 'But one thing we haven't taken into account are the wishes of the maid herself.' He beckons Ya Ling over to him. 'I am a generous master to you, am I not?'

'Yes, Maestro.'

'With a forgiving nature?' She nods. 'A master who will provide for you whatever the future might bring?' He ignores Nicolosia's curious glance. 'Don't I give you all that you need?'

'Yes, Maestro.'

'Feed you. Buy you the sweet wine you love. Clothe you.' He pauses for effect. 'Even in velvet.'

'Yes, Maestro.'

Gentile leans forwards intently. 'Don't be afraid, Ya Ling, answer truthfully. Do you wish to leave the household of Mantegna and come to Venezia with me?'

Silence drops like a stone down a well. Her deep breathing is audible but her voice is clear. 'Yes,' she states. 'Yes, I do.'

Gentile places a heavy pigskin money pouch on the table. 'Then that's settled.'

Mantegna's voice tightens. 'Leave us, wife.'

'But, the slave woman has just said—'

'Get out!'

Mantegna moves behind Ya Ling, his bulky chest pushing against her back as he reaches his arms in front of her. His chin digs into her shoulder as his fingers fumble angrily for the drawstring at the neck of her brown shift.

Still standing behind her, Mantegna cups her naked breasts and holds them out to Gentile as if offering him a gift. She gasps in shame. 'Beautiful, aren't they?' As he speaks softly over her shoulder his hands begin to knead her soft flesh luxuriantly together. She winces at the scraping of his calloused hands. 'Are these what you want?'

She feels Mantegna hard behind her. 'See how the peaks harden like seed pearls. See how she loves being handled. You'll never please a whore like her. She's run away, you know, several times. Once she got as far as one of the dockstations on the river.'

'No I didn't.' She glares balefully across at Gentile. 'He's lying!'

'Now how many sailors did she satisfy on the way to get as far as that, I wonder, eh? And won't you wonder that too, whenever you feel the urge to lie with her? She's like a cat on heat, this one. Sex and survival, that's all she knows. You'll never get any loyalty from her,' he finishes bitterly. 'No matter how hard you try.'

Ya Ling closes her eyes tightly. 'Please, Signor Bellini. Take me from here.' She daren't look across to see if the horrified expression on Gentile's face will turn into one of compassion, or one of disgust. For a big man he makes very little noise. Only the clink of coins in the money pouch as he lifts it up and forces it back into the pocket of his *tabarro* tells her of his final decision.

When the servants are in bed and her husband and brother remain upstairs, Nicolosia appears at the door of the harness room. 'I tried. I did my best.'

'I know.' Ya Ling nods. 'Wait for me in the kitchen.'

Nicolosia's eyes widen when the slave woman comes back with the horns. 'I didn't expect you to do this.'

'I know you didn't. I could use them against you, but I always keep my word.'

Nicolosia gives a furtive glance at the staircase, her fingers slipping in her haste to untie the scroll. Her lips downturn as she reads the lines written on it.

'What does it say?'

Nicolosia throws up a hand in disgust. 'Just stupid nonsense. A list of all the men I am supposed to have slept with. Friends. Neighbours. Even my own priest. Whose name he can't even spell.' She sighs. 'Petrarch needn't worry.'

'Petrarch. Is he the priest?'

'No.' Nicolosia looks sharply at Ya Ling. 'I forget sometimes you are not...'

'What?'

Nicolosia shakes her head. 'Never mind.'

'So why does it upset you so?'

'Because it is a slur on the maestro's honour. He would be livid even though he didn't believe a word of it. He'd lose face if he didn't make accusations and look for vengeance, so there would be a big furore. He'd never find out who did it and all it would do is cause a lot of nasty gossip about me in the *contrada*, which would upset me a great deal.'

'But that is unjust. His enemies are trying to hurt him but hurting you.'

'Exactly. Men jealous of his talent and...' she whispers this, with a wry sideways smile, 'fed up with his arrogance.'

Ya Ling frowns. 'Let me think...'

A warm hand cups her elbow. 'Not everything can be healed with a bag of herbs, little maid.'

Ya Ling's eyes widen at the endearment before she pushes the scroll and the horns underneath a glowing log. Nicolosia brings out the cord from deep within her pocket and throws it on the flames, watching it burn with a sudden vivid flame, noting the way the slave woman maintains the pressure with the poker until an acrid smell of burning horn creeps round the kitchen and the curved contours finally begin to crumble to dust. She turns as Nicolosia's hand rests briefly on hers. 'Go to bed. You look tired out. It's been a long day for us both.' She pauses at the foot of the stairs. 'And thank you.'

Chapter 20

The carpenter's shop is clouded with delicious woody scents. Mantegna picks up a handful of cedarwood shavings and inhales. 'Smell this.' He bends down to pick up some camphor chippings and hands them across to Cecco. 'Watch what I do here. How I get a good price.'

'Framing wood, Maestro? Any preferences? How long?' The carpenter holds out his arms wide. He has three fingers missing, which always fascinated Cecco as a child.

'Hard wood obviously. Deep enough for the carving. Oh, and nothing is to be said about this. This is not a court commission. Understood?' The carpenter nods, but his features fall in disappointment. 'So no boasting about me being a customer, right? If the Gonzagas find out about this, then I'll be on your tail.'

The man nods nervously. 'Some nice oak or chestnut then?' he begins.

'Let me see some oak. And don't try palming me off with pine.'

The door that leads to a small room behind the workshop opens and through the haze of wood dust Mantegna sees a familiar outline stooping to come through it. He feels a ripple of shame when he thinks of their last meeting, when he made enquiries about offering the man Ya Ling's child if it were to be born a girl. The figure locks the door and then looks across and shrinks back into the shadows. 'Dati?' he demands, surprised. 'I would never have thought you were keen on woodwork. Though you no doubt have your finger in many pies.'

'Maestro!' The man's bony features quickly assemble themselves into a delighted smile. 'This is a happy coincidence.'

'What brings you here?'

'Oh, and is this your son? What a fine handsome fellow he is! Look at his broad manly bearing. Just like his father.' Cecco shuffles his feet. 'And where do you come in the family? Firstborn? Lastborn?'

'No. I'm the only one.'

'So far.' Dati gives Mantegna a broad wink.

'Father?' Cecco holds out a tentative hand to Dati, looking from one to the other.

Mantegna shakes his head, his voice rattled. 'So what are you doing here?'

'Just a small commission.' Dati speaks quickly. 'Nothing of any import.' He nods at the carpenter, his face serious. 'Just something for my wife. Now if you will both excuse me, I must be on my way. No time even for pleasantries, and I would so like to have made the acquaintance of your son. What a pity.' He stumbles over a pile of cedar planks behind him, then hurries out of the workshop.

Cecco holds his chest with both hands. His face reddens as he tries to suppress his breathing, until a splutter of coughing overwhelms him.

'What ails him, Maestro?' The carpenter looks at the boy straining for breath. 'What does he need? Water? A bit of fresh air?'

'He's always doing this. His mother spoils him. Just give him some water outside. Stand him in the sun for a bit, see if that helps.' Mantegna looks at the door Dati has just locked. 'But first I'd like to see what he's up to.'

'I've no idea.' The carpenter threads a key off an untidy ring and hands it across. 'Never seen anything like it. He's a shifty sod, that one. Come on, Cecco.'

'Is he?' Mantegna looks thoughtful as his eyes follow the carpenter leading his son outside, before he opens the door and steps inside a small room. A layer of golden dust and long shavings like a giant's curls lie on the floor like a carpet. An odd box lies in the middle of the floor, tightly constructed of thick wood and well jointed. It's made of expensive chestnut wood and looks strong enough to withstand a battering. Mantegna bends down to lift up a corner of the box and feel its weight to see if that might give him a clue as to its purpose, but when his fingers feel for the lip of the handle to slip his hand inside, they trace the coils of a giant brass screw instead, one with a massive thread that curves down around its thick column. There is something about the shape of it that makes him uneasy.

'There's one at the other end as well.' Mantegna nearly jumps out of his skin. The carpenter's footsteps have been deadened by the sawdust. 'Sorry, Maestro. Christ only knows what it's for. Some heathen ritual, no doubt. Something devilish and foreign he wants copied. I've made some things in my time, but nothing like the contraptions Dati asks me to make. I've no idea what they're for. This last one is a bit different to the others, but it's still a puzzle to me.'

'A massive screw at each end?' Mantegna brings his hand to his chin. 'Could it be a wine press? For his wife?'

'That's one of the things Dati said he was experimenting with. And a cheese press too. To try to press curds into cheese. As if we don't have enough cheesemakers round here,' the carpenter scoffs. Mantegna turns one of the screws with both hands, making it squeak in protest against the hard seasoned wood. The end of the box slowly moves inwards. 'You know, there's something about him. Something not quite right.'

'But where's the spout?' Both men look up as Cecco moves to the other end of the box, squats down and slowly turns the screw to make that end of the box slowly move inwards. 'You know, to pour the juice out when the grapes have been pressed. There's only a hole in the lid. It would splash everywhere.' His breath wheezes in his chest. 'How do you know that man, Father?'

'For the love of God! Stay outside in the fresh air when you are told! You stupid boy.'

Cecco stands up, his cheeks scarlet. His folded arms bunch up beneath his ears as he walks slowly to the door.

'Dati's a bastard for not paying too.' The carpenter tries to lighten the leaden silence. 'I suppose I could always use it to squeeze the money out of him.'

'Yes. You could.' Mantegna gives a hollow laugh, then draws an arc in the dust with the toe of his shoe. 'But I've heard his good deeds outweigh his sins. A priest told me that. Apparently he rescues poor children and finds them good homes.'

'Does he? I've not heard that.' The carpenter's voice drops. 'He's wily. No doubt he's generous to the church.'

'Generous, you say? Well, on that subject, I'm going to have to ask you for credit as well. Only for a short time.' He puffs out his chest. 'You know how highly esteemed I am by the Marchese Ludovico –

by all the Gonzagas in fact. I'll pay you once the paintings have been sold.' He tries to make it sound like he's doing the carpenter a favour.

The carpenter gives a troubled sigh, which Mantegna ignores. The bartering doesn't take long. There are too many wood merchants in Mantova for the carpenter to pitch too high. Delivery is arranged and Mantegna gives him a final warning about the need for discretion before he leaves.

Outside, he takes the mare's reins from his son. 'There was no need for that, Father,' Cecco says stiffly.

Mantegna draws the mare level with Cecco so he can reach over and put a hand on his son's thigh. 'Sorry, son, about shouting.'

'Is it about the commissions, Father? About the Gonzagas finding out? You don't need to be worried. Only Settimio and I know and we'd never tell a soul.'

'I know that, son. But don't tell anybody about that man Dati either.'

Cecco's eyes widen. 'Why? Do you owe him money? Is that it? You can skip my wages for a couple of weeks if that'll help.'

Mantegna brushes a smear of dust from his son's cheek. 'That's good of you, son. But I'll need a bit more than that. These frescos will take me about ten years, if I do them as they cry out to be done. And they will be magnificent.' Mantegna's voice lacks its usual bombast. 'I can promise you that. You will be proud to be a part of them. But I've already borrowed a lot against my future earnings from them and we can't live on fresh air in the meantime. The marchese is spending a fortune doing up the Palazzo Ducale, he's investing in foreign wars, and now he wants to make sure his son can cut a dash at the Vatican, so it's not easy getting money out of him. It's risky doing private work, but what can I do?'

'I'll work harder, Father. Get up earlier.'

Mantegna swallows hard. 'You're a good lad. Too soft for the world we live in, that's for sure. Too gentle.' He shakes his head. 'But it's a brutal world out there.'

Cecco nods wisely. 'I know, Father.'

He pats his son's cheek. 'I doubt that, my lad.'

Back at the workshop all three men work hard for the rest of the day. Mantegna watches Cecco pull the candle nearer as he hunches over the border of palm leaves he is engraving round the rim of the holy medallion Mantegna has been quietly commissioned to make. 'You're doing a good job, son.'

'Better be. The monks know every detail of the story of the Passion. They'll be after me if I miss anything out.'

His tongue rests on his top lip as it always did as a child when he concentrated hard. Mantegna smiles at the bent head. 'Time for home. Settimio left a good while ago. Don't strain your eyes.'

Cecco lifts his head from the medal and runs the tip of his burnishing tool against the sharpening stone. 'Can I see what you've done today, Father?'

The study of the Virgin and Child shocks him to silence. He ventures the candle a little nearer. The Madonna looks desolate, with strands of ringlets tumbling down her cheek like tears. The swaddling clothes cocoon the baby so tightly they seem to predict the constriction of a shroud. Cecco feels his own sore chest tighten just looking at it. The Madonna looks downwards with awful resignation, in an image that is both intimate and universal. Locked together in a tapestry shawl to represent their terrible shared destiny, and isolated by the darkness surrounding them, the mother and child look totally together and totally alone. 'It's very touching.' Cecco swallows hard. 'But so sad.' The Madonna's posture is defensive, her hand protecting the infant's fuzzy, vulnerable head. 'She looks fearful, as if she knows the harm the future will hold for her baby but she can't do anything about it.'

He looks up at an odd noise. His father's face is stricken. 'Father? What have I said?'

'Nothing, son.' He holds a coiled fist to his lips. 'I'll be all right.'

Cecco drops his glance to the floor. 'I've been clumsy trying to say what I feel.' His hand hovers over his heart. 'Father, what I meant to say was your Madonnas are always so true to life. Some of them are so real I see Mother in them. Not this one though.'

Mantegna shakes his head from side to side as if shaking his thoughts out of it. He pulls his hand down his face. 'Your mother?

Hardly. I wouldn't call her an icon of motherhood.' He tries to control the tremor in his voice. 'Far from it. But she is miserable. I'll give you that.'

'Well, I suppose she's not got much to be happy about sometimes.' Mantegna shoots him a look. 'With only one son, I mean.'

'Just concentrate on the sketch, Cecco. What does it teach you?' Cecco's mouth begins to frame his thoughts. 'What do you think of it?' There is an awkward pause that lingers too long. 'Well, go on then!'

'She has an eastern look about her.' Cecco gives his father an awkward glance, watching the way his jaw stiffens.

'Well, never mind that,' he snaps.

Cecco holds the picture at arm's-length and then up to his face. 'I hope you don't mind me saying so, Father, but I think it's too sad. It offers no hope.'

'Well, not everybody has that luxury.' Mantegna's voice sounds silted with despair. He pushes his son away and dips his head down into the candlelight. 'It might not be one of my most sublime, but as long as it has my name attached to it, then the merchant who's buying it will be happy enough.'

'But what if the Gonzagas find out?'

'I'll put a false date on it. No one will know when it was painted. All merchants are the same. He's getting a bargain and that's all that matters to him.'

'I'm sorry I criticised it, Father.'

'So you should be!' He holds up a knuckle. 'You'll never have this much of my talent. I carry the whole bloody workshop on my back, never forget that!'

Cecco nods, eyes wide as if mesmerised by the sudden squall of temper that has overtaken his father. 'Father, you are a greater artist than I can ever dream of becoming. It was wrong of me to find fault.'

'When times are difficult, son, even a great artist has to ignore his worries and his conscience sometimes and deal with men he doesn't always trust. I have a great vision, but at the same time I need to provide for us all. This might mean doing things I'm not proud of.'

He thinks of Dati and his promise to find Ya Ling's child a good home, if that is what has to be done. At least it will go to a good patrician family and will be well taken care of. And if he threatens Dati enough, then he will have to pay up. He pushes away all thoughts of Ya Ling's desolation when the child has to go. It's the best he can do. He holds up the sketch of the sad-eyed Madonna nearer to the candle glow. 'And the hard part will be living with what I've done afterwards.'

Chapter 21

Despite all Ya Ling's reassurances, Genevra is determined to make her will in preparation for the ordeal of childbirth. 'It's a terrible time even for a younger woman but for a woman of forty summers like me... Not to mention bringing the birth forwards like we have. I'm frightened we've tempted Providence.' It is a pitifully small amount to leave to Clemente – the dress she wears, her kitchen cap, a threadbare cloak of sheep's wool and a bone comb with a pretty green stone set into the handle – but she feels much better for keeping to tradition.

She has followed all of Ya Ling's advice, rubbing her swelling belly with comfrey oil, eating the oregano shoots that Clemente finds in the market and gulping down the paste of crushed dill seeds that will ensure plenty of rich milk for the baby. The slave woman's gentle touch soothes her backache, and her strong downward strokes on Genevra's stomach prepare the path that the baby will have to forge to enter life itself.

The birth itself proves straightforward. It is as if the baby knows when the maestro is out, and chooses its time carefully. When Genevra feels the first stabbing pain Ya Ling keeps her moving slowly round the kitchen and, after several hours of massaging her back and her contracting stomach, she allows her sips of lavender water until, just after the bell for midnight mass, the baby arrives.

In the first week little Ernesto is contented, making little sighs and suckling sounds and being made much of by all of them bending over the rush basket that lies on a folded quilt in the corner of the kitchen. The weather becomes hotter and Genevra spends her time in her room while Ya Ling takes over her tasks. The baby begins to cry more often.

Ya Ling corners Clemente in the kitchen. 'What's wrong?'

'Nothing, the little one is fretting, that's all. The wife wants to be a bit private at the moment, she's a bit overwhelmed. She says to tell you she's fine. He's a big boy you know, for one born a bit early.' He gives a deep chuckle before giving Ya Ling's hand a squeeze. 'And all thanks to you. He's always hungry,' he says proudly. 'No wonder she's tired out.'

Over the next two days the cries become higher-pitched, sounding through the wall of the harness room. 'I need to see her, Clemente, and your room is too dark,' Ya Ling insists. 'Bring her out here when the maestro and Cecco have left.'

As soon as the outer door bangs shut, Genevra comes into the kitchen and, when she does, Ya Ling knows exactly what ails her. The way her walk is unsteady, the way she cradles her agonising breasts in front of her, and the baby's increasingly hoarse screams tell her one thing. Milk fever. 'You were right.' Clemente holds out a chair for his wife and watches her anxiously as she collapses into it. 'She's beginning to talk nonsense, Ya Ling, she doesn't know where she is. Or even who she is. Do something for her, for the love of San Rocco. What do you need?'

He looks on anxiously as Ya Ling places a cool cloth on Genevra's forehead. The milk has entered her blood and is causing a great flux within her body. Her face runs with sweat and she is becoming increasingly confused. Time is short. Ya Ling pulls the pallet from the bed out of the harness room and Genevra willingly falls onto it, screaming as the movement jars her painful breasts. Ya Ling squats down beside her and opens wide the loosened lacing on her bodice. Genevra's breasts scarcely move. Beneath Ya Ling's gently probing fingers, they feel solid and burning.

It's worse than she thought. Both breasts are blocked. The baby's legs kick above the edge of the basket and his weakening screams of despair threaten the sanity of all who hear him.

Ya Ling begins quickly massaging the hard areas in Genevra's breasts where the milk has settled like stones, and keeps putting the baby to her. It is a long slow job that could take many hours.

The household continues to flow round the two women but Genevra only seems to get worse. She is hot with fever and dips in and out of consciousness. Nicolosia is summoned by Ya Ling and the two women have a hurried conversation by the sink. They both look upwards at the noise of the outer door opening and exchange worried looks.

'What's going on here?' Mantegna grumbles. He sees Genevra lying on the kitchen floor. 'That child kept me up half the night.'

'She will be fine soon. It is just a problem with feeding the baby. All will be well soon—' Nicolosia's voice breaks off when she sees a surge of impatience in Ya Ling's eyes.

Cecco leans down, then shoots a meaningful look at his mother before his gaze drops on Ya Ling. 'Genevra looks awful.' He tilts his head sideways. 'Can't she do something for her?'

'Who? Her?' Mantegna jerks his thumb, avoiding looking directly at Ya Ling. 'The slave? What does she know? Apart from disloyalty and trying to make me lose face. Just tell her to keep out of my way. I've not forgiven her for her behaviour in front of your brother.'

Ya Ling quietly withdraws to her room.

'Please, husband.' Nicolosia's eyes fill with tears. 'Genevra's in a bad way, but we'll manage.' She dabs at her eye with her cuff. 'Now, shouldn't you be getting back to the palace?'

Mantegna pulls his wife out of earshot. 'I've come back to sort out a couple of paintings. I've got Bruzzi the surgeon interested but it's probably safer if he comes here.' He gives a deep sigh. 'And I suppose, as he is coming here later anyway, he could have a look at the cook. He's going to think it odd with all this noise going on if I don't mention it.' He glares at Nicolosia as if it is all her fault. 'But he'll charge.'

A couple of hours later Mantegna brings a stranger to the top of the staircase. The man's glance takes in Genevra's fevered moaning on the pallet and he can hear the faint wailing of the baby. 'I thought it was just the woman who was sick,' he says. 'Not the baby as well.' His voice drops in a quiet aside to Mantegna. 'I expect a bigger discount if I treat both of them. Fifty per cent at least. And that's off the cost price.'

Cecco follows them both down the stairs. 'Wife, let me introduce Signor Domenico Bruzzi, surgeon to the Gonzaga court.' Nicolosia gives an inelegant curtsey. 'He is here to admire some of my work and has kindly offered to cure Genevra and the baby who is making so much noise. I had to ask permission from the marchese himself for his surgeon to come.' He looks round as if expecting praise.

He leads Signor Bruzzi back up the stairs. Once in the salon, he brings forwards one of his impressive chairs, unstraps his large leather portfolio and opens it out on the table.

Bruzzi screws up his face. 'Not this one. Not a circumcision painting. That might not sell well.'

'Sell?' Mantegna's eyes narrow on him.

'Not that that's why I'm buying them, of course, I was merely thinking aloud that traditional themes will probably keep their value better.'

'I see.' Mantegna lifts out three paintings from the bottom of the pile and fans them out on the table.

'Listen, so what if I do part with one of them? There's got to be something in it for me. You know what a risk I'm taking buying any of these, so I want a really good price to make it worth my while. We both know you're in no position to argue, so don't waste your breath.' Mantegna steps back in anger at the man's dismissive tone. 'These look better. I like a nice landscape and you can't go wrong with a Madonna and Child or two.'

'I don't think you realise what you are buying, Bruzzi. This is not mere merchandise. This is great art,' says Mantegna. He opens his palms in a proud gesture. 'My name will live on for lifetimes.'

'Do you want my money or not?'

While the men negotiate, downstairs Ya Ling frantically works on Genevra, who flinches and cries out in pain when the baby is put to each breast in turn and gives determined tugs on each nipple. The milk remains firmly blocked and even the cold waterlogged cloths cannot cool the soaring heat that rises out of her body in waves. 'I've never been able to dance much, but I'll try for you, Vittorio.' Genevra's voice rambles and sounds as if it comes from far away. 'Is that oven door open? My head feels as if it's inside!' Her voice is peevish but her smile comes back in an instant. 'All the girls know what a red ribbon means, Vittorio, you cheeky devil. Those loaves must be ready by now. Shut the oven door!' She tries to get up and cries out in pain.

Ya Ling stretches her aching arms over her head, then backs away as Mantegna accompanies Signor Bruzzi downstairs. He looks puzzled at the horrified look in her eyes as she carefully studies the surgeon. Bruzzi holds himself arrogantly as he throws a bloodied sack of knives onto the floor. A couple of flies hover before settling on the film of slime that coats his leather apron. 'Get me a stool.' Bruzzi sits by the pallet and his hard grasping hands on Genevra make her scream out in agony. 'She has milk fever. Both breasts,' he says to Mantegna. Dragging his sack across the floor, he retrieves a grinding stone and a short squat knife. 'They'll both have to come off or she'll be dead in a couple of days.'

Genevra's guttural yell of panic frightens the baby to sudden silence. Nicolosia holds a hand to her throat. Ya Ling recoils in disgust as Bruzzi picks out a random knife and runs the blade raspingly down a sharpening stone, sending a fine sifting of powdered blood down onto the other knives in his sack. She walks over to him. 'No! You're not touching her.'

Bruzzi continues as if he hasn't heard her. 'Are you the husband?' Clemente has turned pale green but he manages a nod. 'Get the groom. We'll need two to hold her shoulders down, and two more to hold her feet. I suggest your lady wife leaves.'

Mantegna sends a furious fist to Ya Ling over Bruzzi's bent head, and glances at his wife, who seems to be looking to the slave woman for guidance.

Nicolosia sends a pleading look to Mantegna, who points his finger at the staircase, looking unnerved at her lack of gratitude. She makes her way reluctantly up the stairs.

Ya Ling pushes the filthy sack away with her foot. 'No! You're not going to cut into her. Or even touch her. Leave her alone! You're not going anywhere near her!'

Mantegna looks at her, his jaw dragged low with shock. He tries a placatory smile at Bruzzi but the man ignores him. 'Get rid of the whore,' Bruzzi snaps. 'Straight away.'

Cecco tries to intervene. 'Ya Ling, he's famous! He's operated on many, many people.'

'Butchered them, you mean.'

Bruzzi's upwards stare takes in Mantegna's mortified stance as the slave woman answers his son back. The stool topples over on the tiles. 'So the whore dictates what happens in the household? The son must plead with her before I ply my craft? I've never seen a spectacle like this in all my life!'

'You'll kill her,' Ya Ling insists quietly.

Mantegna turns his bulky frame as his wife rushes back down the stairs into the room and holds on to his arm. 'Husband,' she murmurs, clasping both hands out in front of her chest like a penitent. 'Don't let this happen. You know what Genevra means to me. How she looked after me like a mother when my own had died. How she loves Cecco as her own. The loyal service she has given my family all her life. And to our family.'

Mantegna's eyes flick down to Genevra's red, quivering face against the grey pallet. 'But I'm doing my best for her. Can't you see that?'

'There are other healers wiser than him.'

He pulls Nicolosia into the corner, his voice low and urgent. 'Listen, wife, Bruzzi is physician to the court. And we've agreed a price on three paintings.'

Nicolosia looks to Ya Ling with desperation in her eyes. Mantegna sees the slave woman almost imperceptibly shake her head. He looks back at his wife, his heavy brows knitted. 'Genevra means more to me than any money,' she says simply. 'We can find someone else to—'

'What nonsense is going on between the two of you?' he demands. 'What's the damned slave up to now?' He turns to Clemente, who is holding on tightly to the back of his chair, seemingly dumbstruck. 'Get the groom when you are told.'

The surgeon runs his grimy thumb along the blade of his knife. The flies swirl over to the kitchen window, attracted by the smell of the pungent midden heap in the courtyard. Bruzzi glares at Mantegna. 'Either kick the whore outside, or I'm leaving.'

Clemente looks intently at Ya Ling. Her eyes close and her head gives the briefest shake. 'It's not that I'm not grateful to you, Maestro. Far from that. But let's just see how my wife gets on.' Clemente's firm voice surprises them all. 'If she is to die anyway, then why make her suffer more? I can't allow that.'

'No. No. No knife. Maestro…' Genevra's voice is barely audible. Her hand lifts helplessly, then falls. Looking down, he sees a tear snaking down her cheek and splashing onto her exposed breast.

Genevra, always so modest and old-fashioned, but now in too much pain to show decorum. Too weak to cover herself. She must be in agony. 'Clemente, whoever takes my place, make sure she will love our baby.'

Mantegna looks over at Nicolosia and sees her gripping the table to stop her hands from shaking. She turns. 'Please, husband, make him leave.'

'Mantegna?' Bruzzi's voice makes them all jump. Mantegna looks from one to the other and sees that all eyes are trained on Ya Ling.

There is a rattling as the surgeon throws the knife and the grinding stone back into his sack. He leans down into Genevra's face. 'When the priest starts giving you the last rites, you'll have these fools to thank.' There is menace in his soft voice. He turns to Mantegna. 'It's a poor sort of a man who lets his whore rule him, but you let her rule your whole household. You'll be a laughing stock in court tomorrow. And worse. The marchese is going to be very interested in you dealing paintings on the sly, isn't he?' He slams the heavy door as he leaves.

The baby's faltering cries begin again. Mantegna manages a stiff glance round the room. 'I don't know what is going on in my household, but any obedience to me, any loyalty whatsoever has been supplanted by loyalty to her. You! Get to your room.' He follows the slave woman and locks them both inside before rounding on her. 'Have you any idea what you have just done? The complete fool you have just made of me? I had to beg Ludovico Gonzaga himself to let Bruzzi come here. And he wouldn't come at first. Not to treat a servant. A woman servant at that! They all think my wits are addled! Perhaps they're right!'

'I'm sorry, Maestro. You are indeed—'

He stops pacing the room and grabs her shoulder. 'Do you realise I had to sign a promissory note using the Gonzaga frescos as surety, just so I could pay him? Ludovico himself witnessed it! Then, he, the marchese himself, handed Bruzzi a fistful of coins. Once word gets round the court that my whore refused to let the palace surgeon, who had express permission from the marchese, anywhere near my servant, and that all my family defer to her and not to me, then my reputation is ruined.'

Thinking quickly, she holds out both hands in front of her. 'Maestro, if I can just—' She takes a step back as he lunges at her. His breath stings her face.

'Now I have to go and beg Bruzzi to keep silent. To try to salvage something of my name. Bribe him with more money. To apologise to him for your insults.' Mantegna runs a hand through his hair.

'Maestro, please…'

'You made me look stupid in front of Gentile, and now this.' He pushes her hard against the wall. 'Time is running out for you in any case. Your shift is starting to look a bit misshapen. You'd better keep out of my sight until I decide what to do with you.' He tightens the manacles on her ankles until she winces, then clips her chain to the wall before he leaves.

Chapter 22

As soon as Gregorio closes the door behind Mantegna's horse, Nicolosia frees Ya Ling and watches in surprise as the slave woman pulls a thin twig of burned wood from the fire and, crouching on the tiles, sketches out an outline. 'Clemente, find me a cabbage in the store room and snap off the darkest leaves.' He lumbers across the kitchen, glad to have a practical task. 'Mistress, can Gregorio take the mare to the forest?' Nicolosia nods immediately. 'Gregorio, look at this leaf. I don't know the word for it in your language, but it has frothy white flowers that turn into berries the colour of wine. Do you know the one?'

Gregorio kneels down beside her. 'Yes I do. I think it's elder. My mother used to make a drink from the elderflowers. Would that be it?'

'Yes! Yes! That's the one. Be quick!'

'Which do you want? There will be plenty of flowers but no berries yet.'

'Neither of those. I want the bark. But it must be very fresh, so just bring me some young thin branches. I'll strip them here.'

While they wait, Ya Ling alternates laying lemon balm-cloths and cabbage leaves round Genevra's breasts and keeps twisting and turning them, ignoring her delirious ramblings, only stopping occasionally to push the baby's frantically searching mouth to her nipples. Clemente and Nicolosia take turns to sponge her burning body with cold well water to try to allay the fever. Gregorio finally bursts back into the kitchen, rustling, carrying several boughs in his arms. Ya Ling snatches off a green leaf and examines it carefully, then her eyes light up as she smiles at Gregorio. 'Wonderful! Just what we need!' she exclaims. He blushes bright pink, then stands aside to watch her grab a paring knife to strip the bark off in long green ribbons. She then lays them on Genevra's breasts and gently massages their cool juices into her skin.

Genevra continues to murmur, her fevered brain clearly leading her down strange pathways. 'Vittorio!' she moans. 'Don't be sad… I have never seen eyes as dark as yours… such long eyelashes! But you know

I mustn't! I am promised... But I give you my word I'll never throw that ribbon away...'

All afternoon Ya Ling continues applying fresh elder bark and using the cabbage leaves to draw the tight swollen curve of Genevra's skin down towards Ernesto's frantic mouth. Finally they all hear a moan of relief from the mother and the loud gulping of a desperate baby. Peace reigns and everyone breathes. After a few minutes of blessed silence, broken only by the sound of the baby suckling, Ya Ling pulls him away from the breast and he yells in outrage, his tiny arms and legs whirring faster than a windmill in a storm.

'No! Leave him. The poor child starves!' Nicolosia says.

'I have to take him away before he becomes too full and sleepy. He still has work to do.'

The child is put to the other engorged breast and latches on tightly until Genevra sobs as the milk begins to flow swiftly like a river undammed. Ya Ling waits until the child falls into a deep sleep, his tiny red face pushed hard against his mother's slackened breasts.

'That was a miracle,' Clemente breathes, looking at Ya Ling in astonishment. She smiles modestly. 'Or magic.' Her smile fades in an instant.

'No, not a miracle, nor magic either.' She looks at Nicolosia carefully. 'I used to help my parents, that's all. When my mother was busy seeing to the other sick people, then I had to help. I have done such things since I was young.' Her soft voice tapers to nothing as she thinks back to the little willow herb basket she used to carry back to their house when she had been foraging with her father in the woods.

Clemente sits with his arm clasped round his wife and child. Ya Ling can scarcely bear to look at the tight family group they make. Her hands briefly move to the front of her dress. 'I don't care what you say, that still looked like magic to me.' He reaches for Ya Ling and squeezes her arm, his eyes filling with tears.

Both wife and child sleep deeply until the evening bell, when the baby wakes up and grizzles hungrily, as if anxious to make up for the lean time he has recently suffered.

'Drink this, Genevra.'

'What's in that?' Clemente asks, looking impressed at the bowl of aromatic liquid that Ya Ling has prepared.

'Mint and camomile, to keep the fever at bay.'

Genevra sits up on the pallet and curves her arm round little Ernesto, who is still clamped determinedly to her, a chubby hand on each side of her breast. She gulps down the tisane and settles back contentedly.

'Still there is one mystery to solve.' Clemente's voice is good-tempered with the relief he feels. 'So tell me this, wife. Tell all of us. Who is this handsome Vittorio? And pray, why did he give you a ribbon?'

Chapter 23

Mantegna looks up and curses. The clouds against the leaden sky look bloated with rain. Pulling himself upwards, he feels the pommel of the saddle jerk sideways and hears a clicking noise. The saddle needs mending and more beeswax polished into it to keep it supple. It feels stiff and unyielding. More expense. Mantegna sighs.

The bloom has gone off the mare too. Her coat looks brittle, and she needs a good kicking and a slash with a whip to get her going. Thank heaven he's sent Gregorio out for firewood or he'd have been standing there, looking on with a long face at that. He'd even dared ask for linseed to put in her bran mash until Mantegna silenced him with a curse. As if he had money for such luxuries.

'You again?' Dati looks flustered for a moment when Mantegna arrives unannounced. Mantegna likes that. It's rare to feel he has the upper hand. 'Maestro, you must please warn me ahead of your intention to visit me, then I can welcome you properly.' His smile fades uneasily and he sends the big Neapolitan servant out for wine and salted almonds. Leading Mantegna up a third staircase to a room high in the eaves, he sits and waits. Dati's eyes lock carefully on Mantegna, who walks over to the window. 'Just passing, Maestro? Out here?'

There's nothing to be seen in the courtyard a long way below. It's empty apart from a cart with a broken shaft. Then the big Neapolitan walks across, dragging behind him a soiled sack that leaves a dark trail on the cobbles. The guard dog rattles frantically to the end of its chain and lunges towards the sack in a fury of barking. 'Come and sit, Maestro.'

'What's he got down there? In the sack?'

'Who?' Dati looks expressionless. 'The servant?'

'I thought you just told him to go for wine.' The man throws the sack into a wooden shed and locks it, kicking the dog away as it scrabbles at the door. Mantegna feels a prickle of unease, wondering what might be in the sack that was driving the dog to such a fury. He glances upwards. A threatening piebald sky looms from the far horizon. The dog still barks. Rain begins hammering down onto the red-tiled rooftops, then streams down onto the cobbles and washes the trail clean.

Dati's voice is sharp. 'Have you come about the child? The one your friend can't afford to keep?'

'I'll be frank, my friend feels uneasy about this arrangement. He wants to do the right thing and be assured that the child will go to an excellent home.' Mantegna's eyes are clouded with doubt.

'I told you, they are a patrician family. Cultured and wealthy. The child will have a wonderful home with all that any child could desire.'

Mantegna shifts in his seat. 'Well, I heard that you were not always trustworthy. Not always prompt at paying.'

'Jealousy. Something we successful merchants are used to.' Dati's sigh is loud and dramatic. 'Competitors are jealous of my success and of my benevolence.'

'So your charitable work is known by many?'

'Within the grounds of discretion, of course.'

'Of course.' Mantegna relaxes a little. 'It's just that I am a father myself and…'

'As indeed am I,' Dati returns smoothly. 'Five sons and three daughters. Three dowries. So you can imagine the expenses of my household.' His knowing glance looks down at Mantegna's shoe where the stitching has come away from the sole. 'We are all slaves to our families, are we not? We all have to do what is in their best interests. Everything we do is to protect them. You and I, we're no different.'

'I've been wondering what that box might be for?'

'Box?'

'You remember, the one you had made at the carpenter's? The gift for your wife?'

'Oh I forget now. Like you, Maestro, I have many ideas, and some are more successful than others. Perhaps if I had your eye for detail…' Dati nods as if impressed. 'Like all great artists.'

Mantegna waves away the compliment.

Filtering into the silence, an odd grieving, plaintive sound comes up from below. 'What's that noise?' Mantegna asks, tapping his ear with the heel of his hand. There is something unnerving about it. Makes him feel restless. Anxious to be gone.

'Maestro, so many questions today. One might think I wasn't being trusted.' The irritation in Dati's voice is barely reined in. 'That would be a pity. Remember, you approached me, and you are the one who stands to gain.' He glances at the window. 'Going to be a heavy downpour and the afternoon is already darkening – might I suggest that as you have arrived here unaccompanied it would be safer not to delay your departure too long, Maestro? This neighbourhood is not safe when darkness falls.'

'But how much will I gain? You seem reluctant to tell me. It's all right for you. You must make a fortune with your moneylending,' Mantegna accuses.

'You think so? Ah, if only it was that simple. Listen to me, when the warehouses are broken into it's always merchants like me who have their money pledges stolen. Don't you find that a coincidence?'

'Still you seem to thrive…' Mantegna looks confused.

'Trust me, lending money is a thankless task. I am too generous, too trusting. An enemy can denounce me at any time, accuse me of usury, then the debts men owe will go up in smoke, probably alongside me, on the pyre.'

'Really?' Mantegna pauses, his hands outstretched. 'But Dati, if it is a girl-child, it will be well tended and well fed. Promise me that at least.'

'Dressed in velvets and fat pearls. The child will live like a child of the Gonzagas. I've already told you that.' Dati smiles broadly up at the Neapolitan who has come into the room. 'At last!' He pulls the cork out with his teeth and spits it on the floor. 'Right up to the brim! Let's be sociable.'

Mantegna braces himself against the chair-back. 'But all the same…'

'Your concern for your friend's child is admirable, Maestro. Like you, I struggle with my conscience. But you can always go to the confessional and wipe your sins clean.'

The wine tastes astringent and seems to stick the inside of Mantegna's lips to his teeth. 'That's not how it works,' he says shortly. 'As you well know.' He holds up his glass. 'This looks cloudy. Where's it from?'

'It's very special. From Toscana. Perhaps heavier than you are used to. It's interesting to try new tastes. Like you do at home. An expensive hobby to have, is it not?' Mantegna looks hard at him. The man is wily all right. Dati holds up his glass. 'To our expensive households. Long may they prosper.' He takes a long pull at the wine.

The glass feels slippery in Mantegna's hand. The wine is very potent. The level is only halfway down the glass but already his limbs are relaxing as warmth creeps up inside his chest. 'To our financial success,' he slurs.

'So when will the child be ready?' Dati asks suddenly.

'A few months yet before birth. Then you said to keep it for two years, didn't you?' The words tumble out.

Dati raises his glass in salute. 'Well, let's hope for a boy. Then your friend won't have to worry.'

Mantegna slides sideways in the chair as if fending off a blow. 'How much will I get?'

'Oh, I'll pay a lot. Let's see how promising the child looks. How pretty its features. How clever it seems.'

'It will be both.' Mantegna stands up so quickly the surfaces around him seem to turn watery and dissolve. 'I can hear that noise again.' Against the clamouring of the rain that strange noise returns and comes echoing up the stairwell. It sounds like a lament, as if little creatures were keening in chorus. After a furious roar from the Neapolitan the noise stops abruptly. 'I've never heard anything like it,' Mantegna says, clutching the banister as he nearly misses a step.

Dati goes to the window. 'Travel carefully. There are some evil men in this *contrada*. But above all, be discreet about our business together, Maestro,' he urges. 'Be discreet.'

Chapter 24

The Gonzaga Palace

At the Palazzo Ducale, Mantegna paces the black and white tiles of a long corridor. He stops and stares at the staircase that leads down to the Casetta dei Nani, the quarters specially built for the court dwarves. The weak rays of the wintry sun pattern the floor by his feet. He watches the squares of light move slowly down to the next block of chequered tiles. Some of the dwarves pass by him for the second time, and begin staring at him and nudging each other. Despite the icy draughts that blow down the corridor, a cloud of warm musty air seems to rise up the stairwell from where they are kept. They all look so busy, so purposeful, bustling up and down the shallow treads of the stairs, some chatting, some chuckling to each other.

A young female one stops at his side. 'May I help you? Are you lost, Maestro? I don't think you want to go down there, do you?' She smiles, indicating the steps that lead downwards. 'We'd never get you out!' Mantegna leans down to look closely at her. He's never looked at one so carefully before. She has pretty eyes the colour of burned sugar, and dark curls down her back that bob as she walks. She waits, looking up at him with a tiny wrinkled brow. 'You are Signor Mantegna, the painter, aren't you?' He nods. 'Then you are a long way from the Camera degli Sposi down here. I expect the dimensions are a bit confusing for you in this part of the palace. Do you want me to guide you back up there?'

'Thank you. I would enjoy your company. And I may even have a special reason for it too.' She gives him a curious smile. 'But first tell me your name.'

'Maria.'

'And tell me something of your life here. Are you happy?' he asks, suddenly needing to know more about her.

She stops in surprise and smiles up at him. 'Of course, Maestro. Why wouldn't I be happy? I have a good job here, and many friends. Why do you ask me that?'

'I don't know. I just find myself curious.' He follows her odd little gait up and down several servant staircases and along different corridors hung with colourful *contrada* flags and shields.

She wrinkles her nose. 'Sorry about the smell along here, they have just sprayed the tapestries with camphor to keep the moth grubs from burrowing into them.'

'You are very knowledgeable.'

'It's really interesting here.' She gives him a conspiratorial grin. 'Always something going on. Much better than my little home village.'

'Good. I'm glad to hear it.'

Stopping on the cloistered walkway, she indicates a panelled door, through which they can hear Settimio's terrible singing. 'Strangling that cat again, Settimio?' Mantegna demands, winking at Cecco who is in the corner mixing grey pigment. He holds the door for her. 'Come in, Maria. Come in.'

'Sorry, Maestro.' Settimio swirls his brush into the water pot, clouding it to pale blue. 'Sorry about the noise.' Both young men fall silent, raising their eyebrows at each other as Maria comes in. Her eyes peer curiously round the white plastered walls, where she can just make out the faint outlines of several arches and balustrades drying into the damp plaster over the fireplace. 'It's like looking at a map, Maestro…' she begins.

He shoots her an appraising look. 'Yes, child, it is. One leading to a masterpiece.'

'Will you be painting all of it? The whole room?' Her jaw drops as she looks round.

'Eventually, but not for a long time. Not until all the building work is completed. I am merely marking out two walls. Planning the placements. Then the other two will be left blank for other artists to work on. Though when I have eventually finished my two masterpieces, I doubt anyone will presume to dare paint the others.' He turns aside. 'Just wait a minute, you two. Move out of my light.'

Cecco exchanges a worried look with Settimio. 'But Father, do you think the marchese will approve?'

Maria shifts uneasily as Mantegna looks angrily at his son. She jumps back when he gently lifts back a handful of her hair and studies her profile. 'Don't worry, maid. I just want to position you by the fireplace and perhaps do a quick sketch. It's good for an artist to include something different.'

'Me, Maestro?' Maria allows him to guide her to the window, then smooths down her skirt.

'I'll try. You are part of the court, aren't you? But I can't promise.' His voice is kind. He looks across at her, first holding up a piece of charcoal, then fashioning an outline of her shape onto a scrap of rag paper. 'After all Ludovico wants me to paint the court true to life.' His arm makes a lofty circular sweep around the mottled patches of plaster on the empty walls.

'What? Me? On one of the walls in here? Goodness.' She smiles excitedly, furrowing back her curls from her forehead with her fingers. 'But I'm nothing special, you know. I'm only a natural,' she murmurs.

'So you're not a pumilio?' Cecco asks.

'Oh sorry. Forgive me, I'm babbling. I'm just not used to being looked at so closely.' She looks nervously from side to side.

'A natural?' Cecco puts his brush down and looks at her closely. 'I've always wondered what the difference is. Is it true they kidnap little ones? And keep them down? Or is it witchcraft? It's just, my friend heard…'

'No.' Maria fidgets with her sleeve. 'I can't.' She looks quickly from Cecco to his father. 'Maestro. Thank you for the honour, but really, I'd better go.'

'Cecco! Leave her alone. How can I draw her with her face all tensed up like that?' Maria shies away from his pointing finger.

'Sorry, Father, but she must have heard things, she's been here for years, and as it's just us in here, I thought she might—'

'Well, don't think! Nobody is interested in what your friend heard, or in you passing on ridiculous court gossip. Look at her posture. Shoulders nearly touching her collar. She looks terrified. Just leave the poor girl in peace.'

Chapter 25

'Pity.' Nicolosia carefully lays one painting on top of another on the polished table in the reception room. 'Bruzzi wouldn't have paid much but it would have been better than nothing.'

Ya Ling wrings the wet floor cloth into the bucket. 'I'm sorry, Mistress.'

'Don't be. Genevra's life is far more important to me than money.' Nicolosia carefully rearranges a vase of dried roses and flicks the dust from the petals with a paintbrush. 'And a few more lean days won't do us any harm. All this fasting… we're going to end up quite saintly,' she says with a brief smile. 'In any case, Signor Bruzzi has a reputation for talking big and paying small.'

'May I? I have never seen any of the maestro's work.'

'Of course, if you wish. Come over here by the light.' The paintings rustle as she selects one. 'This one is a circumcision.'

'I'm surprised Bruzzi didn't want it. He seems to love the knife.'

Nicolosia laughs. 'You don't like it?'

Ya Ling shakes her head. 'It makes me think of Chen, our family eunuch, and what he must have suffered. What pain he must have gone through. I like to look at beauty, not cruelty.'

'Eunuch? You had a family eunuch? Mother of God!' Nicolosia crosses herself. 'How barbaric they are in eastern lands. Such savages! You would never find anything like that here. The Holy Mother Church would never allow anything so cruel. No. Here we are civilised. Cultured. With great artists and poets.'

'I know, Mistress.' Ya Ling's lips press together tightly as she thinks of the talk in the kitchen of flayings, of burnings, the strappado and the cage. She busies herself lining up two paintings next to each other on the table. 'Are they always flat like this?'

Nicolosia looks bemused, then nods. 'Of course.'

'I prefer scrolls. It's lovely unrolling a painting and a story coming to life. Is this the White Christ and his mother?' Nicolosia nods. 'Then why does he paint two pictures of them?'

'Because these are the kind of paintings most people want, for all sorts of reasons. For their beauty of course, but for keeping evil at bay and keeping in good favour with God as well.' Ya Ling stares at the first painting, holds it with her arms stretched out, then close to, then stares again, her eyes widening and then tightening their focus on the baby the mother holds.

'Well, what do you think?'

'May I be honest?'

'I expect nothing else from you.'

'She looks familiar.' Ya Ling purses her lips. 'The expression on the mother's face, it gives me a pain here.' She taps her chest. 'But he hasn't got the shape of the little one right, has he? The baby's head is too top-heavy for its body, and the face looks too puffed out. Perhaps it's sick.'

Nicolosia leans her head to one side. 'It's a new technique. I know it looks a bit strange when you are close up to it, but you have to imagine it hanging high on a wall. Like this.' She stands on tiptoe, holding the painting as high as she can.

Ya Ling purses her lips. 'It still looks squashed to me.'

'Don't let him hear you say that, for heaven's sake! Of course, both of my brothers are brilliant at foreshortening. At everything really. Landscapes. The human form. Everything.' She brings her face closer to the painting. 'But you're right, in these recent paintings, the Madonna looks far more sad than he usually paints.'

'And what are these?' Ya Ling picks up the next painting and points to creatures with wings that look like chubby little boys, tumbling about the skies and forming a frame around the image of the Madonna.

'Those are called putti.' Ya Ling rolls the word round like a new taste. 'Little cherubim.'

'What?'

'Like little angels.'

Ya Ling shakes her head. 'And what are they?'

Nicolosia's dark eyebrows rise. 'I'm so used to you now, I sometimes forget that you're not Catholic. Not one of us. It's hard to describe what putti are. I suppose they are like a guardian spirit. Halfway between humans and the Divine.'

'I've seen them in Mantova. I knew they came from the spirit world.'

Nicolosia turns with a scornful smile. 'You've seen angels, Ya Ling? Where? Flying over the rooftops?'

'No. Not up there. But I have definitely seen putti coming out of a merchant's house in the big piazza with the mulberry tree in the middle. The day I ran away. I couldn't see their wings because they were dressed. Very expensively too. One even wore a velvet cape.'

Nicolosia's face falls and her finger darts up in warning. 'No. Ya Ling, those aren't putti. They are playthings, the pets of the rich. Poor little souls. It's best not to ask too much about them.'

'Clemente told me the same thing when I saw them in the big procession. Why?'

'Enough! No one really knows how they come to be as they are. Some even say witchcraft is involved. So no more questions.' Nicolosia beckons her back to the pool of light from the window. 'Now come over here. This one is a landscape, see the two saints? San Giacomo and San Giovanni are being called to follow Christ.'

'Landscape?' Ya Ling stares doubtfully for several moments at the stony archway and the stark grey rocks beyond, her expression barely changing. 'Has he not learned to use colours?' she asks politely.

Nicolosia claps her hand over her lips but her deep chuckle threatens to spill out between her fingers. 'Ya Ling! You can't say that! The maestro is the most highly regarded painter in Mantova! Can't he do colours indeed!'

'Or weeping willows swaying in the wind? Or plum blossoms? Or frothing waterfalls? I know he'll never be as good as Dai Jin, because no one in the world could ever match him. And I know the maestro won't be able to do any elegant calligraphy, but I thought he might at least try to put in a couple of cranes in flight. They always look so beautiful, so graceful when painted flying over waterfalls with their black-tipped wings spread out like great fans. Perhaps he hasn't learned how to do those yet. Or perhaps he's tried and he just can't.'

'Weeping willows? Blossoms? Birds? Oh dear.' Nicolosia doubles over as more laughter bubbles to the surface.

'Or an egret or two, if cranes are too difficult for him. Some bamboo. Plum blossoms might be too delicate too, but he might be able do a few if he practised a lot.'

Nicolosia leans over and rests both hands on the table. 'I'll ask him when he comes back.' She gasps for breath. 'He'll really like that.'

Both turn at the sound of a bag being thrown down heavily on the damp floor. 'You won't have to wait that long,' Mantegna says, glowering at both of them. 'I'm already here.'

'Let me take your cloak, husband,' Nicolosia's voice soothes as she reaches forwards. 'The slave didn't mean any criticism of your great work, Maestro, she is just from a primitive land, that's all, with little culture and art of only the most rudimentary—'

'Leave us, wife.' Ya Ling tries to follow her quickly out of the room. Mantegna calls to her before she reaches the door. 'My wife might suddenly seem to think a great deal of you, but I don't. Not any more.' His fists tighten. 'Daring to disparage my work. Be warned. I've heard quite enough from you.'

Chapter 26

The Camera degli Sposi, Gonzaga Palace

The queue stretches all the way down the corridor at the palace, the noise from the courtiers rising like a flock of starlings. At the end of the queue is a quiet group of serving maids and a dark-skinned slave with a black and white headdress.

Mantegna calls them all into the Camera degli Sposi. 'You all know why you are here,' he begins importantly. 'Preliminary planning of who I might choose. Let me introduce my son Cecco, who some of you may know, and Settimio the apprentice. I will start with the maidservants. A chosen few will be on my ceiling. The oculus. It is a great honour.' Mantegna lies on the floor and the women nudge each other and smile behind their fingers. Cecco beckons them to stand in a circle and peer down at him. 'I definitely want the dark one. The contrast against the blue sky will be magnificent. Tell her to wear that same headdress for each sitting. You, you and you two with the headbands. Four of them, with the slave and the peacock, and all the putti should be plenty of detail up there.' Cecco makes a careful note of their names. Mantegna stands and brushes the plaster dust off his tunic. 'Quiet! All of you!' he barks. 'My son and apprentice will now group you according to height and hair colour, then we will discuss the composition of each group. I will then choose those lucky enough to be painted in the fresco that will depict the Gonzaga family and a few of their courtiers.' The room erupts with an expectant buzz. 'I need a respectful silence for this task. Never forget, gentlemen, you are competing for a place in posterity.' The room falls silent. Mantegna turns in irritation at a repeated burst of shrill laughter. 'Who is that?' he demands to know.

A giggling small boy is pushed forwards from where he has been hiding behind a group to the side of the fireplace. 'What's your name, child?'

The boy rearranges his green silk cap, which has slipped sideways on his shiny black curls. Mantegna notices the child's opulent clothes;

his *tabarro* is of figured blue velvet and his silken hose are green and blue, fashioned in a much older style than is appropriate for a child. They are not the only thing about him that is precocious, Mantegna thinks, noticing the challenge in the child's eyes. 'I am Enzio, page to Barbara of Brandenburg,' says the child.

'Well, the joke is over, Enzio,' Mantegna says shortly, then nods at the door. 'You can leave.'

'No. I want to be in the painting.' He jerks his thumb at the wall over the fireplace.

'How old are you?'

The child stares up at him. 'I am seven. And my father is the richest wool merchant in Mantova.' Enzio swirls his little hips around, allowing the pleats of his *tabarro* to fan out for emphasis. 'And he lends money to the marchese, so I don't have to follow the rules.'

The room becomes very quiet. Mantegna steps forwards on the balls of his feet. 'Get out, child, when you're told.'

'But I want to be in the frescos.' He pouts. 'My father will complain to the marchese if I am not.'

All eyes swivel expectantly to Mantegna, a snigger or two is heard from the back of the crowd and one or two of the young men lean together to whisper asides.

'Don't worry, Maestro, I'll see to it.' Settimio holds the child firmly under his arm. 'Come along, Enzio.'

Enzio pulls away and steps boldly forwards. 'Just let me be in it.' His chin comes up in demand.

'No, child,' Settimio reasons. 'The only children in the fresco will be those of the Gonzaga family.'

Enzio stamps his shiny leather shoes on the red tiles and turns to the crowd of courtiers still packed into the room. 'He's not a proper painter, anyway. Bruzzi says he's only a puppet. Everyone knows that. Bruzzi says that even his whore has him on tight strings. Like this.' Enzio drops his head in a sudden twitch and jerks his knees and elbows upwards. A surge of stifled laughter is heard from the back of the crowd, and it ignites into an irresistible flicker that roars round the room like wildfire. Settimio and Cecco catch Enzio midway just as he is attempting a dramatic bow to his audience. Mantegna comes up fast behind, but the child clearly knows the layout of the palace very well and soon disappears from view.

'Father, wait! Wait until you have calmed down.' Cecco's arm is shaken off and Mantegna breaks into a run all the way to the Marchese Ludovico's apartment.

'Why, Maestro, you look quite put out.' Mantegna sits on the bench Marsilio Andreasi indicates. 'Get the Marchese Ludovico for me now!' he fumes. 'I am calling a vendetta against Signor Bruzzi, and I want the Marchese Ludovico to stand witness to it.'

Marsilio draws in a draught of air. 'But this is not a good time, Mantegna. There is a banquet tonight to celebrate the arrival of three cardinals from the Vatican, then there will be a private conclave when we are hoping the cardinalate of the marchese's son will be brokered.'

'I have to see him!' Mantegna's face puckers in fury. 'My honour has been impugned by Bruzzi, and a pageboy called Enzio has just cast a slur on my reputation as a painter.'

'I'll see what I can do.'

By the time the Marchese Ludovico arrives, Mantegna's temper has ratcheted even higher. He sips the glass of wine he has been served and can barely articulate to the marchese what has happened.

Ludovico Gonzaga lays a conciliatory hand on his arm. 'Now is a very sensitive time at court, as I know my private secretary has just informed you, so I will need to ask for your patience on this matter, just for a while. But Maestro, you need to calm down. You look so choleric, I fear for the health of the renowned artist who I am confident is going to make my frescos a wonder of the known world.'

'Let's see.' Marsilio Andreasi coughs. 'Just so I am sure I have all the facts at my fingertips, Maestro, there are rumours that Bruzzi went to your house to buy some paintings. The marchese and I know that these cannot be true as you have promised both of us not to undertake any more paintings, or private commissions of any sort, until the frescos are completed. And they are not even properly begun.'

Ludovico's voice has an undercurrent of steel as he takes up the subject. 'And Bruzzi also gossips that you still retain your mistress, yet you have been warned by me personally just how sensitive such matters currently are. He has even intimated that' – Mantegna strains forwards – 'it looks as if she might be with child. Of course, as a surgeon he is probably more attuned to such matters.'

Mantegna says nothing. The marchese looks into the middle distance as if reminiscing. 'And Enzio is a child indeed. Impudent and irrepressible. As we all were once,' he goes on. 'And whose father is financing much of the rebuilding of the palace – in particular he has promised a donation for the moving of the window and for the restoration of the fireplace in the Camera degli Sposi, where your marvellous frescos will eventually be seen.'

'But, Maestro, even his generosity is as nothing compared to the marchese,' Marsilio Andreasi breaks in, giving his master an admiring glance. 'But who has now decreed with regret that there will be no more advances and no more private sales whatsoever.'

'But stay today and share privately in the feast, which is being prepared for our illustrious guests from the Vatican,' the marchese says. 'You may return this evening to this room and enjoy one of the special carp from my private lake.' The marchese lays a dignified hand on his chest. 'Accept it by way of my personal recompense to you.'

Mantegna knows he is beaten. After the evening bell he returns, and a row of servants bring in a boiled carp with the Gonzaga insignia picked out in coloured rice, the huge gaping head garlanded by a circlet of bay leaves like a Roman emperor. A basket of white bread and a flagon of Rhenish wine are laid on a side table and maiolica bowls of creamy junket strewn with tiny blue borage flowers are put down beside them. Mantegna plunges a knife into the silver flank of the fish and curses as fish juice spurts down the front of his *tabarro*. He swallows several tasteless mouthfuls. He has run out of options. Everything conspires against him. His empty money chest. The new piety of the court, and a mistress soon to be heavy with child. What he might have to do to the slave woman is the worst thing he can imagine doing to any woman. But she has asked for it. Making him look a fool in front of Gentile. Then Bruzzi. And now the whole court thinking him a *buffone* and laughing at him behind his back, tearing his hard-won reputation to shreds.

An image of her holding his paintings up to Nicolosia, inveigling her to laugh at his talent, springs into his mind. Daring to ridicule his artistry and his repute. Mantegna reaches across and stabs the knife into the fish, working it deep between the bones. The fish lies in pieces on the platter, its jaw grimacing open as if in outrage. His churning conscience feels easier when he stands and makes to leave. He'll ask a priest to pray for a boy-child. One that looks nothing like a heathen – then he can apprentice him. And if it does turn out to be a girl, then Ya Ling has brought this upon herself.

Chapter 27

Mantegna waits until early dawn when the house is silent before he strides in and shakes her. 'Rouse yourself. We're going.'

She sits up wide-eyed. 'What? Now, Maestro? Where?'

'Never mind that. Just gather your things and be silent. And if you ever try coming back and showing your face around here, I'll tell an advocate about the bolt of damask you stole.'

Ya Ling's face remains an amber mask. 'But Maestro, you know that I would never steal from your household.'

'Well, perhaps a few jerks on the strappado will loosen your memory. Or when the flames start singeing your feet. You won't be quite so pretty with your nose cut off.'

'What? Maestro, please.' Her eyes flick anxiously from side to side. 'Of course I'll make ready. Of course. But where are you taking me?' With a sinking heart, she quickly dresses and gathers the velvet dress into a neat roll. Mantegna has lost face. She knows punishment is due. It has already cost her a whipping that makes her stiffen to remember.

The bricks come away easily and she tucks the sharpened spoon into her shift, then stuffs the bindings up her sleeve. Mantegna is waiting for her outside the harness room with his mare already saddled and the mule on a lead rein with a wooden box strapped to its back. He scrambles up onto the mare and pulls her up behind him. 'I can't afford to be seen with a pregnant slave, and I can barely afford to feed you either. If it is a boy-child then I might reconsider.' He shoots her a glance over his shoulder. 'But I warn you, if you try to run, I'll have you in the cage by nightfall.'

The Piazza delle Erbe is just beginning to wake up. Merchants shout good-naturedly to each other as they set up their stalls beneath the arcades. Great yellow wheels of hard dry cheese are rolled over the cobbles, and fishmongers prise open their barrels of pike and lay them out in glistening patterns. Mantegna curses and turns the mare's head to avoid the milk boy staggering under the two wooden pails on his yoke. They soon leave their *contrada* behind and turn off, clipping down a series of lanes until they ride along a wide river bank and cross a rickety bridge over the River Mincio.

The smells of the soapworks and the tannery make Ya Ling splutter. After two hours of the mule's stubborn pace, Mantegna turns the mare down a series of mean alleys until they reach the huts on the outskirts of a slum. The sight of all the beggars who come clamouring around unsettles the mule with their flapping rags and their filthy stench. The mud-cracked lanes are paved with small fires, and Ya Ling hates the heat and the pall of acrid smoke that hangs low like a grey shroud and scrapes the back of her throat. Mantegna dismounts and approaches a small, poky hut set back from the rest. Ya Ling follows, waiting nervously while he unlocks it. The hut is round with a roof of branches and a floor of packed earth.

'Here, Maestro?' Ya Ling looks round the dark interior, aghast. There is nothing inside. Beyond, the slum. 'You can't be leaving me here? Not with the child coming. What will I eat? How will I feed the baby?'

He lifts the box down and bangs it on the floor. 'This is the best I can do. I'm not made of money. In any case I'm not even sure if the child is mine.'

'But Maestro, who else could I have lain with?'

He scuffs his shoe on the dusty floor. 'Some masters wouldn't be anywhere near as generous, to rent a room for their whore, not after they've been publicly humiliated. Everyone at court is laughing at me because of you.'

Shouts are heard outside, furious threats, then the sound of running feet. Ya Ling looks over her shoulder fearfully. 'But it's so dangerous. And I will be alone here when my time comes.'

'There will be other women here, they'll help.' Mantegna brings out a padlock and key from the box. He lays out a threadbare cloak and a tattered brown blanket and throws a loaf and a small knife on top of them before he lifts out a small iron pot and puts it on the hearthstone in the middle of the floor.

'When will you come back?' She rests her hand on his plump waist and lets it drift lower.

He moves away and leans against the dusty wall. 'Not often,' he says carefully. 'But if it's a boy and strong, then I might apprentice him.' He leans down into the box and hands her a leather bottle and a handful of coins. She looks at them, her eyes blank with apprehension. 'And you can find work here. Plenty of it around in the hemp fields. I'll come once before you have the child and after it's all over.'

'But giving birth? Here?' She levels her leaden gaze on him, a hand now on her stomach, until he looks away.

'You'll manage somehow. Lots of women do.' He presses the key into her hands before he leaves. 'You should have thought this might happen before you ruined my reputation.' He whips the mare into a trot, dragging the sullen mule behind them all the way home.

Nicolosia reacts in a way guaranteed to infuriate him. 'Ya Ling, a thief?' she asks in that underhand way of hers. Her gaze takes in their quiet kitchen, with its sacks of polenta and chickpeas and the box of chestnuts Gregorio has gathered in the forest. She looks through the thick glass of the window to the outline of the oak trees in the field beyond their wall. In a few months those branches will be wearing snappy white coats of frost. 'Risked food and shelter for a strip of damask? I don't believe it!'

'She stole the cloth, wife. Haven't I just said so? Tell the others as a warning.'

'But she's wise beyond her years. She'll know exactly what lies in store for her outside the safety of our family, the dangers for an unprotected woman like her that lie waiting on the other side of our walls. You should never have let her go.' Nicolosia's voice rises. Mantegna turns to her in surprise. 'Think of all the agues that lie ahead for Cecco! Think of that terrible hacking cough he has every winter when the thick fog from the lakes brings the yellow bile back onto his chest. And have you forgotten him shivering all last summer? When he becomes ill again, where will I turn?'

'What on earth have Cecco's agues got to do with a thieving slave woman?' Nicolosia drops her accusing gaze. 'It's a miracle the boy has lasted as long as he has, and thanks to your disobedience he might be the last son there'll ever be for my workshop.' He gives a mean sideways smile, imagining Nicolosia's face when he presents Ya Ling's fine lusty son to her. How she'll hate that! A free apprentice too. Just as long as the child bears no evidence of its heathen blood. The child is his, after all, to do with as he chooses.

'But husband—'

'Enough. She's gone, I tell you, and I don't want her name spoken again.'

The door bangs behind him and Gregorio barely has time to open one of the doors before the mare canters through as he makes his way back to the workshop.

Later that morning Cecco stands back to admire the bold sweep of his father's brush. 'You seem in a better mood today, Father…'

'I am, son. I am.' He is gratified at how easily the horse's massive muscular neck curves onto the wet plaster. He's done what he had to do. His conscience feels lighter already.

After Mantegna has left, Ya Ling locks the door in a daze and sinks down on the floor, clutching the leather bottle. She feels a surge of loneliness sweep over her as the future opens ahead like a void. Fragments of conversation between her parents and Chen slide into her mind. 'Never let Little Sister out of your sight in the hutong. Guard her from the sun with your parasol at all times.' She remembers laughing at Chen when he tried to avert her gaze from the courtesan being carried in her sedan chair to the Forbidden City. How confident she had been. How anxious to get away and begin her new life. How assured of the golden future with Altan that lay ahead. For several hours she relives fragments of shared memories, snippets of conversation that had seemed so banal at the time, but were now more precious than a casket of jade from the emperor's palace.

As she takes a sip from the bottle she feels a tiny stir from the baby pocketed deep inside her and the bottle almost slips from her trembling fingers. As her heart begins to pump uneasily she makes herself sit up straight and begins to tighten her resolve, aligning it to a firmer shape. She takes on reality like a strong mantle and spans both hands protectively across the swell of her stomach. One of Baba's Lao Tzu sayings springs to mind. *He who knows that enough is enough will always have enough.* Somehow she will have to manage. She looks at her surroundings with fresh eyes. She has shelter. Food and enough water for now, and tomorrow she will find work. She takes out the velvet dress and gives it a hard shake, and her face becomes set and steely. Using the spoon, she digs a hole in the earth floor, hides the coins and then stamps down hard. She tears off a quarter of the loaf and lies on the cloak willing sleep to come. She'll need plenty of energy for tomorrow.

The night is broken by the sound of brawling and screams, and when the door is thumped and the handle is rattled hard she grabs hold of the knife and holds it in front of her until dawn filters down through the branches on the roof and spatters grey light onto the floor. She unlocks the door and follows the straggling queue of people to the hemp fields, where the gangmaster looks askance at her slight frame and her neat shift and pulls in a breath noisily through his rotten teeth. 'You'll not last long here,' he grumbles.

'I will. You'll see.' Her voice is thin and anxious but she grabs the sickle, a straw wreath for her head and the willow basket that sits on it and walks quickly into the hot overgrown field. She copies the next woman in the row. The work is backbreaking, weeding the rows of towering hemp and breaking the dry clods of soil in the next field ready for replanting after the harvest. Fatigue throbs behind her eyes and the glare from the sun makes her head ache. The basket soon fills with weeds and is emptied at the end of the row many times, but she works doggedly on. Finally a bell is rung and the workers collapse under the feathery shade and bring out their bread. No one talks to her and she is conscious of muttering from the grimy-faced men who eye her. They fall silent when the gangmaster walks down the row. The last bell of the day is a signal for the workers to congregate by the wine stall set up at the end of the field.

'Come, maid, shake off your aches and pains with a glass. I'll stand you the first one. You can offer me something in return, I'm sure,' says a big sinewy man with skin like tannery leather. He licks his lips, making the group of men standing next to him laugh. Ya Ling keeps her head down and, ignoring the catcalls, runs all the way back to her hut, where she stays. The knife handle feels insubstantial in her slippery hand but, listening to the door being shaken and the drunken calls outside, she feels safer with it held close.

The next morning as she walks to the fields the mist hangs heavily down, punctured by the church towers and the many turrets of the Gonzaga Palace in the distance. She longs to run back and lock herself in her hut but the tiny scrap of life begins to quicken inside her stomach as if giving her a reminder.

Out of the mist to her right a woman looms up unexpectedly and wrenches her arm round. 'Come here, bitch! This is my territory!' Ya Ling looks straight into a filthy face drilled with pockmarks and purple with the broken veins of a drinker. 'My turf! Nobody gets away with catting on my turf! I'll show you.'

As the woman lifts up her arm Ya Ling sees the glint of a knife and smells the sour smell of old wine. Her scalp prickles with fear but she dodges to one side, then shoves the woman, who topples over heavily, bringing up a cloud of red dust as her head bangs hard on the floor. Ya Ling snatches the woman's knife and her own and holds them one at each end of the woman's throat as she kneels on her chest. Ya Ling's own throat is dry with fear and the words come rasping out. 'One word from you and I'll make these knives meet in the middle.' She presses the blades hard into the woman's filthy neck until she moans and asks for mercy. A crowd has gathered around them and a ripple of muttering runs round it. 'You can keep your territory. I'm not a whore like you. I'm just here to work in the fields. Now what's your name?'

'Gilda.' The woman's voice is coarse. 'Get her off before she cuts my throat.'

Ya Ling looks up and stands, moving both knives slowly round the crowd. Some of the women step back quickly. Her voice comes out unnervingly fierce. 'Remember. I let her go. The next one might not be as lucky.'

The gangmaster walks in front of her along the fence that leads to the field and holds back the straw wreath with a sneer before he drops it on her head like a crown. 'God help you when Gilda sobers up,' he says grimly.

'I'm not afraid of her.' Ya Ling turns the wreath round and round on her head, flicking away the straws as they flake off.

'Well, you should be. She's cleverer than she looks. She runs a lot of things round here and not just the cathouse either. She supplies the wine for the fools who drink their wages every night, sells old clothes and runs a gang of poachers. You're a fool to have crossed her.' His glance drops to the outline of Ya Ling's shift. 'And it looks like you might have need of her other skills.'

She tilts her head back to scan his face. 'What do you mean?'

'She's the midwife round here. There's no one else.'

Ya Ling thinks hard as she toils on, and by the time the sun has dropped low in the sky she has made up her mind. The gangmaster tells her where Gilda lives and she makes her way there, first picking up the velvet dress before fear takes hold of her.

A stale smell wafts out of Gilda's hut and she finds her dozing on a pile of old clothes. She wakens instantly and scrambles to her feet. 'You! What do you want?'

Ya Ling smooths down the nap of the velvet and holds it out in front of her. 'How much for this?'

The woman's eyes open wide but her lips soon crease downwards. 'Not much,' she snaps like a reflex.

'Then get what you can, and I'll split it with you.'

'No chance.'

Ya Ling takes the knife out of her pocket and holds the blade up to the light briefly, then pushes it quickly back into her pocket before it can fall out of her trembling fingers. 'One last time. How much?' she demands gruffly.

'Depends. Who slit your eyes?'

'What?' Ya Ling stares in surprise.

'You stupid or something?' Gilda stretches the skin at the corner of each eye upwards with two fingers. 'Who did that to you? The same bastard who got you pregnant?'

Ya Ling thinks quickly and decides to nod. 'Yes. The same one.'

'Well, you're a tough little bitch, I'll give you that. No wonder you're handy with a knife.' She picks up the dress. 'Come back in three days.' Ya Ling notices how carefully the woman folds the dress and rests it on an empty barrel. 'What you waiting for?' She tries to roll a barrel to the door but struggles.

'I'll do that for you.' Ya Ling steps in front of her and rolls the barrel down the lane to the wine stall, where a restless queue has gathered. The gangmaster waves his whip at the hands already grabbing for the barrel.

Ya Ling turns to him. 'What grows round here that I can eat?' She senses Gilda cocking an ear even as she puts two rows of stained wine bowls on the table.

He nods at the hemp fields. 'You can eat the leaves and the seeds have a bit of oil in them. That's about it. Anything else round here will have been stripped clean.'

Gilda looks irritated when Ya Ling lifts the barrel and starts pouring out the first row of bowls, until her attention is taken by the coins being held out. Ya Ling makes sure everyone there sees her helping Gilda and talking to the gangmaster before they are too fuddled to remember. When they're all sprawling in groups under the birch trees, Gilda is on her third bowl of wine and Ya Ling manages to slip a coin into her pocket.

The gangmaster comes across and puts his whip on the table. 'You can pick up the white rice that's fallen from the barges on the river-bank, but you'll need plenty of patience. My wife picks it sometimes, but it drives her mad.'

'Patience? Oh I've got plenty of that.' Ya Ling stretches her aching back.

'Then you need to look out for the flat-keeled boats coming upriver. The ones pulled by the mule teams. A girl like you might get the odd pocketful given.'

'She'd get a lot more than that given to her if she worked for me,' Gilda says with a sneer. 'But she thinks she's too good for the cathouse. Still, it's early days yet.'

Three days later Ya Ling returns to Gilda's hut. Three *triplo testoni* coins are waiting for her in one of the wine bowls. Gilda stands in the doorway as Ya Ling turns to leave. 'I'll have some of that back,' she challenges, nodding at the curve at the front of Ya Ling's shift. 'For when your time comes.'

Ya Ling tries to keep her lips buoyant as she takes in the rags on the floor, the thick collar of cobwebs on top of the doorframe and the dirt that crunches underfoot. 'I want to have the baby in my own hut.' With a sigh, she holds out one of the coins. 'Do you have any children, Gilda?'

The woman's face shrinks as if she has been struck. 'Mind your own sodding business. Stay out of my sight until you can only count to twenty between the pains. Don't bother me any sooner.' Ya Ling hands her a little sack before she leaves.

'What's this?' she says, suspicious.

'A present.'

The gangmaster looks equally puzzled at the similar hessian sack Ya Ling puts on his table the next morning when she arrives before the others to start work. 'I've picked the chaff out of it too. Your wife's right. It's a very long job.'

His hand bounces the weight a few times and his eyes on her are shrewd. 'What are you after?'

'I want to be picked to work inside. When the cold weather comes.' She pats her stomach. He nods briefly. 'And I'll get you more rice when I can.'

Ya Ling gradually gets to know the alleyways near to her hut. Gilda pays protection money to a criminal family to help her run her businesses in her little *contrada* without any trouble and it's safer to stay inside Gilda's empire. Ya Ling soon knows where to gather acorns and blackberries before anybody else gets to them, where to buy the freshest chickpeas, whose bread has more barley than oak bark and which fruit seller doesn't notice when the odd orange or lemon goes missing up the sleeve of her shift.

The hemp harvest is backbreaking work, made worse by the weight of the baby pulling her forwards and the dull persistent ache in her back. One night Ya Ling can't sleep, and buzzes with a restless energy, sweeping the floor over and over again and rearranging her few possessions. On the hemp row she leaves her sickle embedded in a tough stalk when the baby kicks hard, making her draw in a lungful of hot dusty air that makes her gasp and cough. Hot eddies of pain begin to burn brighter when a juddering of unbiddable muscle makes her fall to her knees and cry out. The woman behind her runs for the gangmaster. 'It's her time. Get her home. Send for Gilda,' he says.

Ya Ling lies on her blanket, hearing the low moaning in her own throat, like the lowing of a doomed animal. Tears run down each side of her face and wet the blanket below her. She sobs in fear behind gritted teeth as if trying to muffle the sound, but it still pours out. She longs for Baba's wisdom, for Mama's cool capable hands, for Ayi's warm lap to lay her head on and have her hair stroked back from her face with a silk cloth soaked in jasmine oil. For Chen to pace anxiously round the courtyard. But most of all she longs for Altan's strong arms and his conviction that everything will always turn out well.

Gilda puffs herself into the hut, hauls Ya Ling to her knees and rocks her roughly backwards and forwards. 'Push now. Then hold back until I tell you.' Ya Ling notices that Gilda's rough-skinned hands are surprisingly pink and clean and feels a moment of reassurance before she is buffeted by the next wave of pain. The church bells ring out several times, marking the passing of the day, and she hears the workers' bell and the nearby market bell signalling the end of trading, but the pains only continue and intensify. At one point a stream of curses comes out of Ya Ling's panting mouth that makes Gilda chortle. Just at the moment when she feels her body being pulled raggedly apart she hears Gilda's shout. 'Nearly there. The head's nearly out. Don't give up. Two big pushes and it's out.' Ya Ling feels a great watery gush and an indescribable feeling of relief. 'It's a girl.' The disappointment in Gilda's voice is palpable. 'But it's fine. It looks all right. You got anything to swaddle it?'

Ya Ling nods at the roll of binding cloths she has washed and watches intently as the baby flails her fists and lets out a trebly yell at the cold cloth Gilda uses to wipe her down. Ya Ling pulls herself up on an elbow. 'No, let me see her first.' She holds out her arms to nestle her tiny pearly-limbed daughter and anxiously counts her fingers. Only five on each hand. Ya Ling sags back onto the blanket with relief.

'I told you she's all right,' Gilda grumbles but there is a brief crack in the hard veneer of her face as she swaddles the baby. 'What are you calling her?'

'I don't know.' None of the auspicious names she has thought of translate well.

'You could try Fortuna,' Gilda suggests as she ties the ends of the binding cloths together. 'She'll need all the luck she can get.'

When the warm swaddled baby is handed to her Ya Ling holds her tightly in the crook of her arm, her eyes raking the baby's face. A shock of tenderness takes her unawares. The baby's skin is pink and translucent like the inside of a shell. Her hand cups the frail downy head and feels a tiny pulse beating beneath the soft dip at the top of her scalp.

Ya Ling holds the child to her breast and at each vigorous little tug she knows with absolute certainty that her life is now inextricably connected to her daughter's. She will postpone her escape to Beijing until she has enough money to do so safely and with enough status to command respect when she gets there. Fine clothes. A little jewellery. Her brows knit together. *Don't adjust the goals, adjust the action steps.* A cover story will have to be carefully thought out – an adoption perhaps. Her daughter is far too precious to her ever to be looked down on as inferior, to be shunned as born out of wedlock, to be seen as anything less than perfect. She kisses the soft mouth and smells her daughter's warm breath. Fortuna. That's what she will be called. Fortuna, after the goddess of luck. To make her way in the world she will need an auspicious name. She makes a silent vow over the dark downy head. 'Fortuna, you will have everything I can give you. I will work myself into the ground to give you the best life I possibly can.'

A week later when Mantegna arrives, his response is less enthusiastic. 'Oh. A girl.'

'Maestro would like to hold her?' Ya Ling offers the child out to him, a winning smile on her lips.

'No new apprentice for me then.' His curls shake. He looks accusingly at Ya Ling, then glances round the hut and makes to go. He pauses at the door. 'It's costing me a fortune to keep you here as well. I'll try for a while, but I make no promises.'

Chapter 28

For the rest of the summer, wherever she works she puts the baby in the shade, where weak sunlight washes through the birch trees and makes the shadows shiver on the ground. When the air becomes crisp with autumn and the chaff burns each day in the wheat fields, she is glad to be working in the indoor drying sheds, stripping the fibres from the hemp stalks and watching over the baby's basket while she beats and combs the hemp into white straggly lengths. The baby starts a troublesome cough, and her tiny fists keep pulling down the little scarf that Ya Ling has made to wind round her mouth. When ice begins to heal over the watermeadows and snow starts to muscle the trees, she bribes the gangmaster to let her keep her job indoors until the warmer weather. The cough worsens and Ya Ling despairs of being able to afford the herbs she needs.

Time passes and despite Ya Ling's efforts the child fails to gain weight as she should. Life remains hard. Ya Ling is often hungry and always exhausted, but Fortuna has survived her second winter. Mantegna has only been to see her twice, once before and once after the baby was born, but at least the rent is still being paid.

One cool March morning when she is outside spring planting with the child bundled against her back, the gangmaster shouts her name down the row and waits as she walks up to his table. 'There's a man come to see you. I'm docking you half a day.'

Ya Ling blinks, then swiftly hurries down the muddy lane. She glances up at the sun trying to break through the leaden clouds and drops a kiss on her daughter's head. 'You are well named, my little Fortuna. Your papa has finally come to see you again. Perhaps he will give us money, then I can find better work and save more so we can get that boat home. So that's what you must call him when you see him. Say Papa!'

The child tries to wind a finger through her mother's dusty hair and pulls it hard. 'Papapapa?' she says hesitantly, trying out the word. 'Papapa?'

Riding across the bridge, Mantegna fiddles with the mare's mane. He's been putting off going to see her, but he has to, otherwise, as Dati told him, the child will be too old to adopt. Already unnerved, having to go out so plain-clothed makes him feel even worse. His status is hard earned and he wears his few remaining fine clothes as if they armour him. The remnants of his finery that he's refused to pawn, the brocade *tabarro* and the emerald green Spanish-style cloak from Genova, still lie in the big chest in his bedchamber. No matter how tightly the household is squeezed, he can never part with those. Any neighbour catching a glimpse of him today might think he's gone down in the world and lost favour with the Gonzagas.

There seem to be even more hucksters in the piazza than usual. Mantegna glances at the rows of pedlars with their wooden trays full of cheap gewgaws, the cardsharpers surrounded by the usual crowd of staring heavy-jawed peasants, and the pimps and the prostitutes now touting their wares more cautiously, aware of the spies who now work the markets for the ecclesiastical courts. Mantegna raises his eyes in thanks that he had the foresight to hide Ya Ling away when he did. Today, he is reluctant to leave the dirt and the devilry behind.

He paces the floor of the hut, crossing its cramped interior. The slave woman has tried to make it homely, putting hearthstones round the fire in the middle of the floor and pinning up a fragment of cotton to keep out the draughts from the door, but no matter how often she sweeps the floor with the broom she has fashioned out of a handful of willow twigs, it still feels dank and cold underfoot.

He's never got the welcome here that he deserves, either. The first time she'd whined and asked for money over and over. 'Something for your son, Maestro. Only a fine sturdy boy could kick like this. I'm definitely giving you a son,' she'd promised him. But she hadn't. The second time, he remembers, the child's limbs were pale and straight and she had a halo of dark curls like him. At least there seemed to be little heathen in her, and her skin tone could pass for a Mantovan child. That will, he hopes, make the patricians welcome her even more.

Ya Ling rushes in, puts the child in front of her and fusses with her curls. The slave woman looks much thinner and less appealing. Working in the hemp fields has darkened her skin, and her eyes look red-rimmed from the smoke inside the hut. Her shift is frayed at the hem and he wonders what happened to the velvet dress. Her wooden clogs clattering across the packed earth floor of the hut make her look like a peasant. 'I've named her Fortuna. A name of antiquity, to remind her of her famous father and the classical paintings he is famous for. I knew that would please you.'

The child gives a little scratchy cough. She is quite frail-looking so he needs to move fast. It's a miracle she is still here. 'I wanted to see her. To make sure she is all right. Unbind her.'

Ya Ling looks down nervously. 'But Maestro, it's quite chilly in here.'

'Do as I say.'

He starts to examine the child, but there is something about the hurried way Ya Ling wraps the grey bindings back round the child's wriggling body that makes him suspicious. The child coughs until her cheeks turn pink, then, as Mantegna drags down several strips of cloth, she stops still and looks anxiously at her mother. The child is no longer perfect. There's a raised, oddly coloured scar high on her ribcage. 'What's this? What the hell happened to her?' he thunders.

'It's nothing, Maestro.' Ya Ling's voice shakes with guilt. 'It's just that one night I was exhausted after a day in the fields and I fell into such a deep sleep that Fortuna climbed over me and fell against the corner of a hot hearthstone. That's why the wound is diamond-shaped. But it's nothing. It will fade very soon, you'll see.'

'But it's bright blue!'

'That's only because I put… I put…' she pauses, 'because I took her to a healer who washed the ash off with verjuice and then put a potion of blue gentian seeds on it to cleanse the burn.'

'Listen to her cough. It sounds terrible. What's going to happen to her here?' She follows his glance up the frayed string to the smoky ceiling, where she has tied a hunk of coarse brown bread to keep the rats off it. 'Tell me that.'

'I can work harder! I can do more hours in the fields. If the maestro cannot spare me any money, then that is what I will have to do.' Mantegna shifts his weight. The damp is starting to soak through the soles of his shoes. 'And I've managed the worst. I've got her through the winters here. Once the weather gets warmer, it will be more pleasant for you to visit us.'

'Listen to me.' He exhales heavily. 'What kind of a life can you give her? How will she end up? No patrons. No family. You're not stupid, Ya Ling. Quite the opposite. You haven't survived as long as you have in a strange land without realising you are a tiny fly right on the edge of the vast web of patronage, of favours, and bribes, of confraternities, and all the brotherhoods that make up Mantovan life. You'll die in this slum. And so will she at this rate.' He squats down and holds out his hands. 'Poor little Fortuna.'

Ya Ling's hem comes up a little higher. 'But if the maestro could just spare a few *grossones* for me to put by for her dowry. For cloth to make a little shift for her.' Her hands scrunch the material tightly. It's pitiful to watch. 'For corn…' she adds quietly.

'Ya Ling, you must pay attention to what I say. There's this patrician family who have just lost a daughter, and the mother is pining badly for the child. The husband is heartbroken too, so they're going to be very generous.'

'No! Never! I couldn't even think of it!' Fortuna catches her mother's eye and rolls over, pushing against the floor until she stands, then, giving a series of staggers, tries to run fast towards her, ignoring Mantegna's outstretched arms.

'The husband wants to find a little girl to replace the one they've buried before the mother sinks any lower.' He stands, carefully keeping his voice low and reasonable. 'It will work well for them and for you too, and most importantly for little Fortuna. Just think of the life she'll have, the velvets she'll wear, the rows of shiny pearls. The connections. The feasts.'

The child holds her hands up to her mother and giggles as she is clasped closely to her breast. Ya Ling turns, her face white with shock. 'But I couldn't!' The child is the only thing that keeps her back from breaking in the fields. Nuzzling her soft skin. Listening to her repeat a new sound she has learned. Her quickness. The sweetness of her laugh. She turns to Mantegna, her voice shaky. 'Every night I pull her onto my chest to keep her off the damp floor and I force my warmth into her. If I couldn't do that, I would have nothing to live for.'

'You're denying her all that comfort. All that security.' Mantegna leans a hand against a wall, then rubs the damp dust off his palms with a show of distaste. 'Think of the good marriage she could make.' He takes a step towards her. 'They'll offer you plenty of money. You'll need a trunk to keep it all in.'

'No! I couldn't!' The child's head nestles against her bodice, then the little oval face looks up into hers and a small yawn sends a soft whisper of breath deep into the fold of her breasts. These small pleasures sustain her. Whatever vicissitudes lie ahead, the warm little body in her arms gives her a powerful reason to keep going. Fortuna lifts her head to cough and Ya Ling pats her back. 'If I didn't have Fortuna, I would have nothing,' she says simply.

'I'm worried about this cough.' Mantegna walks over and moves Ya Ling's hand away and strokes the child's cheek in concern. 'You sound as if you'll never see her again. You can always visit her! They're decent people, kindness itself. They'll take good care of her and nurse her well. I'll tell them you are her old wet nurse. They'll understand.'

'No,' repeats Ya Ling, holding the child close. 'Never.'

The following day Ya Ling is waiting for work long before the others are even awake.

The gangmaster shakes his head. 'More hours? What? Work in the dark? If I let you, then the others will be on my tail.'

'But they wouldn't know,' Ya Ling pleads. 'We could have a private arrangement. I'd share the extra money with you.'

'What, and have a riot on my hands? No chance. Don't talk about arrangements. I've done you enough favours and had no rice for a very long time.'

Ya Ling feels Fortuna's chest tighten against her back and she starts coughing. 'Then I must ask you if I can have today off. To get something for the child. I will go to the rice barges as soon as I can.'

'Up to you.' The gangmaster turns away with a shrug. 'If you can afford to lose a day's pay.'

The warm weight of Fortuna slows her down but Ya Ling walks doggedly along the dusty track, her back aching, until she arrives at the Piazza Sordello as the midday bell is ringing. In his shop under the colonnade, the apothecary sits picking his teeth. The shelves are full of piles of musty leaves. She averts her eyes from the glass jars full of liquid in which lie deformed creatures, calves born with two heads and frogs with missing limbs. No wonder the smell in here makes her nose wrinkle. She shakes her head to lose an image of Baba's immaculate dispensary full of fresh herbs that are replenished each day. What primitives these people are. She has to content herself with a few anise seeds and a handful of rosemary, already dried to brown needles. After pocketing the herbs she pulls herself taller and turns to the apothecary. 'Do you know of anybody who needs a healer?'

'Who? You?' He looks her up and down, his glance taking in her matted hair and ragged shawl. 'Why would anybody let a tinker woman like you anywhere near them?'

'But I am learned and I have a good reputation.'

'Says who?' The man yawns.

'I have cured many…'

'Yeah, it looks like it.'

She leans across the counter. 'Please Signore, just give me one chance to show you what I can do.'

His lips curl. 'Don't waste your breath. Shut the door after you.'

She stops in the market to buy a small pot of honey before she begins the long walk home.

Crossing the cobbles of the piazza, she notices a child standing in a doorway, her unripe fledgling breasts on display and a hungry look about her. A horse reins in next to her and a hard-faced man looks down. The child licks her lips slowly and deliberately and pulls down the front of her shift even further. 'Whatever you want, Signore,' she says dully. 'Anything to please.' Ya Ling's glance drops from the child's raddled cheeks down to her feet, rotted black with last winter's frostbite with gaps where her little toes should have been.

The shock of memory makes Ya Ling put a steadying hand to the wall. Her face blanches as she thinks back to an afternoon in Beijing when she had accompanied her mother, who had been summoned to an ink merchant's house. To his fury, his favourite concubine could no longer dance for him and when her right foot was unbound the cause became obvious. Her toes lay tightly grown into the arch beneath her foot and three of them had suppurated like a row of black grapes. Ya Ling's mother had swiftly cut off the rotting toes and argued ferociously that the footbinder should leave the raw flesh uncovered so it could heal, but the merchant had insisted on the foot being tightly re-bound and the silk lotus-foot slipper being rammed back on. A death sentence for the young girl. Her mother had cried all the way home.

Fortuna's coughing brings her mother back to reality and the sight of the hungry girl. This is what happens to destitute children here, she thinks. Her hands feel behind her in panic and cup her daughter's feet firmly until her breathing settles down. She fumbles in her pocket and a coin tinkles at the child's feet. 'Child, take this and buy bread. Go home.' She shifts Fortuna's weight more comfortably and, ignoring her stiffening muscles, begins the long trek back to the hut.

Chapter 29

'How often?'

'Once a month. Perhaps more.'

She cups a hand round the child's silky head and kisses her. 'No. Never. Once a month? I couldn't bear that.'

'Perhaps more often then. I told you how kind they are. And think of Fortuna's future with them. Her good health. Think of her dowry and the marriage that will bring. The comfortable life she will have.'

For a long while Ya Ling stands very still. She glances down urgently at the dark winding curls that ripple whenever the child coughs. Only the tears meandering down her face indicate that anything is amiss.

Mantegna taps his foot. 'But they won't wait long. They probably have many people out looking for the right little girl for them, even now.'

'I couldn't.' Her voice wavers.

'It would be such a pity if this chance went to another child less deserving than yours.'

'I can't.'

'Look, this isn't easy for me, but I am doing my best. I do worry about the child and I can see she is looking much thinner since I last saw her.' Mantegna stares across the hut. 'And that was barely a week ago.' Ya Ling nods her head, too overcome to speak. The anise and the rosemary have made no difference. The herbs had been too old and had lost all of their potency. 'If you deny her this one chance and her cough worsens until it's too late, then imagine how you will feel. And I can't keep paying your rent here. Nicolosia knows something is going on. You'll have to fend for yourself soon.'

Ya Ling wanders round the hut jiggling the child in her arms, then she stops abruptly. 'Can you promise me that I will be able to see her every two weeks?' Her eyes blaze across his face.

'Every two weeks? At least. I'm sure I can fix that.' He nods and immediately stretches out his arms.

'And that they are good people? And will treat her as one of their own?'

'I told you. She will be loved like the daughter they lost.'

'And you will come back each week and tell me how she's getting on?' Her eyes lock on to his.

'As often as I can.' His hand goes to his pocket and brings out a folded piece of parchment. 'And this might help you make up your mind.' Ya Ling takes it from him and her eyes scan the strange writing before she gives him a questioning look.

'It's your slave contract. Watch!' With a florid gesture Mantegna tears it in pieces. 'Look.' He rolls the slips of paper into a ball and pushes it into the ashes on the fire. 'I'm letting you go. You are a free woman. You can leave here and work wherever you want.' He pulls out a money pouch from inside his jerkin and hands it to her. 'And I've got a little something here for you as well.'

The pouch creases against his chest as she pushes it back to him. Her voice lowers with contempt. 'You think I could take money for her? I will work hard and scrape together a dowry for her myself, so that when I reclaim my little Fortuna, then she will be proud of me.'

He reaches across and takes the child in his arms. Fortuna studies him solemnly. She feels very insubstantial against his stocky chest. 'They'll feed her up and make her strong,' he says.

At his deep voice, the child jumps and struggles to turn, sending a fearful glance to her mother. 'No! No! Maestro, I can't! Not yet. I'm not ready!' Ya Ling sobs as she pulls the child back into her arms. 'Give me a few more weeks with her. Let me get used to the idea. I can't part with her yet.' Fortuna's tiny face crumples in alarm as she feels her mother's chest palpitating.

'You have to. You have no choice. We both know that.'

'Well, I'll let them have her just until they get her well. Then I can discuss with them the arrangements about when I can see her.'

'Good idea.' He pauses at the doorway, looking back at Ya Ling bent double with grief. Despite the small burn mark on the child's chest, the woman has done well. The hempen sun bonnet with the wide brim and the white bean paste on the child's delicate cheeks have done their job. The child's skin is *candido*, as pale as Carrara marble.

He glances down at the child struggling in his arms. Perhaps the child isn't even his. This is hard, but it would be harder to give up a child who looks just like me, he reflects. Fortuna stays still and gives him a wary, watery smile. 'Just imagine her cheeks pink and plump with good health. Her little frame dense with good eating, resting on the patrician lady's lap.' He gives an encouraging smile before rushing out of the hut. All the way to Dati's farm he feels as if a burden has been lifted from him. He is definitely doing the right thing.

Chapter 30

Winter has come hard and early. Despite Nicolosia carrying out all of Ya Ling's advice, the cold damp mists rising from the River Mincio have settled on Cecco's chest. One drizzly mid-winter morning, he walks into the kitchen trying to stretch away his stiffness. His mother rubs her thumbs over his back in comforting circles, kneading the taut muscles. She takes the glass stopper out of the big vial of green syrup, turns it upside down and shakes out the last few drops onto a spoon. Despite how frugal she has been, only using it when Cecco's chest was really bad, now there is nothing left of the batch Ya Ling made for her all those years ago. She holds it against her chest like a talisman.

Gregorio watches her. Now might be a good time to tell her, once Cecco has left for the workshop. The kitchen is quiet but he bides his time, until her worried glance finishes following her son across the courtyard. 'Mistress,' he begins, 'I've seen her.'

Nicolosia whips round. She doesn't need to ask who. 'Where? When?'

'A few times, over the last few months. But I hadn't realised it was her. I've seen this woman waiting, between the tripe man and the chestnut seller on the road outside, but I'd thought nothing of it. Then recently this same woman has run alongside the maestro's mare a couple of times and tried to push a letter into his hands. He gets lots of beggars and people are always trying to give him petitions, but this last time I'm pretty sure it was her. I can't be certain – she was so quick, just darting at him out of the crowd, and her voice was muffled behind her veil… The maestro threatened to put me out on the street if I ever tell anybody.'

'I won't say a word to him.' His shoulders relax at the reassuring pat. 'Do you have the letters?'

'No, Mistress. The maestro ripped them up and threw them into the mud. I heard him telling her she'd end up in the cage if she came near him again.'

'When was this?'

'Nearly two weeks ago. That was the last time. I've been stewing it over in my mind whether or not to tell you.'

'I'm glad you did.' Nicolosia walks swiftly to the dresser drawer and brings out a small piece of her husband's sketching paper. After smoothing it out against the table she writes a few lines on it. 'Next time you see her give her this. Tell no one.'

'I will, Mistress.' He pauses. 'She looks in a bad way, Mistress.'

'How? How could you tell?' Nicolosia's face creases in concern.

'Sacking tied round her. Really thin. She looked desperate… the way she thrust the letters at him. And her feet were all bare and muddied. I can tell she's weak but she does her best to keep up with the mare. The first time she even grabbed hold of the stirrup. She was nearly dragged under. When she can't keep alongside any more, she doubles right over, trying to get her breath back.' He folds the paper carefully but looks askance at it. 'But can she read, Mistress?'

'No, and I doubt she can write either, so she must know about going to a scribe. She'll find a way. I know she will.' Nicolosia thinks hard. 'Remember, not a word to a soul.'

Later, in her room, kneeling in front of the shrine to the Virgin, she prays hard. She has no money spare to give to Ya Ling but, as she prays, a faint thought grows into a firm idea. She knows a lady who could help Ya Ling. One favour deserves another. It is the Mantovan way.

Two weeks later, Ya Ling watches Nicolosia looking down from a first-floor window. The maestro and Cecco leave first. Both seem to be working long hours these days, sometimes not coming back till the bell for vespers. Clemente has chosen to try to strap his long fishing rod to the saddle of a new and skittish-looking colt, who responds by bucking his way across the courtyard. A bag bursts and oranges roll in every direction across the cobbles. Ripe curses and jokes are offered by Gregorio. Genevra squawks like a bustard as both men heave her plump frame up onto the mare, and shouts anxious instructions when Ernesto, now a fidgety little boy, is strapped behind her on the saddle. The long childhood journeys from Beijing to Mongolia, when the entire household decamped for many months, were organised with far less fuss than this, Ya Ling thinks, but the good-humoured banter and the laughter when the procession finally sets off send a shaft of sadness through her.

There is a space between the chestnut seller and the tripe stall, but the tripe man's loud bellowing and the smell of the stinking innards tangled together on his stall make her move further down the road. An orange and green striped awning flutters over the pastry stall and she hides beneath it, her eyes drawn to the tiny syrupy honey cakes and the smell of the warm almond tarts the stallholder lifts out of a wooden box. The owner threatens her with a fist, but she ignores him and continues to wait.

When she sees the blue curtains open and close three times, she slips quietly inside the house. Nicolosia gapes as Ya Ling steps into the kitchen. With her thin stooped posture, the younger woman is almost unrecognisable even after she lifts her veil. The face looking back at Nicolosia is pinched with anxiety. Her skin is burned and wind-whipped to dark brown.

The big pot of soup fragrant with barley and thyme simmers invitingly on the stove. 'I'm calling it chicken because I've waved a few bones through it. Best I can do,' Nicolosia says.

'It smells wonderful.' Starving though she is, Ya Ling looks down at her grimy hands, but Nicolosia has already begun pouring warm water into the big cauldron. Ya Ling strips off and curls herself inside. After she has smeared lead paste into her hair to kill the lice, she ducks under the water to soap it off until the scummy water is peppered with black specks. Nicolosia chases the fleas along each seam of her shift with a lit candle and as they drop, wriggling, on the kitchen table she hits them with her slipper. She finds a bedgown for Ya Ling to wear while the filthy shift is washed and dried.

'How is the family?'

'Well, they won't catch any trout at this time of year, that's for sure, but they were glad of the chance of a picnic.' She turns from smoothing the damp shift over the wooden frame and nudging it nearer the fire. 'Tell me, how have you managed for all these years?' She listens carefully to Ya Ling's story, only speaking once she has finished. 'The hemp fields? No! What a terrible waste of your talents! And a child?'

She nods as she pours out another ladle of soup and hands Ya Ling a thick slice of bread soaked in olive oil. 'I thought that must be it, though you didn't show. And you never seemed sick or feeble. But I knew it must have been something as important as that. Why he sent you away so suddenly, and without a real reason. And yet you gave your precious daughter to him? For others to rear?'

'I had no money at all. We were near to starving. And she had this terrible cough from the smoke and the dust in the drying shed. I did everything I could for her but I didn't think I could keep her alive. And it all happened so quickly. By the time I realised I couldn't let her go, he had taken her. She is with a wealthy patrician family and being well looked after. All I know is that they had lost their own daughter, and the mother was so desperate to have another she was sick with sadness. I know they have given her a good home, I just don't know where they live so I can't go and see her.' She grasps Nicolosia's arm. 'So please, please ask everyone you know. I long to see her! To find out how she is. Where she is. She's never out of my thoughts.' The wet hair clinging to Ya Ling's skull makes her features look skeletal. 'If I can only make enough money then I'll be able to bring her home.'

'Of course I will ask.' Nicolosia keeps the doubt from her voice. It seems a very unusual arrangement. A patrician family wanting a girl-child as a replacement for one who has been taken by the Lord? When Mantova is full of poor families with strapping baby boys they can't afford to feed, who can be bought for next to nothing? And to take on a sickly child at that. One who might die, like their own daughter had done, and sadden the mother once more… It hardly seems likely.

'The maestro promised me that I could see her every fortnight. But once he'd taken her… well, he just ignores my pleas. I've done everything I can to get news of her. I've spent all I had on scribes to send two letters to him begging for news of her. But I've never heard back.' Her eyes look huge with worry.

Nicolosia frowns. 'I'll do all I can. I will certainly ask if anyone has adopted a girl-child and if I hear anything then I will let you know.' Ya Ling eats ravenously, wiping the bowl clean with the last hunk of crust. Nicolosia lifts the pan and pours out another ladleful, smiling at the woman's enthusiastic sigh. 'And I will help in other ways too.

The maestro is working at the Palazzo Ducale every day preparing the fresco room. From dawn to dusk. He has no choice. He's spent years making excuses, putting off starting them properly. And, besides two massive frescos, he's to do an oculus for the ceiling, as well as painting the other two walls to look like leather curtains. Finally last week, the Marchese Ludovico told him that his patience had worn out, and that either the maestro starts work on them full-time or he stands to be banished.' Nicolosia doesn't look too saddened at the idea of his absence, Ya Ling thinks, but nods to encourage her to go on, and she does: 'So I will do what I can.'

'That is wonderful news for me. The maestro threatened me with the cage if I came near any of you.'

'I understand.' Nicolosia looks shrewd. 'So the child is the reason why you have not tried to get back to your family?'

'Yes, of course. I had to give her the chance of a healthier life. A better life. I regret doing it every day.' The grey circles of fatigue under her eyes deepen. 'It cuts me to the bone, mistress.'

'What of your betrothed?'

'Oh, Altan! I am still felled by memories of him. I dream about him galloping into my father's courtyard and lifting me off my feet with a roar of laughter and relief and holding me so tight my breath can't escape.' Her hands clasp tightly to her chest.

'Slow down!' Nicolosia laughs. 'I'm out of breath just listening.'

Ya Ling picks a bunch of glossy rosemary from the kitchen table and breathes in its sharp verdant scent. 'And when Fortuna is well and I have her back, once I have earned enough money, then we can travel to Beijing, back to him and to my family.'

'That might take you a long time, Ya Ling,' Nicolosia warns, her voice heavy with concern.

'I know.' Ya Ling squeezes her arm. 'And I know that Altan will probably have married. But all I can do is go back to my homeland. All I can do is hope.'

'Well, you saved my son once, and God forbid he ever gets that bad again, but before you go, you must show me how to make the potions he needs. In return I have arranged for you to meet Signora Trionfetti. She will pay you very well. Perhaps even recommend you to others.' Nicolosia smiles knowingly. 'But saving the reputation of Marzia Trionfetti is a task I don't envy you.'

'Really?' Ya Ling stops crushing the rosemary leaves with the pestle. 'Why is that?'

'The Trionfetti family is very rich and Marzia has been spoiled since she was a baby. There are no other children, so Marzia has always been their little *principessa*.'

'What is wrong with her?'

'It is not sickness. She has been caught in flagrante with her music teacher.'

'In flagrante?'

'In bed with him.' Nicolosia chuckles. 'She is quite brazen. They don't know what to do with her. Fortunately no rumours have yet reached the Rossi family, who have betrothed their son to her. Now *they* are highly respectable.'

Ya Ling nods with a thoughtful expression. 'So, these Trionfettis, they want their daughter a virgin again?'

'Indeed they do. And I thought of you immediately.' Nicolosia pushes the frame nearer to the fire, watching the steam rise from the threadbare shift. 'But we have a problem. You can't go to the Trionfettis wearing this.'

'Then ask them to pay me in kind instead of coin. A black cloak and shoes. Tell her it will ensure discretion when I visit.'

Nicolosia smiles. 'Of course. Why didn't I think of that?'

Chapter 31

Two weeks later a slight figure dressed head to foot in black is smuggled up the servants' staircase and into the bedroom of Marzia Trionfetti. The girl sits lounging on a chair, not looking anywhere near as penitent as the circumstances demand. She has a full, lush, sensual mouth and a knowing expression in her darkly lashed eyes.

'How long is it before your wedding night?' Ya Ling manages to hone her voice into an air of inquisition, although she is glad that the veil hides her nervousness. So much depends on this.

'Oh, I suppose… around three months,' the girl replies as if making conversation requires far too much effort.

'And how many men have you slept with?' No one in Mantova ever speaks so directly. It is a calculated gamble.

Her stunned expression makes the girl look years younger. The fearful glance she sends over to her mother tells Ya Ling all she needs to know. 'Tell this woman I don't take kindly to her dreadful questions,' she bluffs. 'I'm going to get upset.'

Signora Trionfetti inhales in shock. 'Signora, I know for a fact that it was only the once, and a good while ago. Marzia is very virtuous. It was that blackguard of a music tutor who managed to tempt her from her chaste and maidenly ways only on that one occasion.'

Ya Ling keeps her shoulders still and her stance unperturbed. 'Exactly, Mamma,' Marzia murmurs, before her eyes drop demurely down to the prayer book on her lap. 'As I told you, Mamma, I fell only the once.'

Ya Ling laces her trembling fingers together and keeps her voice even. 'If you don't tell me the truth, then I cannot help you—'

'Once! It happened only the once! I've already told you that!' The girl's full mouth downturns into a sulk as she turns to her mother. 'Why won't she believe me?' Her voice rises in petulance.

Ya Ling's gaze travels up the girl's dress of pale green silk to her pretty pouting mouth and she feels anger swell in her chest. Marzia has known a life only of comfort and pleasure. Her favourite image of Altan enters her mind. There he is, beating out the pattern on her silver necklace, concentration furrowing his brow. How much love there had been in his eyes. How much pride he'd taken in her decorum and her decency. She looks on in disgust as the girl gives a voluptuous stretch and she thinks of how casually this girl has given away what had been forcibly taken from her, Ya Ling. 'If you don't swear on the Blessed Virgin that you are telling me the truth, then I cannot help you. You will disgrace your family and end your days with the Carmelites. How many men?' she asks grimly.

The girl sits up and drops the prayer book on the side table. She flusters. 'Three.'

'Mother of God! Three? You have slept with three men? Marzia! I am disgusted with you! How could you? You have been chaperoned from birth!' Signora Trionfetti has gone white. 'It's impossible! Who are they?'

'Apart from my music tutor, you mean?'

The mother gives a furious nod before she speaks through gritted teeth. 'Yes. Tell me!'

'The silk merchant's two sons.'

'Both of them?' Signora Trionfetti sits down heavily on the bed.

'Well. Who else do I ever meet?' Marzia asks with a pretty shrug.

'And how many times have you lain with each one?' Ya Ling demands. She doesn't need an answer. The sudden flush to the girl's cheeks and the way she plays with a ribbon at her neckline is enough.

Signora Trionfetti tips herself off the bed, her large bolstered bosom quivering with anger as she approaches her daughter. 'How? Tell me! How was this possible?'

'The cypress tree in the courtyard has a branch that runs under my balcony,' the girl mumbles.

'Well, it won't be there tomorrow night!' The girl jumps at the half-hearted tap to her ear, which reddens slightly. 'Do you realise what this will do to us when the Rossis ask their son about your virtue the day after the wedding? Do you?' Marzia flinches as her mother's plump finger now pokes the side of her temple. 'You won't be so pleased with yourself then! Will you? When they ask for an annulment and everyone in Mantova gets to know why.' The girl folds her arms closely around herself. 'No blood on the sheet is one thing. That happens sometimes and people know that. But what will the parents say when he tells them you are as slack as a whore? Eh? What do we do about that?' The mother sits back down on the bed and holds her handkerchief over her face. 'You little *puttana*! Three of them! It's so much worse than I thought. You've ruined us! That's what you've done. Ruined us!'

'Do you still have your monthly bleeds?' Ya Ling asks quietly.

'Yes. I've never missed one.' Marzia sulks as she probes round the rim of her ear with delicate fingers as if she has been mortally wounded.

Ya Ling's sigh of relief is heartfelt. She gives the mother a reassuring smile. 'Then all is not lost.'

The travelling case is unpacked and out of one of the compartments in the wooden medicine coffret she had saved so hard to buy, Ya Ling brings out a small muslin bag and a bunch of bullrushes tied with twine, which she carefully unties and lays on the bed. The pointed seedheads lie on the bedcover like a row of spears. The girl looks on, her eyes suddenly wide with fear. 'What are you going to do with those? Will it hurt me?'

'No. It won't hurt you at all but you must listen carefully and practise exactly what I tell you to do, so that when the time comes you can act quickly. On the eve of your wedding I will get a small drawstring bag like this one to your mother, which she will give to you while she is preparing you for your nuptial night. You must put it somewhere hidden but near to hand in the bedchamber, so when your husband leaves you alone for a few moments…'

'What if he doesn't?' Marzia looks up insolently.

'Then you must act like a terrified maiden, look shy and—'

'Yes, indeed she must practise that,' the mother snaps angrily. 'Though on reflection, her acting ability is clearly beyond doubt.' The young woman looks uneasy at her mother's harsh tone, but gives a sly smile when the older woman begins to dab her eyes once more.

'If necessary, Signorina Marzia, you will have to ask him to leave you alone for a few moments,' Ya Ling goes on. 'Lift up the chamber pot and carry it behind the screen – something like that.'

'Why must I do that?' Her lips purse with distaste.

'Just listen to what the healerwoman says,' her mother hisses. 'And do as you are told for once!'

Both women watch Ya Ling carefully remove the inner filament from the bullrush stem and squeeze a few pinches of cottony fluff at the end of the stalk. She rolls these round and round carefully in the palm of her hand until they fuse together to make a small spongy ball. 'The bag I will give to your mother will contain a tiny corked phial of blood – fresh pig's blood is best because it doesn't thicken quickly. You will soak a small piece of this in the blood. It will draw up quite a quantity of it, so take care you don't get any on your nightgown. Then you must push it deep inside you.' She glances at the mother and chooses her words carefully. 'The ardent young husband's exertions will do the rest.'

Signora Trionfetti looks unconvinced. 'And do you think he will be taken in?'

Ya Ling pauses. 'The young groom is going to be very preoccupied.'

Marzia gives a fruity giggle, until she catches her mother's ferocious look. 'Don't look so triumphant yet, young lady!' the woman warns.

'And you must remember to remove the piece containing the soaked pig's blood the following morning.'

'Why?' Marzia wrinkles her nose. 'What if I don't choose to?'

'Because if you don't, then corruption will fester inside you, and you will die.'

The girl's insolent expression falls, as if she is beginning to realise the severity of her situation.

'But we still haven't solved the other problem that all your impious behaviour has caused.' The mother's voice tightens in accusation. 'He's bound to know he's not the first. I fear there is no resolution to that.' The mother wags a finger in her daughter's face, then strides to the far corner of the room, putting distance between them.

'Yes there is, Signora Trionfetti. Signorina Marzia, bring me a chamber pot.' Marzia sulks momentarily at being asked to handle something only her bedchamber maid should do, then makes a great fuss of holding out the chamber pot at arm's-length. 'Now use it.'

Marzia tosses her dark curls. 'I can't. I don't need to.'

Ya Ling's patience is beginning to unravel. 'I see. So, you are choosing coarse bread and water instead of a wedding feast, Signorina Marzia, are you? A scratchy nun's habit instead of pretty silks? I would have thought that the prospect of a life sentence of silence might have persuaded you to comply with my instructions.' She lowers her voice. 'But of course if you want to disgrace your family, then I cannot insist...' She closes the coffret lid and, after pushing it inside her bag, swings it up on her shoulder and pretends to make for the door.

'Come back! For the love of all that is holy come back!' Signora Trionfetti walks determinedly over to her daughter. 'You cannot insist, but perhaps her mother can.' She winds her fingers through her daughter's thick curls, drags her across the room and kicks her ankles apart until they are on each side of the earthenware rim of the chamber pot. One hand yanks Marzia's silk skirt upwards, the other pulls her drawers down. 'Do as the healerwoman says. Piss in the pot! Now! Or I will go straight downstairs and tell your father exactly what you have confessed to me. Once I tell him that his daughter has lain many times with three different men, then the Carmelites will have a new novitiate locked in a cell in their convent before tonight. I guarantee you that!'

Marzia whimpers as she steps out of the drawers. Ya Ling holds her steady. The girl squats, then looks up, eyes wide with alarm. 'I can't,' she says. 'I'm trying but honestly, I can't!'

Moving in front of the petrified girl, Ya Ling begins to pour water high from a jug until it splashes noisily into a bowl. 'Once you have started to pee, then stop immediately. Keep starting and stopping until you have emptied yourself. Drink large goblets of boiled water all day and keep tightening yourself all day. You will soon be able to keep yourself feeling taut inside for longer.' A trickling sound is heard. The girl sighs and then concentrates hard as she tries to stop the flow. 'That's right. And as you feel yourself clenching inside, then you will know what to do to keep him content on your wedding night.'

Signora Trionfetti goes to the door and calls for several buckets of water to be boiled, then pushes a large goblet into her daughter's hands. Once outside the girl's bedchamber, she clutches Ya Ling's hands in her own. 'It will work, won't it? I am beginning to feel confident that you can save my family from terrible shame.'

Ya Ling nods. 'Just as long as she keeps practising.'

The mother smiles grimly. 'Oh, she will do that all right. She will have nothing else to do before the wedding because she won't be leaving her bedchamber. Now that I know what she is capable of, I won't even leave her alone with our elderly priest. The woodsman will be here first thing tomorrow morning to see to that damned tree. Just promise me that I can trust your discretion?'

'You can indeed, Signora. Why would I say a word to anyone? If the subterfuge I have recommended to you ever gets back to the Rossi family, they will take out a vendetta on me.'

Signora Trionfetti looks thoughtfully at the diminutive figure in front of her. Her features relax. 'Yes. You're right. You understand. We understand each other.'

'And you will ask all your friends if they know of an adopted daughter? A child with black curls and high cheekbones?' Ya Ling's anxious breath wafts out from under her veil.

'Yes. Signora Mantegna has already asked me to do that.' Signora Trionfetti looks puzzled. 'I haven't heard of anyone adopting a daughter, but of course I will do as you ask.'

'And may I also ask you to recommend my services to your lady friends? As a healer? One who is very prudent and knows how to keep a family's secrets.'

'Of course. In fact I have a niece who needs the help of a wise woman like you… but I fear it might be beyond even your powerful knowledge. Her husband strays. He has lost all interest in her.'

Ya Ling's heart sinks. She picks out each word with care. 'You may be right. This is probably beyond my expertise. I am only a healer after all. But I will see her.' This is straying into territory she would prefer not to enter but Signora Trionfetti could prove to be a powerful patroness. With her savings she has just enough money for a month's rent, but the landlord who has shown her a set of rooms in a quiet street near the Rotonda di San Lorenzo is starting to become restless. 'Promise her nothing until I have seen her.'

'No indeed. But I warn you now, making her desirable might need a miracle blessed by the pope himself.'

'Signora, I cannot promise a miracle. No mortal woman could ever claim to do that.'

'No. Indeed. But please see her at least, and do your best. If my daughter's wedding night passes successfully then not only will I recommend you to others, but I will do more besides. I will show my gratitude to you with a gift. Saving my daughter's reputation is no small thing for my family. As the payment for your service was a little unusual…' She fingers the fine wool of Ya Ling's black cloak. 'I wonder, is there anything particular you would like from me?' Ya Ling tells her promptly. Too promptly. Signora Trionfetti stands back in surprise. 'But don't you have a crucifix already? Surely every respectable woman has one, at the very least.'

Ya Ling is grateful once again for the veil that covers her features. 'Of course I did have one, I always have, but… in the upheaval of packing to move to my new residence, I fear I have misplaced it.' She drops her glance quickly. 'And I am lost without it.'

'Well, then we must remedy that loss very quickly.'

After leaving the Trionfetti house Ya Ling calls in to the Rotonda. The mass has already begun and she settles herself inconspicuously upstairs into the matroneum, the loggia for females faithful to the way of the Cross. The priest swings his silver vessel and the familiar waft of what she thinks of as *ru xiang*, but what here they call frankincense, perfumes the air, riding over the smell of sweat and sour cheese that comes from the tightly packed women. Ya Ling closes her eyes and inhales deeply. The smell of the spicy resin that comes all the way from Dhofar takes her back several years. It was one of the many things the Berber had traded. Whenever she is worried she always thinks back to him.

She watches the priest gesture at the people with the vessel, spraying wisps of perfumed smoke over them, and she wonders what it signifies. Sitting right at the back, it's possible just to observe and try to work out all that is going on around her. She is learning the priest's incantation and the response to it syllable by syllable and will keep returning to the church until she is word perfect. Putting her palms together in front of her, like the other women, she prays to any god that might reside in here. What she is about to do for her patroness's niece leaves her feeling very uneasy. Healing is one thing, but this task will be far less easy to explain away.

Chapter 32

The Gonzaga Palace, 1466

Mantegna looks round the dimensions of the bare room. The weight of the work ahead bears heavily on him, but if he can paint the frescos as they live in his head, they will be miraculous. Rushing them would risk his reputation, and he is keenly aware of the many artists poised ready, waiting for their chance, who would be only too delighted to slip into his shoes at the Gonzaga court. Mantegna unties his smock.

Cecco frowns when his father stops painting. 'But what do I say, Father? When they ask me where you've gone? Why you are absent again?' Court spies in the pay of Marsilio Andreasi operate everywhere, and it won't be long before another of Mantegna's absences from the Camera degli Sposi will be noticed.

Mantegna screws up his eyes against the sunlight that pours through the open door. 'Tell them I've gone for pigments.'

Settimio puts down his grinding stone. 'But Maestro, people know that's my job,' he says mildly.

'Then say I am taken with a fever!'

'We said that last week. I did tell you, Father. The marchese threatened to send Signor Bruzzi to our house next time you are ill.'

Mantegna thinks of Bruzzi's stinking tool bag full of sharp knives and crosses himself. 'All right then!' He bristles. 'So tell me, the pair of you, what am I supposed to do? Eh? How I am I supposed to stretch my stipend, and wait perhaps years for the last payoff for this' – he glares up at the curves of two new arches soaring high into the emptiness behind the balustrade – 'and still manage to pay you a wage?'

Settimio's embarrassed glance drops to his plaster-smattered smock. 'Forgive me, Maestro.'

He turns to his son. 'And still put food on the table for you and the rest of the household?'

'Sorry, Father.'

'And go easy on that lapis, Settimio, it's more costly than silver.' Settimio puts down the blue block and looks warily at it. 'And use less walnut oil. That costs a fortune too and it only makes the paint granular if you are too generous, and I can't afford to throw a drop of paint away.'

'Yes, Maestro.' The big apprentice looks chastened.

'I'm not made of money, you know! Both of you!'

'We know, Father.'

'If I don't find other ways to make money then we don't eat! And if I do, I stand the risk of the Gonzaga wrath falling down on me and being banished to God knows where. So I have to look elsewhere for money, it's as simple as that.' He casts a despairing glance up at the ceiling, then around the three bare walls. If that bastard Dati would only pay him what he was owed he wouldn't be in this fix. His features drop. All that heartache for nothing. 'And the irony is, all I want to do is paint. To be left alone to create my masterpiece. But I cannot do that on thin air.' He glances up to where the faint circular outline of the oculus has been traced into the damp white plaster of the ceiling. If his experiments with the new ideas of perspective manage to get the oculus right, then it will amaze all who look up at it for generations to come. It will show all those smirking courtiers who mock his shape and his clumsiness and his lack of breeding just what brilliance he is capable of. Stun them all to silence. He holds his head in his hands. 'I just need peace so I can concentrate. Nobody has ever tried to do what I am about to do up there.' He points a shaking finger upwards. 'I am going to paint an illusion that will astound the world with its reality.' His finger travels round the room to the window. 'My enemies out there can't wait for me to fail.' His hand drops to his side. 'And the pressure weighs heavy on me.' He sighs. 'I just need some respite.' His voice fissures, as brittle as crystal. 'Some peace. And peace of mind.'

He has little enough of that. Palace whores aplenty. Wine until his brain is addled. Opulent feasts at the palace. Court jesters who make the room rock with laughter but who leave him feeling lonelier than ever inside. Nothing has ever matched lying in Ya Ling's arms, no matter how much he has paid. He thinks of the empty hut in the slum. It's too late now; she's moved on. The Lord alone knows what has happened to her. And often, when he lies in the darkness thinking of her, his conscience presses on his chest like a stone. The remembrance of handing over the weeping and struggling child to Dati makes his *tabarro* cling, wet with sweat.

'Are you all right, Father? You look as if a ghost has risen. Is there anything I can do to help you?'

'Or me, Maestro?'

Mantegna looks away from his son's earnest face to the heavy jowls of his apprentice. 'Help me? You're a pair of innocents. How could either of you help me? Neither of you have any idea how cruel the world out there is. Have either of you felt the ache of hunger in your belly? Eh? Ever had to eat grass to try to relieve it?' he demands. The young men exchange a shocked glance, then drop their eyes to the floor. 'No, I thought not.' He sighs heavily. 'Neither of you appreciate how I struggle to keep you safe from the dangers that lie in wait outside our walls. You have no idea of what I've had to do. What I've given away. I can hardly believe it myself. But I'll pay for it. On Judgement Day, I'll be the one who pays.' He rests his heavy head on his chest.

Cecco puts down his dripping plaster brush on the bench and quickly tucks a piece of sacking under it before reaching across to the older man. 'Father, please don't upset yourself.'

Mantegna turns away from his son. He can't bear the loving touch of his son's hand squeezing his arm. His own flesh and blood. Just as Fortuna is his own flesh and blood too.

'Let's get back to it,' he says gruffly, turning aside quickly so that neither of them can see the tremor that runs the width of his shoulders.

Chapter 33

The two nieces could not be more different. The birth-given name must be such a cruel reminder. Carabella – beautiful darling. Signora Trionfetti hadn't lied. It was not going to be easy. The young woman must silently curse her parents each time she gazes despondently into her looking glass. But how could they have known? That the tiny pink bundle they held by the marble font would grow up with a face like hers?

'Keep still.' Ya Ling studies every inch of her carefully.

'I know I'll never look like Venus, but frankly he's no Adonis either. I'm no fool, Healerwoman. It was never a love match. Just the usual arrangement between both families, us and the Faraldos. All I want is just to tempt him into the marriage bed often enough to conceive a son, then both sets of parents will be happy and leave me alone.'

Ya Ling likes the girl straight away. The gifts that nature has bestowed upon her do not include a pretty face, but do at least include quick wits and an attitude to life of calm amusement that might please a man if she didn't have such a defeated air about her. The girl smiles delightedly when Ya Ling assures her of that. 'You need to smile more. It transforms your features,' she says.

'I thought only alcohol could do that. At least that's what my husband seemed to need on our wedding night. Lots of it, too. And he hasn't visited my chamber since.'

'Well, more fool him. You are witty, and your voice is soft and well modulated. Let your humour show. Amuse him. Make him smile. His mistresses won't be able to do that as well as you.'

'Do you really think so?'

'Yes. You are clever and amusing and from a very well-connected family. Speaking of families…' Ya Ling's smile is cautious, 'I don't suppose you have heard anything of a little girl-child, adopted by a prominent family and brought up as their own?'

'A little girl? Adopted? By one of the families we know? How strange. No. I've heard of nothing like that. Why do you ask?'

Ya Ling keeps her voice even. 'Never mind. I thought it sounded a strange story too.'

'Where did you hear it?'

'Don't let it distract us. I need to concentrate on you, my dear.' Ya Ling pauses, then stands back, taking in the pronounced swell of the girl's bosom behind her shapeless dress. 'Your body is firm and I think it is well proportioned but I can't tell. You need the skills of a good dressmaker who will know how to accent your womanliness.'

'Won't this dress do?'

'No, it needs to be tighter and the neckline must be lower.'

Her wide mouth curves downwards. 'I'm not sure my husband will pay for that. My dowry came with plenty of dresses.'

Ya Ling looks unimpressed. 'I'm sure it did. But possibly none suitable for seduction. Confide in your mother. Tell her that your father must oblige with another dress. A very special dress. After all, a precious gift must always be prettily packaged.'

'But I fear this gift already comes with too much extra adornment.' She points ruefully to her top lip, which grows an abundant line of dark hair, and to her eyebrows, which cut across her forehead in a thick straight line.

'Those are easily resolved.' Ya Ling opens her travelling case and takes out a packet of the wishbones she uses to take out splinters. The girl stands still, barely murmuring as each hair is plucked and her eyebrows are shaped. 'Already your eyes look larger, making your skin look very pale and perfect.'

Carabella takes the mirror and, turning to Ya Ling, laughs in delight. Her sour breath catches Ya Ling full in the face. She opens her mouth obediently when requested and Ya Ling sees that one place at each end of the row of her bottom teeth is red and inflamed. 'Are you brave enough to let me remove two of your teeth?'

'Do you really have to?' The girl displays calm courage, with none of the hysterics Ya Ling expected.

'Yes. Shreds of meat are caught under the gum of the last tooth on each side, so by removing them we will cleanse the mouth.' She takes out several small packages from her case. 'I will find you some bark of the darum tree to whiten your teeth. This will turn your lips a beautiful shade of saffron red too. In the meantime, this tooth blanch of cuttlebone will keep them clean. Then we will make your mouth even more appetising with a syrup of mint.'

'Then I must be brave while you pull. What else can you do for me?' She holds up a handful of dry brown hair. 'All his mistresses have been fair, so I need golden hair to please him. Sadly, I think a miracle is needed for that.'

Ya Ling senses another presence in the room. Neither of them has noticed the maid who has quietly let herself in. 'Send her away,' she urges quietly.

'Mistress, I only wanted to see if you required refreshments for your guest.' The maid looks at the dark-clad lady with open curiosity.

'Send her away.'

'It's only Renata. She has worked for us for many years.'

'No. Please do as I ask and send her away.'

'Are you sick, Mistress?' The maid flicks her head from one woman to the other. 'What ails you? Can I help?'

Ya Ling places a finger briefly over her veiled lips, then walks over to the window. She waits for the door to close before she relaxes. 'All right. Fair hair? I can make that possible.' Carabella looks astonished. 'I will wash your hair in lemon juice soaked with dried camomile flowers and afterwards you will have to sit for many hours in the hot sunshine, then your hair will shine and have fine waves like golden corn running through it.'

'The sun? I could never sit in the sun! You told me that my skin at least is a redeeming feature, but once my face is browned like a farmer's wife, then my husband won't come anywhere near me.'

Ya Ling puts a finger to her chin for a moment. 'I will have some sort of circlet of wicker constructed to keep your skin whiter than a pearl. It must have a broad brim, then we will pull your hair through it and expose only that to the sun's rays.'

The girl's tone becomes more confident. More confidential. 'And what other magic can you work for me? In the bedroom, for instance.'

Ya Ling swallows down the sudden rush of unease at the dangerous word. 'I work no magic, Carabella. Nothing like that. If I agree to help you in this way, then you must swear to me on oath that you will tell nobody in the world what I have done for you.'

Carabella looks puzzled. 'Of course. If you insist.' She shrugs. 'I'm hardly going to boast about needing such services. It doesn't reflect well on me as a wife.'

'That's true, but nevertheless I still insist.'

'Then I promise. I swear on all that's holy,' she says solemnly.

Ya Ling brings out a pot of soothing salve and rubs it gently into Carabella's reddened top lip and the inflamed patches around her eyebrows. 'So tell me precisely what else you are asking me to do for you.'

'Once I am transformed, then how do I get him into our bedchamber – and more importantly, what must I do to keep him there? And entice him to keep returning.' The red glow slowly spreads out until it covers the rest of her face. 'Enough times to conceive a son.'

'First of all, when you want him to visit you, you must bathe that afternoon, then draw a circle of this very carefully round each eye. Practise first – it must look very natural. It will make your eyes look very dark against your white skin.' She hands Carabella a tiny wooden box of kohl that comes with its own miniature paintbrush. 'Rinse the mint syrup round your mouth, then rub your lips with this salve of mulberry juice to make them soft and shiny. Wear your new dress, which will cling tightly to your curves and show off your womanliness. When he returns amuse him, think up some tales to tell him that will make him smile. Then leave. Later in the evening find some pretext or other to bring him to the marital room. Just before you open the door to him, put a drop of this at your throat, between your breasts and above your mound.' She raises her eyebrows encouragingly. 'Tell no one of this. It is very potent. It contains musk and attar of rose oil.'

Carabella looks curiously at the glass bottle. 'Does it have a name?'

'Harem perfume.'

'No!' The girl gives a peal of laughter. 'It can't be called that!'

'Here. Try a little.' Carabella leans down into the tantalising scent that drifts up wantonly from her wrist.

'I see what you mean. It smells delicious. But will it work?' Her soft brown eyes look anxious.

'It never fails.' Carabella sneezes loudly. 'And it certainly won't be having that effect on your husband. I can promise you that.'

'Really?'

As they laugh together Ya Ling notices that already the young woman's face looks softer and prettier, and the hand she habitually lays across her cleavage has opened invitingly as if cupping her own soft ripe curves. There is far more to healing than curing the body. Every healer in her homeland learns that in their first lesson, but these Mantovans have still to find that out. She carefully lifts out a tiny pouch from her case. 'Listen and remember this: *Everything has beauty but not everybody sees it at first.*' She gives Carabella a quick confident smile. 'Some people just need more time to see it. To be encouraged to see it. That's all.'

'Who said that? Was it Dante?'

'No, someone even wiser than Dante, a great scholar called Confucius. So when you feel shy standing before your husband, repeat that saying to give you courage.'

'I will. Over and over.' She holds her hands together as if in prayer. 'Is that everything, Healerwoman?'

'Not quite. Use this.' Ya Ling pulls out a tiny silken drawstring bag. 'This is the scented powder of aloe wood and sandalwood that has been crushed to dust, then sieved through silk. Put clean sheets on the marital bed, then sprinkle on a good handful of this and rub it well in. He will find it very difficult to stay away.'

Carabella's hands take the bag and hold it close to her chest. 'Oh, I do hope so. I long for a child. You can't imagine how much.' She sounds so heartfelt that Ya Ling feels her own longing for Fortuna welling up inside. 'But what about the paintings? You haven't mentioned them at all.'

'Paintings?' Ya Ling asks.

'Oh, you know, putting paintings in the marital room showing virile men performing acts of chivalry, to make sure I have a boy-child. Do you recommend any particular artist?'

'Oh, they won't work.' Ya Ling gives a dismissive smile.

'What about a *zibellino*?'

'That won't work either.'

'Really?'

'No. That's just a talisman. How can an ermine skin with a gilded head possibly do to you what only a husband can?'

Carabella smiles shyly but her eyes still question. 'Well, my father has said he will pay for me to go to Loreto. The shrine there has produced many sons.'

Ya Ling's veil shakes. 'Truly, none of them will work. Not without the visits of your husband.'

'But Father Efisio personally recommends them! All of them.' Carabella's eyes widen. 'All the priests do.'

'Then you must do as your conscience tells you,' Ya Ling says hurriedly.

'But you advise me differently?'

'Yes... I think I might.' Ya Ling keeps her voice low and cautious. 'When you lie beneath him, before he enters you, you must place a bolster under your hips.' She remembers her mother's calculations. 'Count the first day of your bleed as one, then somewhere between twelve to seventeen days after that you will need to entice him. Remember the more he visits your bedchamber, the more likely you will be to have a child.'

Carabella looks at her in awe. 'But shouldn't I pray to a saint as well?'

'Of course. Of course.' Ya Ling sends her thoughts back to the masses she has attended.

'Which one do you recommend?'

She grasps a name from thin air. 'San Bernardo?'

'For fertility? I would have thought San Antonio di Padua would have been the one for that.' Carabella looks at her in amazement. 'Surely it should be him? What is your priest's recommendation?'

'Of course! Of course! You're right. I was merely distracted by thinking of how lovely you are going to be.' She reaches quickly for the pair of pincers in her case. 'Now, let's not waste a moment. Are you brave enough for me to begin?'

Carabella's mother and her aunt are as good as their word. Over the next few months commissions start coming in from the most respected families in Mantova. They in turn recommend Ya Ling as a well-bred lady of unsurpassed healing skills who practises her art with the utmost discretion. With the money she has earned she has her set of rooms painted pristine white and equipped with gleaming canisters full of fresh herbs and an expensive set of brass weights. Each time she visits an elite family, she also asks as casually as she can for any news they might have of a patrician family who have adopted a little girl with high cheekbones and dark curls. Hard work helps numb the heartache she still feels at every look of surprise, every negative shake of the head. She even tries the orphanages. Now she is becoming respectable, she needs to bide her time and carefully build her reputation until it is secure, then Mantegna will no longer be able to deny her the truth.

Chapter 34

The Camera degli Sposi, Gonzaga Palace

There is a loud knock at the door. Mantegna turns from painting a swag of curtain with a difficult fold that is annoying him. 'Get that, one of you. Who dares interrupt me? Tell them I can't be disturbed, the plaster is just perfect now.'

Settimio holds the door ajar, looking surprised to see the healer-woman. He's heard of her, even seen her a couple of times, seen people crossing themselves as she passes through the crowd, her black cloak and veil flapping as she hurries to aid some poor suffering soul.

'There's no one sick in here, Signora. I would try the wet-nurse wing. They always seem to be ailing there.' His polite smile fades as she slips past his big frame, steps smartly into the room and waits quietly in the centre.

Mantegna turns. 'You deaf, Settimio? Didn't you hear what I said? I can't be disturbed.'

The woman continues to stand there, her veiled face turned towards him. Her stillness is unnerving.

'Perhaps you didn't hear either, Signora. We are all in good health here.' Mantegna turns back to the wall and is soon absorbed in his work again.

After a few minutes Cecco clears his throat. 'Father?'

Mantegna's eyes widen. The woman is still there. 'Look. I can't be any clearer, Signora. You've got the wrong room. Settimio, take her and find her one of the stewards to show her where she is supposed to be.' He gives a waft of his hand.

'I will, Maestro. This way.' Settimio opens the door wider and gives an encouraging nod.

The woman walks over to the wall and stands sideways as if watching the maestro work. His bulky frame rises in irritation as he turns towards her. Her soft breath feathers his face.

It smells of mint. To his bewilderment, she carefully pulls her veil down from the hood of her cloak so that her eyes are visible. Only he can see what she has revealed. He takes a step backwards. 'Out. Go on, you two. Wait outside.'

'Us? But Father, I thought you told—'

'Now. I've changed my mind.'

'Please don't say you are ill. You've never said anything.' Cecco's forehead creases with worry.

'I'm fine!' he snaps. 'Just do as you are told.'

Both paintbrushes clatter on the table before they close the door behind them.

'Ya Ling? You and the healerwoman are the same person? How in heaven's name did you manage that?' He swallows hard, digesting the shock.

She pulls herself taller. 'Cleverness, knowledge and hard work, I expect.'

His gaze slides down the front of her dress. 'My word. You've done well for yourself. Very well indeed.' He lifts up the heavy silver crucifix that weighs down the thick silver chain. 'So, what's this? Eh?'

'A gift from Signora Trionfetti.' He nods, impressed. 'I have worked for many such families for several years now.'

'I don't believe my eyes. You're now a respectable Catholic widow, no less. And one blessed with the gift of healing, too. How did all this come about?'

'Please, Maestro! Just tell me! When did you last see her? You promised me you would tell me regularly how she was. She is a child quite grown! How could you keep me waiting for so long without news of her? I know that she will have forgotten me but when I tell her of my circumstances when I let you take her, that I cared only for her health, then I am sure she will forgive me. Now that I have money and feel safe in my status, I am finally in a position to bring her home. I have lived for this day for all those years.' Her voice holds the snap of anxiety. 'I would never have let her out of my sight if I thought you would keep her away from me like this. It has nearly broken me.'

Mantegna's mouth dries up. His stomach churns at the thought of the thin money purse he had finally got out of Dati. The soft pleading in the woman's voice could be his undoing, if he isn't careful. Her forehead looks ashen. A memory of the harness room crosses his mind. He feels a jolt towards her, a quickening of feeling, all the more painful because her stance tells him it will never be reciprocated.

'I haven't seen her for a while. You know how careful we all have to be these days. Speaking of which, you can't approach me again. No one is allowed to disturb my labours – Ludovico Gonzaga himself has said that.'

'When will you next go to the family who have her? I must come with you.'

He sees the pulse of a vein at her temple. 'They won't agree to that. I have been to see the man who brokered the arrangement and he tells me she is prospering, still a little frail, but better than when she was first given to them.'

'I would hope she is! But not completely cured? After all these years? Then it is urgent that I see her.'

'Be patient, Ya Ling. They are doing everything they can for her. When I have some free time I will make enquiries again.'

'I will come back in a week.' Her veil shakes with her impatience. 'And every week until I find her.'

'I'm sorry but I can't allow that. I have only just returned to favour with Ludovico, but even so, I sense Andreasi's spies are watching me. If you come again you will find I have posted a sentry on the door.'

'How will I know you have gone to see the family? That you have kept your word?' She gives him a half-lidded glance of contempt. 'You haven't before.'

'If you tell me where you stay then I will come and find you when I have news of her. But give me a few weeks.' He points his paintbrush at the wall, where only a small twist of curtain is coloured a deep orange. 'I have much work to do. Now you must leave, and not return, or there will be trouble for us both.'

Several weeks later, she is leaving the bedchamber of Signora Caponera when a stocky figure mounting the stairs makes her grasp tighten on the handrail. 'Maestro?'

Mantegna looks up and sees her, then recoils in surprise. 'You? Here?'

'I'm tending the wife,' she says briefly. 'A difficult pregnancy. Maestro, you must have news of Fortuna by now.' She lays a hand on his arm and he takes two steps backwards down the stairs. Ya Ling keeps her voice soft. 'Don't back away. Have pity on me. I look for her in every rich household I attend, but no one has heard of her adoption.'

'Calm yourself.' Mantegna looks around blindly. 'I fear she was sickly.'

'Just tell me a few words about her. Please! Are they kind to her? Is she better? Where does she live? You must tell me.'

'I-I...' He stares at her as if willing speech to come.

Ya Ling's breath constricts her throat. 'Was? What do you mean, was?' She stares down at him.

'Dati told me two weeks ago...' He looks into a pair of dark eyes widening with fear and takes a deep breath as if his courage might fail him. The words come out in a tumbled rush. 'She succumbed, she – she... perhaps the lack of nourishment... I know you did your best—'

'No! Please God, no!' Ya Ling sits down heavily on the stairs. 'That can't be!' She remembers the way her own stomach had griped when she had spent her last *sessinos* on buffalo milk to spoon into that pink rose-petal mouth. The way her breasts had been constantly sore when the child had latched on hungrily. Fortuna. So quick, so lively, her tiny features always alive with curiosity. Apart from her cough from the smoke and the dust in the hemp sheds she had never shown signs of ague, or of fever.

He makes to climb past her up the stairs but she steps in front of him. 'What was it? What caused her death? The cough. It worsened?'

'Yes. That must have been it. The cough.'

'Must have been? Don't you know? How could they have let her die? You promised me they would take great care of her!'

Her veil becomes agitated. The heavy outer door creaks. Loud footsteps cross the hallway. Mantegna looks over the banister. 'I must go. Ya Ling, you must understand. I did my best. I'm sorry but I can't be seen here with you.'

'What?' Her legs crumple beneath her. She sits down heavily on the stairs.

'You must go too. Go quietly. Go home to grieve.'

'Go where?' Her mind can scarcely take in what he has said.

Mantegna leaves and the door bangs shut.

'I thought I heard the painter Mantegna's voice. Signora, are you well?' Signor Caponera looks up from the lower floor, puzzled, clearly wondering why the capable widow seems frozen halfway up his staircase. With the assistance of his elderly steward he gently helps her down the stairs and insists on giving her a glass of wine before he instructs his groom to escort her back to her consulting rooms.

Chapter 35

None of her tinctures can stem the ache Ya Ling feels inside, nor can they aid her sleep during the long nights of crying. She buys a black silk mourning cloak and veil. On the rare occasions she ventures out, her tiny form struggling over the cobbles elicits sympathy. She becomes known as the Widow. With no idea of where Fortuna died, or where her body lies, or what rituals accompanied the laying of her tiny body into Mantovan soil, she tries in desperation to find the child's spirit using the old ways. She throws knucklebones and tries to remember Ayi's Bai chants she heard as a child. The spirit remains silent, which is small consolation. Signs of a troubled spirit would have broken her, but there has been no sign yet of Fortuna's spirit resting at ease. Surprised at the comfort the ancient ways give her, Ya Ling makes them part of each day's routine. She grieves, barely eating, unable for a while to respond to the loud rappings of her patients on her door.

Now she lives in a respectable neighbourhood, some of her patients are wealthy and are not accustomed to being kept waiting, and finally they can be ignored no longer. With a heavy heart she pulls back the wooden shutters from the windows and resumes her work. There is little respite; when it becomes known that she is once more receiving patients, they begin waiting outside her door as soon as the cock crows. The queue is a barometer of Mantovan wealth and status; the more prosperous are always at the front and then it tails off, right down to the tillers and tanners who pay in kind, scouring the woods for the fungi and the herbs she needs to keep the rows and rows of canisters full in her treatment room. The Hebrews, always at the end of the queue, start to get restless as the afternoon wears on and the time approaches their curfew, when the ghetto gates will clang shut.

As the years pass, her list of clients becomes more illustrious. Thanks to the many recommendations from all the prominent families she has attended, of her discretion as well as her great healing gifts, the Widow is much in demand. Her reputation is protected by her influential patrons from the slander and gossip of her rivals, who are jealous of her steady rise to supremacy.

Her days are long and exhausting, but she never forgets the hardships and the deprivation she endured in the slums and she never turns anybody away. The money purse hidden behind a roof beam becomes a heavy iron chest sealed beneath the floorboards, but the thought of the accruing wealth brings its own sadness now there is no precious daughter to endow. As she consolidates her reputation, the gratitude of those she has cured gradually helps to give some slight comfort and ease to her soul. Exhaustion delivers some respite from her sleeplessness. Though desperate to return to Beijing, she must wait for a sign that her daughter's spirit rests contentedly here. Only then will she be able to grieve properly, and only then will she be able to leave.

One evening she stands at the window, gently rubbing the tiredness from the delicate angle of her cheekbones. At last the queue is beginning to dwindle, but she sees a flash of scarlet and white as a groom in Gonzaga livery pushes his way to the front and raps heavily on her door. 'Come immediately! You are needed at the Palazzo Ducale. A summons from the Marchesa Barbara of Brandenburg herself. One of her maidservants is dying in childbirth.'

'The palazzo...?' The royal buildings take up a huge swathe of the town, but the possibility of bumping into Mantegna there, after he neglected Fortuna so badly, makes her shudder.

'Quickly, Signora. No one keeps the marchesa waiting.' The groom barely gives her time to collect her salves and instruments. Her glass vials tinkle together against the compartments of her medicine coffret as he bundles her onto a pony and bounces her over the cobbles.

Once at the wet-nurse wing at the palazzo, she recognises the midwife immediately. A dull stupid woman who relies too much on astrologers, votive candles and prayers to San Rocco. On the table, the servant's knees lean slackly open and she groans in exhaustion. One little leg up to the thigh is all that has emerged from her swollen cleft. It looks blue and lifeless. 'I don't know why they've sent for you.' The midwife's tone is defensive. 'Signor Bruzzi was sent for ages ago. It's too late now. There's nothing more to be done. I've begun a baptism on it and the priest is on his way. He can do the last rites for both when he comes.'

'Quick, get me some ice and a bowl,' Ya Ling commands a passing servant before taking out two sharp knives. She carries them over to two candlesticks and burns the blades carefully in the flickering flames. She slits the skin below the woman's opening and catches the baby as it tumbles out in a swirl of purple afterbirth. Using the other knife, she cuts the cord and knots it quickly. The baby lies grey and still, like a marble statue of a cherub. Ya Ling is so busy sucking out the baby's nostrils and spitting into the bowl that she doesn't notice a large woman in the corner, who is watching her every move. Gently inserting a reed down the baby's throat, she draws out the effluvium, then turns the lifeless little form upside down and holds it by its slippery ankles as she slaps hard on the curve of each tiny buttock. A noise emerges, like a wet explosive sneeze, and the tiny arms clutch at the air as if dragging handfuls nearer to its gasping mouth. When a howl of temper rebounds round the quiet room the maidservant struggles to sit up. A burst of joyous laughter turns to awe as the baby's skin beneath the birth coating suffuses with a rosy pink. 'Wash and swaddle him.' She hands the wriggling form to the gaping midwife. 'Get him ready to be put to the mother.' She walks up to the head of the table and whispers to the mother, 'A beautiful boy! Take heart. You are going to feel something very cold below. This will cleanse you and help lessen the pain of the needle. Be brave. I'll be very quick.' The woman nods at her, wild-eyed with shock and elation. Ya Ling freezes the torn skin with a handful of ice wrapped in a linen cloth, then instructs two servants to hold the mother firmly while she stitches.

A guttural voice comes from the corner of the room. 'I am very impressed. A child risen, almost from the dead. When you have completed your task down here, then they will bring you up to my bedchamber.' The voice holds authority. 'Take your time. See to my maid first. I can only move very slowly.' When the woman gets to her feet with great difficulty and steps into a golden haze of candlelight Ya Ling recognises Barbara of Brandenburg, the stately wife of Ludovico Gonzaga, the Marchese of Mantova.

'Of course, Marchesa. I will come to you as soon as I can.' Barbara of Brandenburg nods in approval at the Widow's appropriately spoken *cortesia*, at the way she elegantly bows with one knee to make a reverence.

The double doors bang into the walls on each side as Bruzzi bursts through. He drops his bag onto the floor, then trips over it. His clothes are steeped in sweat and sour wine. 'Where is she? Come on! Wasting my time on fucking servants,' he mumbles.

'You will not be required, Bruzzi.'

He stands stiffly, as if the blood has congealed in his veins. He turns slowly at the anger underlying the marchesa's voice. 'Marchesa! If I had known you were here I would have—'

'It is as well you were tardy, otherwise the Widow would not have been given her chance.'

'But I came just as soon as I heard. I brought my tools ready to do a Caesarean on the woman. None do them better than me.' Bruzzi's words slither over his teeth as he tries to arrange his wayward limbs into a clumsy bow.

'Really? Well, that won't be necessary. The servant has been spared the pain of a Caesarean and both mother and child are healthy. Both have been well tended.'

'By whom?'

Ya Ling cringes behind her veil as Bruzzi follows the marchesa's imperious gesture. She tries to make herself as inconspicuous as she can.

'What? Who?' Bruzzi tries to walk carefully across the kitchen.

'I've told you. The Widow. A blessed healer.'

'Some call her that. I call her the Crow.' He sways slightly on his heels. 'Flapping around in black. And now apparently hovering round my patients like a carrion crow.'

'You can go, Bruzzi. Go and get yourself sober. This woman has impressed me very much. She is to become my healer now.'

As he holds open the door for the marchesa's slow departure his head angles back across the room to Ya Ling, as if he is trying to place some memory of her. Ya Ling flexes her fingers so that she can finish stitching the maidservant's wound, then give the flesh a thorough cleansing with old wine.

'Ouch! That hurts so much!'

'I know, but it purifies the flesh and will help healing.'

'See? She's no idea what she's doing!' Bruzzi shouts across the room. Ya Ling watches his departure with a worried frown, then checks the baby's breathing and, after she has loosened the swaddling round the baby's neck, she lays him carefully against the anxious mother's breast.

The servant leads Ya Ling from the wet-nurse wing, across two courtyards and up a majestic marble staircase to the *piano nobile*, then through six huge reception rooms. They are all draped in swagged velvet curtains the colour of old emeralds and every wall is armoured to the ceiling with paintings of battle scenes in ornate gilded frames. They pass through to an even grander *sala*, which leads deeper into the marchesa's private apartment. All the while, Ya Ling is aware of a film of moisture lying on her palms. Whatever Barbara of Brandenburg suffers from, she had better cure it. Retribution from the family will be swift and cruel otherwise. Trying not to be unnerved by the tall bronze sculptures, the sumptuous Veneziano tapestries and all the iron-bound treasure chests lining each wall, Ya Ling approaches the huge canopied bed where the marchesa lies, stoically staring up at the gilded rosettes that hang like stars beneath the blue ceiling. She points to her stomach and Ya Ling presses her hands tightly together until they are controlled to stillness, before politely folding back the heavily patterned velvet skirt and pulling down the long silk drawers. A leather truss is banded tightly round the marchesa's stomach. 'No! No! Leave it there! Leave it there! It's the only thing that gives me any relief from the pain in my back!' she cries.

'Marchesa, I'm afraid I cannot.' Ya Ling's voice shakes so much she barely recognises it. As she eases the leather binding down over the broad hips, each gentle tug causes a harsh cry of pain. The stomach is bloated and engorged and the guts lower down feel hard-packed like iron pipes under her probing fingers. 'When did the marchesa last...?'

'Over two weeks,' she gasps.

'Two weeks? As long as that?'

'Yes. Bruzzi wanted to take the knife to me, but I am too afraid,' Barbara confides.

'No. You were wise not to do that.' One bed-chamberer is immediately sent to the market for prunes and figs, another to the butcher for a sheep's bladder, the third to the blacksmith with instructions for him to forge a thin metal cylinder, and a fourth has to boil a cauldron of water and to collect a pot of honey and a grinding stone. But the more complicated list is entrusted to Marsilio Andreasi alone, who writes down and repeats back to her the list of things he needs to bring from the numbered canisters in the treatment room in her home. 'Silica, *Bryonia alba*, chaff-flower roots, pulp of laburnum, senna and the husks of the psyllium seed.'

'So what will you do to me?' the marchesa asks.

'A heavy purging, my lady. It will be unpleasant, and I suggest you make no plans to leave the privy in your bedchamber.'

'For how long?'

'All night and perhaps the following day, perhaps less, I hope. You will need to drink flagon after flagon of warm water, Marchesa, and try to keep walking around the chamber as well.'

'And will this purging medicine work?'

'It has moved mountains in the past.'

The marchesa grunts as a spasm of pain courses through her. 'And the metal rod? The sheep's bladder? I've told you, I won't be cut.'

'When the sheep's bladder is tied round the rod and filled with warm water, it is greased and – then it is...' Ya Ling thinks for several moments. 'My lady, the blockage might need to be attacked from all directions,' she says delicately as she massages a soothing salve onto the marchesa's stomach with strong downward strokes, 'but I do believe that the purging medicine will work.'

Less than three hours later loud groans can be heard through the door of the little privy. 'San Rocco help me! This is worse than childbirth!' Barbara of Brandenburg cries. As the night wears on, the sounds become less anguished until at dawn a fainter, more relieved tone is heard. The servants keep the stench at bay by holding pouches of dried lavender to their noses as they wait outside the bedchamber with jugs of purging medicine and leather buckets, until they are all finally sent off to bed. Ya Ling pulls back the drapes and winds them round the classical columns, then makes a bolster for Barbara's broad back before helping the exhausted woman onto the massive bed. She lifts a heavy velvet cloak lined with tan marten fur and tucks it round the marchesa. A cool comfrey poultice is gently moulded around her plucked hairline before Ya Ling drags a heavy walnut box chair across the room and up to the side of the bed.

When Barbara wakes in the early afternoon of the following day, she finds Ya Ling sleeping with her forehead resting on the coverlet and wakes her with a firm pat on the back of her head. Ya Ling wakes up suddenly, startled to see Barbara's broad face smiling down at her. 'Look, Healerwoman! I can lean down to you. I can move once more without pain.' Ya Ling feels the warm hand now patting her back and blushes at the honour that such an intimate touch conveys.

She hurries to prepare a warm infusion of camomile and to send to the palace kitchen for a piece of white wheat bread for the marchesa to break her long fast. When she has finished eating, Ya Ling begins collecting together her herbs and glass vials. 'Wait, Healerwoman.' The marchesa's loud guttural voice calls for Marsilio Andreasi to be summoned. When he appears and his flowery reverences at her return to health are completed, he receives his instructions. 'Marsilio, this woman is now in my household. She is to be my new healer. Arrange a set of rooms for her here and send a mule cart to collect all her cures. Give her the services of Maria, the little maid – she is hard-working and will help her settle into life at the palace.'

Ya Ling looks down quickly, her arms rigid against her sides. Move here? Where Mantegna's presence will be a bitter reminder of all she has lost?

'Are you not honoured to serve me?' Barbara of Brandenburg stares at her. 'Rooms at the palace, and a maid to take care of you? These are high honours indeed. All the luxuries of the court at your disposal, things you will never have seen before.' She flicks a hand upwards. 'Feasts where fish swim in bowls of aspic, and where exotic fruits are nurtured in houses made of glass. Where music is played at lavish entertainments that enthral all who attend.' Her deep voice sounds bemused.

Ya Ling quickly drops into a reverence. She will just have to make sure she works well away from the Camera degli Sposi. 'I am very grateful for the honour you have given me.'

Barbara nods, satisfied. 'You are dismissed for now to move your possessions, but tomorrow I wish for a private conversation with you.'

When she has left the marchesa she feels a puzzling warmth rising inside. She smiles to herself, stretching the tension from her arms. Tucked safely inside the Gonzaga web of patronage and power, for the first time since she was captured as a young girl she suddenly feels safe.

But now that she will live surrounded by hundreds of pairs of watching eyes, she will have to use the old ways very sparingly. The ancient chants and occasional throwing of the knucklebones have not yet reassured her that Fortuna's tiny spirit is at rest here in Mantova, but she cannot stop using them until she knows that her daughter is at peace. The bones always land in patterns that speak of respite, of pain overcome. It's unusual that they never vary in their placement, but Ya Ling feel sure that one day they will tell her more.

The groom leads her to a small carriage. Ya Ling nearly trips over the stepping block when she sees a small person already sitting in the shady interior. It is one of those strange miniature humans.

'Hello. I'm Maria,' the person says pleasantly enough, and Ya Ling takes the offered hand.

'Where are you from?' she ventures later, when the packing is almost completed and they are wedging the last of the blue and white herb jars between handfuls of straw in the big wooden box Maria brought with her.

'Oh, I'm from further south, on the coast, near Brindisi. My father's a fisherman.'

'And are they all like you there?'

'What, you mean in my family?' Maria shrugs. 'Some are, some aren't.' There is a pause. 'I'm a servant of the Marchesa Barbara of Brandenburg, that's what I am,' she says stiffly. Her back lengthens, then she picks up a hammer and begins hammering nails into the box lid.

'I'm sorry, child. I seem to have caused you offence.'

Maria turns round and motions silence, waiting until the groom has carried the box outside and is strapping it onto the carriage roof. 'Mistress, you are so well regarded that it seems as if I am getting above myself to be giving you advice.'

'Go on, child.'

Maria turns her ear to the door. 'Since I am given to you to work as your maidservant, I don't want you to come to any harm.' She takes a deep breath and smooths the seams of her skirt. 'When we are alone, you can ask me any questions you like. You see, I am a natural, but there are others at court who are not. They are educated to be entertaining with their pretty ways and accomplishments, and are highly prized. Often owned by some very powerful men. Men it is better not to cross.'

A natural? Ya Ling puzzles over the difference.

'Then, Maria, what is it that is unnatural about them?' She moves nearer to Maria and watches her intently. 'I have heard tell that witchcraft is involved.'

Maria's jaw drops in shock.

'Shh, Signora.' The groom's step is heard on the threshold. Maria whispers quickly: 'No one truly knows, though there are terrible rumours. I've heard that there is a great deal of money involved, so anyone who asks too closely is likely to…' She pulls a finger across her throat.

Ya Ling blinks. 'I see.' She shivers, remembering Clemente making the same gesture at the Christmas procession all those years ago. 'I thank you for your advice, and for all of your hard work too.'

Maria smiles as she picks up a broom and busies herself while Ya Ling makes a final check of her rooms before they travel back to court.

The following day Maria brings in her breakfast tray. 'I thought you might like a bit of peace and quiet this morning before I show you round. You are asked to attend Marchesa Barbara in her private garden straight after the angelus bell.'

'You are very thoughtful.'

Maria is a good guide but Ya Ling finds her head spinning at the vast number of similar corridors that all lead to different staterooms, each more opulent and gilded than the last.

As they go, Maria proudly tells all she knows about court etiquette and complex matters of precedence.

The small enclosed garden is a haven of peace after Maria's whirlwind tour. Barbara of Brandenburg sits on a stone bench that overlooks a fountain with a gilt statue of Mercury poised in flight in the centre, nymphs and putti pouring water at his winged feet.

The marchesa stands at her approach, her face masked with thin silk to ward off flies, and they begin a stately progress under a marble loggia lined with vines. The marchesa's ladies-in-waiting jostle into a queue behind her, each reaching to lift her long train of purple brocade away from the red dust. 'No. Leave that for now. You may follow at a distance. I wish to talk alone with my new healer.' Barbara throws her cloak over one shoulder to display its ermine lining and they walk past a maze of boxwood trees and through to the potager. The marchesa pauses by the garden wall where peach and apple trees are espaliered against the bricks. Their truncated limbs are wired to the wall and weighed down with budded fruit. Ya Ling remembers the third courtyard of her family's house in Beijing where the little *panjin* trees were starved in their shallow pots. She realises with a start that she hasn't thought of them for years.

'Pick me a peach.'

Ya Ling looks surprised, then reaches across and squeezes several. 'They're not ready yet,' she says. 'Nowhere near ripe enough. They will be far too sour for your stomach.'

'I know. I just wanted to see how forthright you are. Not many people are here.' She inclines her head towards the ladies-in-waiting, who have formed little factions and are chittering like sparrows. 'Come sit here.' She nods at a carved wooden bench in the shade, waving away one of her ladies who is pretending to look admiringly at the pink roses that climb the archway near to where they sit. 'Healerwoman, I want you to examine my younger children carefully. They are not quite as I would like,' she begins bluntly. 'Their foreheads protrude a little and the youngest has limbs that are…' She makes a slight curved motion with her hands. 'Is there anything you can do for them?' Ya Ling takes her handkerchief from her sleeve and flicks away at the cloud of midges that hovers nearby, pretending to brush one or two from the marchesa's silk veil. She uses the brief respite to think hard.

'Well?'

Ya Ling stiffens, feeling that her tenure here could be over as soon as it has begun. The ladies-in-waiting sulk and whisper to each other as they glance across at them. Her future hangs by a thread. But Barbara of Brandenburg is no fool. She must be well versed in the arts of flattery and courtly prevarication and she doesn't seem too impressed by either.

Ya Ling's voice comes out strained with anxiety. 'No, my lady. I am afraid that there is nothing that I can do for them, their bones are set, but I can make them stronger and help make sure that their children are born straight and true.'

The marchesa takes Ya Ling's handkerchief from her lap and winds it round her fingers. Her voice drops low with sorrow. 'I feared as much. But yes, we must keep them strong to secure the dynasty, so tell me what I must do.'

Ya Ling remembers Baba's deep voice instructing his Mongolian family, 'You cannot live on bread and milk and meat and blood.' She swings her knees round so they almost touch the marchesa's. 'You must make them eat fruit and vegetables. Even if they don't want to. And you need to introduce new blood into the Gonzaga line. They mustn't keep marrying into the same well-born families.'

'Really? Is that the case?' The marchesa pauses. 'Now I think about it, many children from the Malatesta family have the same thing and our families have intermarried more than once.' She shakes her head. 'If only it were our choice.' She sighs. 'Marriages are made to forge new alliances, or to shore up shaky ones. But do you honestly think this will help? If you do, then I will speak to my husband.'

'I know it will, Your Grace.'

'You speak plainly, Healerwoman. And that is a pleasant change for me.' The handkerchief drops down onto Ya Ling's lap. 'I want you to start work in the palace tomorrow. You can enjoy the rest of today in the sunshine, but in the morning I want you to start taking care of my family. The wider family too. The courtiers, and all my household staff and servants. There is not much sickness yet but the warmer weather will soon bring that.'

Once Barbara and her entourage have left, Ya Ling relaxes on the bench with the sun warm on her face and the birdsong restful to listen to. As she walks back to the palace, Bruzzi pushes his way through a low hedge and strides down the path to her. Ya Ling looks round quickly. Bruzzi has chosen his time well; the garden is now deserted. He walks right up to her until she is backed against a tree trunk. 'I'd be careful if I were you. All on your own out here. I have many important friends at court and my spies are watching your every move. There are some steep staircases in the palace. Some long drops.' The tree bark is digging into her back, so she pushes her toes into the grass to keep from slipping sideways. 'One word from me and they'll follow my instructions. Then I'll be back where I should be now. Here.' He jabs his fist downwards. 'As chief barber-surgeon to the marchesa and the rest of her sickly clan. Ludovico still admires my skills, so don't make yourself too comfortable, bitch. Not yet.'

He gives her one final push before walking quickly away down the cypress walk. Ya Ling carefully brushes the dust from her back until she feels her knees steadying, then shakes herself down and heads quickly for the relative safety of the busy palace.

Ya Ling soon settles into the routines of life at the palace. For several years she works hard and enjoys the many challenges of all the different ailments brought to her. Her treatment room is immaculate; the canisters are always full to the brim with the freshest herbs and the air is perfumed with crushed medicinal spices. She treats everyone from the ruling Gonzagas down to the lowliest cleaning maid with the same fairness and efficiency. Knowing that she is well regarded helps lessen the nagging feeling that Bruzzi is watching, waiting in the background, biding his time.

One day she is summoned to attend Barbara of Brandenburg.

'My plaything Anna has some kind of flux on her chest, and is unable to entertain, so I wish you to see her immediately.'

Ya Ling has heard all about Anna from Maria. The darling of the Gonzaga court, the favourite entertainer for an unprecedented two years, seeing off all her rivals with consummate confidence. Her pure silvery voice and skill with the *chitarra*, her ability to mimic and tell witty stories have all made her famous well beyond the confines of the court.

Ya Ling drops a deep curtsey. 'Of course, Marchesa. It will be a great pleasure.'

Barbara of Brandenburg holds up a warning finger. 'A great pleasure? Possibly not. You may find that my little Anna, my little plaything, my special *camarade*, will be even more of a challenge than me.'

Chapter 36

The Gonzaga Palace

While Enzio waits for his friends, he twists his body so he can keep looking at every angle of himself in the ornate brass mirror his parents sent from their estate for him. His family still miss him. Though his father's sacrifice in sending him for advancement to the Gonzaga court has reaped many rewards, his mother still pines. He likes how the cut of the red ribbed velour jerkin emphasises his manly shape and the tight hose shows off his fine calves. He knows how to present a *bella figura* and how much they all admire him at court. It's not just his looks either. He has a gift for oratory, reciting honeyed speeches that always delight Barbara of Brandenburg. He can't wait to share his idea, the wonderful knavery he has come up with for carnival. Holy Mother of Jesus! They need some fun before Lent begins.

'So what's this marvellous plan of yours?' Baldassare asks. 'Why can't we just taunt the Hebrews and make them race in their drawers again? We all enjoyed that so much last year. I can't imagine anything topping it.'

'No. I want more of a challenge. One that shows off how well I can act.' He waves an expansive hand round and round in a circular motion. 'A performance with flair. A character role.'

Gerardo chuckles when he tells them what he has planned. 'Anna? She likes you, so it might work. But I bet you'd never dare do that!'

'Why not? She's not watched like a daughter would be. No mother or father to worry about. No family.'

Baldassare thinks for a moment. 'No, she might not be dowried, but it's still risky. What if she tells Barbara?'

'Anna's not special any more. There is a rumour going round that the marchesa's starting to tire of her.' Enzio yawns. 'No gossip gets past me.'

'Where would you do it, though? It would have to be private enough to convince her your intentions are…'

'Completely dishonourable!' Enzio laughs loudly. 'But I want the pair of you to see it,' he insists. 'I need an audience, otherwise what's the point? All my talent going to waste!'

Gerardo thinks hard. 'I know! The laurel arbour. It's really dark there if you go deep inside.'

'Ah... deep inside? Yes, I have every intention of going in as deep as possible.' Enzio smiles complacently as they both double over at his witticism.

'Listen, I'm serious,' Gerardo continues. 'We could rig up a tapestry down one side for us to hide behind.'

Baldassare looks from one to the other. 'She'll never fall for this. Anna's not stupid.'

Enzio's full mouth purses. 'Of course she'll fall for it. She'll be mesmerised. Why wouldn't she be?'

'Look at him. See how your eyes are pulled towards him. Not the others.' Anna points down into the courtyard at Enzio, with his bright blue mohair cape and his matching cap. He is the son of the richest wool merchant in Mantova and his clothes are the envy of every young man at court.

Maria watches Anna's fingers ply her rosary. 'May I ask you, what are you praying for?'

'His safe return from the woods.' Anna blushes.

'But hunting thrushes is hardly dangerous. All they do is tie the cages of the *traditori*, those little traitor birds, to the bushes to lure the thrushes in, then they make the twigs sticky with lime, and once all the poor thrushes have been tempted in and got stuck fast, then Enzio will blast them to bits with all the clay pellets from his crossbow. He's hardly hunting wild bears, now is he?'

'Don't get above yourself, maid. Handling a crossbow takes great skill.' Anna smiles in what she clearly hopes is a sophisticated way. 'Men! Always proving themselves. Honestly!'

Maria dares place a tentative arm round her. 'Do you know much about men, Anna?' she asks quietly.

'Not really. But I hope to learn a bit more. And quite soon too.' She waits until Maria has turned to face her. 'After Enzio's invitation.'

'An invitation? From him?' They both look down from the high casement window as Enzio swaggers to the front of the hunting group and leads them out, laughing, towards the forest. It is impossible not to notice his beauty.

'Are you sure?' says Maria.

'Of course I'm sure! It's the most thrilling thing that's ever happened to me and I'm not having my maidservant spoiling it for me. Enzio has singled me out. So he must think I'm special. Even if you don't.' Anna taps her toe, fuming. Maria is no pumilio. There has been no sign of any artistic skills in all the years they have lived next door to each other in the Casetta dei Nani. 'Please be back here promptly after lunch to get me ready,' she says sharply.

Maria's knock on Anna's tiny door is punctual and she obeys Anna's directions to braid her hair into two little plaited horns and paint her face with lead paste until it feels rigid and looks like the finest porcelain. The tiny pair of cork pattens clipped under her shoes lift Anna up about a foot. Obviously still not high enough, and she feels very wobbly on them, but they are better than nothing and make her feel a little more confident. 'I've waited all my life for a chance like this.' The uncertain spin she gives makes her look much younger. 'So, how do I look?' Her head comes up in a stubborn jerk.

Maria's face puckers with concern as she follows her to the door. 'You look lovely, Anna.'

Early-evening scents are trickling through the garden. The heavy perfume of the early musk roses hangs in the air and the grass is carpeted with daisies. Enzio is already there, waiting for her. All her self-consciousness disappears when she sees him putting the final touches to a little tapestry awning he has rigged up to cover one side of the arbour. How thoughtful. The romance of it makes her breath catch in her chest. He wants their assignation to be kept private, until they are both sure enough of their feelings for each other to declare their love to the world. What a lovely boy he is. Nobody understands him at all. The inside of the arbour is dark and the space is tight. The heavy evergreen laurel branches on each side seem to lock her in. The onset of panic she always feels in a confined space makes her anxious. She pushes all terrifying thoughts of the box out of her mind. She has to bear it. It's as simple as that. She can't say anything to him that might break the romantic spell. Not after he has gone to all this trouble.

'Here my little song thrush, especially for you. You're panting like a little bird. Is that because of me?' His soft lips purse together. Anna manages a nod over the rim of the goblet of sweet wine he holds to her lips. In the wine swim several golden muscatel grapes. 'You look so beautiful I don't know how to describe you. Like an Amazon queen.' His voice seems a little loud, but he often sounds like that. It's part of his character, his love of drama. His wonderful talent for theatricals and flowery poetry.

The wine is definitely helping. She is enchanted at the efforts he has made to please her and tries to relax as he picks up his *cittern*. Made from ivory and inlaid with ebony and with golden fretwork, it has an extravagant bow of scarlet satin tied at the top of its neck. It is the envy of every court musician. He often carries it round with him. He raises his beautiful eyebrows to her as he strums a few chords. It is strung too tightly and there is a definite discord to the top notes, but she wouldn't dream of reaching to loosen the ivory pegs. The song he sings isn't one she has heard before; it seems to be all about hunting and catching tiny birds. She seems to hear a murmuring nearby as if the birds themselves are listening and wanting to enhance their joy. The tune is difficult to work out too as his voice seems to keep breaking. His nervousness must be making him too breathless to sing to her properly, she realises. At his encouragement she manages several large mouthfuls of wine and, watching his dark eyes on her, thinks that her tiny heart is beginning to melt.

'Don't be nervous, my darling,' Anna whispers shyly. 'I know exactly what you are feeling. Such strong emotions. I feel them too.'

'So you share the strength of my passion, do you, Anna? I thought you might! Oh my love, my love.' The notes become strident and he looks down at the *cittern* so helplessly that she gently takes it from his hands and leans it carefully against the laurel hedge. The wind mutters loudly through the thick leaves. Anna turns her head to listen. 'Just finish your wine, my darling Anna, to give you courage for the adventure I'm about to take you on.'

The wine is sweet and delicious, even more delectable because he keeps tilting the goblet to her lips until the last few drops slip down like silk. She feels a burning in her chest and the cooler air under the tapestry roof of the arbour suddenly warms up. He pulls her onto his knees. 'Touch me, Anna,' he demands. 'Feel how my manhood is growing just for you. See what your beauty does to me.' There's a deep rustling noise behind her but Anna is distracted by the feeling of his hands, one minute playing with the hem of her skirt, the next suddenly feeling for the cord round the waist of her linen underdrawers. 'Oh little Anna. You are so willing! So eager! I fear I'll never leave here a virgin.' A sudden gusting sound rattles through the laurel leaves behind them, but Enzio's slow languorous kisses keep her face welded to his. His fingers start to boldly explore the most intimate seam in her body. It is forbidden to let him do this. But this might be her only chance to find out what every woman expects to experience. For one brief moment she is determined to be like other women. To be just like them. Not to be different. Not to be herself. Not to be a pumilio. And truly she has never known a pleasure like this before. A pulling, drowning pleasure. And it is Enzio who is giving her these feelings. The most beautiful man at court. So perfect. Her proud smile feels constricted behind the stiff mask of white. 'Oh Anna. So tiny but so determined to make love to me,' he groans theatrically. The strange sensation rises and rises beneath his probing fingers and she can tell by his reaction that he is feeling the same pounding, the same overwhelming, unfurling spirals of pleasure. The sweep of his long lashes against her throat quickens, she feels his chest vibrate and hears the sound of his laughter echoing against the birdsong in the garden. She stops and suddenly withdraws her eager questing lips.

Laughter? Why would he be laughing at a tender time like this?

But it definitely sounds like laughter, and that of more than one male voice too. And very close by. Anna feels the sharp pressure of her desire deflate. She feels as if her heart has been squeezed tight between a pair of very cruel hands.

At her sudden stiffness on his lap, Enzio withdraws his hand. She gives him a long agonised stare before she climbs down off his knee and pulls the tapestry away from the laurel hedge. Gerardo is there, doubled up with laughter, with a fist pushed tight against his mouth.

Baldassare at least has the decency to look shamefaced. Anna doesn't know which of their expressions cuts her deeper. The spiteful delight at her stupidity, or the pity for her dashed dreams. Mustering as much pride as she can, she retrieves her cork pattens and with difficulty slips her feet into them. 'Oh do see the joke, Anna! Come on! You can't have thought for a moment I was serious!' Enzio idly brushes away a few flakes of white paste from the front of his red velvet jerkin. 'You! And I? How could that ever be possible? How ridiculous to even think, even hope…'

The expression on her face makes him blink as she stands precariously up on tiptoe to pull her face up nearer to his. '*Traditori*,' she says very quietly, so the sound won't penetrate the curtain. 'You are all *traditori*. But you, Enzio, you are far worse than the other two. You are worse even than all the *traditori* birds you used this morning on the hunt. They have no choice. They know no better. They sing because of instinct. Because that is all they know how to do. They do not mean to entrap. But you, you should know better. So be careful, Enzio. I warn you. Be very careful.'

'Why, little maid? What are you going to do? Shoot me with a crossbow?'

'Be warned, Enzio. I will have my revenge on you. I will find a way. You will disappear, I promise you that.'

Anna uses all the strength and dignity she can manage to keep upright on her pattens all the way back down the long avenue of cypress trees that lead through the garden. But once she arrives safely back in her room, the tears course down her face and she crawls under the bedcovers in an agony of shame.

Maria puts down the tray on a side table near to her bed. Her voice is soft and sisterly. 'Please, Anna. Just try a little. It's been two days now.' She gently moves the bedcover back and strokes the stiff little shoulder. 'Here…' She holds out a sop of bread dipped in broth. Anna pulls the damp covers back over her puffy face. Maria persists. 'See, I saved you a honey cake.' The little bed heaves as Anna burrows her face into the covers. 'Enzio isn't worth it, Anna. Making yourself ill like this.'

'You were right, Maria. I should have listened to you.' The voice comes out muffled against the pillow. 'I was so stupid. I can't face anybody. I know how they're all laughing at me.'

'If I could sing and dance like you and had wits as sharp as a lance I wouldn't give them a second thought,' Maria encourages. 'Come on, this plate's getting heavy.'

'Maria, don't you find it oppressive being hemmed in down here like this? Kept in our own quarters like animals. As if this is all we are. All we can ever be?'

'I'm afraid you've lost me, Anna.' Maria holds out the plate.

'I'm sorry. I was very rude to you. I don't deserve such a good friend. Always so kind. I didn't mean it when I said you were only a maidservant. As if being a pumilio is so wonderful. So superior,' Anna says bitterly.

'But you are wonderful. So musical. So witty. Don't let that horrible Enzio make you think you're not.'

'But do you understand why I went with him? Why I let him do such things to me?'

Maria strokes her red cheeks. They feel hot and feverish. 'Not really, Anna. Not with him.'

Anna mumbles, 'All I wanted was to feel like a normal girl for once. To have a handsome man show me the things he would show his sweetheart. Even if...' Maria waits. 'Even if... I knew he might be pretending. That's how much need I feel inside.'

'Oh Anna.' The bed creaks. 'Move over a bit. Here.' Anna sits up and lifts her knees up to her chest. 'Father Anselmo preaches that we must all accept the burden that God has—'

'No!' Anna takes the offered handkerchief and dabs her cheekbones. 'I'm not like you. You must understand that. If I was a natural then I might think differently, but I'm not and I often think, why me? It's so cruel that I might never...'

'Listen to me, the last time I went to confession—'

'Don't talk to me about Father Anselmo!' Anna snaps. 'Or any priest. They all know what goes on and they do nothing about it. They want to keep in with the wealthy families, so that's why they keep quiet about it. And it's a terrible sin! It must be.'

'Stop it, Anna!' Maria looks over her shoulder. 'You can't talk like that, against the Holy Mother Church, even down here. And people have suffered terrible torments for being too curious about pumilios. Some have ended up in the cage. Some have just disappeared.'

'I know. I, of all people, should know to be more careful. But surely you understand why I was so stupid. I just wanted… For one evening I just wanted to be like the ordinary girl I might have been.' Her small face is riven with misery. 'To know what it feels like to be loved by a man.'

'Oh, I know. I know.' Maria sighs as she leans across and squeezes Anna's hand. 'But no more talk like that again. Promise me.'

Chapter 37

Ya Ling waits patiently in her treatment room. An order from Barbara of Brandenburg can hardly be ignored, but if the little maid refuses to even see her, then what can she do? Having been told of the little *camarade*'s self-importance due to her two years of high status in the Gonzaga household, she is prepared to give the girl a couple of days. Late afternoon on the third day she tries again. Maria is apologetic. 'She won't come, *Gentildonna*. I'm really worried. She is so heartbroken. She hasn't been out of her bed for two days now.'

'I never usually have to pursue my patients, please tell her that.'

'I will, my lady. I do wish she would come and see you. She really does need your attentions. I will go and try again.' Maria rushes off and tries her best but Anna refuses to lift her face from beneath the coverlet of her tiny bed.

When the vespers bell has rung from the bell tower, Ya Ling puts down the turmeric roots she has been slicing into her grinding bowl. She asks her maid to try one last time. 'You must tell her that she has to come to me straight away, Maria, otherwise I will have to tell the marchesa that she has refused her wishes.'

When Anna enters the room, Ya Ling is surprised. There is something unusual about the girl, more so than with Maria. She presents a sorry sight as she comes slowly in with her odd rocking gait, pausing now and then to wheezily catch her breath. Ya Ling kneels in front of her and gently wipes away the last faint streaks of white paste from her forehead. Anna's slight frame folds and she gives a chorus of sobs. Ya Ling holds her close until she becomes still, then moves to unlace one of her sleeves. Anna backs away as if horrified.

'But you must! You have to let me, child!' Ya Ling leans back on her heels in readiness. 'If I can look at the Marchesa Barbara naked then I can surely examine you.'

The little face twisting into a sulk makes her look far younger than her years. 'I won't! And you can't make me!'

Ya Ling pulls the girl back into her arms. 'Tell me, little one, what has upset you so badly? If you share your unhappiness with me, then you will start to feel much better.'

The girl begins to babble. Her hot breath warms the side of Ya Ling's face. 'It was the look in his eyes that did it. I can't get it out of my mind. How stupid I've been!'

A fresh wave of sobs overtakes her and Ya Ling tucks a curl of damp hair behind the girl's ear as she pieces the story together. 'Go on, little lady, tell me everything. You can trust me.'

'Stop calling me little! I don't like that.'

'Sorry, child. I wasn't thinking. Hold on tight to my hand while you explain. It will help.'

Anna shakes as she tells Ya Ling what happened. 'It gets worse. He's telling everybody! Later that same evening, when I went down into the servants' hall, I wondered why everybody suddenly stopped laughing. And then I saw him. He was in the middle of telling them all, then he suddenly tailed off when he saw me. He'd been making these small gestures with his hands… I should have known. I fooled myself as well. That's what really hurts. One look from him and my wits went out of the window. That's how stupid I am!'

'No, you are not stupid. Just dazzled for a while. You're not the first young maid to be taken in by a horrible young man. But I'll look after you,' Ya Ling soothes. 'And so will your friends.'

'Some of them.' Anna's breathing calms down to a series of painful sighs. 'The ones in the Casetta dei Nani, they understand.'

'That's where you live? With Maria and… the others?'

'Yes. They've been kind. Tried to cheer me up when I ran back down there to hide.'

The girl's cough sounds like pebbles rattling in a box. 'I hear that the Marchesa Barbara keeps asking for you, and is getting annoyed at your absence from the court. She is waiting to be entertained, and if you can't dance for her and make her smile soon, well… As you know better than me, lives are fragile at court. A rumour, a quip that cuts a fraction too deep, a throat that can't keep a sweet tune…' The handmaid's lips draw in as she thinks hard, then she reluctantly holds her hands aloft ready to be unlaced out of her tight brocade dress.

At first Ya Ling doesn't notice it. She is concentrating on keeping up a slow murmur of conversation to put the girl at her ease while she runs her fingers gently over the curve of her breastbone to feel the compression beneath. But then, lifting up the girl's arm, she sees it straight away. The room grows quiet. A small diamond-shaped scar is embedded in her chest as if stitched there in blue thread. Ya Ling takes the girl's hand and lays its palm against her own, comparing the girl's short stubby fingers to the long slender length of her own. She runs a hand through her soft black curls before staring into her startled dark eyes.

'What are you doing? Staring at me like this! I thought you were supposed to be curing my cough!'

'How old are you, child?' Ya Ling sinks back on her heels and holds Anna's face between her trembling hands. 'Have you seen fourteen summers?' Her voice quivers. Her heart races as her eyes roam over Anna's shortened frame. Her sturdy little arms and legs. 'Fortuna?' Her gaze locks on to the brown eyes set deep in her unusually large face.

'Why do you ask me that? And who is Fortuna?'

'What happened to you, child?' Ya Ling manages through a dry throat. 'Who did this to you? Made you like this?'

'I can't tell you that, however important you are. In any case, I'm not Fortuna, I'm Anna.'

'You must tell me!'

Anna's eyes stretch wide with dread and her small features recoil. 'You must be new at court, to dare ask me that.' The healerwoman keeps staring at her as if she is a ghost. 'Who is this Fortuna?'

'Fortuna is my daughter.' Anna looks afraid at the healerwoman's shaking voice. 'Please tell me what happened to you.'

'I'm not allowed to say a word,' she whispers. 'He said they'd burn me as a witch if I did.'

'Who did? Mantegna?'

'The painter? I don't know him at all. It was a man called Dati.' Anna pulls down Ya Ling's veil and touches the contours of her face. 'How could I be your daughter? I look nothing like you. You are laughing at me. Being cruel. Like he was.'

'No, child, I am your mother.'

Anna's eyes fill with tears. 'You can't be!' Suddenly she pushes Ya

Ling away. 'So why did you let me go? How could you do that to your own daughter?'

'I knew when Mantegna told me you had died that something was wrong. I could sense he was keeping something hidden from me. *Bastardo!* So tell me, child, where? Where did you live? Where did this happen to you?'

Anna's voice drops to a faint whisper. 'At the pumilio house. Dati said I would be burned as a sorceress if I ever told what had happened to me there.'

Dati? Wasn't that the man Mantegna said had told him that Fortuna had died? Her voice tightens. 'You must tell me what you know about this man Dati.'

'He was there right from the beginning. He did the bindings. Every week. We used to struggle to get away but it was no use, we were still dragged off into the binding room. It was so painful. He pulled them so tight.' Anna's voice drops as she remembers. Her face is bleached white with shock.

'So where did he keep you? What else did he do to you?'

'I cannot say! I daren't say!' Anna holds her head in her hands. 'You would keep silent too, if you knew the suffering that went on there.'

'Where? Where did he keep you?'

'Purgatory itself.'

'Oh child!' Ya Ling clutches the girl's hands to her chest.

'It's not far from here. The place where the witchcraft happens. People don't know that. Only changelings are sent there. And really sinful people go there after they die, but I never saw any of those. And you must never tell a single soul. It's a dark place. All I remember is the bindings digging in, and the taste of bitterness. The disgusting food that stung you inside like poison. There were others there too.' Her small frame quivers. 'Dati told me that if this was purgatory, imagine what the real hell would be like. And he can send me back there any time he wants.'

Although she often takes wine to help relax her patients or to help them sleep, it is unusual for the Widow to pour herself a large goblet and stand there gulping it down; still, none of the staff in the palace kitchen show any interest as Ya Ling helps herself from a flagon of wine. She is known to be held in high esteem by Barbara of Brandenburg and so she can do as she wishes. In any case, the kitchen staff are busily scurrying around making preparations for the feast to celebrate the arrival of Francesco, the Gonzaga son who has recently been made a cardinal. He has come to Mantova to see the completion of Mantegna's likeness of him in the fresco, and to admire the portraits of Ludovico and Barbara on the adjoining wall.

So, if it seems strange for the healerwoman to stand for several moments with her veiled forehead leaning hard against the icy brick wall of the meat pantry, no one has time to notice. There are swans to be plucked, mounds of vegetables to be prepared, and ribbons of golden pasta are already drying as they hang from their pine racks waiting to be tossed in oil. Several wild boar carcasses hang from the ceiling hooks, still to be butchered and prepared. A scarlet shiny thread drips from each snarling mouth, the stickiness spreading into a pool onto the tiles. An apprentice cook curses as he slides and slithers and bumps hard into the Widow's shoulder. 'Sorry. So sorry, Signora! So much to do!'

Ya Ling comes suddenly out of her stupor and nods at his apology, then quickly refills the flagon from one of the vast oak barrels that line the corridor to the kitchen and picks up another goblet. She hopes that a draught of wine will relax Anna and help her to unburden herself. Will help her to speak of the unspeakable.

If necessary she will give her a pinch of poppy paste to calm her down even more, but that has to be handled with great care. Some patients can be stirred by such a powerful need for repeated doses that she only uses it rarely. She can't bear to expose her daughter to anything that might harm her even further.

Her daughter? It seems incredible that her tiny daughter has been returned to her now, on the cusp of maturity, in a form she would never have recognised. It isn't just the bodily changes; Anna's face itself holds only a glimpse of her eastern heritage. The slight slant to her cheekbone and the blue sheen to her dark curls are the only signs that Ya Ling is her mother. She curses Mantegna for what he has done to their child, for what he has made her suffer. And she curses herself even more at her stupidity in ever having handed over her beloved daughter to him.

Walking back through the labyrinthine passages of the servants' quarters where hundreds of staff are accommodated, she checks each corridor carefully. Nowhere here is safe from prying eyes and loose mouths. She finds Anna where she has left her a short while before, crouched double on a small stool. She unties her veil. From now on, there will be complete openness between them. Absolute trust. It's imperative that no one else knows of what Anna is about to tell her. Harsh punishments have fallen swiftly on those who have tried to find out about pumilios in the past. Maria has warned her of flayings and the strappado. Of men prepared to kill to keep the sickening process secret. Of Ludovico Gonzaga himself being heavily indebted to some of them. Others talk of vengeful spirits. Of sorcery and of the risen Devil himself.

Anna lifts her head when the goblet is gently pressed into her hands. She takes it wordlessly and drinks deeply. Her eyes are red and puffy with crying. 'You and the painter Mantegna?' Her eyes look dazed. 'How can I trust you? Why should I believe that you are my parents?' A sudden thin, piercing wail comes out of her tiny frame, like a child who has just woken alone in the darkness.

Ya Ling feels a jolt run through her. An image of the Berber's blue turban comes to her and she relives the pain she still feels at his betrayal. Her voice is low. 'I know how you must feel—' she begins.

'No you don't.' Anna looks down at her body. 'How can you?'

'No.' Ya Ling winces. 'You're right, child. I can't.' Anna holds up her small hands as if seeing them anew. 'I could have been like the other girls at court? Tall perhaps, with long limbs and a pretty face? I can't believe it.' Her hands cover her eyes. Ya Ling has to lean down to hear her plaintive broken voice. 'I can't bear it.'

'You are pretty, Anna.' Ya Ling's face is streaked with tears. 'You couldn't be more beautiful to me.'

Anna sounds dazed. 'They told us we were bred to be pumilios. They said we had no natural parents. That we were changelings and that was why we had been sent to purgatory. That was why we had to keep silent about where we came from or we would rouse even worse demons.'

'Every child has parents, Anna…' Ya Ling begins gently, her voice almost overwhelmed by the tenderness she feels inside. She tries to smile but can't control the wavering of her lips. 'Don't you remember anything of the life we shared when you were a baby? When you lived with me as a tiny child. Can't you remember any of that?'

'No! Nothing!' Anna suddenly stiffens and looks up aghast. 'But if what you say is true, then you must have given me away!' she accuses.

'At that time I had no choice. I was destitute. You would have starved, or been on the streets. You had a terrible cough from the dust and the smoke in the slums. Mantegna promised me that you would be cared for by a wealthy family as if you were their own daughter. He promised me I could see you every two weeks. It was only after he told me that you had died that I stopped chasing him for news of you. I used to run beside his mare, begging him to find out how you were.' Ya Ling sinks to her knees. The tears feel cold on her cheeks. 'Child, you must heed me. For the love of Heaven, believe me when I tell you that I spent everything I had paying scribes, begging him for news of you, but he threw my letters into the gutter. I asked for you in every single house I went to. Then when he told me you had died, I thought I would die of grief myself.'

Anna stumbles into her mother's outstretched arms, and they lean tightly into each other. 'But him! Mantegna! My father?' Anna looks down as if suddenly shocked by her own diminutive frame. 'How could he do this to one of his own bloodline?'

'I cannot imagine. Maybe he chose not to find out what Dati's plans were for you. So he is either very cruel or very careless. Either way, we will find a way to ruin him. *Justice can overpower a hundred evils.*' She leans down to trail a hand through Anna's soft hair. 'But first, my child, painful though it is, you have to tell me exactly what happened.'

Anna's eyes open wide with fear. 'No. I cannot speak of it. Who knows what terror might be visited upon me?'

'You must trust me, Anna.'

'Trust you?' Anna shakes her head. 'How can I do that?'

Ya Ling stands and reaches into a small wooden coffret pulling out a scrap of creased cotton. 'See these stitches? I made you a little shift and I made myself a matching veil so that when we met I could prove that I was your true mother. Don't you remember the little shift? The pattern round the hem?' Ya Ling shakes out the veil eagerly.

'No,' says Anna. 'We didn't wear clothes. Not until we were much older. When we were young and growing we were always kept bound.' Anna scrutinises her mother's face. 'But you are from an eastern land. I barely look like you,' she whispers. 'How can I believe you?'

Ya Ling bites her lower lip. 'Wait! I know you have an excellent ear for music and can remember many tunes. Do you remember any of these?' She begins to sing scraps of the folk songs and the lullabies she had sung to Anna as a baby. Her voice quivers above and below the tunes but she ploughs on determinedly.

Anna frowns in concentration, shaking her head. 'Sing that last one again.' As she nods her head in time to the music her tense features begin to soften. 'Yes, I think I do remember,' she says carefully. She hums the first chords of the tune.

'I was the one who sang that to you!' Ya Ling claps her hands in relief. 'Then you must believe me! It's an old folk song that my mother taught me in Beijing. So you must know I am telling you the truth.' Ya Ling slips a reassuring hand over her daughter's smaller one and pulls her closer. 'I need all the information you can give me. If we are to get justice then I have to know every detail.'

Anna grinds her jaw from side to side. 'Dati will find out and he will send me to hellfire. He has done that to others.'

'No he won't. You are safe now. Safe in my arms. Do you think I would stand by and let further harm happen to you?' Anna could hear the suppressed anguish in her mother's voice. 'As long as there is breath in my body, I will keep you safe.'

Anna takes a deep draught of wine and sits back on the stool with both arms wrapped tightly round her chest. 'Then I will try.'

'You must, Anna, for all the other pumilios who have suffered.' Ya Ling's voice tightens with tension. 'And to save the other children who have not yet been taken. Begin, child.' In the long silence Anna's breathing grows less tattered. 'Have courage, child. You must begin.'

Anna stares up into her mother's eyes, her fears heightened. Ya Ling has to stoop down to catch her words. 'Then I will, but my memories of life in purgatory are very few. It was so awful there that I have tried hard to forget the terrible things that happened to me.' She plucks at the fabric of her dress.

'Please try, little one.'

'I remember a dark room…' Her voice sounds younger, its tone tentative and terrified. 'It was down some wooden steps. There was straw on the floor and it rustled when it was fresh. I remember snatches of sound. Of floorboards creaking overhead. Of the small noises we made to each other, noises of comfort but usually of fear too. There was a trapdoor looking up into the light, which made me blink when it was opened.' Ya Ling clutches at her chest, remembering the rising panic she herself had felt in the ship's hold when she had been captured, the smothering darkness, the tiny strips of light that came through the gaps in the planking of the deck. 'We were brought up into the light every now and then and we hated it.'

'Hated it? But why, child, why?'

'It was really frightening. So bright it made my eyes water. The hot sunshine made them sting. They used to line us up and look at our progress. Every now and then there would be one that wasn't right. I remember one little boy was very weak, he had stopped eating and his legs began to curve round like a pumpkin. Dati didn't like that and he took him away. We didn't see him again. He told us he had thrown him into hellfire. After each of the bright days Dati and the big terrifying man who worked for him would pull and pull on my bindings until I thought I wouldn't be able to breathe. I used to dream of my arms and legs bursting through the bindings, because that is what it felt like they were trying to do. Being in the cellar was better. I was used to that. It felt safer down there…' Her voice becomes a thin sliver of sound.

Ya Ling fights the instinct to lift her daughter up into her arms; she thinks that if Anna stops she might never start talking about it again. 'So did they not feed you, child? Or did they just keep you hungry? Is that how it worked?'

'Always hungry. Every little stomach in that cellar growled day and night. The big man used to come down the steps once a day with a bowl of green slops and a bucket of water, but often the food was so bitter that no matter how hungry we were we didn't want to even try it. But we had to. We were beaten if we didn't and threatened with hellfire. The man used to teach us a few words too. We soon understood what the word fist meant.' Wine spills out of the goblet. 'Later on our lives were better when the dwarfing had been achieved.'

Ya Ling removes her hand from her open mouth. 'And when was that, child?'

'I don't know.' Anna's voice drops low. 'They kept measuring us so I suppose when we were small enough for our age. When they were satisfied that we wouldn't grow any more. Then we were sent to a different house and fed properly. We had a tutor for language and a music tutor to teach us to sing and play different instruments. My skills at singing and the *chitarra* made me very valuable so that's why I was sent here to court. I've tried to keep remembering those happier times, but sometimes at night when I can't sleep, and sometimes in a really bad nightmare, the memories line up to taunt me. They tell me that happiness won't last. Only the fear, and the hunger and the gnawing pain in that pumilio house in purgatory will always stay with me. I don't know what was in the food, but you can't imagine how foul it tasted, or how it scalded your insides.'

'They must have put herbs in your food. Stunting herbs to stop your growth. Some plants like foxtail, daisy root and rye grass have dwarfing juices in them. Walnut and elder leaves too, but knotgrass is the worst for hindering. When I learned my skills I was taught their properties as a warning. Of course as a true healer, I would never ever need to use them. I leave that to vicious men like Dati.' Ya Ling shakes her head in disgust.

'Well, I must have eaten all of them, because they certainly worked on me.'

The despairing lift to her tiny shoulders makes Ya Ling sink to her knees and enfold Anna in her arms. 'I can't bear to think of the agony you went through and what other children are going through now. We must use our cleverness together, you and I.' She gives her daughter an encouraging squeeze. 'No matter how powerful these men think they are, with all their terrifying tales of witchcraft and threats of hellfire, we will find a way to stop them. We just need to think hard and apply the knowledge we find out.' She hugs Anna fiercely. 'But for now, you are safe, child. Nothing cruel like that will ever happen to you again.'

'But when I sleep I go back there. Many nights I return to purgatory in my dreams.' Ya Ling feels fear undulate down her small frame. 'I return to the worst part. The very worst part of it all. I feel I am back in the box.'

'The what?'

Anna's attempt at a whisper erupts with sobs. 'I can't…' She burrows her head into her mother's shoulder. 'They will certainly send me to hellfire if I tell of that.'

'Child, you must. Cling to me tightly and know that I will keep you safe. You must finish this dreadful tale. I promise you that when nightmares are taken out and shaken in daylight, then they lose their power to terrify.'

Anna makes several attempts to begin. The back of her dress is soaked in sweat. Her mother simply kisses her damp hairline and holds her close. The effort required to speak through her clenched jaw makes her voice sound as brittle as spun glass. 'It was a small box with a big metal screw at each end. After the bright days when we had all been examined, if any pumilio looked as if they had grown too much then they were taken away and bound so tightly they couldn't even struggle, though believe me, we all tried to get away once we were carried into the room with the box waiting with the lid open in the corner. It stopped us growing, you see.'

Ya Ling feels her heart beat the same rapid tattoo as her daughter's. 'Go on,' she murmurs, 'have courage.'

'You were laid in the box and both arms were forced into short slots in each side. Then the screws at each end were tightened until it felt as if you were going to be flattened to nothing. They put a weight on your stomach so that you couldn't lift your aching back up from the bottom of the box to gain any ease. They knew exactly what they were doing.' Her voice drops bitterly. 'Then they… then…' Her voice comes out in a long vaporous plea.

'Then they what, child?'

'Then they closed the lid and strapped the box shut.'

Ya Ling feels the small body shake violently and she tightens her arms around her. She finds it hard to keep control of her own voice. 'In God's name, why would they close it and strap it shut as well?'

'To lessen the noise. Every pumilio screamed and screamed when they were put in the box, and it upset the rest of us very badly. We couldn't eat or drink anything. So they made a lid with only a tiny hole to breathe through so the sound was not so loud. But we could still hear it though, that awful high-pitched screaming, and we used to join in.'

Ya Ling wipes away the sudden tears that run down her cheekbones before her daughter can see her weakness. 'And for how long did you have to bear that?' she murmurs.

'Many days. It seemed like many lifetimes. In summer the heat was intolerable. We were taken out and given water, then put back inside. Each joint seemed to cry out for space. It felt like your bones themselves would break through the frame of the box, but they never did. They were too clever for that in purgatory.'

Ya Ling's heart constricts at the thought of the pressure on her daughter's tiny bones. Of her lying in agony in the darkness. How could she not have sensed her torment? Then a sudden insight strikes home. The knucklebones did not lie. The chants she used asked the bones to show if a dead soul was in torment, not if a live one was in agony. She quickly pulls herself together. 'Child, listen to me. You must never call it purgatory again. It is far too dangerous. It is a sin to do so, and the people of the Cross and their priests will be very angry and bring down heavy punishment if you call it so. But it is something we can use to our advantage when we plan our revenge.'

Anna rubs her eyes with her fingertips, then takes a deep shaky breath and looks at her mother calmly. 'Then I will never call it that again. You are right, Mother. We must make a plan. We must work together and find out as much as we can, then our crossbow will be primed and ready. No other child must suffer like I did. Like I still do.'

Ya Ling manages a fragile smile. She recognises the strength in Anna's bruised soul. She remembers the tiny *panjin* trees in Baba's courtyard, still cleaving their roots to the soil in their cruel shallow pots. 'You will endure, Anna,' she says. 'That is what life teaches us. All things must pass.' Her gaze on her daughter is full of admiration. Anna's determination and endurance come straight from her Mongol forebears, but her shrewd understanding that revenge works best when patiently planned and calmly calculated comes straight from the land of the Han.

Chapter 38

'Everyone at court knows how fond he is of you, Anna. He sees you as a daughter, so you have to tell him. All of it. He will be a powerful ally for us.'

'Do I have to?' Her reluctant eyes scan her mother's face.

Ya Ling puts her hand to her heart, realising how painful it will be for Anna to relive the terrible ordeal she endured in the pumilio house. 'You must. I know it's going to be hard, but you must. I now have enough money for us to travel safely to Beijing and to arrive with dignity. I can't wait to show you—'

'What? Leave here?' Anna looks shaken. 'But, Mother, why would we do that?'

'So we can live there! So I can show you the city where I was born. My family, and Chen, who brought me up.' Her eyes light up as she clasps Anna's hands in her own. 'And perhaps a man called Altan, who I once—'

'But what will they make of me there?' She glances down.

Ya Ling opens out her hands. 'Well, once they know you, then…'

'But here I have friends. A home.'

'But child, this is what I have longed for, for years. All that I have worked towards.'

'How would I be introduced to your family?' Anna insists. 'A child birthed out of wedlock? A very different child to one they would want to claim as their own?'

'Listen, child…' Ya Ling pauses and her face falls as she thinks hard. 'We could tell them you are my handmaid.'

'Your handmaid?' Hurt tightens Anna's eyes. 'Oh, Mother.'

'Sorry, child. That is not what I meant at all. I spoke too quickly, without thinking.'

Anna's expression is earnest. 'You see, over the last few days I've been hoping you will teach me some of your skills, then I will be respected for my knowledge.'

'I see.' Ya Ling sits down heavily.

Anna waits several moments. 'We will have to discuss this another time, Mother. Firstly I must go and talk to Marsilio. We agreed that while the pumilios continue to suffer, their needs must come first. Even before such an important decision as this. So I must go. He will be a powerful ally.'

Her mother watches as Anna realigns her shoulders and then strides purposefully across the room to go to Ludovico Gonzaga's private office. 'And make sure Marsilio knows to keep it secret that I am your mother,' Ya Ling calls when she reaches the door.

The private secretary is in his office, sitting behind a tidy pyramid of scrolls, the Gonzaga ring poised ready to be impressed against the red wax melting in a pot over a candle. 'A walk? Now? I would like to oblige you, but I am very busy.' His deep voice lifts in surprise when he notices her agitated fingers. 'All right. Three more to seal, then I will join you by the fishpond.'

His steps along the cypress walk are hurried. Anna taps the space next to her on the bench and begins immediately. 'I have something to tell you that may take a while. It isn't a pleasant tale but it is one I have to tell you. Do you have the time now to listen?'

'I have always time for my little friend.' Anna feels a hand on her head. 'One who reminds me so much of my dear daughters. And who always will. They might not have been your age, Anna, but they were both about your height, when the last plague struck and the Lord decided to call them to Him. So whenever I see you, I will always think of my little girls, frozen in time.' He notices Anna's hands trembling so violently that she tucks them under her skirt and sits down heavily on them. 'If it's about that bastard Enzio, don't worry, he's on my list. He has many powerful connections but I'll stop his cruel tricks one day, child, see if I don't.'

'No.' She sighs. 'It's far worse than that.' He turns to her in concern. Anna's deep breathing is audible above the slight breeze that rustles the reeds round the rim of the pond. At the first mention of the pumilio house, Marsilio glances quickly behind and his finger comes up quickly to caution her, but Anna ploughs on determinedly and tells him everything, about Mantegna giving her away, and every brutal detail of what happened to her when she was handed over to Dati.

Marsilio's beaky profile pales. He instinctively reaches out to pull her onto his knee but she indicates the tiers of palace windows that overlook the pond, where shadows lurk and curious eyes look out. 'My child…' he mutters, 'my poor little *camarade*. On one level, of course I knew they existed, but I assumed they were a variation of children born like that naturally. I knew that some kind of process was involved, but I thought it had more to do with their education, teaching them music, and how to entertain, that sort of thing. I dismissed all the nonsense about witchcraft as a trick because I knew large profits were made dealing them.' He turns to her and takes her hand. 'In all truth, I had no idea of the degree of barbarity involved, and I am ashamed of that.' He shrugs awkwardly. 'I should have known. In my position, I should have made it my business to know.'

'But now you do know how children are being tortured, then you must help the Widow and me stop it from happening.' She folds her arms determinedly.

'That's impossible, child.' He lays his thumb across his throat, the private sign that binds together their unlikely friendship. 'Let me explain. As you well know, having a pumilio is a sign of great status. They cost a fortune to buy and – ironically after all the cruelty you have just told me about – having one is a sign of culture and refinement. Their oratory, their acting and their musical skills are seen as assets to any great family.'

Anna scowls. 'Marsilio, I know all this! But you can't just admire the skills the pumilios have acquired. You have to help the Widow and me to stop this dreadful business happening in the first place.'

'Child, now I understand why the provenance of pumilios is wrapped in secrecy. Why even asking about it has caused some people great trouble. There are far too many influential men involved. Not just here in Mantova either, but in other cities too. They supply the courts and the wealthy families of many other countries with pumilios. The marchese has treaties and alliances with some of them, and the others he won't want to annoy.' Marsilio's voice thickens with worry. 'Do not proceed further with this. Promise me.'

'So you are telling me there's nothing we can do?' Her voice rises. 'Then what about Mantegna? Don't you think he should be punished for giving me away to Dati? Either he knew what would happen to me or he didn't – but even if he didn't, then he didn't even bother to find out where I had been taken. Either way, punishment is due. And Dati even more so. His servant too! I've just told you all the terrible things they did to me. Will you just let them carry on doing it to other children?'

'Unfortunately Mantegna is now too powerful to touch. The fresco that he is currently painting in the Camera degli Sposi is said to be the finest ever seen. It is so true to life, some say it's a miracle. Mantegna himself has boasted of that. Listen, child, the Gonzagas would only allow a man they really admired and trusted to paint such an intimate portrait of them.'

'So there's nothing we can do?' Anna's eyes fill with tears.

Marsilio shakes his head. 'It's too dangerous, Anna. You must not get involved in this. I would do anything for you, you know that. My wife is always asking me for news of you.' He smiles briefly and reaches over to pat her cheek. 'In a court like ours, full of spies all eager to trade in the merest rumour to gain advancement, the loyalty and discretion we share is a rare pleasure.'

Her small frame tenses. 'Then surely…?'

Marsilio's voice rumbles lower with regret. 'Little one, everyone's life at court is precarious. Even mine. All I can do is give you my relic of the true cross to keep you safe.'

'Oh. Thank you.' Anna nods in gratitude, then slumps against his side. The morning's heat rises around them as they both stare out into the glare above the still water. A mother duck emerges from the reeds, fussily encouraging her brood of fluffy yellow ducklings to venture into the water. They fan out across the surface in a straggling golden arc. Suddenly a pike rears its head and snaps its powerful jaws round the smallest duckling, which gives a squeal before it is dragged down below the surface of the water.

'Did you see that?' Anna leans forwards to get down from the bench. 'Be quick! We must do something.'

Marsilio gently pulls her back. 'No, child. It is nature. And the will of the Divine. That's how life is. Cruel and unfair. We may question the injustice, but we both know we are powerless against it. I know this even more now after what you have just told me. I'm very sorry, Anna.'

Anna turns a surly face to him. 'No, Marsilio. The pike is hungry. That is why he grabs what he can. It is his instinct to survive and he is unthinking. What I have just told you is about man's cruelty, inflicted over and over again on the helpless, just to make money. That is another level of evil altogether.'

Marsilio gives a sigh of regret. 'Come, let's return to our duties before tongues begin to wag. Tell the Widow she can trust in my silence. I have already forgotten everything you have told me.'

'So you won't help us?'

He holds out a courteous elbow in silence and helps her down from the bench. He twists the large sealing ring, easing away the heavily carved G from his finger. 'Come, little one. There is nothing more to say.'

Ya Ling has tried to keep herself busy straining tinctures through muslin into small bottles, but it seems too dainty a task for her fingers. The bottles' neck rims are too narrow and the sticky green fluid keeps splashing onto the bench. She crushes juniper leaves furiously in her big black mortar instead. She looks up quickly when the door opens. 'How did it go, child? What did he say?'

Anna screws up her tiny features. 'Hopeless. He says there's nothing we can do. It's too dangerous.'

'That's nonsense! There's always a way.'

Anna's voice is edged with bitterness. 'And he also warned me that Bruzzi is asking questions about you all over the court, so he said to tell you that you must be careful.' The pestle pounds hard into the leaves, releasing a ferny woodland scent. Anna fears the thick walls of the mortar will shatter under the heavy thumping and grinding. 'He says we're not powerful enough. Not strong enough. Without allies. There's nothing we can do. Although he did promise me a relic of the true cross to keep us both safe.'

'Another piece of wood from the White Christ's cross? Well, how big could it have been? It must have been enormous because everybody in Mantova seems to have pieces of it!' Ya Ling rolls her eyes.

'And how many bones did these saints have? Must have been thousands! Not like any skeleton I have ever seen.'

Anna's voice is shocked. 'Mother! Shh. You can't say things like that! Not here in Mantova.'

Ya Ling rattles on, unimpressed. 'There will be a way, Anna,' she insists. 'There always is. We don't need physical strength or powerful allies. Remember what Lao Tzu tells us – *Nothing is softer or more flexible than water, yet nothing can resist it.* We just have to use our intelligence.'

'But Marsilio Andreasi is the cleverest man at court. In all of Mantova, probably. I bet he's the wisest man ever! If he says there is nothing we can do, then we have to believe him.'

'The wisest man ever? Him? No, child. There have been many men far wiser than him. Confucius for one. *He who learns but does not think is lost. He who thinks but does not learn is imperilled.*'

Ya Ling is delighted at the way Anna focuses on her as she listens. 'So take heed, Anna, we must learn from each other. You can teach me more about the ways of the court and the church, and together we will think anew.'

Chapter 39

Everywhere is a sea of red faces. The most elevated elite of Mantovan society, flamboyant in their finest velvet and flounced silks, all parade into the Great Hall. Court servants scurry around, resplendent in the scarlet and white Gonzaga colours. Flagons of emerald green Murano glass are passed round as more wine is demanded from the perspiring servants, who can barely keep up. The noise level rises like the roar of the sea, trapped between the tapestries and Mantegna's bright festal awnings, which are pinned to each wall.

'I can't face Mantegna,' Anna whispers to her mother, seated next to her. 'When I see him, now that I know what he did, I'm not sure I'll be able to control myself.'

Ya Ling slides a reassuring hand over hers. 'You will, Anna, you'll see. We both must.'

'It's hopeless. Look, he's just come in. I can't bear it! Look where he's been placed. Only three down from the cardinal!' They both glance at the top table. The cardinal, resplendent in his new scarlet robes, surveys the room. At his cursory nod, the guests sit down. 'He rides very high in the Gonzagas' esteem. I've heard that they think the way he has painted some strange device on the ceiling is a stroke of genius. Oh, I wish I could relax.' Anna tightens the silver pegs on her *chitarra* for the third time and swallows some cold water. 'It's not just him in here either. It's Enzio too.' They look further up their table to where a group of young courtiers sit enjoying the spectacle they present with their noisy sense of entitlement. Their fine clothes. Their jewelled fingers making flowery gestures. 'I've heard that Enzio is even in one of the frescos too, in the one with all the Gonzaga family, painted right at the front. I wonder how much that cost his father,' she says bitterly. 'He'll be even more of a show-off once the public are finally allowed into the Camera degli Sposi and they see him there, up on the wall, in pride of place.'

Nervous fingers play with the strings of her instrument until Ya

Ling gently takes it from her and rests it next to her on the bench. 'Patience, child, and stay calm.'

Anna's small teeth worry her bottom lip. 'Normally I sit at Barbara's left hand and tend to her before I entertain. But tonight I was sent right down here.'

The scent of roasted meat rising from the kitchens overrides the spicy perfume of the immense beeswax candles that drip from the curlicue sconces on the walls, as the heat in the room continues to rise. Waterfalls of green grapes and split pomegranates whose jewelled seeds catch the light like tiny rubies spill from great onyx vases. The fruit looks mouth-watering but it's the tempting savoury smell of the roasted wild boar when they are carried in on great steaming platters that brings a great roar from the guests. In the centre of each platter is a boar's head and each gaping mouth holds an apple studded with cloves. When Barbara pulls the apple from the boar placed in front of her, and takes a hearty bite out of it, that is the signal to begin, to slice into the carcasses on each table and hand round portions of meat, and tear at the long flat wheaten loaves that serve as trenchers to catch the dripping fat and juices. Men pull out their knives, already sharpened in readiness, poised to demonstrate their chivalry by carving dainty pieces for the ladies.

The platters of meat are all laid on the tables, but Barbara continues merely to smile and wait. The grumbling is hushed and an air of anticipation runs palpably down the lines of hungry guests. The Gonzagas are famous for not merely feeding their guests but for entertaining them as well. Their favourite cook, a fat-cheeked Frankish man, likes to surprise. He has been holed up in his own chamber in the kitchen for weeks. Rumours have spread round the court that he's been practising in secret for a very special dish, the like of which has never been seen before. The evening justifies it. The promotion of Francesco Gonzaga to cardinal has elevated the Gonzaga family from being seen as mere landlords and *condottieri* to becoming Lords of Mantova. Ludovico has insisted that Mantegna devote one whole wall in the Camera degli Sposi to Francesco's honour. He has always been a favourite with his father and the feast is a further demonstration of Ludovico's gratitude towards his second son.

The crowd crane forwards to see what is being carried through the room and what the sudden hush signifies. Each pewter salver holds a plate on which sits a huge swan still covered in white feathers. The crowd look on in silence as a swan is placed in the centre of each table. Swords are raised again but this time they look to the Frank for instruction. He speaks with a thick glottal accent and relishes his moment of showmanship.

Ya Ling frowns. 'What does he say, child? I find it hard to understand the way he speaks.'

'It's full of boned birds all reassembled. First a boned swan, inside that a huge capon, and inside that a cockerel, then a chicken, then a pheasant, then a grouse, then a partridge, then a pigeon, then a quail – and there is also a special surprise inside as well.'

The cook takes off his floppy white cap and bows low to the marchesa, who nods back at him. Swords come down and cleave each swan in two with a huge theatrical swish. There is a gasp of surprise as two halves of feathered baked clay fall onto the tables, leaving behind massive rounded sections of meat. The crowd roar approval when from out of the shattered clay fly several tiny and terrified thrushes, who desperately seek to hide themselves away up in the cooler branches of the rafters. On Ya Ling and Anna's table falls one scorched little bird that has been caught by the sword and lost most of its wing. It flutters round and round in circles on the tabletop, spraying tiny gobbets of blood onto the white linen and making the crowd convulse with laughter.

'I can't bear to think about how terrified they must have been, beating their tiny wings in panic.' Anna's hand presses hard against Ya Ling's chest. 'Dark and imprisoned, like in the box.'

'It's all right, Anna,' she soothes as she slips a hand over her daughter's.

'But I must stay calm. I daren't take my eyes off Barbara in case I miss her summons. I always begin and end the entertainment, that's what the court favourite does.'

After the last of the meat is eaten, and the mounds of fruit are almost finished, four uniformed heralds arrive and blast out on their silver trumpets the announcement that the entertainment is about to begin.

The room falls immediately silent. Ya Ling manages a confident smile as Anna picks up her *chitarra* and begins the lonely walk between the two long tables to the raised dais in front of the top table. She notices that her daughter's posture becomes rounded with embarrassment when she passes Enzio, Gerardo and Baldassare.

'Ah, it's my little *traditori* bird,' Enzio says in a loud aside as she passes. 'One too ungainly to fly up to the rafters.' Anna tries to ignore the barely repressed titters, which tail off to silence when both she and the audience realise that there is already someone else standing in front of her on the dais: Barbara's new *camarade* at court. A young pumilio called Crispino with jet black ringlets and a large exaggerated velvet codpiece, who bows low to her as if throwing down a challenge. In the awkward silence Anna decides not to try to catch Barbara's eye. It's too late for any imploring looks and in any case, she is busy laughing with her husband. The walk back down along the rows of guests seems interminable.

Cruel laughter billows round the room. Ya Ling's lips draw into a rigid line when she sees how Enzio lies in wait for her daughter. 'Oh dear! How sad! Demoted at court! But perhaps a new profession lies ahead for you, Anna. Why don't I bring some of my friends to the arbour again to see how well you perform? But you can't charge much, can you? There is so little of you, after all.'

Ya Ling simmers inside but merely smiles when Anna returns to her red-faced and close to tears. Once Anna is seated beside her she takes her hands tightly between her own. 'After that fool has entertained us, and we have applauded, then you must perform your songs and only then can we retire to my room,' she tells her. Anna's tear-filled eyes look up at her in desperation, but Ya Ling continues to hold her hands, transferring the steely weight of her own resolve to her daughter.

Crispino's repertoire of silken songs of unrequited love soon tug at Barbara's heartstrings and make her dab her broad cheekbones with her frothy lace handkerchief. She is then reduced to husky laughter by the bawdy songs he sings, about lusty stable boys and cuckolded husbands, accompanied by suggestive winks and ribald thrusts of his preposterous codpiece.

'How pathetic he is! You would never behave like that!' Ya Ling comforts. 'Now go and show them all.'

Anna's repertoire of folk songs usually delights the audience and has them joining in each chorus, but tonight her voice sounds reedy and her fingers mispluck several times. People look at her on the dais and then at each other with downturned lips. They have another hero now. The applause is muted. On the long walk back to her seat Enzio's voice is slimy with sympathy. 'Now what was that noise I just heard? Not a song thrush, that's for sure. An imitation of a screech owl perhaps? Even the marchesa's shrieking peacocks sound more in tune than you!'

Anna manages to reach Ya Ling's room, her mother close behind, without any outward show of the hurt that pounds inside. Once the door is closed she collapses into a bundle on the bed. 'You controlled yourself. You did well.' Her mother's voice resonates with pride.

'How can you say that? I'm finished. It's so unfair!' she sobs. 'Now I have lost my place at court, no one will want to know me.'

Ya Ling strokes her back and waits until Anna's tears have stopped. 'Now you will discover who your true friends are,' she says.

'I hate Enzio! He is despicable! Did you see him paying court to Paola Gonzaga? Making her laugh? No doubt at me…'

'A Gonzaga daughter for the son of a wool merchant? Enzio is aiming far too high. No matter how wealthy the father might be, or how much Ludovico might be in debt to him, there would never be any possibility of a marriage. Anyway, Paola has already been bartered and traded to Leonhard of Gorizia to make the best alliance for the family.'

Anna's bottom lip comes out. 'The Gonzaga children are not even beautiful. Susanna and Dorotea both have hunchbacks like their uncle the cardinal, and little Ludovico and Paola have foreheads curved to a dome. But that won't matter, of course. Not for them! They'll all be married off, but there will never be a suitor for me.' Anna's tears darken a patch on the bedcover.

'The formal betrothal takes place next year when Paola is thirteen. So tell me, Anna, is that what you would really want? A doddery and bad-tempered old man slavering as he waits for you in your bed each night? The Gonzaga bloodline is tainted by too much intermarriage. You can see that by just looking at them. Your Mongolian family go to a great festival each year called the Naadam, where many different tribes come together for matchmaking, so each man's seed is widely sown. That is what the Gonzagas should do. Don't worry, Anna, you have Han cleverness and Mongol courage bred into you. For all their wealth, you must never envy any of those feeble Gonzaga children.'

'But look at me! Of course I envy them.' She curls up into an even tighter ball. 'No handsome man will ever look at me!'

'What? You mean handsome like Enzio? Being admired by a preening fool like him? Remember Lao Tzu! *Character becomes destiny.* One day you'll see the truth of that. For Enzio, and for you as well. Looks mean very little, my child. Vanity seldom goes with a keen mind, and I have met very few young men as vain as him.'

Anna turns to face her mother and manages a weak grin. 'Actually, Mamma, he's even vainer than you think. One of the maids who cleans his chamber told me he has a row of potions on his mantelpiece to make himself even more beautiful.'

'He does?' Ya Ling's eyes quickly narrow. 'And who supplies him with those?'

'Bruzzi.'

'Bruzzi? I see.' She looks down thoughtfully at her daughter. 'Are you sure about this?'

'Oh yes. He makes a fine living selling them.' Anna wipes her eyes with the back of her hand. 'Maria heard Enzio tell Gerardo that there was one very expensive salve that Bruzzi had sold him that was guaranteed to make his… his… man's part even bigger.'

'Really?' Ya Ling allows herself a cautious smile. 'I don't suppose Maria would tell you exactly where Enzio's room is, would she?'

'Oh, I already know that. It's right at the end of the senior courtiers' corridor, next to the Hall of Weapons.' The amusement drains from Anna's face. 'You see, when he began flirting with me I thought I should find out where his chamber was, in case… in case…' Her face crumples with shame.

'Have patience, child. We will be avenged. You'll see.'

'I doubt that. Both Mantegna and Enzio are so powerful at court, we can do nothing but watch from the sidelines and see them prosper,' she says sadly.

Ya Ling's heart tugs at the resigned expression that has settled on her daughter's features. 'Don't look so hurt, child.'

'But it's hopeless.'

'Have courage. Have faith.' She cups her daughter's face between her hands. 'Listen to me. When I have sourced some poison ivy and some sap from the lacquer tree from my supplier in Venezia, and collected a bottle of that filthy blue scum that settles on the backwaters of the River Mincio, then Enzio will be the one who is hurting. Believe me.'

Chapter 40

Over the next three weeks, happiness seeps through Ya Ling like sunshine. Each day she sits with Anna in her treatment rooms and recites the names of the herbs and spices that she lays out in a row on the table, and her daughter recites them back perfectly. She misses nothing. Information is quickly stored and just as quickly retrieved. 'I'm very impressed, Anna. In only two days you have learned how to cure fevers and tomorrow I'll show you how to set bones with a paste of barley flour.'

'And is that good progress?' Anna smiles at her mother's enthusiastic nod. 'But I still have a list of questions from yesterday.'

'And knowing you, you won't be content until you have mastered every explanation.'

When Marsilio Andreasi enters the room his face is worn as if with pain. Ya Ling stands quickly and pulls out the bench by the table where they are working. 'How can I…?'

He shakes his head gravely. 'I'll come straight to the point, though it grieves me to do so. I am very sad to tell you that the Widow has been summoned to the ecclesiastical court, which convenes next week.'

'Me?' Ya Ling goes ashen. Has she been spotted entering or leaving Enzio's room? Has she made a blundering mistake during one of the many masses she has sat through? She struggles in vain to keep her voice light. 'Me, Signor Andreasi? Pray tell me, what am I accused of?'

'The situation is grave. I came as soon as I heard. You are right to be fearful, Signora. I am afraid you have been denounced by Signor Bruzzi, the surgeon.'

'How can that be taken seriously, Marsilio?' Anna demands. 'He is just jealous of her success! The Widow has never lost a patient. Her cures are well documented and she is held in high respect, while the long list of Bruzzi's patients who have ended up on a slab in the death-house can only—'

'It is not her healing skills that are being challenged.' Ya Ling clutches the edge of the table. She can guess exactly what Bruzzi will have accused her of. 'I do not wish to be the one to impart such awful news, but your mother has been denounced as a sorceress.'

'No! Never!' Anna gasps.

'Thank you. For informing me so quickly.' Ya Ling manages a tight nod for her daughter's sake. 'At least it gives me a little time to prepare.'

'Us, you mean,' Anna says, recovering herself quickly. 'You are not alone in this. We'll work on this together, night and day.' Her jaw tightens in determination. 'The court convenes next week? Then we haven't a moment to waste.'

The courtroom is set high up in one of the forbidding towers of the San Giorgio castle. When Ya Ling enters the room, only a timid shaft of sunlight filters down through a small arched window. She feels as if she has already been found guilty and has been condemned to a prison cell.

At her arrival, a group of common citizens shift about eagerly at the back of the courtroom. Both Barbara of Brandenburg and Ludovico are in attendance, which is unusual. Ya Ling hopes that it's a sign that this hearing might be fairer than most. Perhaps the bigger purse of the accuser won't decide the outcome as it often does. Barbara sends her a brief nod, but even the status and power of the marchese and his wife cannot overrule the vote of an ecclesiastical court. Only the cardinal and his jury of priests can determine the outcome of that. As the most senior cleric in Mantova, their son Francesco is to preside. He is a man known to want his cardinalship to be seen as punitive in cases of witchcraft. His mother's high opinion of her healer will count for little.

There is a sudden hush and the crowd of priests parts. The cardinal looks intimidating; his scarlet silk chasuble is stiff with embroidery, the cincture at his waist is looped with gold thread and the jewels on his pectoral cross glint even in the dim light. The scarlet biretta sits squarely on his head, and beneath it a pair of watchful eyes survey the scene. The room falls silent at the first imperious knock of his silver crozier on the wooden floor.

When the priests file in and sit on each side of the cardinal, Ya

Ling's spirit lifts a little when she sees that the rotund figure of Father Vitale is among them. She has cured two of his illegitimate sons of lung fever. Then her spirits plummet when Maria, her maidservant, comes limping into court and is led to the witness bench. Both her eyes are swollen with dark bruises and wide with fright. Another, older, woman is led in to sit next to her. Ya Ling stares at her and tries desperately to remember where she knows her from. There is something familiar, but she can't place her at all. It disturbs her.

The advocate that Signor Bruzzi has hired has a long thin face and a straggly white beard. He looks wily and experienced. The cardinal indicates that the advocate should begin and he jumps up and starts shuffling a large stack of papers together.

'Let us begin. The woman before you, known as the Widow, is accused of witchcraft by Signor Bruzzi, who is known by all as the former barber-surgeon to the court. He is concerned that the woman's foul and unnatural practices are not just putting lives at risk, but placing Catholic souls right in the path of damnation. The Widow will answer every accusation against her. Speak up!'

'Yes.' Ya Ling's voice barely ruffles her veil. Though her head shakes, she manages to nod.

'The first accusation is that you put the *malocchio* on Signor Bruzzi and caused several of his patients to worsen.'

If anybody deserves the evil eye then it's Bruzzi. 'No, sir. It is not true. My skills are only used for healing, never for laying curses.'

'Is that all you have to say?'

Ya Ling lowers her head meekly. If she speaks of Bruzzi's filthy blood-soaked apron and the trail of flies that follows him everywhere, his quickness to reach for the knife, then they will surely accuse her, a mere woman, of appalling conceit.

'Then I call the maidservant known as Maria.' A court servant carries over a box and Maria climbs onto it so she can be seen over the rail. Her movements are very cautious, as if her joints are made of glass. 'Tell the court, have you seen the accused woman indulging in heathen chants and throwing bones, like a primitive?' Maria nods. 'How many times? Speak up!'

'Three.' Maria's head sinks to her chest.

'Three?' His voice drips suspicion. He looks meaningfully at the cardinal before he turns to the bench reserved for the accused. 'What say you, woman, to this charge?'

'My profession means I have to keep my hands supple.' Fear laces into her throat and she has to swallow hard before she can continue. 'So therefore I play the child's game of jacks. I have seen the Gonzaga children playing it at court and one of them showed me how. Their little tokens are made of ivory but I cannot afford such a luxury, so I have to make do with knucklebones. The Frankish cook favoured by the Gonzagas has supplied me with them.' That at least is true and she knows the cook will speak up for her in court. She has cured so many of the cooks and kitchen apprentices of livid burns and scalds that a favour from the kitchen is long overdue. Out of the corner of her eye she sees Barbara nod in agreement. Such support might not be lost on the court.

The other woman is asked to rise. It is only when she stands that Ya Ling recognises her as Renata, the maid of Carabella Faraldo. This is a body blow. The advocate uses his papers like a fan. 'This woman brings a far more serious charge. She claims that the Widow bewitched the husband of her employer, Carabella Faraldo. That the Widow's spell made the signora's looks improve beyond measure and her hair turn much fairer so that the husband barely recognised her and he couldn't stay away from the marital bedchamber. Furthermore, the maid Renata has told me that the spell also made Carabella Faraldo fall pregnant. The gift of a child is bestowed only by God himself, yet the Widow by her spells impregnated Signora Faraldo and made her conceive a son.' There is a horrified intake of breath from the row of priests. 'What say you to this?'

'My learned advocate, I do not use spells. I will confess that I helped Signora Faraldo improve her looks. Her hair was lightened with lemon juice and dried camomile flowers, nothing more than that. Every woman feels more desirable if she is more content within herself.'

A murmur swells out from the women among the common citizens at the back of the courtroom. Barbara gives a wise nod to her husband and brings out her golden rosary. Whether it is for protection from the sight of a sorceress, or whether she is praying for the Widow, is impossible for the priests to decide.

'And what say you to the accusation that you helped the lady conceive? Signora Faraldo herself told this maid, Renata, that the Widow had worked magic. That she had been barren before you, the Widow' – he turns dramatically and points a long finger – 'you, and your pagan ways, helped her entrance her husband back into the marital bed.' There is a further collective intake of breath.

Ya Ling gathers every ounce of courage and chooses each word with delicacy. 'It is known by all here present that the more frequently a husband visits his wife, the more likelihood there must be of God's gift of a child.' She looks down modestly. 'There is no magic to that.' A slight wave of amusement spreads round the court.

'But you used strange spells and anointments, admit it.' The advocate rocks back and forwards for effect. 'Which came from heathen lands?'

'No, sir. All I used came from either a trader in Venice who sends me rare spices from the east, or from the spice merchants in the Piazza delle Erbe, or from some of the plants and herbs gathered from the forests near here.'

'Then why do you always go about fully veiled? What have you to hide? It is an old custom that is beginning to fall out of favour in these enlightened times.'

'In my profession, decorum is very important.' Turning to the table of curious priests, she fights to lower her trembling shoulders. 'Many of the old customs have fallen out of favour. Obedient children, faithful husbands…' she pauses, 'and chaste priests.' At the murmur of agreement at her answer she turns her face towards Father Vitale. Having a string of illegitimate children, he should know that more than most. He returns her glance with an almost imperceptible nod. 'Not all the old customs should be discarded.'

'So do you make claim that you are not a heathen? I have heard that you only wear the Holy Cross of Our Lord to make a semblance of being a respectable Catholic widow. Is that true?'

Ya Ling takes a deep breath. 'I am true to my beliefs.'

'Then prove it.'

Ya Ling marshals her thoughts and tries to keep the strange words in the exact order she has committed to memory for such an occasion. '*Pater noster qui es in caelis sanctificetur nomen tuum.*'

'Very impressive.' The advocate shoots an irritated look across the courthouse towards Signor Bruzzi.

'*Confiteor Deo omnipotenti beatae Mariae semper Virgini, beato Michaeli Archelangelo…*'

'All right! All right! Enough! Be seated and wait in humility for the summation of the cardinal.'

Ya Ling sinks down onto her seat. When the cardinal stands, the short scarlet cape that covers his hunchback swings and shimmers behind him like a ring of fire. She hopes it isn't a portent. The breath tightens in her chest. The cardinal has the deeply clefted Brandenburg chin, which he sticks out in the posture of a man used to having an audience hang upon his every word. The room goes icily silent. His voice rings out, heavy and ponderous, and to Ya Ling's terrified ears it sounds full of foreboding.

'I have listened to the evidence brought before me, and I wish it to be known that though the case against the Widow does not appear to be fully proven, there are aspects to it that fill me with grave suspicion. Due to the sensitive nature of the treatment accorded to Signora Carabella Faraldo I wish to have further private discussions with her and her husband. I also need to ascertain if a woman can indeed have her hair turned to gold, or if this be some trick of the sorcerer's art. Therefore for the sake of fairness, I demand that both Signor Marsilio Andreasi and Signor Bruzzi will test the recipe given by the Widow on two maidservants of the Gonzaga household in front of witnesses. However, I am most horrified by the accusation that she has enabled the conception of a child, for that is a gift known only to God, and heresy is one of the most serious crimes ever to come before an ecclesiastical court. Moreover' – his voice holds the pomposity of a man used to wielding absolute power – 'I will state publicly that in this case, as with all denunciations of witchcraft, my foremost concern is for the protection of all righteous Catholic souls. I have severe reservations about this supposed healer brought before me. Any mortal who is proved to have assumed the mantle of our Lord will face summary execution. That is what the ecclesiastical court has always done and I will always uphold this precedent. Once I have been satisfied with the findings of my investigation, then I will give my verdict on whether the Widow is, or is not, a sorceress.' As he turns towards her, Ya Ling clutches the rail in front of her and though her legs almost buckle beneath her, she manages to stand. 'The practice of witchcraft is a heinous sin. If I have my suspicions justified, I may wish for more proof…' he pauses for effect, 'then I will use the strappado. If further evidence of your guilt is furnished as a consequence, then you will burn.'

To her pounding ears it is as final as a death sentence. The strappado. People confess to every sin imaginable to stop the cruelty of those thin leather straps. The continued drops from the ceiling, plunging down and down until every joint in the body is pulled violently apart and every tendon is stretched to breaking point. During the torment no one keeps silent. Victims confess to every sin imaginable. No one ever recovers. Ya Ling has seen those crippled by the strappado begging in the piazza, holding out their shaking alms bowls, and she has looked on in sympathy at their twitchy gait across the cobblestones, as even the slightest movement causes moans of despair.

Two prison guards take Ya Ling down several flights of slippery stairs to the prison. It is pitch black. There are no windows and only one thick, treble-locked door. The oozing walls of the empty cell indicate that it is below the level of the moat outside the castle. Her stomach knots with terror as the darkness draws around her. There is no noise except for the pitter-patter of rats in the damp straw and the rasping of the thick drawbridge rope. Ya Ling feels on the floor for the driest patch, pulls her skirts tight around her and sits down to try to think. Her nerves are drawn tighter than they have ever been. She concentrates her mind on breathing in, then releasing each breath very slowly.

Indeterminate shapes loom in the darkness, vague outlines of the walls and the door. Something large and feathery blunders into her face, and with panic-stricken hands she flaps it away. In the darkness her breath sounds as fast and shallow as that of a hunted animal.

The air tastes stale and soiled with the foul commingled breaths of the other prisoners who have used it before. She forces her churning thoughts away from what might have happened to them and focuses instead on counting the beat of her heart until it becomes more regular, then she pulls in *qi* with every shaky breath until her thoughts become calm and Confucian. *To see the right and not do it is cowardice.* Anna has a right to revenge. The prison makes the harness room seem luxurious, but the rustling of the straw makes her think how her daughter must have suffered in the cellar of the pumilio house. The smothering darkness reminds her of her daughter's torture in the box. If Anna can survive being locked inside that, then she can survive a prison cell. And survive she must, and rise above whatever lies ahead so that Anna will be avenged. She knows Anna will be working tirelessly to have her freed, but it might not be enough. Ya Ling braces her back against the rough stone wall. She hasn't travelled so far and achieved so much just to founder here. Escape is impossible. For now. Pushing her folded arms into her chest, she allows herself an ironic smile. Ridiculous though it seems, her last remaining hope lies with Enzio.

From outside comes a slight intermittent noise. She lifts her head curiously. A flapping sound, like an approaching breeze. With every sense alert, she stares into the block of darkness, swaying her head from side to side to conduct a thorough search of every wall. Sure enough, high on the opposite wall there is a patch that appears a little lighter than the rest. Her heartbeat sounds thunderous in the empty cell. The walls are furred with moss but her fingers scrabble along each hewn stone for gaps in the mortar, until she finds two fingerholds. She pulls her wiry frame upright and stabs her toes into any tiny ledge where they can find purchase in between the stones. Inch by inch she hauls herself up the wall until her hands find coarse hessian instead of slippery stone. She snatches and snatches at a corner of it until a handful of fibres comes away and a chink of blessed daylight seeps through. A rusty grille lies behind, and she is able to thread her fingers through it and hold her balance until she can bring her eye up to the gap. She finds that her sight line is just above the moat that looks out across to the grass leading down to the lake. She shrinks back behind the hessian when two pairs of boots march past on the wall above the moat and the sentries exchange passwords. The sentry stand is visible from the window. Escape will have to be at night. Her arms ache but she pushes off from the wall, still clutching the grille, and making her weight as leaden as she can, she drops heavily, pulling against it. The iron struts dig cruelly into the skin under each knuckle but she persists, trying to swing from side to side to loosen the grille from its fixings. She clambers back up the wall and lets herself drop over and over again but no matter how hard she tries to use her weight to heave downwards, the grille is embedded into the wall as solid as a tomb. Tucking the hessian back over the hole, she slides down the wall and crumples onto the straw, blowing hard on her fingers to cool the burning pain. It's going to take several weeks and she might not have the luxury of as long as that… but she summons up Confucian thought once more to stiffen her resolve. She thinks of the mountain and the stones. Slipping off her under-chemise, she tears a strip from the hem, but the rattle of the first lock sends her scurrying back into her dress.

The rumble of Marsilio's deep voice comes through the door and she stands to greet him, apologising for the smell in the room. The shaft of light that accompanies him into the darkness is almost as welcome as his sturdy presence, but the serious expression on his face tells her he is not bringing good news. 'My dear, the court has reconvened twice, but there is no clear verdict as yet. Although several people have come forward to give testament to your virtues, I must warn you, it does not look promising. The cardinal's record in cases of witchcraft has always been harsh, and he has stated publicly that unless Bruzzi retracts his accusation, which I fear is unlikely, then—'

'But what about the marchesa?' she demands, 'Hasn't she spoken up for me?'

He bows his head. 'I have heard nothing. In all probability she cannot be seen to contradict the wishes of her son in his new position.'

'How long?' she says. 'How long have I got?'

'Four days perhaps. Possibly less than that.'

'No!' She clutches her hand to her throat.

'Signora, there is nothing I can say to console you, except to let you know that Anna is working day and night to free you. She petitions Barbara constantly and gathers many of your patients to speak for you.'

'And still Barbara says nothing?'

'Nothing,' says Andreasi.

'Oh, Anna.' Ya Ling's voice breaks. 'My Anna.'

'I am so sorry for your predicament. I too know the pain of losing a daughter.' Marsilio's head lowers in sympathy before he quietly withdraws.

Ya Ling swallows back her tears and feels in the darkness for the length she has torn from her under-chemise. She tears it in half again. 'Anna.' The name is a talisman she carries to help her bear the pain of dragging her weight down on the grille hour after hour.

It must have been three days. Three hunks of sour bread lie on the floor uneaten and the water trough in the wall has been refilled three times by the taciturn jailer who is terrified of entering her cell; he holds his dagger out towards her, never turns his back and is always very quick to make his exit. The sound of voices and banging comes filtering down from outside. Dragging herself up the wall and pulling herself up to eye level, she stares out, scarcely hearing the loud cheer when the tall wooden stake is pulled upright on the grassy mound beyond the moat and secured tightly.

'Let's see her magic her way out of this!' one sentry calls to another.

A long line of prisoners stands ready, some holding faggots of branches, some bundles of brushwood, which they stack neatly in turn until they have built up a mountainous pyre.

'And it's all unseasoned wood, so it'll burn very very slowly. Be a good one to watch. Nice and slow.'

The other sentry shouts back with a satisfied tone: 'No wonder they need all the barriers putting up. There'll be thousands wanting to come and watch the burning of this one. This one's well known, not like all the others.'

Ya Ling sinks to her knees, barely turning her head when the jailer briefly opens the door and throws in a last hunk of bread, too afraid to even enter now that her sorcery has been proved. She readies herself in the darkness, pushing away all her fear of the crackling flames beneath her feet, the flickering fire slowly consuming her legs, the molten fat making the flames spurt blue. Instead she breathes in *qi*, all the while giving thanks for the love of her parents, the gentleness of Ayi and the loyalty of Chen. She tries to remember the feel of Altan's cheekbone pressed to hers, the scent of him, the brief flare of heat on his skin when her face was held against his, but it is Chen whose face is etched on her mind. The laughter lines round his eyes. The sound advice she would never take. Keeping watch so she could slide down the yellow lions and shrugging off the beating he got for it. She remembers the splash the turtle made when they tipped it into the fishpond. Like Anna, Chen's growth may have been stunted but his spirit is undimmed. Like Ya Ling, he might have been a slave, but he could never stand by and watch the freedom of others be curtailed.

Last of all, she holds fast to every happy memory she has shared with Anna during the short but blessed time they have been together. She rinses her lacerated hands and her filthy face in the water trough and by iron willpower forces her quaking head to a semblance of stillness, ready for Anna's sake, to face whatever lies ahead with dignity and strength.

When the door opens wide, the light falling across the straw brings her out of her reverie and makes her suddenly blink. She pulls herself shakily to her feet. 'I'm ready,' she says quietly.

Marsilio Andreasi steps into the cell and wades through the straw. 'The news is very promising for you, Signora. The denunciation has been suddenly withdrawn.' His tone is formal, but his arm is supportive when he feels her knees sag with relief.

'What? How?' The squeeze under her elbow indicates that he considers further discussion inappropriate in front of the guard.

'Anna is waiting for you in your bedchamber.'

Anna flings herself into Ya Ling's arms. 'Look! See what I have arranged for you. I knew exactly what you would want first!' Anna has assembled the biggest bowl she could borrow from the kitchen and organised a relay of female pumilios to each carry in several buckets of warm water. A surreptitious finger across her lips indicates that nothing can be said until they have all left, but though Ya Ling sits dazed, she can tell that Anna is bubbling with excitement while she gently wipes away the rust stains from her mother's hands and binds the cuts on her fingers. After Ya Ling has washed herself, Anna winds a wiping cloth round Ya Ling's damp hair and gives her a plate of ricotta pastries and a dish of poached apples. 'Sent up from the kitchen just for you. The cook and all the kitchen staff have asked for news of you every single day.'

She continues chatting blithely until the pumilios have drained the bowl and finished mopping the floor. Once Anna has seen them out, she goes to the doorway and carefully glances down each corridor before rushing back in. Standing in front of her mother, her dark eyes shine with excitement. 'It worked, Mamma! It worked better than our wildest dreams! Not only has Bruzzi been banished from court, but so has Enzio, who is now covered with such blisters and pustules he looks like a victim of the plague! And it's not just his face that's suffering either – apparently he started rubbing his burning private parts and trying to pull down his underdrawers right in front of Paola Gonzaga herself! She thought he was going to attack her maidenhead and screamed for the palace guards! Then he accused Bruzzi, who claimed there was nothing harmful in his potions at all, just coloured olive oil and tallow wax – so then the other courtiers who had each paid a fortune to have their man's part made massive, well, then they all began to lay down challenges, saying that he was a trickster and they would all take him to court. It was pandemonium! So when the Marchesa Barbara heard all about it, she announced that if Bruzzi and Enzio wanted to avoid prison, they should pack up and leave Mantova immediately. And never come back. So they both have.'

'Bruzzi's gone! I am so thankful for that.' Ya Ling still sits as rigid as a stave, unable to settle back in her chair.

'Apparently Barbara told her husband that as Bruzzi was so dishonoured, then there was no case for you to answer to, so the denunciation could not possibly stand, and you should be freed immediately.'

'I am fortunate to have such a powerful patron.'

'Not quite as powerful as poison ivy and the sap from that lacquer tree, though?' Anna looks thoughtful. 'Mamma, I know Enzio was vain and horrible, but he won't be scarred and in pain for ever, will he?'

'No, child. Only for a few days. Then the blisters will heal.' Ya Ling stretches out her stiff arms and manages a smile. 'It's good that you remain compassionate even for one such as Enzio. Using your gifts wisely and well is the mark of a true healer.'

Anna blushes at the compliment. Walking behind her mother, she reaches up on tiptoe and begins to knead her rigid back. 'Mamma, I know you are still badly shaken, so let me reassure you even further. Several powerful men came forward to speak up for you. Some spoke very ill of Bruzzi and the damage he has done to members of their family. Many women also came forward to attest to your skills and to your decorum. Many patrician families too – the Caponeras, Signora Trionfetti and Carabella Faraldo. Even Mantegna's wife and servants came.'

'What? Nicolosia came?'

'Yes. And two servants called Genevra and Clemente, and their groom as well.'

'Did they?' Her hand slaps against her chest. 'How wonderful. What did they say?'

'Well, Nicolosia said that her son had had severe chest agues for years and that when he was at death's door, you cured him. That you were honest and discreet.'

'And Genevra?'

'Well, she started to say something but nobody could hear her, so she got very red and flustered and sat down, so then Clemente took over and said you had brought his precious son Ernesto safely into this world and when his dear wife had milk fever, you saved her from going to the next. People were very impressed by that.'

'This news makes me feel very happy. The confidence others have in me helps allay my fears,' she says, venturing to stretch out her legs, conscious of feeling fresh and clean under her newly laundered shift.

'And we're going to be very busy too, Mamma. We already have a steady stream of new customers for tomorrow.'

'For chest agues and childbirth, no doubt.'

'Oh no. Nothing like that! Look, I've bought these in readiness. Guess what they're for.' Anna carries over a large wooden box of lemons and a sack of dried camomile flowers.

Ya Ling smiles knowingly at her daughter. 'Don't tell me. Now that the word is out, every gentlewoman in Mantova wants us to help her look beautiful and give her golden hair!'

'And tempt back their straying husbands, I don't doubt.' Anna giggles.

Ya Ling's face becomes suddenly serious. 'Marsilio told me a new word. He thinks I am now almost inviolable. But I'm not. No one ever is. Especially' – she smiles – 'Mantegna.'

Chapter 41

The Camera degli Sposi, Gonzaga Palace, 1474

'Will this work?' Anna whispers.

'Yes it will. Remember, information is more valuable than salt.' Ya Ling smiles as she repeats her father's words. Excitement runs through them both. It's a risky business. Only the most favoured patricians have been allowed into the Camera degli Sposi to see the frescos.

A special invitation has to be offered and Mantegna insists on being present at all times. Temperamental and litigious, he wants to hear every single comment made about his masterpiece. So they wait until Mantegna and his apprentice have left for home. Marsilio turns the key in the lock. The light is still good enough for the jewel-bright colours of the frescos to dazzle in the small square room.

'Look, Marsilio, that's you there!' Anna's voice rises as she points to the fresco on the north wall. 'Just look! He's got your nose exactly right!' The fresco shows Ludovico talking in a confidential aside to his secretary. 'And look, there's Rubino too!' The massive auburn-coloured hound waits patiently, curled under his master's chair as if sated after a good meal. There's the hated Enzio, his arm aloft in an extravagant gesture as if he has been captured in the middle of a flowery paean about Ludovico Gonzaga.

As Anna's gaze flicks between the painted walls, Ya Ling moves in closely to give her undivided attention to the family fresco. 'Very clever,' she says. 'See how he's painted them as if they stand on the fireplace itself. It looks as though real curtains have been pulled back to show the court come to life.'

'Yes. His technique is brilliant.' Marsilio turns to Ya Ling. 'It's all there, isn't it? As if they've been imprisoned, stuck beneath a coating of almond varnish. It's eerie, the way he's captured the court to perfection, the intrigue, the manoeuvring, the flattery, the *sprezzatura* strutting for effect. The likenesses are uncanny, are they not?'

'It's magic!' Anna says fearfully.

'No, it's definitely not that, but it is brilliantly done.' Ya Ling stares at the fresco, absorbing every detail. 'Mantegna must be very secure in the Gonzagas' affections to paint the family in such a lifelike way, to capture them looking so relaxed but with all their flaws too.' Ya Ling's careful eyes rake along the wall. 'It's almost as if he's one of them, as if he's entered into their bloodline himself. I expected them all standing to attention and looking perfect. Not like this at all. They're almost too lifelike. He doesn't flatter any of them at all, does he, Signor Andreasi?' Her voice drops low and confidential. 'Might that not perhaps cause him a problem?'

'No, you're right, he doesn't. I knew you would notice that.' She looks impassively at him and waits, sensing more to come, but he remains as careful as ever and shifts the line of questioning with practised ease. 'And he's even painted his own face in here somewhere. Over here. Look! Next to the door, between the putti and the cardinal fresco.'

Her eyes widen. 'How did he get away with that?'

'He might not have. We'll have to see.' Something in his cautionary tone makes them both look expectantly at him.

'Go on,' Anna says. 'You can trust us. You know you can. Both of us.'

He points to the panel over the door. 'See how boldly he has written OPVS HOC TENVE in his dedication to the Gonzagas.' Both women wait in silence.

'I don't understand.' Anna smiles sweetly.

'Well, that phrase could be taken to be a modest statement, something like "this slight work". But "tenve" can also mean "subtle" or perhaps "fine" and, knowing Mantegna, that's exactly what he has in mind. And, on top of that, just look at the inscription he's put above the door. We all know how sensitive he is about his modest background. How much he has to keep proving his genius to anyone who will listen – but here, I fear he has boosted himself far too much. "Suus Andreas Mantinia"! *I am Mantegna* indeed! As you well know, little one, no one puts himself above the marchese. And not far from his appalling boast, he's included his own image against a golden background. Neither Ludovico nor Barbara are entirely happy about that, as you can imagine.'

Both women stand on tiptoe. 'So tell me, is he out of grace?' Anna asks.

'Well, child,' Marsilio looks down at her with a thin rictus smile. 'Let me just say that though the marchese and marchesa are impressed by their own likenesses, Mantegna has included details in the family fresco that do not please them quite so much.'

'Because they are too lifelike?' Ya Ling's shrewd glance studies the fresco above the fireplace.

'Exactly. He has taken the marchese's instruction to paint exactly what he sees a little too far.' Ya Ling turns to the fresco that celebrates Francesco being made a cardinal. 'He's cleverly covered up Francesco's hunchback with that little cape' – she turns back to the family fresco and looks doubtfully at it – 'but on this one, I can see why the Gonzagas aren't happy with the way he's painted the two youngest children. Look how he's shown that odd bump on their foreheads.'

Anna screws up her face. 'I agree. They might look like that in real life, but I'd have thought he'd have made them look a bit less mis-shapen.'

'Ssh, child! You mustn't say that!' Marsilio glances anxiously at the locked door. 'And don't forget he delayed starting the frescos for so many years that he's only now putting the finishing touches to them. And he's known to have taken private commissions during this period, which has caused even more delays. He's asking for more money too.'

'So is he out of favour?' The two women wait patiently.

'Not while he can do this.' He leads them into the middle of the room and motions to the ceiling with a raised hand. 'The oculus!'

'When was that built?' Ya Ling asks, surprised.

'It wasn't.'

'I know her!' Anna points upwards, open mouthed. 'The African slave. The one with the black and white headdress. She's a good singer. What's she doing climbing up there?'

'She's not.' Marsilio looks on amused as both of them lean back, twisting their heads from side to side.

Above them in the ceiling a circular balustrade looks out as if open to the heavens. Over the rim five serving maids still continue to smile mockingly down. A peacock looks upwards to the cottony clouds set in a blue sky. 'Look out!' Anna tugs at her mother's sleeve. 'Come away. Marsilio, you too! If that stone urn slips off that pole, it will kill us all.'

Ya Ling's face behind her veil tips upwards. 'It's not real, is it? But how could any man paint a flat surface to look like that?'

'Exactly. This shows Mantegna's genius. It's called an illusion. And nothing like it has been seen before. He may be somewhat out of favour, but while he can produce such feats, and doesn't overstep the mark, then his favoured reputation with the Gonzagas will remain secure.'

Anna looks up at the ceiling warily. Nothing has moved. The peacock's profile remains still against the blue sky, the vase still rests precariously on its slim pole, the four women and their African slave woman still continue to smile down in front of the halo of heavenly clouds exactly as before. 'Where's the peacock's tail?'

'Well, that's another thing. Apparently its squawking drove Mantegna mad, so he would only do a quick outline. Ludovico had sent to the Indies for a pair of them at vast expense, so he isn't too happy about that either.'

When Ya Ling and Anna focus on the flock of tiny putti fluttering around the rim of the oculus, their miniscule wings whirring as if to keep their truncated little forms from tumbling down to earth, they exchange a look. Pumilios, that's what they look like. Pink and larval. 'Do you think the maestro has unearthly powers, Marsilio?' asks Anna.

'He can certainly do things no other man can do.'

Slipping a hand into his, she looks up at him gravely. 'Can his paintings rescue souls from purgatory?'

Marsilio stands back in shock. 'Child! You must never ask anybody a question like that! That is heresy.'

'Really? Heresy, you say?' Ya Ling asks, composed. 'I have heard that he says such things to his son and to his apprentice.'

'Well, he must be a boastful fool if he does. It goes against the most profound teachings of the Bible. It's a terrible crime! Don't you understand that, child? Whispers spread faster than the plague at court, you both know that. Rumours, rivalries, no one is ever safe. Listen to me. Mantegna is very talented, but he is only a man. I fear your remarks might get you into terrible trouble one day. The ecclesiastical court would deal with such claims very harshly.'

Anna turns her attention back to the family fresco of Gonzagas, marvelling at the way the artist has captured the expression on each face. 'But he can make people immortal, can't he?'

Ya Ling holds her breath, waiting for the private secretary to answer.

'For the love of God, child! Wherever did you hear that?'

'Settimio, his apprentice, told my mother that Mantegna often says that when he is pleased with a day's work. That's why he is confident that the Gonzagas will eventually come round and accept how brilliant the frescos are.'

Marsilio shakes his head sternly. 'This conversation is straying into lethal territory. Tell me, child, what is prompting these kinds of questions?' Anna avoids catching her mother's eye.

'Let me put it this way for you, Anna,' Marsilio goes on, 'Mantegna has painted many sublime Madonnas while he has been here in Mantova, and many other religious pictures that seem to be brought to life by his genius. Heaven must surely smile on a family who have enabled him to do that.'

'So is he saying that the Gonzagas won't go to Hell then, because of the frescos?'

'Enough. I am not prepared to say any more, Anna.'

'But tell me please, would you say Mantegna's position at court is now invio… inviol-lable?'

Marsilio gives a brief smile. 'No one's position here is ever really that. Only a fool thinks otherwise. Come…' He pauses by the door. 'They are very nearly completed now.' He pats Anna's curls as they pass. 'On Barbara's orders there are to be no more household staff included in the frescos. She just wants them finished.'

Walking down the corridor arm in arm with Anna, Ya Ling begins hatching a plan. The information Marsilio has given away has been invaluable. Not only will it banish the memory of Enzio, but her revenge will also finally settle her account with Mantegna and punish him for what he has done to her daughter. More importantly, it will begin the rescue of all the other tormented little pumilios. Anna has a plan too. One that will lessen her mother's guilt at having given her to Mantegna and the tortures she suffered in the pumilio house.

Chapter 42

In the Camera degli Sposi the day is dragging on and on. Despite his bravado, both Cecco and Settimio know that the way the Gonzagas are giving the maestro the cold shoulder is worrying him to death. For the last two weeks while he has been putting the finishing touches to the frescos, he's been snapping like a hungry catfish.

'Is this better, Father? I've slightly altered the angle of Rubino's head again and had another go at the way the paw hangs.'

'No! Do it again! You've made the head far too big. He looks more like a lion than a hound, you idiot. Do I have to do everything myself?'

He finds fault with everything his long-suffering apprentice does too, making him re-grind pigment until his hands are raw, forcing him to hold the torch so close to his face in the darker corners that his skin crackles like the rind of a roasting pig. Settimio turns at a slight rustle behind him. He has no idea how long they've been standing there, quietly watching. 'Maestro?' he murmurs gently upwards. Any loud noise can result in a fist in your face these days.

'Be quiet.'

Cecco's voice is louder. 'Father!'

'I've told you, just narrow down the shape of its head. Go and look at a hound in the kennels if you have to.'

'Maestro, we have visitors.'

Cecco wipes his brush with a cloth and looks curiously at the two women. 'It's the Widow and the marchesa's little handmaid.'

Mantegna's face looks sharply over the edge of the scaffolding. All goes as quiet as if he's resumed work.

'We need to see you now, Mantegna.' Anna's voice rings up clearly. 'And on your own. It's very important.'

Cecco coughs loudly. Settimio's glance twists from Anna up to the top of the scaffolding.

In all the years of working together neither of them have heard the maestro spoken to like that. Up near the ceiling, Mantegna's face appears again briefly but his scowl hides any trepidation he is feeling. He's had no contact with any senior member of the Gonzaga entourage for over two weeks now, but it would be very odd to send a serious summons through two women, and one only a young plaything who is no longer a court favourite. Though Ya Ling is known to be held in high regard by Barbara of Brandenburg, it's still very unusual to send a confidante to speak to him instead of a senior courtier. And the unexpected sight of the two of them together makes him curious. To give himself time to think, he feigns reluctance as he climbs slowly down the last few struts of the scaffold.

'What do you want?'

'I said we need to speak with you alone.' Anna puts her hands on the hips of her tiny brocade dress. There is something in the way she walks confidently over to the corner where he stands that brings a wave of unease.

'Settimio, wait outside.' She looks insubstantial enough that a puff of wind might knock her down. Settimio closes the door behind him. Cecco leans against a bare patch of wall.

'I said alone, Mantegna.'

'Is everything all right, Father?'

'Just leave us.' Cecco shrugs and leaves. Mantegna's voice is stirred with anger as he turns to her. 'I don't like the way you address me. I don't like it at all.'

'What do you expect, Father? Gratitude?'

Both Ya Ling and Anna notice his great chest deflate as he tries to maintain contact with her piercing brown eyes. 'Father…? Who…? Me?' he stammers. 'I don't know what you are talking about!'

'We both know the truth.'

'What truth? She's a pumilio, for heaven's sake. How could I have fathered one such as her?' His eyes wheel round to Ya Ling, his mouth suddenly dry. 'I'll have her tongue in a bridle if she tries to defame me with a claim like that.'

'Oh yes! Of course you would need to do that, wouldn't you, Father? My tongue is the only thing you haven't yet curbed.'

'Me? Curbed? Curbed what?' His face drops in astonishment. 'What is she talking about?' He turns to Ya Ling. 'Has the child addled her wits?'

'No. You knew full well when you sold your daughter' – her voice shakes with anger – 'I repeat, SOLD your daughter to Dati, that he makes his money stunting children horribly until they become pumilios.'

'What?' Mantegna sits down heavily on a stool. 'You mean little Fortuna?' His painstaking look takes in every detail of Anna's appearance. 'God help me. No, it can't be.' He wipes the sweat off his brow with his smock, then stares again at Anna. 'He told me you were going to be brought up by a patrician family who had just lost a daughter. That you would be a replacement for her. Brought up with love and kindness and every luxury.'

'And you didn't think to make sure that that was the case?' Ya Ling's voice is icy. 'You just sold her and handed her over like a parcel? Just like that, and walked away?'

'But you spurned me in front of Gentile, you ran away and made me look a fool in my own *contrada*, you made me a laughing stock at court. A *buffone*. I acted in anger, but as God is my witness I've often thought of her. Just as I have thought of you.' He puts his two hands together as if in prayer. 'But I daren't make too many enquiries after her. Not with my good name to keep.'

'Well, that's all going to change now,' Anna says. He looks across at her in dread. 'Unless you do what we want,' she goes on.

He stares into space for a long time, then looks back at Anna, his eyes glazed. 'Anything. I'll do anything I can.' He glances up at Ya Ling, needing time to focus. 'When I went back to the hut in the slums and found you gone, I hoped you were still alive. I have hoped that many times.' He keeps looking at her but her face is inscrutable behind her veil. 'When I gave you back the slave contract, I knew of your intelligence. How quickly you learned and how strong you must be up here.' He taps his forehead. 'How resilient. And I hoped you would prosper.' He has the grace to look away.

'You will listen carefully to our demands and you'll do what we say.' Anna smiles grimly. 'Despite all you have done to us both, we now have mastery over you. Just like Ludovico has. Imagine that! Who would have thought we would be in this position? But we are.

Thanks to my mother's cleverness, your reputation is completely in our hands.'

'Perhaps more than that. Perhaps your life as well.' At the familiar lilt of Ya Ling's voice Mantegna feels a knife slowly turning in his roiling stomach.

'Tell me.' Anna looks down, and gestures at her diminutive frame. 'What kind of man does this to his own kin for money?'

He can't meet her eye. 'But I didn't know this terrible thing would happen to you. You must believe me.' His apron comes up to his face.

'Don't expect sympathy.' Anna pulls herself taller. 'There are certain things you have to do for us.'

'Things? And what if I won't?' His wary glance slips between them both. 'What if I can't?'

'Then we will ruin you.'

'You are too late. I am ruined already.' He turns to Ya Ling. 'Deep inside, where it matters most. Do you think I will ever be able to go to confession or sleep easily in my bed after this?' He waits for several moments, his hands pressing down on his knees, then he suddenly stands. 'Then what is it you want of me?'

'I want you to paint us both in the frescos. My mother and me.' Ya Ling turns in surprise.

Mantegna's face falls. 'There is absolutely no chance of that. Ludovico Gonzaga would never stand for it. For a start, he vetoed my idea of including Maria with the court servants – he's already chastised me for what he calls my presumption at painting in all the family frailties. So far he has refused to make any more payments because the frescos are too true to life for a family who enjoy the delusion that they are all-powerful and physically invincible.' He shrugs, his voice bitter. 'It's a pity he told me to do just the opposite when he first commissioned me.' He turns to them both. 'So for me to paint Anna in now would be a direct challenge to his orders and would remind him even more of his children's frailty. It would be unthinkable to provoke the marchese any further.' The thought of his waning favour makes Mantegna feel suddenly bilious. 'In any case, there's no room.'

Ya Ling speaks with conviction. 'Then take out Enzio. Scrape off every last bit of him!'

Mantegna flings his hands open. 'You must both be very naive to think that's even possible. His father has Ludovico tied to him by a tight skein of debt.'

'But when I last saw Enzio he was covered with red pustules, and the Gonzagas won't want any reminders that during their reign, the city harboured the plague.' Ya Ling's voice is cool and businesslike.

Mantegna looks helplessly from one to the other.

'So once you have removed Enzio and his silly pose, then there will be plenty of space for us both.' Anna's eyes flash a look of pure hatred at him. 'After all, I don't take up much room, do I, Mantegna? Not now. Thanks to you.'

'You can have a portrait,' he says tightly. 'And I'll have it framed in gesso and embossed with pure gold leaf.'

'No.' She looks disdainfully across. 'I want us both in the fresco. I want my mother painted in an attitude of sadness and piety because she worries that on the Holy Day of Judgement she will never be given redemption after the tortures I suffered when you took me to Dati.'

Ya Ling rests a hand on her daughter's head. 'Thank you, Anna, I am very touched that you have thought of me like this.'

'I can't do that,' Mantegna says flatly. 'There is no chance at all.'

'You have to. When I was accused of being a sorceress, Cardinal Francesco stated in court that anyone who assumed the mantle of our Lord would face execution. Yet you have claimed that your paintings are so miraculous they could rescue souls from purgatory. You have even said that they will bestow immortality upon the Gonzagas. Both of these statements are sacrilege.'

Mantegna staggers back as if he has been struck. 'But that was idle boasting. I'd taken wine. I never meant…'

When Anna exchanges a sceptical look with her mother, Mantegna sees his prestige and his patronage dissolving like a pastel landscape left out in the rain. No wily advocate can get him out of this. 'Have mercy on me, Ya Ling! Remember my kindness to you. The things that passed between us when we were alone. The sweet wine I used to buy for you. The velvet dress I gave you.'

'And the shackles. And the beating. And the shame. But worse than any of that, my daughter's terrible suffering.'

Mantegna's gaze on each of them becomes thoughtful. 'But you can't prove anything. Haven't you both thought of that? It's just your word against mine.'

'Oh, we can. If you don't do as we want, my mother and I will get the other pumilios at court to testify. Some of them are bound to be from your friend Dati's pumilio house. And Dati won't keep quiet about your involvement, now will he? Not when he's accused. He'll want it to appear that you were part of it. The more prominent the people involved, the better. He'll say anything to save his own skin. Dati told us we were in purgatory. And that he could throw us into the flames of hellfire. Heresy, Mantegna. Heresy! And my mother tells me that's a hanging offence. Still, when the monks have finished interrogating you, you will no doubt be grateful for the noose.'

'Who else have you talked to about this?'

'Marsilio Andreasi knows. Yes, he knows what you did to an innocent child. Your innocent child.'

Mantegna's shoulders sag. 'Look. How much money do you want? Now that the frescos are almost finished, I can start commissions again and soon I will have some big advances…'

'Do you honestly think money would ever compensate me? For the nightmares I still have of being buried alive? For the painful joints? The fighting for breath every winter? The cruel jokes played against me? The fact that the only glance I'm ever likely to get from a young man will be one of pity?' Anna thinks of Enzio. 'Or of mischief?'

'Never forget, child, you would be nothing without me! You were once a favourite in the Gonzaga household! It wasn't my fault you fell from grace…' His voice lacks conviction, as if all his usual bravado is seeping out.

'A favourite? But how long did that last?' She struggles to keep her voice from breaking. 'I was only ever as good as my last merry little pout! My last amusing caper!' she says bitterly. 'My mother is heart-broken at what you have made of me. She is sorely troubled by guilt at what I suffered after she gave me to you. She feels it is her fault, that if she had managed to keep me at her side then I would never have been stunted and in such pain. She dreads facing the wrath of God on Judgement Day. And so should you.'

'But there must be something else I can do for you?'

'No.' She looks disdainfully at him. 'I want us both in the fresco. I want my mother painted in an attitude of piety, and I want to be painted just as I am. True to life.'

'I just cannot do what you are asking. It's not possible,' Mantegna says flatly.

'If you have any decency, Mantegna, you will think first of your daughter's suffering and how best to make it up to her before you consider your own position at court.'

Mantegna stares at Anna as if truly seeing her for the first time. 'Did it pain you much, child? What they did to you?' Anna tells him slowly exactly what happened. Her voice is quiet and purposeful; her eyes never leave his. He staggers back, his conscience wounded. His voice drops in weariness. 'If I had my time over again I would never have taken her. I would have somehow found the money to pay your rent. I would have done things very differently.' Mantegna's eyes are dulled in defeat. 'I would never have let Dati anywhere near you.'

'But what of those who still suffer?'

'What of them? There is nothing I can do. Only a fool would dare to take on families like that. Even just showing too much interest is…' He pushes his thumb downwards.

'Oh, you can. We have thought of a way.' Anna moves to stand in front of him and looks up in defiance. 'For such a great artist, you have far less imagination than my mother and I.'

'What you have asked me to do to the family fresco will finish me, and that's a fact. What else can you possibly expect of me?'

'Mother?'

'You must go to Dati and release the pumilio children imprisoned in his house. If they can be returned to their families then they must be. If not, then you must find homes for them where they will be treated with care and with kindness.'

'I see. That's all, is it? And Dati will just be happy to do that, will he? No arguments. No questions. You must both be deranged.' He begins pacing the floor.

Ya Ling's voice is steady. 'No. No, Maestro. I promise you that isn't all. Secondly, you will find out if there are any other pumilio houses in Mantova and have them closed down as well.'

'What nonsense! I haven't that kind of power! There are men with savage reputations involved. You can't imagine the enemies I would make. There will be immediate vendettas on my life. I would live in fear.'

'Then there is justice.' Ya Ling walks up to him and draws herself to her full height. 'As your reputation means so much to you, not only will we both swear to secrecy about your heresies, but we will also keep quiet that Anna is our daughter and that you sold her to a pumilio dealer.'

'Still. You have no idea what you are asking me to do.'

'There's more.' Her smile is confident.

His tone is guarded. 'Go on.'

'I have spent the last two weeks nursing the marchesa of the croup and I have been busy reminding her of her age, and how precarious life can be. She now realises that for the sake of her immortal soul she must do this. Fortunately Cardinal Francesco is currently looking for a new crusade against sin, to make his name at the Vatican. Of course, the church has known about the cruelty the poor pumilio children have suffered for years, but chose to pretend not to, for fear of tightening the wallets of those involved. But now apparently Francesco claims he has only just been told of this barbaric practice and has decided to have it banned. Ludovico agrees with him, so I have suggested to Barbara that you are given the task of intermediary, as you are such a devoted family man.' Her glance is scathing. 'You will be accompanied to the pumilio houses with a regiment of the ducal guard.'

'The ducal guard? But they won't protect me for ever! There will be a price on my life after this.'

'Why should that worry you, Maestro? If, as you claim, you can dispense immortality?'

Chapter 43

'You are doing it again, Anna,' Settimio's deep voice chides. She tries to keep still but it's very difficult. The urge to look over her shoulder at the fresco itches like a mosquito bite. Mantegna finished painting Ya Ling standing just behind her in penitent's robes weeks ago. He had laboured many days over it, as if trying to engrave her image on his mind.

Some days Ya Ling sits in the corner as chaperone, but most of the time she goes about her business. Both trust Settimio. She hasn't interfered with Anna's wishes for the fresco and has let Anna make her own decisions, watching her daughter's growing confidence with quiet maternal pride.

Settimio's brush holds a blob of coral-coloured paint, so he must be putting in the last few details of her dress. Anna's favourite dress. The one that she herself has made, in a lovely heavy Veneziano silk. She was delighted when Anna chose that. His wide sturdy face keeps nodding from Anna up to the wall behind. 'Tell me something. You can be truthful with me, Anna. I'll understand. You must be so disappointed that it's me painting you and not the maestro.'

'Of course I'm not!' she snaps. 'I much prefer you. You're far more honest.'

Ya Ling smiles. She knows how hard it has been for Anna to trust the apprentice, to judge whether Settimio's conversation was just to keep her still or if he is genuinely interested in her replies. Now Anna knows him better she has confided that she feels the warmth of a tentative friendship between them.

Settimio remains diplomatically silent. He's learned a lot of self-control working for Mantegna, but he had to clench his teeth hard to stop his jaw dropping down onto his apron bib when Mantegna first told him what he wanted him to do. He hadn't been the only one – Cecco's eyes had nearly popped out of his skull. 'Of course, Maestro,' was all he'd said before spending two careful days obliterating the image of Enzio from the fresco. Two days of gently flaking away the young man's extravagant pose and the swaggering gesture of his right hand. He'd saved the best bit till last. The confident contours of Enzio's smirking smile had come off in two easy strokes and Settimio had saved the last one for Cecco. Both had loved doing it. Loved using their scalpels to consign Enzio to oblivion. Both knew just how much the courtiers and the servants were all speculating and gossiping about his fall from grace, every one of them thrilled that for once, Enzio's all-powerful family couldn't restore him to greatness.

'I like your style so much more, Settimio,' Anna says confidently. 'Mantegna painted the Widow very well, but you remember how he first painted me. Awful!'

Ya Ling's lips rise. How little Mantegna knew his daughter. How he had underestimated her honesty when he'd attempted to idealise her appearance. In the gap left by Enzio's disappearance from the fresco, Mantegna had painted what he thought would be every young girl's fantasy. He'd made Anna beautiful. Much taller, with a delicate dress mosaicked with jewels and a luminous aura around her. An angel at court. All three painters had been astonished by her reaction, but Ya Ling had not been surprised at all. She'd been gratified at the way her daughter had responded. Anna had looked at her image in fury, imagining the snide laughter, the comments that would be made by the courtiers and in the servants' quarters. Not to mention what they'd say down in the Casetta dei Nani.

'No!' Anna had shouted. 'No! This is not what I want at all! Look at me, Mantegna, and paint what you see. Do for me what you have done for the rest of them.' She had jabbed her finger up at the fresco, at the Gonzaga family and their entourage. 'Be truthful. Treat me like one of them! Do it again!' she had demanded. 'Accept the responsibility of how I am. For once in your life, be honest.'

Mantegna's second attempt made her into a simpering, prettified court servant looking across at the marchesa adoringly. The brushwork was crude. The maestro's hands seemed to shake, as he worked, with barely controlled frustration. 'Then let one of them do it!' she ordered. 'Your son, or the apprentice.' Mantegna walked out of the room, flexing his big hands. They heard a roar like a wounded beast coming from outside.

'Perhaps, Signorina, if you...' Cecco's voice quivered. 'It might be safer if you...'

'Yes.' The apprentice nodded. 'I'd scarper if I were you.'

'No. I'm staying.' Anna didn't move for several minutes, until the maestro stormed back in.

'Congratulations, Settimio.' Mantegna's voice sounded as if only willpower had got it past his vocal cords.

'Maestro?'

'You've just landed your first commission.' Mantegna walked to the workbench and flung his tools into his burlap bag, giving a long, agonised glance towards the Widow, who sat quietly embroidering a shawl in the corner. He left for Firenze the following night, taking Cecco with him.

'Come on! I'm going to burst! How much longer?'

'Be patient, Anna. Either keep that handkerchief still, or stick it back up your sleeve.'

'No. I'm so glad it's you, Settimio.' Everything about him is measured. A big calm presence in the room. Plain-faced, not handsome like Enzio, but not nasty like him either. Married to Filomena, the daughter of a cheesemaker from his village just outside Mantova. It's strange how his big solid hands can transform the blocks of pigment into such miracles on the wall. Such delicacy. Tiny deft strokes. Such colours – it's like standing in front of a box of shimmering precious stones. 'Settimio, are you disappointed not to go with the Mantegnas to Firenze? I've been worried that it's my fault. That I've put you out of favour with the maestro.'

'No. I've had enough. I miss Cecco though,' Settimio says gruffly. 'My apprenticeship was well over but the maestro wouldn't help me get commissions. Now he's had to. Thanks to you. And my life is here. It's where I'm happiest.' That's how he speaks. Simple and direct. At first he hadn't spoken to her at all. He'd never been alone in a room with a girl who wasn't a wife or a sister, and Anna is nothing like any of them. She is like a tiny exotic doll with her fine clothes and the row of pearls the Widow has given her. Her mind is like quicksilver and she knows all the sophistications of court, the elegant nuances of expected behaviour that are completely beyond him. She dazzled him at first, but as the sittings have progressed he's become aware of the loneliness that lies beneath her confident manner. He always feels better after they've talked. More like a man of the world.

'So Settimio, are you really the seventh-born?'

'Yes. I was rightly named. Four sisters and two brothers. Then me. Last but not least.'

She stares back at him calmly. A watery white is dripping off the tip of a very fine brush, so he must be finishing off her gauzy little head-dress, or perhaps adding sheen to the ermine hem of her cloak. Her eyes roam up his big square frame. 'No. I don't expect you are. And how many still…?'

'Five of us. God's been good. We lost two to the pestilence but those He spared are strong and in good health.'

'Good. I'm glad to hear that.' He notices the slight plaintive look come back across her small, defined features. 'It must be wonderful when you all get together. All of you, being part of a family.' Ya Ling puts down her embroidery and listens.

'Well, it's crowded! That's for sure. And noisy too! Children running in and out. Dogs chasing them. Chickens flapping about too sometimes. Nothing like here.'

'It sounds…'

'What?' Ya Ling's voice is soft.

'Never mind.' Anna sighs.

'Well, you can come and meet them if you want. My father said that to celebrate my first commission we're all going to— but no. It won't be anything like what you're used to. A bit of meat and millet bread, that's about it really. A few olives. But there will be some good cheese. Filomena's father will see to that.'

Anna sends a questioning glance over to her mother, who nods. 'Yes. Yes. I can't wait!'

'Well, I warn you, they're a noisy lot even before the wine flagon gets passed around.'

Anna's eyes shine. 'It all sounds wonderful. Being there. Meeting them all. Your family and everyone.'

'Well, Marsilio Andreasi is very fond of you, isn't he? Like a father, some say.' Settimio often does that, seems to know what she's thinking. He's a kindly man.

'Yes. Yes he is.'

'And' – he jerks his head to the corner – 'you and the Widow are very close, aren't you? A mother couldn't be kinder.'

'Yes, we are very close.' Anna turns and smiles. 'And she's teaching me her skills. I don't think I'll ever know as much about herbs and healing as she does, but when I've learned a bit more, then I'm going to work for her.'

'So you do have a family after all.' Settimio grins at her.

'Yes, I suppose I do.' Anna looks across at Ya Ling, who seems lost in thought. 'And I have my friend Maria, and now you as well. Can I turn round now?'

'Shh. Soon enough. It's going to take longer if you keep hopping from foot to foot.' He smiles down at her. 'So you might stop entertaining then?'

'Yes. I'm a realist. Crispino is the talk of the court, his star is in the ascendancy. But I've heard his songs are becoming bawdier by the day – he's treading a fine line between honest vulgarity and being obscene. A priest from his own *contrada* has refused him communion, and Barbara already has another *camarade* lined up.'

'You're well out of all of that.'

'Yes I will be, once I have learned my trade.'

'And during your working life here in Mantova, you will earn the respect of all the people you cure.' Anna sends her mother a questioning look. 'Not in Beijing, but here where you belong. And where we will build our life together.' Ya Ling notices her daughter's head dip in relief and keeps her smile fixed despite the clawing inside her chest. She will never see them again. Never feel the soft warmth of Mama's cheek or hear the deep rumble of Baba's voice. Ayi, already an old lady when the Berber took her, would have passed away by now, and Altan would be long married with daughters of his own. Her dream of rescuing Mei Ming had been a fantasy. Deep in her heart, Ya Ling knows that she too would not have survived. And Chen. What of matchless Chen? She hopes he would not have taken the honourable path, but fears he would have been true to his conscience. Swallowing down a wave of emotion, she holds out her arms. Anna has suffered enough. Her wishes are all that matter now.

'Come on then.' Settimio puts down his brush. 'You can both look.'

They pull apart from their embrace and walk over to the wall. The colours are new and breathtaking. They both look quickly along the row of faces. There behind Anna is Ya Ling, looking down at her daughter with a look of such tender regret, of such heartbreaking piety, that on Judgement Day the everloving God must surely grant her redemption.

'What do you think, Anna?' he demands.

Anna feels her mother leaning against her and knows that she, too, is feeling the same strong emotion. Her own face looks straight back at her. Pinched and anxious, as it sometimes is. But it has courage too. 'It's just what I wanted,' she whispers. 'It's truthful but you've given me presence. Don't laugh, Settimio, but you've given me a kind of stature.'

'I'd never laugh, Anna. I've never known anyone as fearless as you.'

'I agree.' Ya Ling's voice catches with pride.

'It's me. Just how I really am.'

'So it's what you wanted?'

'No. It's much better.' She has escaped from a place worse than purgatory and has survived. There she is, a member of the Gonzaga court. Just like all the others. She answers the question Settimio would never dare to ask. 'Better than the maestro. Much better than he could have done.'

'I'm glad.' She feels his big frame exhale with relief as they stand side by side.

'Goodness!' says Anna, shocked at the way her position right at the front of the fresco means that all eyes are drawn straight to her. She laughs nervously. 'You've even put my hanky in.'

She slips her hand over where her mother's hand rests on her shoulder. She has Ya Ling. At court, only Marsilio knows of their kinship, but it's enough. And now she has a new friend in Settimio. And Maria too.

Ya Ling murmurs quietly down to her daughter. 'Let Enzio's face heal so he can flounce and flirt with every girl on his father's estate.

Let Crispino's voice entrance, let his leering and his thrusting little codpiece amuse. For a while anyway. There will be more to your life, Anna, more of worth. Much more. At the holy gates of Heaven they will know you straight away. A person who rose above life's cruelty. More than that, you have worked boldly and with courage to help put an end to the suffering of others, and stopped wicked men profiting from evil.'

Anna's image is already drying. Once trapped beneath its film of almond varnish it will be there for ever. Looking at her daughter's painted image, Ya Ling catches a glimpse of the qualities she herself inherited. Besides the many practical skills her parents taught her, Dorji taught her how to think, and Ya Zhi taught her how to love, but Chen taught her how to endure. Only she knows how great the distance is that she has travelled and what she's had to do to survive.

Anna has learned the same hard lesson that out of cruelty can come courage and compassion. Ya Ling feels small fingers interweave with her own. As she locks her eyes on to her daughter's steadfast gaze looking out from the fresco, Ya Ling realises that the truth isn't always what people see, but they have both done their best to reproduce it. Her heart quickens with what she sees.

It is her daughter.

Seemly.

Dignified.

It is Anna.

Acknowledgements

Family and friends have been wonderful, especially Mike, Lucy, Alice, Greg and Jon. I would also like to thank everyone who has pledged. I really value the support of both the usual suspects and those who were willing to take a risk on a complete unknown.

Xander, Annabel, Rachael and Holly at Unbound, and Sadie, Jacqui and Petra have all given me invaluable editing advice and shown great enthusiasm and commitment to the novel in its various stages.

Pam, Tricia, Neil, Felicity, Phyllice, Claire and Guy have always given me constructive suggestions.

Born and bred in Mantua, Alessandra Smith has helped me with local insights, advice and superb restaurant recommendations. Both Elisa Gasparini and Diletta Piazza from the Tourist Comune in Mantua were keen to share their local expertise and very generous with their time.

Thanks are due to Lorenzo Bonoldi for his tour of Mantua, which was both entertaining and erudite. Closer to home, the staff at Lewisham Library have always been very interested and helpful in directing me towards effective research material.

I am very grateful to Mark Ecob for designing such a wonderfully arresting cover.

Patrons

Derrien Allen
Sara Aragao
Martin Archer
Ian Ashcroft
Toby Baldwin
Helen Ball
Jason Ballinger
Clare Barker
Becky Billups
James Bushnell
Edward Carefoot
Lyn Carr
Jeff Chapman
Grace Cheung
Lillian Chou
Robert & Heather Cox
Emily Cox
Natasha Cox-Abeysinghe
Aisling Dunne
Debi Edward
Lisa Ellis Schafer
Emrys Evans
Felicity Everett
Micaela Facino
Camila Fernandez
Claudia FitzGerald
Antonia Galloway
Gretel Hallett
Theresa Hemminger
Nicholas Heyworth
Brendan Hogan
Bryan Hollier

Craig Houston
Sarah Keenlyside
Timothy Keiser
Samantha Khachik
Ewan Lawrie
Ray Lee
Li Lei
Clare Lew
Gillian Lewis
Kai Lun
Fiona Maine
Vincent McInerney
Philip McNaughton
@muirinho
Silke Neugebohrn
Sinead O'Brien
Penn O'Gara
Anna Oberhauser
Sam Palmer
Tom Pattinson
Ray Pereira
Francesca Polato
Dee Rawlins
Amelia Rynkowska
John Sabido
Rosarii Sabido
Clare Sabido
Evan Hoffman Schouten
Alex Schroeder
Lynsey Searle
Eleanor Short
Verity Smith
Kerri Smith
Maria Snow
Sue Soave
Melody Soave

K Sommerville
Sinéad Stack
Mandy Straka
Sigrid Straka
Angela Straka-Johnson
Deborah Stuart
Wendy Summers
Mark Vent
Susan Wagner
Lauren Wellman
Holly White
Sophia Wickham
Gretchen Woelfle
Sally Wynn-jones
Margaret Wynn-Jones
Curry Xu